SOLSTICE LUNARIE

BY OCHRE ASH

SOLSTICE LUNARIE

First edition. August 25, 2015.

OCHRE ASH

Copyright © 2015 Ochre Ash.
ISBN: 978-1-943970-02-5
Written by Ochre Ash.
Published by Ochre Ash,LLC
Cover Art by Sarah Callen

To my wife Rachel, without your unfaltering support for my questionable plans this novel would not exist. I love you and I don't know what I'd do without you.

For Kirk, you're my target audience and my sounding board. Thank you, I hope you love it.

Table of Contents

I. CHARADES AND CHANTS

Here

Who feeds alphabet soup to schizophrenics? Honestly, where else does that pass for care? It defies belief that the line between torment and treatment is that fine, and yet he takes time and care to stamp dough into letters. It's a farce, this place, a cruel charade, and it's all for my benefit. Bob and the others are truly sick. But the joke's on me.

The messages Bob received in his soup bowl were real to him, just as real as the white gloves that grabbed him and dragged him off and strapped him to a gurney. I know where they took him. He's in the closet at the end of the corridor, rolled into the corner beside the pile of restraints and the vats of lubricant and hand sanitizer. He's been left to the voices. I've been there once or twice. If he doesn't stop yelling soon, they're going to sedate him.

It's time for me to return to my room. I am lucky to have a room, a private space if you ignore the round-the-clock surveillance. The other patients all share bunks. It's easier to monitor twelve loons in a room than it is to split them up, suicide risk being what it is. That's what they say: it's for their own protection. Just as my faux-segregation is for mine, or theirs, depending on whether I, or one of the loons, asks.

I suppose I'm better suited to this environment than most. He knows this, the Professor. I do well in a low stimulation environment, white walls, low illumination, white sheets and white noise. I like a clean space, for living and for work. Though I haven't worked in quite some time.

He is breaking the others down. He is breaking them down and forcing me to watch because he hopes to break me down. But he will not secure my cooperation. He knows me well, perhaps better than anyone else, excluding myself of course. But I hold one secret from him. He does not know about the jewel. I have seen the jewel. I will see it again, and the knowledge that I will see it again is my strength. The day approaches.

Orchestral Gnomes and the Jewel in Lotus

I first saw the jewel in the lotus on my eighth birthday. I immediately lost sight of it. After thirty years, three months, three weeks and three days spent slowly defogging my reality goggles, I will see it again. But that event is yet to occur, and being far removed from the first viewing of the jewel let us put it aside and return to my eighth birthday. It's over here, off to my right where all my birthdays are, about three feet away, practically arm's length. I wish it were closer to me, but at least it's easy to find. If only the jewel were as easy to find...

My eighth birthday was a brown day. All of my birthdays are brown days because October is a brown month. A skeleton in the corner, its white bones luminescent under the black lights, played Grateful Dead guitar riffs on a fishbone-shaped Fender. Orange and black streamers hung above its head along with a sign: 'Happy Birthday Riley!' Each letter was painted its own color. The colors matched my colors, only brighter, my mother's touch, and it set a vanilla-sugar sweetness melting on my tongue.

A strobe pulsed behind the skeleton. The other partygoers, children and adults, hovered at the fringes of my awareness. A sensation preoccupied me: an emanation above my left shoulder, a vibration, then...release. The pulse of the strobe slowed with the action on the Fender. The chord passed and gelatinous blobs of pale blue light slid left out of my field of vision, replaced by the next chord bending, slowing, *waaaaw-waaaaaaaaaaa* as the pace waned and the blue blobs frayed into drifting purple banners. The sound shuddered, halted, and the strobe locked stationary as a spotlight.

Again, the sensation occupied my mind. My eyes fixed upon the light. A sensation the same as before, a vibration, I felt its importance. Even now, recalling this, I *feel* its importance. But there was no taste. *Feeling without taste?* No matter how many times I recall this experience I am always surprised that I tasted nothing.

There is one light. The sensation built above my left shoulder. *There is one light but a million eyes.* The vibration grew more intense. It rolled in from my left and sunk into me. Then it was gone. No. Not gone. No longer in me, but around me. I sat at the epicenter of the vibration and looked out from above my left shoulder. It emanated from here: sensation… vibration… release.

There is the one light and the one eye, but the one eye is many. The multifaceted eye reflected inward across a thousand lenses and the thousand lenses within those lenses, forever back down the inner corridors of the visual cortex; synapses fired at machine gun pace, an internal fireworks display in perpetual grand finale, implosion upon implosion coupled with spasmodic electrical surges until the internal cacophony of sound, imagery and energy drowned out all bodily sensation save a vague entomic impression that somewhere above I abandoned my exoskeleton and left it to its final throes, cracking and dying in a fit of violent shakes.

I fell. I say I fell, but it all fell. From the moment I fell, until the moment I opened my eyes to see a crying princess and two paramedics, all fell away. The brown day on my right, an arm's length away, no longer held this moment. It fell away with the world.

You may rightly question the veracity of the experience I recount, given its absence of temporal definition. But understand this: the truth of my experience will be born out in two days time, exactly thirty years, three months, three weeks and three days after my eighth birthday.

So again, I fell. I have never been afraid of falling, a good quality in a surfer, but fell is the right word only in the sense that I lacked control, pulled by an outside force, but that force was not gravity. I can never recall whether I fell down or flew up or left or right or any other direction. What I experienced was motion, the sense that I was not at rest but being carried along, almost like floating atop a river, but without the wetness and in the dark, with no clear visual reference points. The only real referent was the motion itself, which I interpreted only as velocity, which was either very fast or very slow, but the blind motion so thoroughly skewed my perceptions that I could not be certain. The only thing I was certain of was that I traveled away from whatever it was that I left behind, shaking and dying.

The place which I traveled through, and I say through not to, because there was no final destination, was unlike anything most people ever experience, save the first time on Space Mountain, and even then only if experienced at a young enough age to fully appreciate with awe and wonder the sense of being lost in space and time and yet still quite secure with only the slightest hint of fear and not a hint of danger. I never felt threatened or in danger, not even when the first gnome appeared.

How odd.

The gnome was a tiny creature no bigger than my forearm. He wore only a pointy red hat, Birkenstock sandals and a snow-white beard. His penis was nearly a third as long as he was. He looked like Santa on summer vacation as depicted in National Geographic. The gnome carried a lengthy crank and he sang, to my surprise, in a deep baritone:

> *Turning the gears of the universe,*
> *turn, turn, turn*
> *Carry a shaft as big as me*
> *Can you learn?*
>
> *Turning the gears of the universe,*
> *turn, turn, turn.*
> *Wheels and cogs*
> *swamps and bogs*
> *rainforests and ferns.*
>
> *We run gears*
> *for joys and fears,*
> *granite worn away*
> *by waterfalls*
> *and river crawls,*
> *we work 'til end of days*
>
> *The secret's out*
> *that the devout*
> *are gumming up the works.*
> *Entropy.*
> *Dark Energy.*
> *Behind the scenes it lurks*

The bottom line,
is out of time,
all energy's conserved.
So what is there?
It all goes where?
All energy's conserved.

Turning spokes
It's all a joke
Our job's to wind the watch.
A special few can learn the truth
'bout how it's never broke

Perpetual
Motion Machine.
The gears of the universe.
Is is when.
It never ends.
Same forward or reverse.

Turning the gears of the universe,
turn, turn, turn
Carry a shaft as big as me
Can you learn?

A Gnome Orchestra accompanied the Baritone Gnome. They played on bizarre instruments shaped like industrial equipment. As the Baritone's song ended, the gnomadic music factory slowed to an upbeat end full of joyful honks and squeaks. And then, silence.

Children have a way of noticing the most important aspects of the world around them. Most adults lose this talent. Whether you retain your age when you step out of time I do not know, but I was childlike in that I saw the rhythm and felt it reverberate inside me.

I realized that the music never stopped. Even when the gnomes stopped playing the music never stopped. Even in the silence the music never stopped. I was that eternal instant. MUSIC.

I swam with notes and beats as ribbons of color. We flowed together, and along with the movement they became my points of reference. Their colors varied according to tone and pitch and their movement ran with the cadence. Endnotes dropped off rich chestnut stripes that snapped open like flags in a fall breeze. The higher, quicker portions ranged from lime to banana in freeway slivers like the broken bars between passing cars.

Hundreds of gnomes, male and female, swilled frosty mugs of foamy amber brew and pounded out the rhythms of the Baritone's song. They banged on the snaking ductwork of the universe with pipes and hammers, fists and knuckles, wrenches and ratchets. Sprockets spun gears connected to an endless maze of levers and pulleys being twisted and yanked by numerous gnomes as balls dropped splashing into buckets of rose elixir and chains supported sweeping butterfly nets balanced against broomhandles. Doors poked open to mirrored halls. Images reflected into prisms creating rainbows of funhouse lights as scattered photons drove feathered turbine-tops like bass spinnerbaits to power the pump for the massive keg and dispense the yeasty nectar of the universe, nourishment, energy for the gnomes to continue their all-consuming work, banging on the innards of Rube and Goldberg.

The whole gnome nation went along with their work. They frolicked, sang and fucked the universe forward across the stage as strobe lights flashed in the background and silhouetted flipbooks of debauchery writhed against perfectly synched mechanical madness.

Bear in mind that I was only eight and had never seen such adult conduct before, much less the universal fuck and work.[*] Yet I took it all in stride. Perhaps this was because I didn't know any better, or because I already knew. Or perhaps I had already determined to keep it secret.

The singing Baritone inched toward me and stared deep into my eyes. The multifaceted eye of one? Or the green doe eyes of Riley Sparx, son of Rainbow through Water, Sky and Surf Divinity? Baritone Gnome smiled a sinister grin baring a mouthful of jagged triangular pills, rows of razors. Most grown men would have flinched in the face of this miniature from Grimm nightmares, but I simply smiled, and in a voice that emanated from a place deep within, a place from which no voice will emanate again until the day I see the jewel, I said, "I see you sing in the key of E."

---

[*] TANGENT: The gnomes, it should be noted, could fuck and work simultaneously. Humans are usually limited to one or the other, despite having become sophisticated multi-taskers in recent years. However, the world's oldest profession does prove that the two are not mutually exclusive.

14

The Baritone Gnome roared a deep basso belly laugh. His features softened. He bowed deeply and I returned the bow. Numbers floated forward shimmering like waterfalls of pastel purples and pinks and yellows. The gnomes began chanting in unison, in singsongy soprano tones at a pace with the fluctuating colors of the advancing numbers. "Hoo-ray!" they cheered after each number. "Eight! Hoo-ray! Seven! Hoo-ray! One point two! Hoo-ray! Seven point eight! Hoo-ray! Seven! Hoo-ray! 7.317808219178082191780821917..." on and on they sang the decimal, a constant repetition that lasted for days, or years or centuries, but I simply listened, as time neither passed nor was passed through. I kept my patience and sat, contented with the gnomes and their *ad infinitum* chants.

The chant and the motion and I became wound as one, the golden lasso, sans knot. I fixated on the flowing texture, the tightly woven fibers of existence that simultaneously encircled and released the gnomes and me, snip snap like a Chinese finger trap its flax bowed low, pulled taut in the very fibers of the golden lasso, the spiraling ribbons of gold upon gold and wound-up spokes of lotus rope. I moved in wisps and twists and spools of smoke. I scratched across the beady black shine of the Baritone Gnome's eyes. The movement changed. My direction upended. I slid further and further down a steep incline through nothingness. But I knew somehow that I was falling toward my voice, toward the place from where my voice emanates. That's when dark became light and row upon row of shimmering shields receded, pulled back to the wings of the set to show layer upon layer of Faberge and haberdashery, the drunken drapes drawn back in folds to reveal the mirrored soul of the universe, the infinite eyes and arms and lingams and yonis, the many faces of God, and finally, the jewel in the lotus, flecked in gold, and gold bejeweled. And all revealed again.

I smiled as only a child can.

Control

"I saw her name in my soup," I tell him. He sits there like he always does and stares at his clipboard. I feel a tickle on my lower back and sputter on, "A coincidence of course. It's only that the color stands out so vividly that I can't miss it." I don't need to justify myself to him. So why do I? "Black bean alphabet. I suspect that's for my benefit. But you could just be fucking with the schizo's. You trying to induce additional hallucinations? Not enough to snap one a day. You want me to see Bob cry again?"

The Professor sighs and looks up from his clipboard, "Patient Six had a relapse. It was his third psychotic episode in seven months. I'd hardly blame the soup."

"Testing for correlates between synesthesia and mental illness?"

"If so you should be happy. We're trying to solve your problems after all."

"You're my problem. I'm only here because you need me, because I won't give you what you want."

"We both know why you're here. Although if there were a more positive contribution you could make to society we might be able to make certain accommodations to overcome the obstacles created by your violent proclivities."

"I'm not violent and you know it."

"The People of California respectfully disagree. I, on the other hand, think that your less desirable traits can be managed with counseling and proper psychiatric care. However, the first step to your recovery is an effort on your part. You need to show me that you want to correct some of your anti-social behaviors."

"I'm no psycho."

"One shouldn't throw that term around Riley. I spoke merely of certain tendencies. You push people away like you're pushing me away now. I'm not your enemy Riley. How long have we known each other?"

"Go make your own monsters. I'm not going to find them for you."

"Very well, Riley. You appear to be regressing. Cooperation is essential to the patient-therapist relationship, as is trust. I've spent three decades helping you. Surely I have earned some measure of trust?" I sneer and resist the urge to speak. It's the tinny flavor in the back of my mouth that both gives me the resolve and chokes me back. It is a small victory but one that I needed.

"Paranoia," he continues, "an unwillingness to trust old friends, suspicion of the motives of others. Yes, I am afraid you are regressing. I'll check back on you soon. In the meantime I'll adjust your medications. I think anxiety is blocking your recovery. That's all for today. Shall I send Colin in to look on you?"

"He's dangerous you know."

"He's not going to hurt you."

"Oh he's no danger to me."

The Professor crosses and uncrosses his legs. I know what he's thinking. He wants to ask, but he won't. *To whom is Colin dangerous?* If he were to ask that's exactly how he'd ask it. He wants specifics and he wonders if I have them. He knows I know things in ways he cannot. So I might know more than he does. But he doesn't ask. He won't ask. He'd rather guess. It's more important that he keep up the appearance of control.

Finally, he speaks, "Colin has some new artwork for you to take a look at."

My body betrays me. I shudder at the pressure, a cool metal cylinder down my spine, a rolling pin slotting between the vertebrae. I cannot hide my aversion to Colin's artwork anymore than you could avoid turning up your nose at a plate of fetid meat teeming with maggots. Unfortunately my reaction to Colin's aesthetic is becoming more visceral. The Professor leaves and I hear Colin greet him in the hall. Dread. I try to think of the jewel as pain rolls down my spinal column like water down a riverboat wheel. This is going to be unpleasant.

II. CHALLENGES

First Impressions

I am responsible for my present predicament, but the series of events that led me here began when I met her. I was a twenty-nine year old freshman on the campus of the University of California, San Diego. It was late September, a blue day, because September is a blue month, ice blue, like the bluest portion of a glacier.[*] I limped up the series of hills from the east side of campus over to the old part of campus closest to the ocean. I remember the glum sting of salt in my mouth at the sight of young, fit men whizzing by on skateboards and bicycles. That used to be me. All my Yangs were flowing, a wash of taste and texture and feeling: the anticipatory tickle on the back of my knees, a taut, anxious spine, and the picante, the spicy, the burn on my tongue at all the skin, the nineteen year olds in tank tops and shorts, curved and firm and oh so tan. But most of all I remember the salty sadness at the reminders of what I once had that was now lost.

I didn't have to walk there. I could have taken a campus shuttle. I could have applied for a handicapped placard at any time in the previous seven years. I chose to walk. My cane clapped along, *clackety-clack*, for more than two miles from east-campus to Muir: I passed ball-fields and the pool, then onto Warren Mall between the engineering buildings and the Vices and Virtues, uphill past the Price Center where I paused briefly to take in the view of Geisel Library, the eight-story geometric concrete and glass wonder named for Dr. Seuss, before I turned down the grey brick path of library walk, and then headed uphill once more through the eucalyptus trees past the public art installation known as the 'Giraffe Catchers,' tall metal poles strung some fifteen feet in the air with blue wire nets, harmless to students but deadly to long-necked ruminants, and with a worsening limp I passed the Sun God sculpture and the hill affectionately known as 'the Hump' and reached my destination, Mandeville Hall.

I reached the classroom with two minutes to spare. The glum feeling had gone leaving behind the tickle at the back of my knees and a faint pressure on my upper spine. I chose a seat near the door and leaned my cane against the desk leg. The desk faced a whiteboard at the front of the

---

[*] Dear Reader, you may object that because September is a fall and summer month it ought be red or orange or some other color better related to the season. However, my colors do not work this way. I assure you that September is indeed blue.

class and was large enough to accommodate two students. Surrounded by youth I had no expectation that anyone would be joining me.

She plopped a large black tote next to me on the desk. I looked around. There were a lot of empty chairs.

"What's your name?" she asked.

"Uh, Riley. What's yours?"

It could have been love at first sight were it not for a spelling error on my part.

"I'm Ren," she said.

She dug through the tote with the ferocity of a honey badger. Jet-black hair streaked with pink slashed across her face. Her lone visible eye sparkled jade under the bad classroom lights. Large and round, yet shaded with the barest hint of an epicanthic fold, her eye was made all the more alluring by its invisible partner and the small band of freckles that crossed the bridge of her nose.

She wore black boots with pink laces and black and pink striped stockings that rose up over her knees. Her skirt was black leather and rivetless with military pleats. A belt of silver loops matched the bracelets dangling from her thin wrists and a tight pink tank top revealed toned arms and that she did not wear a bra over her small but lovely breasts.

She finally found what she was looking for in her tote, a dry-erase marker. "You're kind of old to be in this class aren't you?" she asked.

The color of her name had predisposed me to irritation, but this last comment blunted any hint of spice with sour dill.

"I guess I'm kind of old for any class," I said.

"What's with the cane?"

"I use it to walk. What's with the anime outfit?"

"I use it to spot old pervs." She snatched up her bag and stalked to the front of the class. "Excuse me."

"You're excused," I muttered. I watched her skirt sway and a hint of spice came back to my palette. I couldn't help it.

She strode straight to the whiteboard, dropped her bag on the floor, and wrote on the board: SORRY. My palette went pasty with confusion. She turned to face the class. "Good morning everyone. My name is Ren. Welcome to Vis Arts 207 'Introduction to Abstraction.'" My spine tightened like a bowstring and I nearly choked on the non-descript protein taste[*] that always accompanies surprise. Ren smiled at me. I squirmed in my chair and tried to smile back. The quarter was off to a bad start.

"The powers that be intend this to be a survey of abstraction from impressionism to cubism and fauvism, as well as the post-modern forms of abstraction like geometric or 'cold' abstraction, lyrical abstraction and other various forms of expressionism. The so-called artists that run the department want you to spend upper division units studying and comparing other peoples' art.

"We are going to make art not study it. If you want to study abstraction and compare Picasso to Cezanne that is certainly worth doing and there is another class that meets on Tuesdays and Fridays taught by Professor Vernon where you can do so. I won't be offended if you leave now, as I am certain to have upset some of your expectations. So, I'm sorry."

I thought briefly about leaving, but I didn't. No one else left either.

"There is great value in a sincere apology." Ren looked at me again, then continued: "It's ridiculous to talk about abstract art. All art is abstract. Our entire world is abstract. We occupy a world of symbols and impressions and signs. There is little left of the natural world, so little that we marvel at it when we encounter 'wilderness' in our national parks. Even when we encounter the natural world we use our eyes, ears, noses and fingertips to see, hear, smell and touch it, right? Wrong. We use these senses to send data in the form of electrical impulses to our brains, which then assemble 'reality' for us. There is no way to prove that any one of us experiences a reality identical to any other of us. For example, there is no objective basis to compare my subjective experience of pink and Riley's subjective experience of pink." She snapped the strap of her tank top. My face and mouth burned with embarrassment.

"All we can really say is that both of our eyes perceive the same wavelength of reflected light off of a surface and that we both agree to refer to this wavelength and the manner in which our brains subjectively construct it in an image as the color 'pink'. Pink is not pink. 'Pink' is a symbol that allows us to communicate an aspect of our subjective experience to another person who has their own subjective experience of

---

[*] Dear Reader, you may be thinking chicken, but the surprising taste of surprise has taught me just how flavorful and distinct chicken is.

that same object, in this case, a wavelength of reflected light. Pink is an abstraction. Therefore, even the most realistic of realist painters, even photographers, deal in abstraction, because any recreation of a subjective experience is inherently abstract. Communicable mediums are the basis for art and reality. We are going to make art. We are going to communicate. So, let the communication begin. Are there any questions?"

A woman in the front of the class raised her hand. "If all art is abstract then what's the point in studying abstraction? I mean is there even anything to study? If everything is abstract doesn't the word abstract lose all meaning?"

"Excellent questions. Yes and no. There is value to studying abstraction and to examining the abstract in the world. First, by examining it we can become more aware of the abstraction that we take for granted, the filters and symbols by which we process and communicate our realities. More importantly, we can become aware that there are varying degrees of abstraction. That is what this class is about. Picasso is inarguably more abstract than Da Vinci. This doesn't mean that Da Vinci's work isn't also an abstraction, the expression of his reality through a visual medium. For this class we will create works of art and study where we ought to place them on our continuum of abstraction. This continuum should not be any sort of value judgment with respect to the art, but simply a method of categorization. Also, I do not intend to limit the use of mediums, except that for each work you create there must be a visual element."

A longhaired young man seated at the back of the room called out: "Do you have a last name Professor."

"Yes. And don't call me Professor, call me Ren."

"What is it?"

"I am an artist. Creators create. Call me Ren."

I ventured to ask a question of my own, one that had been on my mind since she called me an old perv. "How old are you?"

"Twenty-six," she said with a sardonic grin. "Old enough to be an old perv?" This drew blank stares from the rest of the class, not being privy to what I hoped was now an inside joke.

The woman in the front again raised her hand. "You already have your Ph. D.?"

"M.F.A., but it's really irrelevant. Artists need degrees like I need a third arm, a slide rule, and a pantsuit. Look, what you learn in here you won't learn from me, except indirectly. You don't learn art so much as you grow as an artist. You grow by making mistakes and either changing them, or allowing the beauty of the mistakes to become the art itself."

"Have you made any art that we would know of?" asked the longhaired dude.

"You mean have I made any art that sold? No. But if that's your criteria for art I suggest you drop this class and focus on graphic design. There's no shortage of demand for logos."

"So how did you advance so fast if you're not a doctor and haven't sold anything?"

"Enough about me. First assignment. Create a work of art, make it as abstract as you can. We'll reconvene next week and place them on a continuum of abstraction."

"How do we know what the criteria are for the continuum?"

"We'll decide that next week. There's no right and wrong here, just subjective distance from so-called 'objective' reality. I'm tired of talking. I want to paint. Go make art." She picked up her bag and walked out of the room.

An Unexpected Experiment: Personal Questions and Private Letters

Six days later and I still hadn't made anything for art class. I chewed my saliva and thought about Ren's mic-drop, no mention of office hours or workshop time, no syllabus, just, "go make art." Grade school paste taste, thick and sour, sent me to Café Roma before I had to go fulfill my research participation credit. I meant to remedy my situation the second best way I knew how, with coffee. I purchased a large and took it to the sugar station, where I pulled out my digital thermometer and measured the coffee's temperature, 190 degrees. I added a full pour of milk and allowed it four minutes to cool before drinking.

For reasons unknown caffeinated beverages calm my Yangs. I prefer coffee, but Mountain Dew has a similar effect. The buzz cleansed my palette although it did nothing to diminish the emotion I was feeling, or to slow the questions racing through my brain. Who was Ren? She had a passion for art and the philosophy behind it, but claimed not to teach anything. Why not teach? Or was she teaching by not teaching? She dressed how she wanted, taught, or didn't, how she wanted. How do you impress a woman like that?

I wanted to impress her.

My gummy cottonmouth lifted for an instant, trailed by a fleeting Christmassy taste of mint and nutmeg. I thought about my project due the next day: What medium? Carving? Painting? Drawing?

I checked the time on my phone. My schedule had worked out well; time enough for coffee and a stroll across campus at a cripple's pace. You simply have to love San Diego in September. I took in the frosh fashion show with delight and a touch of fire on my tongue, old perv that I was, but for all the low cut sundresses and short shorts, I couldn't shake the image of a pleated black skirt swaying above a pair of pink and black thigh-highs.

I limped through the campus of UCSD Medical Center and arrived at a squat grey building far from the hospital. I entered through a side door, opting to use a handicapped ramp rather than negotiate the stairs. Inside were shiny floors, white walls and drop ceilings.

All psychology classes required the students to participate in a minimum of ten hours as research subjects for professors or graduate students. This didn't necessarily entail the taking of experimental drugs, but I signed up for a study comparing the palliative effects of synthetic versus natural tetrahydrocannabinol.

I hoped I would walk into some sort of locker filled with pounds upon pounds of vacuum-packed, cellophane wrapped, university created strains of high-grade marijuana. Instead I entered yet another utilitarian box and encountered a frumpy receptionist behind a grey desk. She handed me a clipboard and told me to sign in. "So am I getting the synthetic or the natural stuff?" I asked.

She glared at me with disapproval and fingered the cross hanging from her neck. "I don't know. You should sit down and wait."

I waited and stared up at the flimsy panels of the drop ceiling. I have always found it odd that the interior spaces of most universities and hospitals would be entirely at home on a military installation. The utilitarian characterless nature of the spaces seems at odds with an ethos intended to foster learning, or healing, or creativity. To its credit UCSD had done much to remedy this with its newer buildings. I wondered if I would ever escape these uniform rooms, most Americans die in one.

The door burst open and a man flew into the room. Wild white curls bounced about his shoulders as he bee-lined to the reception desk and snatched up the clipboard. "I need to borrow this subject," he panted, and then hastily crossed something out.

The receptionist was befuddled. "He's signed up for Dr. Herriman—"

"I assure you Dr. Herriman will understand. Come along Riley. There's been a change of plans." Neither I, nor the receptionist, were in any position to argue, so I was whisked off to another room that, naturally, looked very much like the one I had just left.

The man sat me down in an uncomfortable metal backed chair and took a seat across the table from me. A stack of large white cards lay on the table next to a stopwatch. "Riley I am going to show you a series of cards. I want you to identify the largest letter that you see."

"Who are you?"

"I'm the Professor."

"I figured that. But who are you?"

"The Professor."

"Professor of what?"

"Psychology. Professor is both my title and my name. I profess it a noble one and I long ago decided that I needed no other: for what is a man but what he does?"

"Professor I was actually signed up for the THC study."

"You're in college aren't you?"

"Yeah, but what does that—"

"It means you'll have to pay for it like everyone else. Now please focus. This is a timed examination."

"Examination? Am I being graded here?"

"No. No. It's part of a larger study. I haven't time to explain it to you. Please, just focus and identify the largest letter that you see." The Professor picked up the stopwatch and showed me the first card:

```
        EEEEEEEEEEE
       EEEEEEEEEEEEE
      EEEEEEEEEEEEEEE
     EEEEE        EEEEE
     EEEEEE       EEEEEE
     EEEEEEE      EEEEEEE
     EEEEEEEEEEEEEEEEEEEEEEEE
     EEEEEEEEEEEEEEEEEEEEEEEE
     EEEEEEEEEEEEEEEEEEEEEEEE
     EEEEEEEE     EEEEEEEE
     EEEEEEEE     EEEEEEEE
     EEEEEEEE     EEEEEEEE
     EEEEEEEE     EEEEEEEE
```

I froze. All I saw was a blurring, bleeding, leaching, stream of tequila sunrise: a beautiful but disorienting and fluid combination of pink and orange. Every instinct I had screamed 'E', but I was aware of a larger shape, and that was the letter the Professor wanted. I stared for several seconds, trying to take in the scope of the larger form that I knew was present. Then, like someone had flipped a switch, the flowing hues turned to static orange and the form of the letter 'A' popped out at once. "A," I said. The Professor looked at the stopwatch and frowned. He jotted numbers down on a yellow legal pad.

The exercise continued with the Professor showing me cards. Each consisted of a large letter comprised of smaller letters. As the test progressed I became more adept at viewing the larger image, but always the first color to emerge was that of the small letters and it took a mental effort to bring the larger image forth in its proper color.

After the first round the Professor pulled out another set of cards and we repeated the test, only this time with digits, numbers comprised of other numbers. Again the smaller numbers popped forth in color and I had to rearrange the forms in my mind to obtain the correct result. All throughout the exam the Professor frowned and grimaced as he jotted down my times. After we had gone through all of the number cards he looked me square in the eye, scowled, and asked me point blank if I was fucking with him.

I denied that I was doing any such thing.

"If you were it could skew the data and foul the entire experiment. You're sure your answers have been proper and timely?" I assured him they had, at which time his scowl flipped to a broad smile and he said: "Fascinating." He excused himself and returned less than a minute later. "I sent my assistant to gather two more sets of cards."

"Is Professor your real name?"

"Has been my entire life. I am what I do, and that is my name. Of course you probably were referring to legalities, in which case it has been my legally recognized name for the last thirty-two years."

"What was it before that?"

"I'm afraid that information is highly classified." He said it with a straight face and I had no idea if he was joking. His assistant returned with two more sets of cards and we repeated the exercise, only this time I was tasked to identify the smaller set of letters or numbers. I answered each time in the span of a finger snap.

When we finished the Professor sat a moment with slightly glazed eyes then said, "Fascinating." Then he looked up through the ceiling as though studying some far away planet.

After what seemed like a long time I asked if we were done.

"Have you ever had a girlfriend?" he asked.

The question caught me entirely off guard and I spluttered to answer with a mouthful of paste. "Uh, uh, emm… yeah."

"Lots of girlfriends?"

"I guess. What do you consider a lot?"

"It isn't important. You hug and kiss these girls?"

"Yeah."

"Did you hug your mother as a child?"

"Yeah. What does this have to do with your research?"

He ignored my query and pressed on with his odd line of questioning. "Your girlfriends, you had sex with them?"

"Some. I'm not really comfortable answer—"

"Do you consider yourself a loner? Do have many friends?"

"I don't know, I guess—"

"Do you talk to yourself? Masturbate frequently?"

"What the hell? How is this—?"

"Forgive me Riley, I'm getting ahead of myself. We've been at it for an hour and a half; I'll credit you with two hours. I'd like to see you this time next week. Plan on going longer." He hopped from his chair like a jackrabbit and was out the door before I could open my mouth.

****

For a week I heaved a heavy chest and tasted savory herbs. It was the Professor. I couldn't get his weird questions out of my head. And not just the sex ones, but, as I sat there alone, day after day, in my enormous 'house,' the question about being a loner seemed prescient and creepy. I'd never thought of myself that way before, but now I realized my only 'friend' was my weed dealer. If you're always alone, can you say you're not a loner?

I limped to the research lab with the clap of my cane echoing off the walls. I was anxious and slapped my cane down harder than normal, but upon entering the room I felt a reprieve, a lifting of pressure, because at long last I could get this day over with.

The Professor ambled in with a thick stack of paper. "Here it is. The questionnaire. Please answer all the questions honestly."

I looked down at the first question. '1. Do you prefer: a) reading a book or b) going to a party.' It seemed harmless enough, but before I began I asked a question that was weighing on my mind and body. "Is all this anonymous?"

The Professor thought for a moment. "Any data used for the research study will be part of a composite, an aggregate set, so yes it's anonymous.

However, if it makes you feel better I also promise you that doctor-patient confidentiality applies to anything you say or hand in to me."

Somehow that didn't make me feel any better, but this wasn't optional, it was part of my ten required hours, so I shrugged it off and spent the next two hours completing the questionnaire. The first few pages were all preference questions, but then it got weird. The questions about sex and masturbation started popping up here and there amidst the preference questions. I sort of expected this, so I just answered honestly figuring I really had nothing to hide. As the questions went on there were fewer preference questions and more 'yes or no's' and 'have you ever's,' and 'fill in the blanks'. Then I got to question 87. I did a double take: '87: What color is 'A'?' I wrote down 'orange' in a shaky hand. Then question 92: 'What color is '9'?' I grabbed the papers from the desk and stormed out.

I found the Professor out in the hall and spat a mouthful of bilious citrus paste, "What the hell is this?"

He looked amused. Calmly, he asked, "what question are you on?"

"Ninety-two."

"Quick. I thought you were a sharp one. Well since you're out here why don't you tell me what it's about?"

"Screw you." Why was I angry with him? Because he knew something personal about me that he couldn't? Or because he knew something personal about me that I didn't? How much did he understand? And how much did I not understand? Questions flipped by too fast to process. "I'm done with this. There's no study is there?"

"Oh there most certainly is a study. I am no false Professor. But your questionnaire may have been modified slightly."

"I didn't sign up to be a lab rat."

"Actually you did. This is part of your ten-hour requirement. Remember? What exactly do you think a research subject does?"

"Well I didn't sign up for your study and it's not much of a study if you're singling me out."

"Sorry Riley but you still owe me six hours."

"I'll sign up for another study. I'm not working with you."

"I'm afraid you can't."

"I'll go to the Department Head."

"I am the Department Head."

"Then I'll go to the Dean."

"Be my guest. But then you'll never get to know."

"Know what?"

"Know how I knew of course." I just stared at him. He frowned. "Oh don't play dumb. I already know you're not. You're smart. That's why you're out here. And the fact that you're out here and angry also tells me that I was right. If I were wrong you'd be out here asking me how the heck you're supposed to answer question eighty-seven. You're already on ninety-two. So tell me Riley. What color is 'A'?"

I stood there, exam clenched in my shaking fist. A sick burning in the back of my mouth left me short of breath. The Professor was right; I wanted to know. But I stayed silent. I didn't taste the cinnamon, but it must have been there, only pride could have stayed my tongue.

"Is it really such a big secret?" he asked. "I'll be honest with you if you'll be honest with me. I'll even go first, as a sign of good faith. That questionnaire is three things: it's a Meyer-Briggs personality inventory, it's an autistic-spectrum diagnostic tool, and it is a customized screening exam for synesthesia."

I threw down the papers and raced away as fast as my cane would carry me. "Six hours," he called out from behind me.

****

I confronted him at his office the next day. I wasn't about to sit through another week of agony and angst. I was out. Either he let me out or I went to the Dean. I got stoned, stoned like a Muslim adulteress, stoned like granite boulders, stoned... you get the point. I didn't want a messy repeat of our conversation and I wanted my palette dulled. In retrospect this was not a sound strategy because although my palette was clear my head was not. So when I confronted the Professor and refused to participate and he agreed to drop the whole issue, I didn't know how to react. I entered prepared for a fight and got instant acquiescence. I stammered for a few seconds until he finally said: "Go. If you're not curious why should I be?" I had no retort.

Retort or no, it wasn't fair. I *was* curious. I just wouldn't be manipulated. No. I couldn't be manipulated. It was against my character to allow such a thing. It was an affront to my personhood. How dare he suggest I wasn't curious! It was equivalent to saying I wasn't interested in self-knowledge: "an unexamined life is not worth living." I knew Socrates as well as him. I was of a mind to march right back there and tell him he had to study me. That's when I realized he had already manipulated me. If I didn't go back I wasn't curious. When I did go back he got what he wanted. Either way I lost. Fucking psychologists.

Peacocks and Passes

I had other classes, that quarter but none bears mentioning except to note that one was a math class, statistics, which I barely passed. I despise math. The quarter passed along quickly as quarters are wont to do.[*] I would like to say that I came to some great new insights and knowledge, but I did not. I would like to say that I made many new friends and had an active social life, but I did not. This is not to say that I learned nothing, but it was only the beginning of the things I was to learn. This is not to say that I formed no new friendships, but the people I grew closest to were Ren and the Professor, and I hesitate to call them friends as both were more and less than that. Mostly, I painted, drew, carpentered and wrote. In short, I spent my time trying to impress them.

It turned out that Ren did have office hours. I learned this after we presented our first assigned works of art and she handed each student a slip of paper with his or her grade on it. My paper had no grade on it, but was instead a note:

Riley,

Please see me during office hours. Tuesday 2-4 #0108 McGilt. Bring your project.

Wren

It hit me like a bolt of lightning: 'Wren!' with a 'W,' like the bird. She was a hotty before, but now... The deep shimmering blues of 'W' absorbed the leaching pink-orange of 'E' and changed what had been a clash of color into a magical continuum. My favorite, 'W,' if only I had known when first we met, it would have changed everything. It did change everything. The spice was still there, the desire, but now it was so much more, sophisticated, rich, with all the complexities of flavor that any dish could hold.

I practically skipped to her office hours, which is difficult with a cane. Her door was open. The room was tiny and the walls were bare, despite a plethora of painted canvasses strewn about. A tall bookcase filled with art supplies occupied the corner nearest the door, and her desk was a stout rectangle pushed toward the back corner. The remaining half

---

[*]For this reason I consider quarters superior to semesters, more knowledge is crammed in and the classes do not bog down with excessive weight.

of the room was cluttered with several easels and the aforementioned canvasses, every one painted with flowing curves of bright colors intermixed with dots or starbursts and set against a black background.

With some difficulty I weaved my way to the lone chair across from her desk. She sat behind her desk facing sideways, palette in her lap, painting on a small easel: flowing colors against solid black. She didn't look up or acknowledge my presence. I sat down and waited.

"Did you bring it?" she asked, as she added another brush stroke.

"Bring it?" I tasted a slightly sour thickening. "Oh. My project." The taste faded. "Yeah I have it here." I pulled it from my backpack. It was a crude avian carving with taut wires extending from the back and splayed out like the blades of a fan. Affixed to each of the wires were oblong and almond shapes of varying sizes and colors, some were painted, others were bare, and still others had human eyes cut from magazines pasted upon them.

Wren contemplated her painting, still not looking at my project or me. I stared at her profile. If possible she was even more attractive from the side. She had a small, cute nose, and the upturn was slightly exaggerated from the profile. She had bleached out the pink stripes in her hair. "Explain," she said.

"Explain?" More paste.

"Explain what the hell that is? Explain how it's abstract?"

"Well like you said, everything is abstract—"

She cut me off. "Don't spit my words back at me. I know what I said. I want you to explain how and why that *thing* is abstract." I started to speak but she interrupted again. "Wait, better yet, answer me this question first: where did your project rank on the continuum?"

During class all of the projects were displayed. Then Wren instructed everyone to vote in a secret ballot and rank the projects in order of abstractness, one being the most abstract and thirteen the least.

"I don't know. You didn't tell us the results."

"So guess."

"I don't know. Seven."

"Try again."

"Nine."

"Thirteen," she said, finally looking at me. "Least abstract." Her voice and look were stern, but I was thrilled to meet her eyes. They sparkled like emerald cut in perfect circles. I no longer felt anxious or confused. I just didn't care: the unknown, unnamed taste overwhelmed me with its complexity and beauty. Dumbstruck, I stared into the silence between us and held her gaze with infatuated eyes.

"Well?" Her voice broke through the spell, but I still had no words on my tongue only taste. "Hey! I asked you a question."

"I can't really control how the class voted. I thought mine was middle of the pack."

"And if I told you I agree with the class?"

"I guess I'd be disappointed." And I was. My mouth went dry. I wanted to say more but the sudden lack of saliva made it difficult.

"You know how many voted yours thirteenth?" I shook my head no. "Twelve. I'm guessing you're the one who ranked yours seventh?" She took the palette from her lap and set it on the desk in front of her. She folded her hands in her lap and leaned back in her chair. My eyes flitted involuntarily to her chest, another tight tank top, bright yellow, no bra. It matched the streaks in her hair. "Explain it to me," she said.

"It's wandering eyes." I made that up on the spot. It sounded good when I said it so I kept going. "They're unconnected to any face. Each stares in a different direction, each looks at something different."

"It's a peacock," Wren interrupted, "and a poorly carved one at that. The assignment was to make a piece as abstract as possible. How is a peacock abstract?"

I wanted desperately to impress her, but the words stuck in my throat. "Just because it has form doesn't mean it's not abstract."

"No. The fact that it is not abstract makes it not abstract." My face must have given away my disappointment because her voice softened. "Look Riley, I don't hate the piece. But it didn't fit the assignment."

"It's a peacock, yes. But the eyes make it abstract."

"It makes it a double entendre, it doesn't make it abstract. I don't want it explained to me, I want to see the abstraction within the piece, this is a *visual* arts course."

"Fair enough. But set aside the question of abstraction. You like it right?"

"No."

"But you said you didn't hate it at least."

"I take it back. I do hate it. You know why I hate it? Because it's a fraud. Everything about it screams fake, not only is it not abstract, it's not you."

I went from disappointed to pissed in an instant. I nearly retched at the bile in the back of my throat. Who did she think she was calling me a fraud? "You don't know the first thing about me."

"I know you don't strut. Peacocks strut. This isn't you."

"All you see is my cane. Is that it?"

"You could strut with a cane. But you don't. The only honest thing about this piece is the wandering eye."

"I used to strut." I said, less forcefully than I would have liked. She had cut me down, or I had. I had for years, ever since my injury.

"I know," she said. Her tone was kind.

"Do you really?" I asked.

"I've got a Sparx. Two in fact: a fish and an eight-footer, an egg. It was my first board. I know who you are."

I was surprised, but I tried not to let it show. "That doesn't mean you know me."

"No. I don't know you Riley. But I'm getting to know you."

I flashed a look I hadn't given a woman in a long time. She didn't bite. "Don't look at me like that," she said, but she smiled as she said it. "I'm not some pro-ho."

"Usually girls who aren't don't know that term."

"I'm sure you know plenty who are. Besides you're no pro and I'm your professor. Code of ethics and all that."

"I thought we were supposed to call you Wren. And you don't strike me as overly concerned with the University's personal conduct policy." I looked her up and down as much as I could with her behind the desk. "Or the dress code."

"Like I said, a means to an end. Weeding out the old pervs." Her smile was definitely sarcastic now, not flirty. "I'd have to say it's working pretty well."

I tried to change the subject. "So you just like blew off the curriculum for our class, are you seriously tenured?"

"Yep."

"How did you get tenure at twenty-six?"

"Wouldn't you like to know." It was a statement not a question.

"I would."

"Let's just say I've got friends in high places."

"That's all you're going to tell me?"

"For now. It's more than the rest of the class got from me."

"Still that hardly seems fair, seeing as you already know who I am."

"It's more than fair, seeing as how I'm not going to give you an 'F' on this assignment."

"What's my grade then?"

"No grade. You got a free pass. But there's only going to be two more assignments so you better make them count. You used to compete, so here's my challenge to you, put yourself into these next two projects. Try to follow the assignments, but it's more important that the art rings true. Don't give me any peacocks if you're not going to strut."

"Okay. I accept your challenge. But tell me, what's with all the flowing colors? What part of you is in these paintings?

"You meet my challenge and maybe you'll find out."

I tried my come-hither look again. "I love a challenge."

Wren laughed, "I'm counting on it. Now get out of my office before I have to break out the ruler."

"I'd love that."

"I know you would. Just don't forget the difference between a frog and a peacock."

"A frog and a peacock?"

"It takes a spell to turn a frog into a prince, but it doesn't take any magic to turn a peacock into an ass."

Fraternizing

I felt old and broken. I'd see the kids running through campus or walking toward the cliffs with surfboards under their arms and I'd taste the salt water. A weight built over my sternum, slowly at first, but it grew, and the stinky-sweet taste of overripe mangoes crept in. I thought I'd left that mood behind in a bottle of Prozac.

It's difficult to convey the real sense of what it's like to taste your emotions. The stronger the emotion the stronger the taste, and it's not just feelings, but moods, and moods are worse because the taste lingers. That's how I know pain isn't in your nerve endings, pain can linger. I've tasted pain, tasted it for months, even years, at a time.

Since my tastes have nothing to do with what's physically on my taste buds I can't brush them away or rinse with Listerine, to do so just stacks up the tastes. It's a weird concept, but I can taste two different flavors simultaneously with no blending, just both tastes present at the same time. As my mood deepened it became hard to eat and the weight upon my chest grew into a two-ton boulder pressing me to earth so that rising from bed each day required Herculean effort. I turned to an old friend to get me through.

One of the great things about university life is ready availability of drugs. You remember I said coffee was the second best thing for dulling my emotional flavors, well the best thing is marijuana, and it was easy to get.

This kid came up to me after my literature class, and offered to buy me a beer. His name was Sean and he recognized me from old issues of Surfer Magazine. It turned out that he was only twenty so he couldn't make good, but I bought a pitcher at the Round Table on campus and snuck him an extra glass.

Mostly he just wanted to talk about surfing and be able to tell his buddies that he had a beer with me, but when I asked if he knew where I could get some chronic he smiled a big ole grin. Sean was a dealer. He wasn't big time or anything, and it's hardly fair to call him a drug dealer since he only sold pot... well pot and occasionally mushrooms... and ecstasy... ok so he was a drug dealer, but he was cool, and we worked out an arrangement. Every Friday we'd head to the supermarket, he'd give me sixty bucks and I'd stock him up on beer for the week. Then we'd get blazed before I headed to Porter's Pub. About every other week I'd hit him up for a bag and he'd sell me a half-o for a hundred thirty bucks.

I started floating around high all day. It staved off the depression, dulled the piercing salty sad moments and most importantly kept the taste of Wren out of my mouth. Her flavor was tough to hold back. She was an obsession, a crush. I doodled her name in my notebooks like a giddy schoolgirl; it was just so pretty.

One brown Friday I bought Sean his quota, blazed up, then headed to the pub for some brews, when who should walk in, all by her lonesome, but Wren. I immediately called her over. "Can I buy you a drink?"

"I really shouldn't be fraternizing with students." She sat down with an impish smile. "But I've been told I don't seem like a woman overly concerned with the University's Code of Conduct."

"What are you drinking?"

"I'll have what you're having."

I ordered two Sierras and I watched Wren's backside as she headed for the restroom. More than sex appeal, swagger, the way she carried herself, there was a confidence there. Wren's garb was more modest than usual, although her grey long knit sweater was tight, revealing her unhindered fashion sensibilities. It hung to mid-thigh, cinched at the waist by a thick black strap with no ornamentation save a single silver buckle. Her black tights were full length, as the mid-October weather had been grey for a couple of days, and unseasonably cold on the bluffs where UCSD sits.

I took a big slug of Sierra and my Yangs fired off, fleeting hints of chocolate, cinnamon, coriander and cumin, stood out on the tip of my tongue, but greater depths of flavor lay beneath in unidentifiable layers. She stopped to chat with a man I didn't know, mid-twenties, probably a grad student. I wanted to punch him in the face. Sour pickles, not sour grapes, but still preposterous, as I had no claim on her at all.

She touched the man on the shoulder then made her way back to the bar. "So I hear you're an aspiring novelist," she said as she sat down next to me.

"Who'd you hear that from?" I didn't remember telling anyone about my book, not that I remembered everything, especially on leaving the pub.

"You know, on the wind, you pick things up just shooting the breeze."

38

"Well I've got to try something new. My Vis Arts professor keeps telling me my work is uninspired."

"I think the word I used was fraudulent." She frowned and clucked her tongue. "Now I hear you'd rather traffic in words."

"A wise woman once told me that our world was made of symbols. I figure it doesn't matter which ones I use, just so long as I communicate." I smiled at her and she rolled her exotic eyes. "But I have a little something cooking in the workshop. A piece of me, I hope."

"And a piece of nature as well?" Our second assignment was to take something from the natural world and express it through an abstraction.

"Of course. I got a 'needs improvement' on my last assignment in the 'follows directions' box. Teacher's a stern headmistress. Threatened me with a ruler."

"Shut up." She slapped me on the arm. I winced, only half faking as my bad arm is quite sensitive.

I raised my glass. "Salud."

"Salud," she echoed and we clinked.

I took a long sip. "You've got a very distinct aesthetic, the flowing colors and shapes. But how come they're all the same?"

"Not the same. Similar. But they're in response to different stimuli."

"What's that mean?" I asked.

"Never mind. I sculpt too. You haven't seen any of those."

"Do you chisel blocks of marble into naked dudes?"

"Not hardly," Wren laughed. An annoying laugh is a real turn off, but her laugh was inviting and sonorous. "I actually use clay. And you're more likely to see some boobies in my work than any dude's junk."

"Now I want to see these sculptures."

"Maybe if you're lucky. But you'll probably be disappointed. Remember I teach *abstract* art. Just because the breasts are there doesn't mean you'll see them. My sculptures tend to be more abstract than my paintings."

"I'm amazed you have room to do anything at all in that office. Do you always paint in there?"

"Not always, sometimes I work outdoors or get time in a studio room on campus, but real studio space is expensive and I already spend enough money just buying materials. Despite what you may have heard, us professors don't exactly make the big bucks."

"Sounds like you need a space."

"Yeah. And I have to figure out what to do with my paintings. No takers yet to show them, much less buy them. I don't really want to put them in storage but... You've seen my office."

I don't if it was her flavor, or the weed, or the spice, or the beer, but I decided to take a chance. "I have a space you can use. It's huge. And I won't charge you a thing."

"For real?"

"For real."

"Wow. Thanks Riley, that would really help. Where is it?"

"Here in La Jolla."

"Say, after these beers you wanna go puff?"

"Huh?'

"Come on," she said, "I'm already fraternizing. May as well shred the Code of Conduct now. Besides, you're obviously baked."

I nearly spit my beer out across the table. I had popped in the Clear Eyes before I arrived. I composed myself and played it off. "Alright, let's get ripped. We can go check out the space too." I pounded the rest of my beer. "You good to drive? We'll go to my place."

"Wait," said Wren, "I thought we were going to check out that space."

"Like I said let's head back to my place."

Wren groaned, "The space is at your house?"

"Relax. You're not committed to anything. Come check it out and you can make up your own mind. You can follow me over there."

"All right," Wren sighed. "My bike's out front."

"Bike?"

A Former Factory, Skinny Ankles, Iron Lungs and an Offer

I flipped a switch. The factory lighting buzzed and illuminated the space in pale fluorescent light.

"You live here?" Wren asked. Her voice echoed off the concrete walls through the massive rectangular space. "What is this place?"

"Some of the finest surfboards in the world were made in this room."

"You mean?"

"Yep. This is all that's left of Sparx Surfboards. Let me give you the grand tour. This is the main room. It used to be the factory floor. Bay doors, front and back. You can see my furniture." Halfway down the south wall sat an old futon with speakers on either side. In front of it was an old scratched up coffee table. The stereo was on the floor next to the far speaker. A beanbag chair and a couple of wooden crates formed a small sitting area. I pointed across to the north wall. "That's my workbench." A crude bench made of two by fours stood against the wall. A small toolbox and my art project, draped with a sheet, sat atop the bench. An old wax-covered longboard hung high above on the wall.

I led her to the southeast corner of the factory where a rectangular drywall box framed the only interior door. On one side of the box, sat two neatly tied trash bags, next to them cases of beer were stacked, six high and five across, next to them were a dozen wine boxes fronted by several rows of empty spirit bottles. "Holy shit," said Wren when she saw them.

"That's like three years worth of empties," I lied; it was more like eight months. "They don't pick up recycling here."

"You're like the neatest drunk in the world."

"You're right about me being neat." She was also right about me being a drunk.

We entered the drywalled area. I turned on the lights to reveal three small rooms. "Kitchen: stove, microwave, refrigerator. Bathroom. And the biggest room used to be the office but now it's my bedroom." I let her glance inside. My room was Spartan: a bed neatly made, a nightstand, a lamp and a dresser with my bong on top, no paintings or photos adorned the walls. The only decoration in the building was the surfboard mounted in the main room. "Head on out. I'm going to change the water in this thing." I emptied out the dirty bong water and filled it with cold bottled water from the fridge.

When I came back out Wren stood studying the line of colored sheets that hung on a wire stretched from the north wall over to the drywalled section to create a makeshift screen. "What's back here?"

"Don't go back there." She started to peek behind the sheets. "Hey! I'm serious don't go back there."

She jumped a little. "Sorry."

"No. I'm sorry. I didn't mean to snap, but you can't go back there."

"Why? What's back there?"

"That's where I keep the dead hookers." She didn't find that funny. "I just don't want you to see my project while I'm still working on it."

"So it's not under that sheet on the workbench?"

"Only part of it," I lied.

She shrugged, walked over to the futon, crashed down and crossed her legs. Even in tights she had nice legs. I'm into ankles. Skinny ankles are sexy and cankles are a deal-breaker. Her anklebones protruded over the tops of her hush puppies.

I crammed a big pinch of bud into the bowl and handed the bong to Wren. "Ladies first."

She took a second to admire the bong. "Nice piece, I like the colors." Then she ripped it, and I mean *ripped* it. The water bubbled for a good fifteen seconds before she pulled the bowl and cleared a monster column of thick white smoke. She blew a cloud and gave two dainty coughs before she handed the bong to me.

"Wow," I said. "A woman after my own heart, er, lung." Then I packed a smaller bowl and tried not to embarrass myself. I snapped it and exhaled without a hacking fit. "So what do you think?" I asked Wren. She looked at me blankly, eyes glassed over and looking more Asian than ever. "About the space," I clarified.

"Oh yeah. It's awesome. Plenty of room. You sure it's okay if I use it."

"I'd love for you to. It can feel pretty lonely in this place. I'd love the company... don't get me wrong, I won't bug you while you're working. I'm just saying..."

"No. I got you. I think this could work."

"The lighting isn't great. I mean it's bright enough, but the fluorescents are a little weird and I know you like to work with colors, but there is a switch over there that opens the bay doors on each side. When they're up you can get a fair amount of natural light in here during the day."

"I would love to work here. You're really helping me out."

"Great. I'll get a key made and you can come and go as you please."

"Really?"

"Yeah. Why not? I trust you."

Schmuck

Silent night. Not the song. My night. How long can you sit with someone and not say anything?

I tried not to look at Wren. Then I looked at Wren. Then I looked away. An interminable amount of time passed, the encounter patterned like instructions on a socially awkward shampoo bottle: Look. Don't look. Think. Repeat. It felt like a high school date where you're not sure if you're going to make-out.

I wished I had a television. I put on Pink Floyd, Dark Side of the Moon, which just made the whole experience more surreal. The cannabis veil descended and I took an inward turn, the external world subjected to an internal monitoring. I sat inside my head, awash in the stream of thoughts analyzing actions and taking none: *Is this awkward? Why doesn't she say anything? What should I say? Would she let me kiss her? My legs are bouncing. I should stop bouncing my legs. Should I put my arm around her? But she's my professor. Is she as uncomfortable as I am? Why am I so uncomfortable? Be cool. My leg is bouncing again. I have to stop fidgeting. Does she notice? Should I look at her? Should I pack another bowl? God she's pretty. I really want to put my arm around her. She's right next to me. Why am I being such a chicken? Put your arm around her Riley. Shoot, you're alone, she hasn't left, try to kiss her. But what if she doesn't let me? What if she's not into me? I think she likes me. But if I try and kiss her will she think I offered her this space just to try and sleep with her. Would she sleep with me? Tonight? You're such a schmuck.*

"Does it hurt?" she spoke? She spoke!

What did she mean? My bouncing leg, my injury. What should I say?
"Not really. Sometimes it aches."

"How'd you hurt it?"

"I don't like to talk about it."

****

The first words out of her mouth were, "I'm sorry." I stood there dumb in glue-gummed confusion, until she added, "...for the other night. I didn't mean to be weird. I was just really stoned."

My cervical column loosened and I dismissed it with a wave of my hand. "No worries. I wasn't talking much either. I was worried you thought I was a weirdo."

"Oh I do," she smirked, "but not because you weren't talking."

"Ha ha. I brought you a key." I handed her the freshly cut key on an old Sparx Surfboards keychain.

"Thanks." She looked at the surfboard shape attached to the ring. "Collector's item?"

"Oh yeah. It's worth less than the plastic it's made out of." Her office seemed more cluttered than the last time I'd been in it. "You need some help taking stuff over?"

"Yeah. Do you think I could borrow your car? Wren's bike was a pink Vespa. Somehow this made more sense than a Honda or a Harley, but with Wren nothing would have surprised me. She bit her bottom lip and looked away with the shy hesitation of little girl, and pivoted her right leg atop a pointed toe. The pose was irresistible, if she'd asked for the pink slip instead of to borrow it I would have said yes. I wondered if she knew the power of her posture. Probably, most cute girls know they're cute and don't hesitate to use their cuteness to get what they want. Then again, Wren was not most girls.

I borrowed Wren's faculty parking pass. She was stunned to learn that I didn't have a handicapped placard. Call it pride or stupidity, but the only time I'd ever used my injury to my advantage was when I applied to UCSD. I don't consider myself disabled. I'm able. Though I was mostly unable to load Wren's things into my car. Wren did all the heavy lifting, five trips of easels, boxes, and canvasses both painted and blank. In the hour it took to pack I examined Wren's paintings. They weren't just flowing colors against black backgrounds, though they all had a quality I can only describe as "flow" or "motion." Some used brightly colored shapes like crosses, exes and spirals, others were less geometric, more like starbursts or fireworks, still others reminded me of graph paper. But none were stationary. Static, yes, they were paintings after all, but not stationary. Every shape was doubled, tripled, quintupled across the canvas or connected by colored streaks, even the flat squares and triangles. They moved.

"If I were exhibiting these I'd call the collection *Color in Motion*," I said as we left with the last load.

"I call it *Music*."

Music

The music hit me like shrapnel. It rattled my bones, and slashed my eardrums from all directions as it echoed through the factory. My stereo was incapable of this decibel level. Then I noticed the head-high monitors and monster woofer in front of the open bay doors at the opposite end of the room. Wren stood before an easel, her back to me. I put a finger in one ear to damp down the full-fledged orchestral rumpus from Beethoven and clinked past Wren. I found the stereo and turned it off. Wren jumped and spun around, then spun back the way she had been facing. "Riley! You scared me."

I cocked my head. "No thanks I'm not hungry!" I shouted.

She scrunched her face like a pug. "What?"

"No you are!"

A look of recognition crossed her face. "Very funny."

"The music's pretty loud."

"Sorry."

"No worries. I like the speakers. You putting in a flatscreen too?"

"With your living conditions a ten inch Toshiba would be a major upgrade. Why is it that you don't have a TV?"

"I don't watch TV."

"Because you don't have a TV. Anyway, I usually paint to music unless I'm just doing touch ups. Your stereo wasn't cutting it, so I brought mine from home."

"You didn't have one in your office."

"Headphones."

"They don't work here?"

"This is better. You mind turning it back on. You can turn it down but I was sort of in the groove here."

I turned it back on. Then I went to smoke a bowl. I was nearly out of pot. I made sure I had another hit left for bedtime and packed a little one, just a toke to mellow out and ease that flavor I got when she was around. It bothered me that I couldn't place it, the taste. It existed, but as a mélange, no single element stood out, flavors moved and shifted like the shapes in her paintings, subtle flavors and hints of flavors vying, ebbing, coming forth, falling back; an edible chameleon, it hid against the background of the other flavors around it. I let it disappear in an exhalation of cool grey smoke.

Colors

The music was off when I woke up. The Brother's Karamazov lay open next to me on the bed. I went out into the main room. It was dark. I flipped on the lights and heard the familiar buzz start up. The room was empty.

Wren's painting was on the easel. Words don't do it justice. The familiar dark background was present only at the edges, the bulk of the large canvas was covered in whorls of brilliant color: golden spirals turned to flattened ochre ribbons and spun off a mishmash of movement where tiny magenta squares popped forth vermillion diamonds fitted to flying crimson crosses. It was round and angular, tiny and giant, and all of it whipped outward from the center. I had to look away, overcome by a powerful sense of vertigo, falling. A thought struck me in the spin: *there was something I had to remember*. I pushed the thought aside.

I collected myself and looked back to it, studying the way she made movement occur on a still canvas. It was awesome, the panoply of color neither jarring nor garish, nor beautiful. It was awesome in the truest sense of the word: it inspired my awe. I tasted her flavor. Only she was capable of this. This was what she meant when she challenged me to put something of myself into my art. How and why this was her I couldn't fathom or explain, but it was. She was on this canvas. My hands shook. I squeezed my cane's grip to stanch the sense that I was falling into the colors.

Collapse

Wren was there nearly every day until the collapse. Each time a different soundtrack blared, classical mostly, some jazz, but no matter what played it was always set to repeat. It was obnoxious and it caused me to smoke more in an effort to blanch my palette, but I never asked her to stop.

I returned home on a white day, mid-quarter, after an early afternoon round of drinking, to find Wren but no music. She was using an ultra-fine brush to add color to a canvas she painted several days earlier. "I was going to call you in for office hours," she said with her back to me, "but I figured I'd just talk to you here."

I knew right away what she wanted to talk about. Earlier that week we had displayed our second projects in class. Mine was a cross between a diorama and a mosaic. I spent days creating balsa wood cutouts and combined them with construction paper backgrounds to render an ocean scene using only angular geometric shapes. The highlight was a balsa wood plank with triangles affixed to the bottom. I set it in the foreground floating in a small dish of water dyed with green and brown food coloring. Boat or surfboard, kayak, canoe, it was up to the viewer.

"I'm giving you a 'C'. And trust me, it's a gift." She rinsed her brush in a jar of water then used a rag to wipe the excess from the fine bristles. She faced me. "I don't know how to say this exactly, so I'm just going to say it. It's not good. I think you tried, and I think you put something of yourself into it. That's why I'm not failing you, but it really isn't abstract, and your technique…"

"I know." Saltwater stung both my eyes and my palette, but I could see it was hurting her to criticize me, and that made the criticism hurt less.

"It's okay Riley." She walked over and put her hand on my arm.

"No. No it's not."

"It is. It's just one project for one class."

"No, it's not. It's more. It's…"

"What is it you want?" Her voice was so tender it reminded me of my mother.

I want your love.

But I couldn't say that. "I want to be great."

"You are great."

"What's so great about me?" There was a pause; a vacant silence filled the empty room. "That's what I thought."

"I don't understand. Why would you expect to achieve greatness in comparative arts class?"

I didn't. I knew its power. Greatness was a means to an end. I wanted her.

"You'll find it Riley."

"Find what?"

"Whatever it is you're looking for." But the lines of pain on her face confirmed what I already knew deep down, that she already felt pity for me, as empty and useless as the bottles in the corner. Art or no art, I knew I wasn't good enough, but I had hoped. I felt a stabbing pain in my gut and choked on my own hot breath. It was the second worst I'd ever felt in that room.

And then she hugged me.

I scalded my tongue on saffron tea. My legs buckled, my body insisting that I drop to my knees, that I genuflect before my own shame. But she propped me up. Her tiny arms kept me from falling.

"You'll find it," she whispered, "what you're meant to do. You'll find that thing you're great at."

I broke away from her.

She reached for me, her blouse stained with my tears and now hers.

"What did I do?"

I threw my cane across the room. "I found it and I lost it! And I'll never get it back!" I flopped onto the beanbag and punched my bad leg with my good arm, again and again I punched until Wren caught my arm and hugged me. But even her hug couldn't soothe me this time. Rose petals, delicate, floral and bitter lay upon my palette. My leg throbbed and for a moment I was transported back to that instant, the injury, the thrashing wild pain that presented with such subtle sapor.

Synesthesia

She was there when I awoke, seated on the edge of the bed. "You're still here," I said.

"I was worried about you."

"Don't be."

"Well I was. Am."

My cane stood in the corner. She must have brought it in. "Can you bring me my cane?" I sat up. My leg throbbed. My world still dripped with rosewater and rotten fruit, but that was unlikely to change anytime soon. She brought the cane over and set it next to me. "Grab the bong and the weed too."

"Are you sure that's a good idea?"

I ignored her and struggled to my feet. I got the bong myself and smoked a bowl. I felt better at once, as my tastes and feelings faded away.

Several of Wren's paintings were displayed in the main room. She'd been working while I was asleep. They were amazing, and for a moment I was envious, but then I decided to ask: "So what's with the music?"

"What do you mean?"

"What do I mean? Come on. The name of your collection is 'Music'. Every time I come home the bass is shaking the foundation of an eight thousand square-foot factory. Why the music?"

She blushed. "It'll sound weird."

"Come on. I had a fucking nervous breakdown in front of you. You can tell me about your paintings. Besides aren't artists supposed to be weird anyway?"

"You can't go telling other people."

"Who am I going to tell?"

"I don't know. The other students in class."

"Like they even talk to me. But if it makes you feel better I promise not tell anyone. Come on, you say it's weird and swear me to secrecy. I was curious before but now I have to know."

"Fine." She took a deep breath. "I call it 'Music' because that's what I'm painting. I'm painting the music. That's why I'm always playing different stuff, every song is its own muse."

"Oh," I said, underwhelmed, "so it's abstract. You convert one set of symbols, the musical notes and beats and stuff, into visual symbols. You paint what you think the music would look like if it were colors."

"Not exactly. It's abstract like everything is abstract. But the paintings are realistic depictions."

"I don't understand. What does that mean?"

She walked over to a group of canvasses turned to face the wall. One by one she flipped them around, eight in total. They were large canvasses, each one several feet across. None were alike, but all had similarities, shades of the same yellows, oranges and blues, but with different levels of brightness and different patterns. The shapes were similar, mostly loops and pentagons, but the sizes of the shapes and the bursts of color were different. The first painting and the final painting displayed prominent grid patterns I would liken to an outdoor trellis. They were remarkable. All of the paintings conveyed the sense of movement characteristic of Wren's work.

"This series is Beethoven's Third Symphony in E Flat Major. The first three paintings are the first movement, the next two are the second, the next one is the third, and the final two are the fourth.

"I see music. I guess you could call it a condition. But it's really just how I perceive music. Certain sounds evoke images. What I paint is what the music looks like."

"So you imagine what the music looks like and then paint that on the canvas."

"No. I paint the music. But I don't imagine. To me music, and some other sounds... I just see them. Music has shape and color and movement. I don't have to imagine. And the same music played the same way; it always looks the same. It's called synesthesia."

"So seeing music is called synesthesia?"

"Yes. But not just seeing music, some people taste shapes, or have colored letters, like every letter of the alphabet is a specific color."

"There's a word for that?"

She ignored me and walked over to another canvas leaned up against the wall and covered by a sheet. It was much smaller than the canvasses she'd been using of late.

"Synesthesia?" I asked.

"It's where one sense triggers another sense. Scientists have known about it for a long time, but they've only recently begun to study it in depth. They still don't really understand it. At least not that I know of, no one's been able to explain why I have it. It has something to do with my brain."

"So are emotions a sense? Like if an emotion triggers a taste is that synesthesia?"

"I don't know. Maybe. That's a really odd question."

I hobbled over to her. "Did you know that in ancient times people were forbidden to speak the name of God? It's the same reason you didn't let anyone outside your tribe know your true name, to name something was to have power over it. In fact, Ya—"

She gave me a long hug and for a moment all the weight and pressure and salt and rot wafted away like smoke on the breeze replaced by Wren's seductive sapor. We were still friends.

"Is that a new piece?" I asked.

"Yes," she answered, "I painted it at my office. But I did the sketch here."

"More music?"

"No. Something new."

"Can I see it?"

"Not yet. We need to talk."

"Look I know what you're going to say and I'm sorry." I inhaled deeply, fighting my anxiety. "I shouldn't have flipped out. I'm just relieved that you're here. I hope you don't think less of me, sometimes it's just…it's hard you know? I mean I used to be a pro-surfer and now I can hardly walk. I had everything planned out, I was coming up the ranks, the company was growing, and then… it just fell apart. Everything. And then I got hurt and anyways I'm sorry. I won't freak out on you again I promise." The words tumbled out of me. I think I'd been waiting to say all that, to someone, for a very long time, even if I did make a promise I couldn't keep.

Wren smiled at me. She has a giving smile. It gives a little bit of her happiness to you. "That wasn't what I was going to say, but I'm glad you said it. And you didn't need to apologize. Well, not for that anyway. I think we both might owe each other an apology though."

"You don't owe me an apology. Keep coming over, keep painting, your work is amazing and I'm lucky to get to see it, and to get to see how you work. No apology necessary, let's just go back to normal."

"Riley you lied to me. But I only know you lied because I violated your trust. So the way I see it we both have something to apologize for, just not what you were thinking it was." I didn't understand. When had I lied to her?

Her beige tea length skirt didn't sway so much as flow, beneath a long-sleeved brown orange paisley print, as she glided the two steps back to the canvas. It was very bohemian compared to her normal attire. I realized that I hadn't been noticing her clothes of late; her style had been subsumed in her identity. I wondered how she'd feel about that? I wondered if the more subdued tone in her clothing was a statement, and if so, was the statement directed at her or at me? Was this her serious outfit? An artist's equivalent of a business suit?

All these thoughts and observations were quickly set aside when she picked up the work and set it on an easel. "You need to see this," she said, and removed the sheet. A stepstool, metal with yellow plastic on the top step, lay overturned in the foreground at the bottom of the painting. Empty grey space dominated the center of the canvas. A large bay door, corrugated metal set in concrete, filled the background. A thick iron pipe flecked with rust ran the length of the painting's foreground at the top of the canvas. A rope hung from a heavy knot tied around the pipe. Its end dangled, severed and frayed, above the toppled stepstool.

"I didn't know how to bring it up, but once I saw... I couldn't just ignore it. So I painted this."

"You had no right."

"I know. And I'm sorry, but Riley, it's not healthy keeping it like that, untouched, like some kind of sick shrine."

"I'm sick? Is that right doctor? I'm sick?"

"Yes it is sick. And you know it. That's why you hide it back in the corner behind that screen of sheets. You know it's sick."

"Well thanks for the diagnosis, but you're still a snoop. And I don't owe you an apology. I'm entitled to keep some things to myself. That's private."

"You don't owe me an apology?"

"It's my life! Who are you? You're just my art professor. I don't know anything about you. Where are you from? Who are you? You don't share so why should I."

"You're right Riley. You don't know me. And I don't know you. You don't owe me an apology for hiding it. You owe me an apology because you wanted me to find it."

"Bullshit! I owe you an apology because you're a fucking snoop?"

"You give me a key. Tell me I can come and go as I please. Set up those sheets. Come off it, that little screen isn't for privacy; it's for curiosity. And you made me curious. You could have walled it off. Or locked it up. Or cleaned it up. For God's sake why is it still hanging there?"

I didn't have an answer. It wasn't like I hadn't thought a million times to take down the rope or to move the stool. Shit, I half-tried to sell the whole place. I even called a realtor. I just couldn't.

"Riley, you've got to let go of whatever it is that you're hanging on to." I glared at her. "Sorry, the pun was accidental I promise."

I marched back to my bedroom, as much as one can march with a limp and a cane, and came back with a surfboard under one arm. I set it lengthwise on Wren's largest easel. "Since we're being so honest. Here's my final project." Wren had assigned the class to do an abstract self-portrait. "There were some blanks left in storage so I shaped a brand new board. Have at it."

But she didn't criticize. She stepped closer and examined the board intently. She touched the jagged cracks in the rails where I'd taken out chunks of fiberglass and foam. She ran her fingers gently around the edges of the gaping hole in the board's center and the fragments of shattered mirror affixed without pattern to the board's surface, scattered amidst red streaks and spots of pink and grey. She silently mouthed the words scrawled above the tattered stomp pad: 'NEVER AGAIN.'

"Well?" I asked.

"The red is it...?"

"Yeah it's blood."

"Oh God." She grimaced and pulled her hand back.

"It didn't hurt as much as you'd think."

"And the other bits?"

56

"Scar tissue. Dead nerve endings. You said to put something of myself into it."

"It's brilliant," she mumbled, then looked at me, "and sad."

I couldn't stand the pity in her eyes, so I sneered at her and said, "I'm broken, right?"

"Everyone's broken. And you can't always repair the breaks. Sometimes all you can do is try to find some other pieces that fit."

"More honesty, eh?"

"You've got to figure out for yourself how to fill the hole in that board. But whatever it is, the pain of the past... I don't know, I just know that whatever you're holding onto is holding you back." She put her hand on my arm. "You're not alone."

I looked into her eyes, green and glimmering, and unique. I felt a tinge of hope, and tasted the fullness and complexity of Wren. Everything else washed away. "You want honesty?" I grabbed her around the waist and kissed her.

III. CHANCES

Focus

Colin's 'artwork' is predictably horrible, but I have learned to suffer it. I observe it, knowing that it will cause feelings of sadness, revulsion, anger, confusion, and pain. But instead of dwelling on these feelings, I observe them. They are beyond my control, they are *of me*, but they are not *me*. It took many long hours of sitting in silence to learn this lesson.

I suffer through his exhibition. The relief that follows is my reward. It's like getting a shot at the doctor's office. You see the needle. You feel the alcohol swab. You know it's coming. Then there is the pinch, as the needle penetrates the skin. Then it's over. The pain ends the anxiety and you discover that the anxiety was far worse than the pain.

Colin leaves and I grow an inch taller before I'm rushed to the cold white tiles of the open and empty shower room and I shrink. The orderly pulls the knob and starts the stream of water. He tells me to get in. He hasn't tested the water.

Ice water in my own mouth, I tentatively reach my hand into the stream. It feels fine, but the fear and pressing dread remain. I look back over my shoulder. "Strip down," he says. The orderly stares, to him I have no name, just as he is nameless to me. They all are. Names breed familiarity, and familiarity breeds compassion. Compassion is incompatible with forced isolation.

I tremble at the cold flow. The cold rushes in but ebbs out slow as a moonless tide. I swallow at the hard coin cast at the back of my throat. I try to observe my feelings, but I cannot, they have a hold on me.

I strip. I need my thermometer. Again I reach in a hand. I put it gingerly into the water then quickly pull it out. "Get in," he says. I am meat. He is authority.

I give one final glance behind me and step in. I wash as quickly as I can. Like a crackhead scratching my hands lather then scrub scalp and body. I'm done. But still the oxidized terror remains in my throat, and the frigid wet recedes as with the turning of the earth.

I think of my story.

Second Grade

April 4, 1982. April is a green month, bright green like spring foliage. It's directly to my left, tight against my hip:

I squirmed in my orange chair, the short kiddie-kind with metal legs and a plastic seat. Second-graders sat in groups at square tables. The girls seated to my left and right, had names that started with brown; I think Carla and Chelsea or something like that. Maria Gonzales sat across from me. Ms. Hoenikker had me with three girls because she said I acted up when I sat with the boys. It wasn't true. It was that Kevin was always picking on me, calling me dork and stuff. I hated him and his barfy name.

I stared at Maria. Her hair was black and shiny and pretty. It made my legs feel tingly to look at it. She had a pretty name, grey and orange.[*] Her name was easy to look at. Maria was easy to look at too.

My leg tingled. I kicked out. I didn't mean to. I caught the edge of the table with my foot and my chair slid back. The metal legs screeched against the floor. Green dots flashed then spread out.

"Riley!" Ms. Hoenikker called on me out of turn. "Sit up. Do you know the answer?"

"What's the question?"

"Why haven't you been paying attention? Page one fifty-six, number seventeen."

I fumbled through the pages of my textbook. Red-blue-brown. 1-5-6. I looked for red-blue-brown. It was hard because they all looked red unless I looked really close. I found it, page 156, but there weren't any problems, just a couple bubbles filled with words and a picture of a smiling black man in a sweater.

"Page one hundred fifty-six," said Ms. Hoenikker.

"I'm on page one fifty-six. There aren't any problems."

She came over to my desk. She moved fast. "Riley Sparx you are on page one sixty-five." She turned the page for me and walked back to the blackboard. "Number seventeen." She picked up the chalk. "Go ahead and read the problem aloud for the class."

---

[*] CLARIFICATION: The red 'r' and primrose 'i' blend to make a red-orange bracketed by two orange 'a's.

60

I started to read number 17. "Fifty-one minu—" Her chalk screamed against the blackboard. Electric pain seared through my left temple behind another burst of green dots. I cried out. There was a taste, not entirely unpleasant, but at the time I didn't know what it was. Now I know it far too well.

"Riley. Enough with the outbursts," said Ms. Hoenikker. "Please finish reading the problem."

"Fifty-one minus fifteen," I read. Ms. Hoenikker wrote the rest of the problem on the board. Her chalk didn't squeak and I didn't see any more flashes, but pain and the funny taste lingered in my mouth.

"Come on Riley you can do this," Ms. Hoenikker said. "What are your rules? Look up in the corner. Rule one, where do we start? What column?"

"The ones column."

"That's right. So what is one minus five? Oops, right? We can't do that so what do we do?" I tried to swallow. "We borrow from the..." she waited for my answer. It was hard to swallow, like my mouth was full of glue. "Look at the rules," she said.

I tried not to look at the colored digits on the wall next to the list of rules. The list was written in black magic marker. Black letters were good. They looked right. I read rule number 2: "We borrow from the tens column."

"Right, so how much do we borrow?"

I was ready for this one. Rule number 3: "Borrow one."

"Good, so we cross out the five." Chalk. Blackboard. Flash. Pain. Green dots. That taste. "So Riley, how many are left, what is five minus one?"

5 - 1. Blue minus red. I looked to rule 4, but I caught a glimpse of a 5 on the wall, a red 5. Disaster. 5 - 1. Blue minus red. No. Red minus blue. No, that was the ones column you couldn't do red minus blue. But wait, 5 is blue. So: 5 - 1. Blue minus red. Blue minus red is purple. No. That's blue plus red.

"Riley what is five minus one?"

"Purple," I blurted out. The class laughed. A pinch slid down my spine, neck to my tailbone like grips on a guide-wire. My tongue burned like hot tea.

Ms. Hoenikker looked furious. "Stop goofing around Riley! Now what is five minus one?"

Red minus blue. Purple. It was the numbers on the wall. *Which numbers am I using? Fuck!* I had just learned the 'F' word like two weeks ago. It was the only pink curse word in my repertoire. Red minus blue. Purple? On the wall purple was 7. "Seven." Wrong. Everyone laughed at me. I wanted to cry. She wrote the 4 in three sharp lines: screech, screech, screech, more green dots, more pain.

"How many do we carry?" She finally stopped picking on me. "Class?"

"Ten." They said in chorus. The burning on my tongue eased. I tasted hints of sweetness.

"So, what is eleven minus five?"

Eleven is two ones. Red, red. 5 is blue. Red minus blue. Wait, I already tried that you can't do red minus blue; we had to borrow and carry. It must be blue minus red. Purple. 4. Why'd I say seven before? 4 is purple, but 7 is on the wall as purple. Blue minus red is purple. "Four." I yelled without raising my hand.

Ms. Hoenikker thought I was acting up. "Recess," she said. I never got to go to recess.

"But five minus one is four." The class roared again. My whole mouth burned. I hated math.

"Thank you for that Riley. But what is eleven minus five?"

God, why couldn't she just leave me alone? "Stupid." I muttered it under my breath but she still heard me. I was lucky. I wanted to say fuck.

"What did you say?" asked Ms. Hoenikker.

"Nothing."

She was not buying that. "What did you say Riley? You want to say it again?" Tin taste, heat on my neck, I couldn't do anymore math. "What did you say, Riley? What did you say?"

"I said it's stupid. Your rules are stupid. This problem is stupid!" I threw my pencil. It landed at Ms. Hoenikker's feet. I expected her to charge across the room, but she didn't.

Instead she took off her glasses, stared me down in front of the whole class and said: "Tell me Riley, is it stupid or are you stupid?"

Needless to say this confrontation drew the attention of my mother, Ms. Hoenikker, and Ms. Glisan the principal. Ultimately things were smoothed over and Ms. Hoenikker sat me down and told me that I wasn't stupid and that she shouldn't have lost her temper. She never actually said, "I'm sorry."

A few weeks later we had 'placement testing' which I now know consisted of an I.Q. Test and a modified Minnesota Multiphasic Personality Inventory. That's right, they gave a psych-evaluation to seven year olds. To this day I do not know if this was a common practice in California public schools, or if my school was targeted for this type of testing because of my presence at it.

That whole year was horrible. I hated second grade. Especially math, the numbers on the wall were not just wrong; many were inverted. 1 was blue and 5 was red when 5 should have been blue and 1 red. When I managed to add up a sum or figure a difference I often lost it by reference to an improper color. I constantly had to translate colors to numerals and vice versa. Even if I wrote out all the steps, I often carried the wrong digit or carried a digit the wrong direction. To this day I remain terrible at math.

Shortly after the incident with Ms. Hoenikker I was diagnosed with a learning disability, which turned out to be a blessing in disguise, but at the time was humiliating and traumatic, no less so because of my mother's reaction to the news. She flipped and demanded to meet with the principal right then and there.

Now I didn't hear everything said at the meeting from my seat outside the principal's office, but it was loud, and rumors flew around the school that I got expelled and that my mom accused the principal of doing 'the devil's work,' threw a stapler at the wall, spit on the carpet and attacked the principal with her shoe. I can neither confirm nor deny the veracity of all of the rumors, but I wasn't the only one in the family prone to throwing things in school.

Mom pulled me out of school that same day. I spent the rest of the afternoon locked in my room listening to my mother alternate between sobs and loud mournful prayers. Meanwhile my father smoothed things over with the school and I returned to class the next day.

The taunts and gossip for the rest of that year were nearly unbearable. I was the kid with the crazy mom. The day I came back my older brother Billy got suspended for fighting. He punched a boy and kicked him in the face while he was on the ground. It broke the kid's nose and chipped one of his front teeth. I knew the kid. His name was Jack and he was one of the popular fifth-graders. I heard Billy tell my Dad that Jack said Mom fucked the principal to get me back in school.

That night I asked Billy what that meant. Fuck was just a bad word to me.

"Retard! This is all your fault." He threw me to the ground and kicked me in the stomach.

Father

Perhaps I shouldn't have started telling you about second grade. I don't want you to think I had an unhappy childhood. This couldn't be further from the truth. Tragedy touched my life, but never as a child.

I spent my childhood in the ocean.

My father was a former professional surfer and one of the early practitioners of the art of surf forecasting. My father surfed when the purses were less than a tenth of what they are today, but he parlayed his surf career into a successful surf shop and custom surfboard shaping business, Sparx Surfboards.

My father knew interesting people. He made custom surfboards for several professional athletes in San Diego, including the Charger's starting left tackle. The board was a thirteen-foot blue and gold behemoth, over four inches thick at the center with concave rockers and steep rails. It was as big and fast as the man that rode it. There was no more fearsome sight in the summer surf during the five years he played in San Diego. Clad only in his yellow baggies, he'd go ripping down the line with surfers duck-diving and bailing, and spongers flailing to escape. He called spongers 'buoys' and treated them as such. He'd charge straight at them and shave away at the last instant throwing up a vicious spray. He could do that on my father's boards, they were that good. My father was part of the shortboard revolution, but as long as he shaped he never stopped making true performance longboards.

I grew up in paradise. When he retired from surfing my father opened his surf shop in La Jolla and built my childhood home on a half-acre of land above the north shore of Lake Hodges. He sketched the design himself. It was a modest home, but perfectly suited to the lake and the unique features of the property. The house set at an angle to the lakeshore, and at the rear of the house a redwood deck jutted out to overlook Lake Drive and a panoramic expanse of Lake Hodges. An American flag flew year round atop a hill across the lake. The deck wrapped around the home giving views of the lake from unexpected angles.

My father and the architect envisioned every detail of the property when they designed it. The home angled so that the front porch faced away from the lake, and in the afternoons when the sun was at it's hottest, the porch and the entire length of the house received the shade of a sprawling live oak at least eighty years old. Beneath the deck, down a gentle hill, was a small garden with two orange trees, two lime trees and small planters for herbs and tomatoes and carrots. It was here in this garden that my mother spent much of her time. It received the best light in the morning and a respite from the sun in the afternoon, when the hills cast shadows across the lake. Oak trees and cacti dotted the hill above us, and willows lined the arroyo to the east.

My father built fifteen miles inland despite being a man of the ocean. He said it made each trip to the coast a pilgrimage, a small reminder to respect both the ocean and the time you have to commune with it. "I gotta have a buffer," he once told me. "If I started every day at the ocean I'd never get out of the water." I sometimes wonder where that wisdom went in my father's final years. Most men gain wisdom with age, but my father somehow lost it, lost perspective.

My father's status in the community was based upon his talent, first as a surfer and later as a shaper and a businessman. He stood six foot four, buff and bearded; it was once a red beard, but for most of my life it was sandy and then grey, like his hair. My brother inherited more his build and look, but I inherited his talent for surfing. And it was my talent, along with my oddities, that afforded me the status of privileged child within my own privileged family.

Second grade ended, and third grade began with the same sorts of torment as before. Children can be cruel. It was harder on Billy. He went to middle school and not only saw all his old tormentors, but new and older tormentors as well, eighth graders. In retrospect I doubt it was much worse than middle school is for most kids, but Billy took it hard. I lived in a sort of dream world, my Yangs present, but not understood. I spent a great deal of time trying to figure out what I was feeling and thinking. I knew I was not normal. Mom was the only person I could talk to about it. She said I was an angel. Mom said a lot of things.

A Secret From Myself

I was two months into third grade when I turned eight. Two months into third grade, my first and only viewing of the jewel. I remember coming back to time.

I lay on my back. Two paramedics, both skinny blonde guys no older than thirty, crouched above me flanked by a princess. One wore glasses. He pulled out a flashlight. The other paramedic stuck out a gloved hand. "Please ma'am give us some space. We need to check him out."

The princess did not back up but instead pressed forward and knelt at my side between the two paramedics. It was my mother, complete with pink frills and tiara. "My angel. Thank God." Her face went pale. "Your glow is red."

My mother referred to my halo, not my cheeks, but the paramedic mistook her meaning. "He's just a little flush, ma'am. Please let us examine him."

The ambulance ride was less exciting than it should have been. My father watched and mouthed 'I love you' as the paramedics closed the double doors at the ambulance's rear. My mother rode beside me holding my hand. The immediate danger of my seizure apparently passed, the driver did not use the sirens. My Yangs were quiet, though I didn't yet call them Yangs. My head was heavy and I had a muddled taste in my mouth, a nonsensical taste, not connected to an obvious emotion, a taste that didn't exist.

There is something I need to remember. I couldn't shake this thought.

I searched my mind deliberately. I fixed upon the day: today, birthday, brown day to my right. I reached out and touched it with my fingertips, neither hard nor soft, simply there. Time, space, color, location, all fixed, all set in the layered hoop of personal history that encircled my body.

I try and recall the day's events. I see myself in the mirror getting ready for my party, I have on a white robe pinned back at the waist, a rope belt and sandals. My mother stands behind me wearing a gown of pink sequins with ruffles on the sleeves. She puts a plastic halo on my head. "Now you have two halos," she says.

I see the costumes of every guest: my father the skeleton, my mother the princess, a doctor, Adam and Eve, two vampires, a ghost. I see Billy dressed as Han Solo. I see a fraggle win the costume contest. His name is Jake, my only friend from school. That was the last time I ever saw him, his family moved away before I 'recovered' from my birthday experience. I bob for apples and carve a jack-o-lantern. The adults in the corner throw darts and guard the 'grown up jug.' I see chocolate cake with the letters 'Happy Birthday Riley' carefully written in icing with my colors. I see the silver streak of the 'y' dance happily away. I see my father smile as he plugs into his amp and pulls up his hood. I see him slip on his skeleton mask and start to play his guitar. I see strange colored shapes wax and wane with the sounds of my father's music. I see the strobe become a spotlight. I see the room shake, and then I open my eyes to see my mother.

All these images were and are emblazoned upon my mind's eye. I remembered every instant, every moment accounted for, image after image in sequence, my whole birthday, the people and their positions and what they said. I saw it all and I could not decipher what I was to remember. I kept a secret from myself.

Admission

I was admitted to the hospital and put into a loud machine. Around my head it whirred and clicked. I saw patterns of dots expand like starbursts and contract to a point. They flexed with the pace of the *whir-click-click*. They stuck me with needles, and then we waited.

For hours we waited, my mother in unceasing prayer, my father coming and going with food and drinks, getting up to use the restroom and pace the halls, any excuse to escape my mother's utterances. Then the doctor came in and said I was normal.

Actually, he said: "It's not epilepsy. We can't find any tumors or lesions. Everything appears normal." He told my mom to keep me hydrated and watch my condition, and to not overstress me or let me near another strobe.

To most this would seem like good news, but my mother didn't hear 'normal.' She heard 'epilepsy-tumor-lesion' and became convinced that I had nearly died. She was unsurprised that the doctor had no answers as she put little stock in science. Her prayer vigil in thanks to God lasted several days and culminated with my parents pulling me from school. My mom didn't want me to have another seizure without her or my father around. My father didn't like the idea, but my mother and her fears prevailed. For a woman of great faith, my mother feared a great deal. I don't think I was unsupervised for a minute over those next few years. For the first few months after my seizure I did not leave the house. My mother doted on me day and night. Billy was not so lucky. He was thrown to the wolves of middle school hell, unpopular sixth grader in an eighth grade world. Though my mother sheltered me, my father did not.

The Dr.'s J.

Without school my life took on a pattern of its own, a pattern that followed the swells and my father's forecast of them. Among the interesting people my father knew were two oceanographers at Scripps Institute, Dr. Jamie Rasmussen and Dr. Jack Cahgey. I knew them each as 'Doctor J.' and together as 'Dr. J's', to which both endlessly delighted in correcting me each time that it was actually 'Dr.'s J.,' they were brilliant and they taught me as much scientific knowledge of the ocean as my father did practical.

The Dr.'s J. worked together, as best I could tell, on a single project that spanned two decades. Many times I heard each of the Dr's J. describe their work to someone unfamiliar with it, and they always used the exact same words: "Our project maps bathymetry and ocean shelf topography to measure how relative swell heights and periods correlate to wave formation in geologically significant coastal areas." This was code for studying surf breaks to see what makes them big, and they got a huge grant from the US taxpayer to do exactly that.

My father met them at Black's Beach on a fall day in the late 70's when the surf was breaking double overhead. My father was amongst a handful of experienced surfers out that day. Black's Beach is about a mile north of Scripps Pier and is difficult to access, requiring a walk of half a mile down a steep road that winds between the bluffs. As my father recounts it, he emerged from the water, shivering after a three-hour session, to see a pair of odd-looking men with windblown comb-overs sporting black-rimmed glasses, scuffed black dress shoes and button-up short sleeve shirts. They were dorks, obviously, but they were also intently watching the waves. One held a stopwatch while the other jotted down sequences of numbers in a small notebook. Upon encountering my father, one of the Dr.'s J remarked that he was glad to see my father was wearing shorts. My father then suggested that he might want to do the same, and perhaps some sandals as well. The Doctor laughed and motioned to the north end of Black's, where the nudists were known to congregate.

After introducing themselves, the Doctors explained that they had been taking ocean measurements all morning, but had received a number of offers to measure things other than waves. My father, being known at any surf break worth a lick from Trestles down to Tijuana offered to stand watch for them and keep away any unwanted advances. He assured the Doctors J that the north-enders were harmless exhibitionists and that their group was largely self-policing. My father was on good terms with several of them in those days and could ensure that the Doctors might continue their work unmolested. In exchange the Doctors explained to my father the nature of their work and the measurements they were taking, which on that day consisted of measuring the time between successive sets of waves. And with that commonality of interest a lasting friendship was forged.

Many times I heard my father say that there were three things he learned from the Doctors J that day that he would never forget. One: that the longest penis measured that day was roughly eight and three-quarter inches, flaccid. Two: that the break at Black's was so tremendously powerful because of two undersea canyons offshore, Scripps and La Jolla that funneled and redirected westerly and northwesterly swells and caused a rush of water that jacked up when it hit the shallows of the ocean shelf forming huge hollow barrels. Three: the Doctors J could predict good surf two days before it arrived. It was this last revelation that blew my father's mind and ultimately changed his life.

In the late 1970's the Doctors J had developed prototype ocean measurement devices. By the time my father met them, these devices had been placed on fifteen buoys in the Pacific Ocean, some as far as 600 miles off the coast of California. The buoys were outfitted with radio transmitters that allowed the data to be transmitted to fleet vessels, NOAA oceanographic vessels, and when overhead, US government satellites in geo-synchronous orbit. Each of these retrievers individually transmitted the data to stations on shore. Eventually the information worked its way, either directly, or by fax relays, from the various boats and stations back to Scripps Institute where the Professors analyzed the raw data. From the collective data they attempted to discern large-scale patterns of ocean swells and currents, and also began the earliest attempts at surf forecasting.

My father immediately recognized the revolutionary potential of forecasting and the Doctors jumped on board. It was a perfect business plan.

They created a network of surf shops up and down the Pacific Coast that both relied on, and contributed to, the forecasts. No longer were surfers required to make the trek to the ocean each morning to check the surf. Instead, surf shops like my father's posted a surf-forecast. Surfers just had to drop by every few days for the forecast. It kept customers coming back and let them arrange their schedules around the surf so they never missed an epic day.

In exchange, the surf shops provided an expanded network of contacts, and not just surfers, but commercial fishermen, open ocean divers and competitive sailors, adding a new group of data retrievers for the existing stations. The Doctors J had a larger more reliable data stream and over time increased the number of buoys. The forecasts became more accurate increasing their value to both surfers and the surf shops. Bear in mind that the forecasting technology was still crude at this point, nothing like the modern ability to forecast nearly a week in advance. Sometimes the forecast was wrong and when it was surfers would grumble to my dad about having spent an hour floating in flat conditions. But the forecasts were accurate often enough that surfers were quick to adopt this new tool and foot traffic in my father's shop increased three-fold over the next two years.

And so my father patterned my childhood around the ocean and the Doctors' forecast of its movements and a sort of routine developed. Days when the forecasted surf was up we would rise early and be in the water when the first rays of sun came up over the bluffs. I caught rides on the early morning glass with my father, and less frequently my brother.

I dreaded days with no surf. I got to sleep later, but then came the religious readings and the grammar exercises. My mother taught me, but I also had some excellent tutors. Mrs. Bloom, our next-door neighbor, was a retired math teacher and she taught me with endless patience. She was a God-fearing woman and the only tutor of whom my mother approved. The other tutors were invariably acquaintances of my father's, often scientists and liberal arts professors who would stop by the shop to chat with my father or order a custom shaped board. I don't know how many boards he gave away in exchange for my lessons but I am sure it was not an insignificant number. Other tutors were grad-students strong-armed by the Doctors J into providing instruction free of charge. All of this was further supplemented by my father's eclectic reading list, which included nearly all of the classics. By the age of seventeen I'd read Virgil, Homer, Melville, Fitzgerald, Tolkien, Joyce, Herbert, Clarke, Shakespeare, Shelley, Cervantes and many more.

My father once bet me a hundred dollars that I could not give a report to him on the first chapter of Finnegan's Wake. He won the bet, but didn't collect, saying that asking a man to explain Joyce's work was as fair as betting him that he couldn't drink a gallon of milk in a half hour without becoming ill* or eat a box of Saltine's without taking any water.

---

* TANGENT: I once won this bet at a pub in San Francisco. They make a pill that allows lactose intolerant persons to eat cheese. I ate half a box of these pills and kept down a gallon for twenty minutes. The fellow I won it from was incensed and called me a cheat, but he couldn't renege without losing face. For the record I puked out something akin to churned butter an hour later.
DO NOT ATTEMPT! I have since learned that this poses significant gastro-intestinal risks. DO NOT ATTEMPT, UNLESS THE WAGER JUSTIFIES THE RISK!

Billy

Billy was just coming into his own when I celebrated my eleventh birthday. As a freshman he was the starting outside linebacker and running back on the varsity football team. I remember that summer the coaches asked him to come to some summer lifts. He stopped wearing shirts around the house and begged my dad for dumbbells. I caught him everyday flexing in front of the mirror. I never teased him though. He'd have pounded me if I did. I thought he was such an idiot. But I didn't realize how alone he was. He was the spitting image of my dad. I know my dad loved him, but there was always something between them. I think Billy thought that something was me.

Billy was good, at football, not as a human being. He was big for his age, undersized to play against some of the eighteen year olds. But what he lacked in size, which at six-one wasn't much, he made up for with foot-speed. He was broad shouldered, lanky and nimble. He had eight sacks in ten games his freshman year. He looked graceful on the football field and in step with his teammates, like he belonged. It was such a contrast to how I knew my brother, everything except the big hits on smaller players. Football is a big deal everywhere in America. Billy's high school was no different, and a freshman starting on varsity was liable to get a big head and take a few liberties in class. Billy was no exception, but whatever pride and satisfaction he gained, he displayed no joy at all.

I hated football season because Billy got all the glory. It didn't have to be like it was. I should have had an older brother to look up to. He should have looked out for me. Instead he put me down and beat me up. Billy kept up the swagger in public, but at home, whenever he wasn't eating, which is to say infrequently, he was sullen and a threat to throw an unexpected punch. He mostly sat in his room with headphones on or lifted weights. I tried to stay out of his way. I hated and envied him. I didn't know that I should pity him his faults. I didn't recognize my own privilege.

If you think envy is an emotion you're wrong. Envy presents in many forms, but always some combination of anger, sadness, annoyance, disappointment and pride. So it tastes, in combination, of vomit, salt water, pickles and cinnamon, with possible dry mouth, but never the same combo twice. Envy is anything but sweet, and I got my first real taste of it

74

that year. It got so bad that I tried drinking sugar water in an effort to confuse my senses. It didn't work. I could still taste the envy but I tasted the sugar too. It was weird, like my feelings and my food both had taste, but the sensation of the feelings wasn't really in mouth... only it was, it had to be, because I didn't know where else to place my taste. There were two tastes, one the food and one the feeling. It was the only upside of envying Billy. I discovered weird flavor combinations and I experimented with others for many years after that.

During football season, in addition to my routine of follow the surf and church on Sundays, Friday nights were added. It was the first time in years that my parents heard other adults say nice things about Billy. They had a right to be proud too, but I hated it. I couldn't wait for the season to be over. Then the season ended, Billy was home more often, and I couldn't wait for the season to come back.

Business

That year my dad opened three new Sparx Surfshops with the help of an Israeli businessman named Yhitzak Beshev. Yhitzak, or Zak, as people called him, brought his wife Lena and two sons Nehud and Ezra to live in San Diego.

My father met Zak through a mutual friend, a surfing buddy named Aaron Greene. Aaron met Zak while on a two-month pilgrimage to Israel. It turned out that Zak was looking for an investment opportunity in America and Aaron had a parcel in University City that needed to be developed. Zak had connections to suppliers on three continents and an American attorney. In twenty-four short months he turned Aaron's parcel into a thriving office park. More critical to my story is a piece of information Aaron picked up on his pilgrimage; they were surfing in Israel. On the shores of the Mediterranean dudes were catching waves. There weren't a lot of them and it wasn't organized or commercialized, but there were surfers, and one of the best was Zak's eldest son, Nehud.

Upon coming to the States, Zak realized that this fad his son was into was considered an actual sport[*] in San Diego, and what's more, a thriving business. Zak saw another opportunity and Aaron put him in contact with my father. They partnered up and opened three new stores.

Suddenly, my dad was away from home a lot. This caused some issues between my parents, not the least of which was what to do with me, since public school, while alright for Billy, wasn't an option for me. My dad wasn't one to argue so he quickly agreed that history and Bible study with mom took precedence, unfortunately this made it difficult to avoid Billy in the afternoon and evening. I took to going on long hikes or reading in my room when the surf wasn't up.

The stores were successful, at least the ones in San Diego and Orange Counties. The SLO location was too far away, and my father wasn't nearly as well known up there.

I still spent a lot of time at the original store and I developed a friendship with Nehud and his brother Ezra. The original store was the

---

[*] My father would object to the use of the term 'sport' in connection with surfing. I use it in this instance is merely to clarify that its broad social acceptance legitimized the activity for Zak.

closest to the Beshev's home, so the boys spent a lot of time hanging around. Nehud was like a god to me. It didn't take long for everyone in the surf scene to know who he was. He was sixteen, two years older than Billy and to my eyes he had it all. He could shred. I don't know where he learned because he said the waves in Israel aren't as good, but he had no trouble with the waves in California.

Zak decided Sparx should sponsor Nehud and have him surf contests. All of the other surf companies were doing it. My dad said yes. So far, everything he and Zak had done together had worked. As it turned out, this worked too. Nehud was good. He became better known. He had his trademark Jew-fro, hazel eyes and olive skin. By the time he was twenty he was the fifth ranked surfer in the world and had over one hundred thousand dollars in career contest winnings. In the process of doing this he'd effectively become the face of Sparx Surfboards. People still came to my father because he was one of the best shapers in the world, but to an entire generation of young surfers Nehud Beshev was synonymous with Sparx.

Colors, Letters, Words and Names

My name is Riley Sparx. I have no middle name. My mother's name was Rainbow. You'd think her parents were hippies with a name like Rainbow. They weren't. Neither was she. My father's name was Saul but everyone called him Skip. I have a brother named Billy. We aren't close.

Names are more than words. Names carry power. Names are their own first impression, meaning they are sometimes a second chance at a first impression.

'Rocket' is a red word, because it starts with 'r' and 'r' is red.[*] 'Rainbow' is red too, unless 'rainbow' is not *a* rainbow, but *the* Rainbow, my mother. When I think about a name, any name, I see all of its letters and colors, in all their vibrancy or ugliness. This isn't true for other words. When I read or think of a word it generally takes on the color of its first letter. When I think of mother I see grey. Brother is blue.

My name starts with 'R' but it looks very different from my mom's. Hers makes an actual rainbow with the last two letters shaded opposite: R-red, a-Orange, i-yellow, n-green, b-blue, o-purple, w-deep shimmering indigo. When I think about my mom's name I see a happy word with a happy-spelling. It is what it spells, visual onomatopoeia, and when I spell it to myself I can picture her sipping tea on the deck in the light of the morning, smiling as she stares out over the lake. How I wish that spelling were more reflective of reality.

'M' is grey. 'B' is blue. 'S' is maroon. 'I' is a color I call vanishing primrose, a pale yellow so faded that I sometimes can't see it. Most of my colors are rather pale or flat, with a few exceptions. 'R' is fire-engine red and very bright, 'W' is a cold color with the shimmer of water like the surface of a deep mountain pool cast in the shadows of last light. It is purple trending toward midnight blue. It is my favorite color and my favorite letter. 'N' is a vivid and healthy green, as contrasted with 'K' which is a putrid vile shade of green that I liken to regurgitated curry. Because of my distaste for 'K' I prefer to think of my father as 'Dad' to avoid the 'k' in 'Skip'. 'Dad' is a grey word, just like 'mom'. My Dad is grey-orange-grey.

---

[*] Capitalization has no bearing on coloration. 'R' is red and 'r' is red.

'Y' is silver and is the only letter that moves. It starts where all my letters start, about a foot in front of my face, then it moves off to the right. It moves faster when I'm tired, then it's like a silver streak running off to my right. 'Riley' sometimes looks like a red streak that runs to my right and vanishes with a silver flash. This is the influence of the 'Y' as the last letter of my first name.

Sometimes letters blend in combination, but there are only two letters that consistently alter the coloration of a word from the color of its first letter. 'Y' is one, and 'E' is the other. 'E' is the only letter that I consider a burden because it can make words difficult to read. 'K' is distasteful, but only 'E' is a burden. 'E' is actually a lovely color, more complex and more vivid than most of my letters. In fact, I find it very pleasant to read or think of words that begin with the letter 'E'. If I ever have a daughter I'll name her Elizabeth. It's a beautiful name, a soft, sparkly name,[*] with the pink-orange of the 'E' and a dazzle of jade from the 'Z' in the middle of the name. I can best describe the 'E' as the color of the middle third of a tequila sunrise. The problem with 'E' is that it can ruin a word for me. It blends easily. It is often the second letter of a word and when it is it always affects the coloration of the first letter and thus word coloration. It bleeds like a watercolor and it clashes with most letters but it can also make beautiful and unexpected blends.

This was the problem when I met Wren, I thought Ren, R-E-N, like Ren and Stimpy. The 'W' changes the entire composition. Ren is annoying because of the muddy interplay between the 'E' and the red and green bookends. Whereas Wren: sparkling twilight devours crimson clouds as orange flames snap to the green flash of sunset on the Pacific horizon!

---

[*] TANGENT: For this reason, the Queen remains an enigma to me, as she is neither soft nor sparkly. A 'dour Elizabeth' is an oxymoron in my chromatic grapheme scheme.

Church

Have you ever spoken to someone who grew up in a religious household about their experience of church? If you have you may have heard any number of experiences recounted: the sense of awe and mystery that accompanied the rituals, the profound sense of alienation that arose from an inability to believe that which others so readily accepted, the majesty of God as reflected in the architecture of a cathedral, the enjoyment of the stories told from the Good Book, the singing and the communal joy that accompanied it, the fear of hell, or the shame of a sinner. However, all of these experiences, positive or negative, undoubtedly shared one common trait for the churchgoer, a sense of consistency. For people who go to church, the church is an ordering principle in their lives.

This is why my experience of church is so foreign to most. I went to church every Sunday until my fifteenth birthday. Yet it was a chaotic force in my life.

I went at my mother's insistence. We all did, Dad included. For Dad religion was in the ocean communing with the waves; church was for show and for Mom.

I attended thirteen different churches between the ages of four and fifteen. All were Protestant denominations of varying ilk. The longest tenured was a community church in Escondido that lasted eighteen months. The shortest was a one-day stint at a non-denominational* church in East County.

We lasted nearly a year at most churches. Usually we stopped going because my mom found some aspect of a sermon, or service, or ritual unacceptable. On occasion we were kicked out. Or more accurately, Mom was kicked out. A notable example of the latter was at a Pentecostal

---

* CLARIFICATION: Non-denominational does not mean moderate or just generally 'Christian.' Any church that describes itself as 'non-denominational' has specific doctrines that it adheres to and often these doctrines are dogmatic and fundamentalist, albeit idiosyncratic. These churches are 'non-denominational' in that they are not affiliated with established and recognized denominations within Protestant Christianity, e.g. Lutheran or Baptist. I refer to churches that are more moderate and espouse generalized 'Christian' beliefs common to many denominations as 'community churches.'

congregation we attended for six months or so. Every Sunday the Pastor would call up members of the congregation who were ready to accept Jesus as their Lord and Savior and then he'd lay hands on them and cry out for them to embrace the Holy Spirit, at which point they'd start writhing and shaking and speaking in tongues. It was frightening and fascinating and as a child I wondered what caused the people to act that way. Of course it was just that, an act.

One Sunday my mom answered the Pastor's call. She accepted Jesus before the whole of the congregation, but when the Spirit came upon her she just stood there. The Pastor frowned and laid hands on her, and she just stood there. He said, "Rainbow! Allow the Spirit into your heart!" And my mom just stood there and stared intently at his forehead. "Rainbow! Do you accept Christ?" There was anger in his voice. Then my mom said, in a loud clear voice: "Your halo just turned black." Now unlike other congregations we joined, this group believed in angels and demons and possessions and all that, but you didn't go around seeing halos much less accusing the Pastor of having a black one. The uproar from the crowd was like nothing I'd experienced. They shouted vile epithets at my mother most of which I was too young to understand. People frothed at the mouth, convulsed and screamed in tongues. Chants of 'devil' and 'demon' rang out. A woman in the front row seized and fell to the ground. My mother, her expression calm and quizzical, looked at the woman and said: "Quit faking you fat cow!" My father, ever practical, told Billy to keep me close and run to the car. He emerged from the church a minute later carrying my mom over his shoulder and we high-tailed it home ahead of a potential lynch mob.

As a result of my churchgoing I read the Bible every week. I must admit, that though I'm no longer a Christian, if I ever was one, I do like Jesus. Of course this has very little to do with Jesus the man, or Jesus the god, and everything to do with his name.[*] 'J-e' is a wonderful combination, pink into tequila sunrise. It is one of the best combinations for words that have 'e' as a second letter. The 's-u-s' also has a pink

---

[*] TANGENT: Before all the Jesus Freaks get too excited saying, 'just as long as you love Jesus, Jesus loves you,' you should know I like Judas for the same reason, pink-pink-grey-orange-maroon, he's very pretty. Also, I think Yahweh is a coward, because his entire name runs away to the right before I can read it.

center, maroon-pink-maroon, and the whole name gives me the mental image of a mixed bouquet of roses.

The same principle holds for the written gospels. Bibles have a practical yet potentially annoying habit of labeling the top of each page with Book, Chapter and Verse. I like Matthew and John better than Mark. I like John the best because it starts with the Word, "In the beginning was the Word, and the Word was with God, and the Word was God." 'Word' is a beautiful word and whenever I read John I read it slowly so I can savor every letter in the Word. Mark ends badly, but Luke is the worst. I can't read Luke without thinking of a long night of partying gone horribly wrong, L-U-K-E, gold-pink-puke-tequila sunrise. It's a night that ends where it starts, like a blackout drunk where you drink, dance, pass-out, wake-up, dance and drink. It's vomit book-ended by Cuervo. I never could give much credence to that gospel. For the record I'm not a fan of Kings either.

Gracious Clarifications

To clarify, when I say that the letter 'R' is red or that the letter 'Y' is silver and moves, I am not speaking metaphorically, nor am I imagining or visualizing the letters as colored. I am speaking literally. I mean that 'R' is red. Always. And I didn't choose or make 'R' red; redness is a quality inherent to 'R,' there is no 'R' without red. Red is a part of the whole. That's why I call them Yangs.

I see my colors when I read a word or sometimes when I think about a word. The sound of a word does not trigger my colors unless I also visualize the word. Sometimes this occurs automatically, but usually if a person speaks I simply hear and understand. Names are the words most likely to aurally trigger my Yangs.

I hope you can understand me. I am a great deal better at explaining my Yangs now than I was for much of my life, but it remains difficult to explain something that only I experience.

I owe a debt to the Professor for this. You may find it odd, my regard for the Professor. He is after all the one keeping me in here. I haven't forgotten. But I also haven't deluded myself that I am in here solely because of him or that my present circumstance was the result of forces beyond my control. My choices led me here, my desperation to be sure, but also my vanity and my hope. I enabled him. I volunteered. It's my fault. But it doesn't do any good to apportion blame, that's part of what I've learned, and I owe much of my knowledge to him. Now before you leap to a conclusion that starts with Stockholm and ends with '–yndrome' let me explain to you how gratitude toward my captor fits into my larger conception of life.

We're all captives, captives of the force that binds all life together. The mind is the captive of the body and vice versa. We are captives of each other. We are the pressures that force life to action. It feels chaotic because at once you are a force and yet forces act upon you. Life is the perpetual meeting of forces, a connection of mediums, and a balance of opposites. Humans can be attuned to our connections to each other in surprising, even inexplicable ways.

It is not action but interaction that defines life. Where lies the boundary between self and other? Part of my understanding of myself comes from him. You see it comes full circle. That's why the gratitude is necessary along with the resentment, the respect with the loathing. Balance isn't positive. It's neutral, yin and yang. He took my thermometer. He gave me a surfboard. He took away my rest. He gave me my awakening. He injured my mind. He aided my knowledge. He gave scientific validity to my Yangs and gave me the vocabulary to describe them.

I often hear his voice in my descriptions and as long as I am going to borrow his words I might as well borrow some big ones. Neurologists refer to my condition as polymodal synesthesia. That's a lot of Greek that is fairly easy to understand: *poly* meaning many, *mode* meaning type, *syn* meaning joined, *esthes* meaning sensation: *poly-modal syn-esthesia* - many types of joined sensation. Thirty. I was thirty years old when I learned these words. By no later than age four I was aware that I was different, but I didn't learn these words until I was thirty, a form self-illiteracy, unable to fully name or comprehend that which made me different from everyone else, or even to perceive the difference itself. Imagine walking around for twenty-six years doubting whether what you feel, see and taste is real or whether it's all in your head and then a doctor comes along and tells you that your experience is real *and* it's all in your head, and that there are others like you. Now do you understand? Whatever the Professor has done, I am grateful for those two words, "polymodal synesthesia," many types of joined sensation.

Note this is "joined sensation," not blended, not mixed, joined. This is critical to the other aspect of my synesthetic vocabulary, the part unique to me, my early language. "Yangs" I got this word from my mother. How she came to it I can only suspect. I once found a DT Suzuki book in a box of her clothing. At the time I assumed it belonged to my Dad and she had confiscated it. Now I think there was time before the church chase where my mother was open to other perspectives.

The Legends of the 'X'

My last name ends in 'x'. It's uncommon, a name that ends in 'x'. It's uncommon to have an 'x' in your name at all. There are two competing versions of the origin of my last name, the 'Legends of the X,' if you will.

Both legends agree that my great-great grandfather was born poor in the hill county of West Virginia, an inauspicious beginning so far from the ocean, and that he wound up working for the railroad.

In the first version this particular branch of my lineage had yet to start using branches to scratch out symbols more sophisticated than 'x'. All of my great-great grandfather's relations had always signed their names with an 'x'. When my great-great grandfather worked his way up out of West Virginia and joined up with the railroad, Standard & Pacific, the company man handed him a paper to sign, but before he did he sketched in the letters 'S.Pac' below the signature line. My great-great grandfather, signed off with the customary 'x', but being unfamiliar with signatures, he placed it below the line so that it appeared 'S.Pacx'. The company man told him to hurry off to his post, as the train was due to depart. My great-great grandfather was to present the contract to the conductor where upon he would be assigned to his post. Upon arrival my great-great grandfather presented himself to the conductor who took the contract and assigned my grandfather to his position. He then forwarded said contract, by post, to company headquarters. At some point the 'c' in 'S.Pacx' became worn, or perhaps the company man simply neglected the lower hook of the 'c', but in any event, it was transcribed as 'Sparx' in the company records.

After twenty years working on the railroad, during which time he was paid exclusively in coin, he left the company to live a quiet life with his wife, I shudder to say it, back in the hills of West Virginia. His final payment was made by draft on the company accounts and made payable to one 'Mr. Sparx.' Rather than make a fuss, my grandfather took the draft to the bank in the town at the foot of the hills, and in order to cash the check he attested to the fact that he was indeed Mr. Sparx.

In the other version, the one favored by my father, my great-great grandfather worked as the brakeman. When it was time for my great-great grandfather to throw the brake the crew would yell back, 'Sparks!!' in reference to the sparks thrown from the tracks when the brake was engaged. Because he was the brakeman the rest of the crew took to calling him 'Sparks', since that's how they always yelled for him. My great-great grandpa, not being much of a speller, adopted the name, but spelled it 'Sparx'.

I think the first version is more likely, few things as common in those days as a scrivener's error, but I choose to believe the version my father told. In his version of the story my great-great grandpa never went back to West Virginia. He traveled the country on those trains. He chose to live out his days crossing the earth on the iron horse 'til one day he saw a sea so bright and beautiful that he decided he'd never leave, never far from the ocean again, but on account of his roving spirit he did from time to time book passage to nowhere, or work a run to the Indies or the Sandwiches and since then our family was watermen. As my father put it: "salt and sand runs through our veins."

Junky

It was a sky blue day, like all days in July, but the weather was grey. I went pull to pop-up smooth as silk with no wasted motion, reached my feet at the top of the wave and dropped in on a head-high left. I tasted the rush, the zing-tang of sharp lemonade. Thirteen years old and already addicted. The wave pitched my board forward and down and I zipped down with it, flexed knees pulling gravity to my abdomen like the center of a black hole. My board was fast. My father's design: 6'3", lightweight, four-fin thruster setup, 1 ¼ inch mid-rail thickness, black stomper pad, true-white color palate. It might as well have had a jet pack attached the way I rode it. My board was to water what an F-14 was to air, and I was mother-fucking Maverick.

I felt the biting rush of speed. I gulped saccharine sour and lemon-drops with the gusto of a dry drunk going back to the bottle. My hips pivoted a swift switch and I dug in the rail shooting speakeasy spray off the tail fins and exposing the Sparx logo on the bottom of the board. Just as quickly I snapped back into the wave face and leveled the board allowing the natural force of the wave to catch and then drive me down the line. I raced the ocean. An involuntary pucker pursed my lips as the breaking wave chased my back.

So sour and so sweet, I craved it, crave it, the rush. No other way to describe it, the sound of the wave, the speed of the board, the pull of the water, the taste of the emotion, it is all the rush. A couple more cutbacks and the wave petered out. My pucker turned to a cinnamon smile. It was my tenth wave of the morning and I wanted more.

Pot

You gotta understand two things: one, it was everywhere, and two, it made me feel good because it turned down the volume on my Yangs.[*]

By toning down my Yangs pot actually helped me to concentrate. This was an unusual effect for it to have. It made me more focused, but also had the contradictory effect of short-term memory loss. This included the usual sort of gaffes: misplaced items and words, forgotten or flitting on the tip of my tongue and the edge of my awareness. Misplacing items was the one I found most frustrating, owing to my semi-obsessive need to order my surroundings. Weed also made many memories less exact, but the overall feeling of them was more pronounced.

My Yangs are like your senses. I can pay more or less attention to them just like you can pay more or less attention to any sense. Do you feel your clothes against your skin? You probably didn't until I reminded you that you could feel them. What do you smell right now? What do you hear? Get it? Our senses are always on, but we aren't always aware of everything that we sense. Sometimes a sense will assert itself: when there is a loud bang near you your hearing sense is immediately devoted your conscious attention, you turn your head and orient to the sound before you are even fully aware that you heard the sound.

When these impressions are strong and repeated it becomes very difficult to ignore them or pay less attention to them. It's like if you were constantly hearing loud bangs. Your attention would be constantly diverted. To some extent your system would compensate, like the factory worker whose environment is filled with loud bangs. This worker doesn't find himself unable to concentrate on his tasks because of the noises, but rather becomes accustomed to the noise so that only unexpected noises trigger a reaction. My system compensates too, but we must not overlook a key fact concerning our hypothetical worker's adaptation, the

---

[*] Dear Reader, I don't want to give you the impression that I dislike my Yangs. I don't. They are a part of me and I can't imagine living a full life without them. That said, they can be somewhat overwhelming, particularly when I am repeatedly subjected to unpleasant emotions that reinforce themselves as tastes or touches. At times in my life where I have been depressed or anxious, the ability to turn down the volume on these reinforcing sensations has been greatly helpful to my sanity.

consistency of his environment. The worker's ability to ignore loud bangs stems from the constant crash-bang din of a factory floor. When the worker returns home he will jump at the sound of a dropped pot like anyone else. The compensation is environmentally dependent.

To be bombarded by a sense without the ability to reduce your awareness of it is a horrible experience. This is why the military plays loud rock music twenty-four hours a day when executing a siege. The constant activation of the hearing sense pushes the people inside to a breaking point and eventually makes them want to come out.

I have an additional problem: reinforcing synesthetic feedback loops. Certain experiences trigger emotions, which I experience as a taste. Sometimes the taste triggers a memory, which in turn triggers the emotion again, which triggers the taste, which triggers the memory creating a closed circle of emotion and taste, like a racecar doing laps around a track.* The self-reinforcing nature of the reaction makes it exceedingly hard to break free from the cycle. These are dangerous to my sanity. They are not rightly called moods, even though they share the characteristic of being feelings experienced for an extended period of time that change my perception of other experiences. No, I understand moods. The feedback loops are different. As the Professor would say: they have a pathological character, like the depressive's chain of self-defeating thoughts.

I compensated for my flavors by creating a consistent environment, the same principle as the factory worker accustomed to loud background noises. My room grew progressively more Spartan and organized with each passing year. Even as a kid my room was always neat. I needed things to be in their place.

As I entered adolescence I frequently resorted to the tactic of drawing away from stimulus. An outsider would probably have labeled it depression, but it wasn't. I was depressed, but depression is a mood. Depression has a taste and a feel; it is a pressure on my chest and a sweet sticky flavor like rotted berries or melons. My desire to pull away from the outside world wasn't depression. It was a means of evading

---

* CLARIFICATION: The taste of the emotion does not re-trigger the experience of the emotion. The taste triggers a memory, which triggers an emotion, which triggers the taste. This is an important distinction to draw. My Yangs operate in one direction only, emotion triggers taste, not vice versa.

depression, to move inside, to be alone with my thoughts, and the weed became and remains my ally in this.

Awbrey

The last church we attended was my favorite. It was a community church in Rancho Bernardo, the kind with a moderate generalized Christianity that boils down to: believe in Jesus, be nice, try not to sin, and ask God for forgiveness. The doctrine had nothing to do with my affinity for the church. I liked Awbrey. You can guess why from her name. Also, she was cute. Also, she talked to me. Awbrey went to this church, so I liked this church.

On my fifteenth birthday my Mom told me we were going to a Church meeting. She wanted Billy and me to attend a youth group that night because we were starting at a new church. I was pissed. First, it was Halloween and I had a party to attend which I intended to follow-up with trick-or-treating and egging. You know, good old-fashioned American fun. Second, this meant we would no longer be attending Awbrey's church.

I refused.

Awbrey was the first and last connection I ever had to a church, such was the oddity of church life for me. All of the things that define a normal church experience have one thing in common, community. Whether you feel you belong or you feel ostracized, whether you feel saved or fear hell, the common thread is that you feel it in conjunction with others. There is a sense of shared experience, of belonging, or not belonging as the case may be, but the group aspect and influence is always present. I never even belonged enough to feel ostracized.

My mom's problem was that she expected the religion to work even though we weren't part of the community. She was the only one who tried to belong, but she didn't try very hard. I never knew my grandparents, but I think my mom was searching for a past experience, the experience she had as a girl. She seldom reached out to other members of a congregation, or even the pastors. When she did try to connect she had a way of alienating others, and we usually left the congregation shortly thereafter. She expected the church to fit her beliefs, not the other way around, and so something was always amiss. She approached religion like a two-year old without a proper concept of shape; she was always trying to put the square block that was her concept of religion into the round hole of a new church. She kept banging the same square block against the puzzle frame. She tried every opening, but it never fit. She never understood that she was playing with two different toys. Eventually she got frustrated and quit.

I got frustrated and quit.

On my fifteenth birthday I snuck out with my costume, a horny devil. I went to my party. I collected candy and I egged cars. I never went back to church.

First Time – Party Time

It was a chartreuse January day set in front of me like the rest of my life. No one noticed when I walked into the party. I stuffed my hands in the pockets of my cords and hung back by the wall. Everyone was crowded around the big screen watching a longhaired dude I'd never met before setup a camcorder for playback. Nehud had warned me we'd be treated to shaky handheld footage of the day's surf contest: the Black's Beach Winter Wave Classic, sponsored by Sparx Surfboards.[*]

"Hey! There he is!" Nehud called out in his Hebrew accent. "Aaron get the Champ a beer!" I got a round of applause and a few people called out my name. Simultaneously out of place and the man of the hour, I knelt down to pump up my Reebok cross-trainers and hide my face as heat filled it and cinnamon touched my tongue. I was the youngest person in the room by at least five years, but it was also my victory party.

Aaron handed me a red plastic cup full of light beer. "Glad you made it Riley."

"Thanks. So this is your place?"

"Yeah, come up to the roof you gotta check out the view."

I followed Aaron up a narrow staircase and through a small trapdoor in the ceiling. From the small rooftop deck I could see the Pacific Ocean stretched out to the endless grey horizon. Cars passed below on the streets of Pacific Beach. The cold January weather had largely purged the streets of beach cruisers and skateboards. To the south I could see the Giant Dipper, the old steel roller coaster at Belmont Park in Mission Beach. "Wow, that's a sick view man."

"I know right? I love it up here man." We stared at the ocean drinking our beers, listening to the sound of the waves. "So your folks let you come, huh? That's good."

"Yeah Nehud promised to look out for me."

"Right on. It'll be fun. It's your party after all." Aaron flipped up a beach towel to reveal a pony keg in a small tub of ice. "Don't tell anybody, but the good beer's up here." He covered the keg back up and

---

[*] This was a clever bit of marketing Zak cooked up. First year in existence and it was already a classic.

clapped me on the shoulder. "We should go back, everyone wants to see the champ."

I would rather have stayed up on the deck, but I followed Aaron back down to the party. I wanted to fit it, but I had never been to a real party before. The first real parties of a young man's life, those where people are drinking and sex is in the air, usually happen in high school, but I never went to high school.

The contest started with four men visible only as dots on the TV screen bobbing peacefully in the surf. Skipped over entirely was the struggle through the violent surf: paddling as though my life were at stake because my lungs told me it was, the panic at being trapped inside as three consecutive waves hammered me back and under into the cold dark wet. These were the parts of the contest I remembered most vividly, but they didn't exist to the camera.

I picked out the surfers in the lineup: the world champion, Chad Doering, posted up in the first position farthest left on the screen, while I was scarcely visible positioned to the right at the end of the lineup far apart from the other surfers. Nehud and a Hawaiian surfer named Apo Kukui were bunched close to Doering.

I turned away and left the room feeling sour and every bit the amateur, both on screen and at the party. The others had set up in the correct spot and I knew if it had been an ordinary contest I would have lost. Only the odd format, best wave, had saved me. Usually a surfer's two best waves during a half-hour heat count toward his score, but in this contest only one score, the best wave, counted. As it turned out one wave was all I needed.

I forced myself back to the living room and the camera zoomed to Nehud as he dropped in on a huge left. The camera captured the scale of the wave from a distance, showing just how small Nehud was in comparison, but the force and immediacy of the moving mountain of water was somehow lost. He took a beautiful line carving S-shaped patterns into the wave and getting covered up in the pipe for a brief second.

The camera zoomed back out just as I caught a glimpse of Doering shouting at me across the lineup. I recalled his words: "This surf ain't for kids. Leave the real waves to the real surfers." I wished I'd come back by asking him about his fiancé who'd recently been photographed at a South Beach club with one of the Miami Dolphins, but I hadn't. I left the room again and pounded my beer not wanting to watch Doering shred the next three waves like I knew he had.

I snuck back into the living room as the heat was winding down. Only a few minutes remained. Everyone else had caught at least two waves and I hadn't made a single ride. I watched myself paddle further outside, a good fifteen yards beyond the lineup. I remembered Chad's voice in the air above the roar of the surf and they conjured up a sugary smile: "Giving up Sparx? Good call. Better stick to the amateur events!"

All the days I'd spent watching the break at Black's, all the time talking to the Dr.'s J., all my time in the water, it all came to a head as my instincts took over in a single perfect moment.

Nehud broke cautiously from the lineup and paddled toward me with slow even strokes. I smiled to myself, knowing he'd seen this play before. A passing wave lifted me up and my eyes confirmed what my intuition already knew. It appeared as a bulge in the water ten yards beyond me. By the time the others saw it and started to paddle it was too late. They were caught inside; even Nehud wasn't far enough out. I remembered the feeling in my shoulders as I spun and started to dig, like they might pop from their sockets as I strained to build momentum. But on television I appeared to be standing still, arms spinning without motion, all stasis except the wave.

I don't know whether I went to the wave because it was going to appear or whether it appeared because I went to it. I just felt it. A sneaker set. Black's is an oddball spot, notorious for these seemingly random waves that form and break far beyond the established peaks. It jacked up behind me like an angry thunderhead. I popped up and dropped in with one smooth motion. For the first time since the video came on I didn't feel like an amateur. I was cool. I whipped down the face at a steep angle and the crowd oohed and aahed.

The familiar sticky sour rush surged through me in a cascade of adrenaline and lemonade. It felt just like riding the wave, only touched with the crowd-crazed blaze of cinnamon. Do movie stars ever sit in the audience at the theatre with a fake moustache and tinted shades just to feel the adoration of the crowd? If I were a movie star I know I would.

I watched the wave gobble up the other surfers as skegs shot through the top and boards flipped in wild spins against taut leashes. Doering took the full impact of the break on his head. I smiled schadenfreude; sugar tainted with bitters.

I skimmed down the fifteen-foot face, the wave of the contest. I flew bouncing in sections, gaining speed until I neared the trough and snapped off a wicked bottom turn, a hard ninety degrees, and raced back up the wave face. Snap-back again, off the crest and back down the wave face. I repeated sharp turns at the top and bottom, one, two, three in a row. I turned back into the wave and slowed and eased back into the curl, the foaming edge of the wave's break and the focal point of its power.

I settled deep into the pocket until I disappeared from view. I relived the rush and envisioned the flat-glass curtain of aquamarine spinning before me. On screen there was nothing but the wave. I was into the tube, the greatest move in surfing, and even though they knew the outcome the audience held their breath in anticipation.

Boom! The wave crashed down with a thunder audible even on the low quality recording. I shot free into sunlight in a crouch so low my butt touched my heels. I stood proud, tossed back my hair and pumped my fist to the sky.

I couldn't discern between the cheers in the room and the cheers on the tape. Everyone wanted to congratulate me on the win. It was an extreme ego stroke, a full-fledged high. But the novelty soon wore off, and I was just a sixteen year old trying to fit in at a pro-surfer keg party.

In truth, I have never grown comfortable in a party setting. The sheer volume of stimulus makes them disconcerting. There is always music, and everyone, myself included, agrees that a good party needs music. However, music makes it difficult for me to hear people speak. Worse still, the more I strain to hear any one individual the less I can hear any other person. Couple that with the constant concern with how I appear to others, the conscious shifts and fidgets in posture, my thoughts ever returning to my outward appearance, then to whatever is said by the person I'm speaking to, and then if I see them later conversing in secretive whispers to another I assume that she secretly ridicules me, which draws me further into my shell, and we have not yet spoken of my Yangs, to which my attention is also pulled, and faced with an avalanche of shifting feeling, the response to all of the stimulus of the party I get caught up in my loops of feeling until all of those shifting feelings are drawn into the vortex of alcohol and mood. This could be positive or negative, but it

96

always goes in one direction or the other, and it's always fueled by alcohol. So I tend to stand next to the keg.

I stood next to the keg that night too. At first it was easy to mingle and make a little conversation. But after a handshake and a congrats I had nothing to talk about. I had nothing in common with all of the 20-somethings at the party.

I slammed three beers and I started to come out of my shell. This cute blonde girl sat next to me. Her name was Jamie and she had on tight jeans and a chest-hugging bodysuit. Her name was beautiful too, pinks and oranges bookended the grey 'm.' For an hour or so I was conversing free. Jamie seemed impressed that I won the contest. Picante fired my tongue and electricity shot through my body when she touched my arm and said, "I think surfers are totally hot." Then Doering walked in and she was on him like wax on a surfboard. Things took a turn to the dark side. Rage, rotten rage, plus the envious cocktail of cinnamon, bile, salt, pickle juice, and the lingering heat of lust, filled my heart and mouth.

Nehud almost came to the rescue. We smoked a bowl and he kept introducing me to people as 'The Champ'. "That girl Jamie," he said, " Be careful. She's a pro-ho."

"What's a pro-ho?" I asked.

Aaron brought out the beer bong. "You talking about Jamie?" He asked drawing a laugh from Nehud. "Oh yeah," Aaron said. "That girl's dirty."

"A pro-ho is a chick who sleeps around with professional athletes," Nehud explained. "A girl like that can be fun, but you gotta be careful. If you know what I mean."

"You're up Riley." Aaron held the funnel full of beer up over my head. It was high-tech as beer bongs come, complete with XL funnel and a plastic valve at the end of the three feet of plastic tubing. Beer sloshed out of the funnel onto the patio. "Hurry up."

I put my mouth on the end and twisted the valve. Cold beer shot into my mouth and I gulped and gulped. I drained it in less than five seconds. The cinnamon overwhelmed the flavors of alcohol and envy when I got a cheer from the crowd and a high five from Nehud.

But that feeling soon turned back into lethargy, simmering rage, and envy. The beer bong held at least three beers and I weighed a buck forty-five soaking wet. I sat, slumped down in my chair, and watched the procession to the keg.

No one talked to me until a man I had seen that day at the beach approached me. He was ancient to me, at least thirty. He had been arguing with my father that afternoon. He'd congratulated me on the win and shaken my hand. When he told me I could be great like my father was, my dad pulled me away, puffed out his chest and roared, "Not interested!" My dad promised to explain later, but the experience left me frightened and confused, full of cold wet paste. And now here he was, at the party, red keg cup in his left hand, his right hand extended for me to shake. "Hey Riley. We haven't been properly introduced. I'm Preston Maxwell. I'm with 'Surf Company X'."[*]

I shook his hand. "So what were you and my dad arguing about at the beach?" The alcohol had loosened my tongue.

"You," he said. "I think that you have the talent to go pro and my company wants to sponsor you. Your father doesn't agree."

That stung. I nearly choked on the acrid bile that burned at the back of my throat. Was he telling the truth that my dad didn't think I was good enough to go pro? Or did my dad not want me to go pro for some other reason? Either way he was blocking my dreams. This was my big chance, right after my big win. He was ruining my life!

"Anyway," Maxwell continued, "I don't want to get in between you and your father. He probably wouldn't appreciate me talking to you at all, so, nice to meet you."

"My dad's not here," I said. "Tell me about Surf Company X. Could I still surf for Sparx, too?"

"Of course," said Maxwell. "We just think you're gonna be big and we want to get in on the ground floor with Riley Sparx. That was an impressive win today. You beat a field that included the world champ." Maxwell pulled out a glass pipe with blues and golds blown through it. "You toke?"

---

[*] LEGAL DISCLAIMER: For liability reasons and pursuant to a Confidentiality Agreement signed in connection with the sale and dissolution of Sparx Surfboards, Limited, I refrain from using the actual name of the surf company involved and refer to it herein only as Surf Company X.

That's the point at which the night becomes blurry. I remember smoking with Maxwell and mellowing out, the bilious anger fading into an undefined hope. The whole conversation was one long ego stroke.

At some point after Maxwell had left Nehud came up and smoked me out again. I remember him saying, "Doering's been fucking maddogging you all night." He kinked his neck in Doering's direction. I looked over. I probably stared; it's hard to know I was so drunk and high. Doering had a beer in one hand and Jamie's ass in the other. He removed it to flip me off then whispered something in Jamie's ear. She looked over at me and smiled.

I remember at least one tequila shot with Jamie, and I remember her taking my hand and putting it on her thigh.

I woke up next to the toilet. There were towels all over the floor and smelly bits of brown vomit stuck in the grout between the tiles. There was more vomit on the wall.

Nehud came in with a bottle of bleach and a stack of towels. "Morning champ. You ready to clean all this up. My boy Aaron is pissed."

"Ugggh. My head."

"Yeah you had a rough night. What do you remember?"

"Drinking and smoking. I did the beer bong and tequila shots. I was out on the patio all night. How'd I even get in here?"

"You don't remember coming in the house?" Nehud sounded concerned. The soured blancmange flavor returned to my mouth. I gagged and dry heaved into the toilet. When I was done Nehud asked, "Do you remember what happened with Jamie?"

"No. Wait, what?"

"Oh that's bad."

"Why what happened?"

"You two were in the bedroom." He looked me in the eye. "She said you did it. Doering put her up to it."

"What do you mean Doering put her up to it?"

"I told you, she's a pro-ho. She would do anything Doering asked. Gangbang. You. Whatever."

I dry-heaved again, the variety of emotion and flavor too complicated to process. "Was that your first time?" I nodded into the toilet bowl. "Oh," his voice went flat. "I hope you wrapped it up."

I heaved again. I didn't have any condoms.

The Talk

"You recognize the guy in this picture?" my father asked.

I did. It was a much younger version of my Dad, his long hair and trademark beard flaming red instead of sandy grey. He stood between two other men and hoisted a large silver cup, a trophy.

"That's you," I said.

"So what do you think about the guy in that picture? He looks pretty cool, right?"

"Yeah." He did look pretty cool. The muscles in his arms rippled under the weight of the trophy and his lean frame revealed washboard abs. He looked happy too, with a huge smile stretched across his face. Pretty girls clad in string bikinis stood in the background captured in the moment, mid-clap. Dad looked like a conquering hero, a champion. I wanted to look like that. I had looked like that. *Was this the day I got to go pro?*

"Yeah you do look pretty cool."

"You'd think so, right? But you'd be wrong."

I stared at the picture trying to gather what he meant. A familiar pasty sensation crept into my mouth, but not alone, a hint of cinnamon accompanied it. The man in the picture was the epitome of cool. My dad was cool. I thought to myself: he still is cool, compared to other dads, but the man in this picture is cool like a Charger or a movie star, cool by any standard.

"Not cool at all," said my father, his tone suddenly very serious. "You know when that photo was taken?" I shook my head no. "1972. You see your mom and Billy in that photo?" I looked carefully at the picture, but my father's was the only face I recognized. The girls in the background didn't look like my mom, and Billy would have been...what? One, maybe two. I didn't see a baby anywhere. "You don't see them because they aren't there." He shook his head and looked at the floor. His voice sounded far away, like he was speaking to himself as much as to me, "Jesus I thought I was hot shit back then." The language surprised me, my father rarely swore, especially in front of me. A third taste entered on the center of my tongue, the uniform blandness of boiled chicken breast.

My father put the photo back in a cigar box stenciled with the word "Presidente" and closed it with a sigh. "All sorts of people told me how great I was, how I was gonna put surfing on the map, make it a big time sport. I had people fawning all over me, girls swooning, guys quick to buy me a drink or clap me on the back or invite me to their parties and their bonfires on the beach. I had a sponsor: 'Jud's Burger.' Went out of business a long time ago, but I was twenty-two years old and I thought it was pretty cool. I was living the life of Riley... different meaning son. I was traveling and surfing and I left your mom and Billy to fend for themselves, left them in the desert...but that's not what this is about, this is about the man in that picture and the things that he let people put into his head." He looked me in the eye. "People like that asshole Maxwell that came up after the contest."

"You knew him back then?" I asked, surprised.

"No, no. But I knew people like him. People really interested in themselves. People who see others with talent and who want to use that talent to make a buck. People who pervert the real spirit of surfing. People who convince a kid who's young and dumb and incredible in the water that what he really needs is competition, a way to prove that he's not just good, that he's better than other surfers who are good."

"But what's wrong with competition? What's wrong with being better than everybody else? You won."

"I lost. Riley it's important that you take the right message from this. What you see in that picture might be what you think you want, but it's not. And even if it were and even if you got it, it doesn't last forever. It can't last forever. And it's only after you're done with all that *winning* that you can look back with some perspective, because while it's happening you're in it and that desire to win can consume you. Once you have that chance, that space, and you look back, only then can you see what you've lost while you were busy winning."

"I don't understand."

"What do you like about surfing?"

"Everything."

"Okay everything. What's that mean? You like the ocean? You like being in the ocean?"

"Yeah of course."

"You like your buddies? The guys you surf with?"

What buddies? The guys I surfed with were my dad and his buddies. But I didn't say that. Instead I just agreed. "Yeah. That too."

"You like the rush? You like the freedom? You like the sense of accomplishment when you catch a big wave, one that's bigger than you've caught before? You like all those things right?"

"Yeah."

"That's my boy. You like the hunt for a better wave? A better ride? You always looking for the perfect wave?"

"Yeah."

"Me too. I love all those things. That's why I've taught you. You're mom takes us all to church every Sunday right? And I go along. She says its good for you boys and she has her rights and I smile and shake hands. That's where she wants you to learn, but where do I take you?"

"The ocean."

"You know why?"

"Because you love to surf?"

"Yeah, but you know it's more than that. Least I hope you do. The ocean is my church. It's where you can see God's hand. The evidence of the ever-changing. The way the water changes with every wave, the way it slowly pushes and pulls at the sand, the way the it erodes the bluffs and how the salt in the air is always new always moving past your nostrils on the sea breeze."

"But what does all this have to do with Maxwell? Does he want to sponsor me or something?"

"Yes. But he's not going to."

"Why not? I get things didn't go right for you, but I want to go pro."

"Not with Maxwell. He's a snake."

The bile overtook me. "You're the snake. Keeping secrets from me when I should be getting sponsors. Are you gonna sponsor me?"

"No."

"Why not? I know Zak wants to. I want to go pro damn it!"

"Eventually you can do that if it's what you want, but not now. You know Riley, you and your brother are getting to that age where I can't control things as much, pretty soon you're gonna have to start making choices for yourself. "

"Then let me choose!"

"Not today." He tapped the lid of the cigar box with his wedding band. "I know you may hate me for it, but not today."

"You're right," I said, "I do hate you."

"Careful with that. Someday you may regret it. Until then I'm your dad so you're stuck with me anyway. And if I teach you three things I've done okay: Respect the ocean. Love thy neighbor. Commune with both."

I boiled with bile and stared pure hate at my father. He met my eye without flinching, just a sad smile, and started to get up. Then he stopped and sat and turned to me. "Could you ever imagine me not surfing?" he asked. "I don't mean for a day or two, or even weeks or months, but years. Could you imagine me spending years away from the ocean?"

I shook my head no. It was unthinkable. The longest we'd ever gone without surfing was maybe two weeks. Even if it was flat for days on end we still wound up in the water with our longboards, hoping for a wave to get us through the flat stretch.

"You were born in 1974. I put you on a longboard, put you on your first wave in 1977. You remember that?"

I did. I remembered it as clear as the day itself, June 27, 1977, but not a trace of the June gloom. My father took me out into the whitewater and set me up on the board then he pushed me forward and told me to stand up. The board was like a canoe to me, so big, but I stood up and rode it to shore. My mouth puckered, my taste for the rush already present. I rode and rode until the single fin caught the sand and I pitched into the ankle high water. My father was there in an instant to scoop me up. He was worried that I would be scared from the fall, but I got up giggling. I couldn't wait to go again.

It is my earliest memory.

"I remember that day," my father said. "June 27, 1977. You know why I remember that day, right down to the date itself."

"Because it was the first day you took me surfing?"

"That's part of it, but I remember because that was the first day I'd surfed in over four years."

That should have been enough to impart my father's message. It should have been enough to make me heed his warning. It should have made me wary of Maxwell. But what I took away from that conversation was not a single word said, though I recall it clearly enough. What I took away was the picture of my father hoisting that trophy above his head. I heard every word, but I didn't listen.

104

I listen now. Had to run around deaf 'fore I figured out how.
You lead a boat by the bow, a man by example
I've sampled ways of living that I finally couldn't handle
I've surfed the seven seas and thrown my future to the wind
I've buried both my mom and dad and led a life of sin.
I know the taste of misery and the color of my name
Misfortune chased me underground. I've had my share of fame.

The next stanza detailed my return to freedom and coming heroics by proceeding to such cliché lyrical delights as 'walls torn asunder' 'delivered from chains' 'lions mane' and 'rightful throne reclaimed'. I was twenty-eight when I wrote it, more than ten years ago, when I wasn't yet resigned to my fate, and when I hadn't yet remembered my only source of true hope because I was busy chasing falsehoods. I had already resolved to tell the story, if not consciously, but I hadn't accepted my role. I thought to tell my story as an epic poem. I see now how foolhardy that was. The material is not suited to an epic. It's either serio-comedy or a tragic farce, depending…

Void: A Legal Primer for Teenagers

When I was seventeen I went through a particularly dark period. I was a moody teenager to begin with, but this was worse. I had the rage. Rage is more than anger. Anger is a component, the sick back-bile flavor, but it's fouler than that. The main taste is a gross sweet, the sweet you can almost taste when you smell raw beef, but the beef is not merely raw but rotten too.

I have felt rage directed at people or a person, but this rage was different. This was the rage of adolescence, an undirected hate I projected into the world. This was the rage of self-doubt and impotence. To get past my rage I did a foolish thing. I signed a deal with Maxwell behind my father's back.

If you are a minor, i.e. not eighteen years of age, then you do not have the capacity to enter into a contract. Any contract to which you are a party is voidable. This is a pain in the ass when your father steps in to void your surf sponsorship, but it is a legal principle that can also save your ass if you make a bad bargain.

My father voided, summarily, my contract with Maxwell and Surf Company 'X'. I ran away. When I went to run I realized I had nowhere to go. I suppose I had something of Kerouac's adventures in mind, my father's fault for putting 'On the Road' in my hands. However, this was the nineties not the fifties and I didn't know the first thing about hitching or hopping trains. So I wound up walking the back way round the Lake to the mall. I came back ten hours later and nobody even knew I was gone.

Impotent. Rage.

Finally, after three days, my parents each declared me in a foul mood. This truly exasperated me. It wasn't my fault this flavor followed me. My mom understood. She'd had the same thing. "Bad Spirits, lingering about maybe. Sometimes you can't see them or hear them. You just feel 'em. Or taste 'em in your case."

She told me that God would look out for us and not to worry it would pass. No doubt she asked our pastor of the day to pray for bad spirits to leave us. I do not wish to dwell upon this bit of conversation with my mother, except to comment on the casual manner in which she accepted odd phenomenon and integrated them with her piety by attributing all things to God's Greater Plan. This gave her an odd serenity about unfortunate events, but I suspect it was not healthy for my development.

My father gave his standard piece of advice and insisted that I get in the water. This worked to a degree as a temporary salve. My general malaise and rage were covered over with the sour rush of the surf, but it also reminded me that I wasn't free. He said I didn't understand, but I would one day. I didn't want to understand. I wanted to go pro. And he was in my way.

Three months later my eighteenth birthday came. My dad finally relented and I was gone. I left, lips upturned on a chartreuse day, my future in front of me and my present on my belt-buckle. I was booked for nine months of photo sessions and contests surfing for Sparx Surfboards on a promotional-tour sponsored by Surf Company 'X'. It was nearly four years before I returned.

Dad knew he couldn't talk me out of it and he was in a dispute with Zak about the future of Sparx. The whole thing centered on sponsorships and growth. Zak wanted more sponsored surfers, more publicity, more branded lines and more stores. My dad wanted to stay away from the competitive stuff and the branded gear and stick to custom boards and the products that both new recreational surfers and life-long surfers needed. Zak insisted that to reach those people you had to be seen. They had to have access to our product. They had to have stores they could go to. Bottom line, we had to be bigger and more visible. I was part of that plan.

Nehud was basically carrying the entire marketing side of the company. At the time he was far and away the best Israeli surfer in the world and he was the only sponsored surfer on the company payroll. I surfed the occasional contest, but this tour was my biggest foray into the pro-side of things. About two-thirds of the tour stops were photo shoots. Seven stops were contests. I wasn't technically on the pro-tour but I had sponsor's exemptions to some of the biggest pro-events.

One of our most profitable lines was Nehud's. It only sold in Israel, but it was the best selling surfwear line in the entire country. People who had never seen anyone surf knew who he was and people with no interest in surfing wore his clothing. He had sparked people's interest back home; fully forty percent of the custom boards we shaped were shipped to Israel.[*]

Funny thing happened on that tour. I didn't win. I don't know if my Dad thought I would, but I did. I thought I would win. When I say I didn't win, I mean I didn't win anything, nothing at all. I got worked. I beat Doering at Black's and I thought I was hot shit, but I got schooled all over the world that next year.

In retrospect I don't think I could have prevented the company from being swallowed up even if I had won. Skip came from a generation where the best surfers in the world weren't pros. By the time I was nineteen that world was gone. I think my Dad hoped if I made a good showing it would prove that we didn't need to expand the sponsorship to expand the business. He didn't directly say it. In fact he kept up his outward opposition to my surfing competitions, but I felt the pressure of it. It was what I'd been pushing for, and after the blowup over Maxwell I finally had my chance to shine. I didn't know all of what was going on between my Dad and Zak, but I knew something was up. Looking back, it wasn't my fault. I was only nineteen and even if I hadn't failed, Zak would have kept pressing for more.

I should clarify that Zak is not a bad guy. My dad never should have got into business with him. Zak always had his eye toward expansion, to greater revenues, greater profits. He was a businessman from go and he made no attempt to hide it. Sparx Surfboards was an income stream to him, not an expression of his deeply held beliefs about life and surfing. When we first expanded my dad was happy for the additional business. It was what he wanted too. But Zak never stopped searching out ways to expand, and he was right to do it. He had put his time and treasure into the business. But Dad always wanted to go back. He spent way too much time at the original shop, not because it needed greater oversight, but because he liked chatting up his surf buddies and helping long-time customers. He liked the money that came with three stores, but he didn't like running them. He wanted to bring people into a lifestyle, not a sport. You didn't just bring in hordes of people and turn them out with as much merchandise as possible. It was antithetical to his vision.

---

[*] Some of the earliest commercially available boards in the Middle East were Sparx models.

So he and Zak were working at cross-purposes from the start. Much as I'd like to say it was Zak's fault the way things went down, it was only part. Zak didn't deceive him. My dad just couldn't see that things were changing. He kept trying to go back, to tighten his hold on that first little surf shop he built up. Eventually he squeezed so hard that it all squirted through his fingers.

I kept Dad's original shop and the shaping room. The Beshev's took everything else: three locations, all inventory, all materials, all equipment, and Nehud and his Israeli surfwear line, to Surf Company 'X', in a deal that included a very lucrative sponsorship for Nehud. But that deal came later, when all my other options were gone.

For now I can tell you this much, Surf Company 'X' acquired Sparx Surfboards, Limited, with two conditions:

One. *The 'Sparx' brand is retired, effective immediately.* **Two.** *All other terms of the buyout are to remain confidential, with Riley Sparx to sign a Confidentiality Agreement. Said Confidentiality Agreement is attached hereto as Exhibit 'B.'*[*]

At this point I must address what some may find to be a glaring omission, my mother. Not that she has been entirely omitted, but that the discussion of my adolescence has focused on my relationship with my father and my desire for a surf career. I say this so that I might tell you the most important fact you should know about my mother; she's gone.

She was gone before I came home from my travels. I avoided San Diego for nearly four years, no small feat for a professional surfer. I would call home from a tropical location every three or four months, but I was happy to have left. I loved the life, the girls, the weed, the waves, not necessarily in that order. I was happy to be away from home, and away from them. Perhaps this makes me a bad person. If so, perhaps the regret I've felt since that time provides some redemption.

I returned home just before my twenty-second birthday. My dad got in contact with me through Maxwell and said I had to come home. I hate him for not telling me to come home earlier. Mom had developed early-onset Alzheimer's and within a year of the diagnosis she had deteriorated to a shell of her former self. I visited her once at Glissen Home, the live-in facility where she received round the clock care. For most of the visit she

---

[*] Sparx Surfboards, Limited Buyout Agreement, Page One, Paragraph Four.

stared at the wall. At the end of the visit she called me her little angel. A week later she was dead.

Angel's Tears

I spoke from a pulpit in a church I had never attended, the last one Mom joined before she died. "I'm thirsty because sad is salty. And I'm sad." When I get sad I get thirsty, a bad combination when there's beer around. "She used to call me her angel. But now she'sss mine."

The purest sadness, not depression, but grief, is concentrated salt, the taste of angel's tears. Mom would have liked that description.

I pointed at the crowd with my finger. "You didn't even know her. You's. Didn't know…didn't know nothing. You see my mom…the thing about my mom'ss—" A bright yellow suit at the back of the congregation caught my eye. I pointed at him, another face I didn't recognize. "Thasss disressspecful! She was a Rainbow. She loved me more than anyone ever will. She's the reason 'R' is red and she's every color of my rainbow. She's all bright colors and you're all…" I looked out at the pews less than half full and saw only strangers and a few of my dad's friends.

"You're not her friends. She deserved friends." I spoke more to myself than to the mourners in the pews. I started to cry. Intense salt flavor overcame me. The weed was wearing off and the Johnny Walker was taking over. "I'm crying angel's tears." I sang the words aloud, "Angel's tears. Angel's tears. Angel's tears. I'm glad it's October, 'cause October's a brown month. And today is a brown day. Today is a shitty brown down— I mean day. Shit. Shit. Shit."

The pastor snatched the mic from me, and my Dad and Billy restrained my arms and propped me up as they escorted me from the pulpit. "Pour out a little liquor! Where's my whisky? We gotta pour some out for mom! Where's that dissrespecful fucker? I'm gonna kick his ass." Thankfully the yellow suit was nowhere to be seen. "Angel's tears!" It was not my finest hour.

I miss my mom.

Cut Down, Burn Up, Paddle Out

I found him on my twenty-fourth birthday. Billy was overseas. It was a little over a year since we had scattered my mom's ashes in the ocean. He knew I'd find him. What's that say about how he felt about me?

He tied a thick rope to an iron pipe at the back of the shaping floor. I found the footstool kicked over underneath him. I just looked at him, hanging there. I didn't feel anything. I had just smoked, but that wasn't it. In that moment I just wasn't capable of feeling anything. There was no desperate scene where I tried to hold him up by legs so he wouldn't strangle. His face was already pallid and grey and his bare feet were swollen and purple, the hypostasis already complete.

My dad didn't get a paddle out. A paddle out is a funeral rite for surfers. The surf community paddles out on their boards with flowers and leis and forms a big circle in the ocean. There is a moment of silence. Kind words are said. Sometimes ashes are spread. The life of the deceased is celebrated and remembered fondly. My dad didn't get a paddle out.

If you've never been to a suicide funeral, consider yourself lucky. If you've got one coming up, I strongly suggest you come down with a cold.

Standing at that second funeral, alone amidst a sparse crowd of sullen faces and handshake condolences, I became aware of my solitude for the first time: empty faces, empty words, and eyes filled only with pity and relief. Pity always involves relief. They are two sides of the same coin. Every time it is said, 'sorry for your loss,' the unspoken corollary is, 'glad it's not me.'

I paddled out for my dad, alone. I picked the urn that was painted with rainbows. The guy at the mortuary looked at me funny, like he wanted to ask if my dad was gay. It didn't matter. I knew why I picked that one.

I opened the urn and looked at the ashes, torn, not wanting to touch them, to touch him, but wanting to know how they felt. They didn't look like regular ashes. The ashes were little pebbles, like oatmeal only thicker, with more substance, like pebbles. I didn't touch them. I said goodbye and poured my father's remains into the ocean. It was where he would have wanted to be, forever in the water, forever in the same place as my mom.

112

Most of the ashes sunk from sight, but others floated and swirled in a foggy cloud. They turned the water a mix of aquamarine and aluminum teal, it was beautiful and sad, and no part of the rainbow.

The death of my parents was the end of my childhood. I have to believe that it was my rite of passage. If I weren't an adult then, then I never will be. For the first time I glimpsed the only certain truths of existence: I am alone and I will end.

IV. CHANGES

Meanings and Mottos

When the kiss ended and our mouths parted and I met her eye and her self-conscious smile it took every ounce of self-discipline I had not to pucker my lips in excitement. But what my first kiss with Wren meant to me was far more than mere excitement. There was a touch of spice, of lust, that lingered, and the familiar tingle at the back of my knees in anticipation of what would follow. There was also Wren, a taste as complex as my feelings, and cinnamon, pride at finally having mustered the courage to plant a kiss where I'd been wanting to for months, but the mélange went beyond all that. Though perhaps nothing could really go beyond Wren. Coupled with the intimacy of that moment I could only say that she left me buzzing. It was as though every taste bud, every hair, every epithelial was vibrating and though it may have been my imagination, I felt that every bit of her was vibrating at the exact same frequency.

Pretty good for a first kiss, right?

A first kiss always means something, even if the only meaning is 'I'm drunk.' Sometimes it means the same thing to both the kissers and sometimes it doesn't.

The problem with a hot first kiss is: where do you go from there? For Wren, the answer was home. She left as abruptly and unexpectedly as she entered and left me alone in a cavernous former factory with an equally cavernous hole in my understanding of what had just happened and a ghoulish painting that for some reason I could not bring myself to cover up. I attempted to fill the lacunas with marijuana smoke and spent the rest of the day staring, emotionless, at a realistic depiction of the aftermath of my father's suicide.

Two excruciating days of weed and worry followed. Finally Wren called in a cheerful mood giving me instant relief and a concomitant lifting of pressure. She proffered an invitation. "I'd like you to come to a meeting with me. It's more of a party really. It's difficult to explain."

"Why don't you try and explain over dinner?" My anxiety returned. I hadn't planned this, using her invitation to leverage a date. I'd wanted to call and ask her out. I wanted to tell her how I felt, which was silly since I wasn't even sure how I felt except that I was aroused, confused and anxious. Of course all are good signs by which to judge your feelings for a woman, if she doesn't make you feel those three things then she's probably not your type.

She hesitated at my invitation, and the silence that followed caused me physical pain and a hit of rosewater. Finally her voice filled the void, "Sure, but let's do it early. The party starts at seven."

I primped for an hour before leaving to pick her up. Ridiculous, I know. Even more ridiculous because my hairstyle was prototypical surfer, which is to say, unkempt. I put on my best pair of jeans, no slacks in an effort to keep it cas, and a green and grey checked button down to dress it up. Black skate shoes completed the ensemble and complete with cane I took a final look in the mirror, un-tucked my shirt, then left, satisfied with my attractiveness.

Sitting across from Wren in a booth an hour later, fingers covered in humus and olive oil, I was less satisfied. She looked sylvan and stunning in a tight green tunic with brown laces high across the chest, a brown skirt, burnt-orange tights and soft suede slip-ons that matched the skirt. Her hair was dyed a brilliant red with a sheen and luster suitable for a shampoo spokeswoman. Hints of rouge accented her cheekbones, and her jade eyes flashed against the flecks of red and gold in her eye shadow with the mischievous air of a woodland nymph.

"I can't believe you hadn't been to Mama's. I thought you grew up around here?"

Her comment irked me. "North County. And it's not like I know every restaurant in San Diego."

"This isn't 'every restaurant.' This is the best Lebanese food in the city."

"That remains to be seen." I couldn't keep the sour dill taste from leeching into my tone. She grinned and shot me a knowing glance. Somehow she managed to look down on me while looking up at me. "What? Are you Lebanese?" I asked.

"Ha!" she chortled. "Not even close."

I was disappointed that my first guess was wrong. The question of her ethnicity had piqued my curiosity since the first time I met her. And you could hardly blame me for reading into her choice of restaurant, we were well north of Downtown and Balboa Park, so it wasn't a neighborhood you were likely to travel by chance.

"You have to try this." She handed me a wrap as big as her arm. The aroma of garlic was pungent. I took a bite. It was about the best thing I'd ever eaten, succulent flavorful chicken and oodles of garlicky goodness.

"Mmmmm."

"I told you this place was the best."

"It's delicious." I handed the mammoth wrap back to her. "But I guess this means you don't want to make out."

"Riley!" she laughed, but there was sadness in her voice and my heart dropped along with my back. I heard it loud and clear, but I had to try. No matter how awkward, even if she regretted the kiss we shared, I was past the point of no return. "Come on Wren. That was quite a kiss we shared."

"I know. But I don't want to lead you on."

"Then don't. I like you."

"I like you too."

"What's the problem then?"

"School for one. I'm your professor. This can't go on."

"Is that it?"

"It's a big deal. I could lose my job."

"I thought you had tenure."

"I do, but that's not a free pass to fuck my students."

"Is that what we're going to do?" I flashed my best seductive smile and raised an eyebrow. It worked. I got another laugh out of her.

"I really do like you," she said, "but I need this job, at least until I can sell some paintings. And in six years nothing I've painted has sold."

"Well, the quarter's over in two weeks. I can wait until then."

"I don't know…"

"Look let's wait until the end of the quarter. Give me whatever grade I deserve. I promise I won't hold it against you if you give me an A-." She rolled her eyes at that. "Come on, you said yourself my final project was great."

"And sad."

"Anyway, grade me like you would any gorgeous, former pro-surfer that you want to have sex with, and once grades are in we can go out again." This elicited another eye roll.

"You may not like me so much after tonight."

"You know something I don't?"

"Lots of things."

"So what's up with this party tonight?"

"It would be an opportunity to seduce you if I weren't your professor. Darn."

"Okay. Just try not to fantasize too much. I don't want to put your job in jeopardy."

She laughed. "I am a little nervous about tonight. I mean I'm sure you'll fit in..."

"You're worried about me fitting in? The girl who sees music, rides a pink Vespa, and changes her hair color every week, is worried about me fitting in?"

"This group is important to me. It's one of the only places I do fit in."

"Must be some kind of group."

"It is. It's kind of a social club. Just try to enjoy yourself, and don't hold the company against me, okay?"

I took a huge bite out of my gyro. "Social club. Sounds exclusive." I chomped through thin sliced lamb and lettuce. "I never pegged you for a social climber."

"Not that kind of club."

"So how does someone like you get into a club? Joining things doesn't really seem like your style."

"Sometimes misfits fit."

"That's cheesy. Is that the club motto?"

"Actually the club motto is 'Beer is proof that God loves us and wants us to be happy.'"

"Ben Franklin."

"You know your quotes."

"A few," I said. "'To become the ocean, you have to drown.'"

"Who said that?"

"Rumi...I think. But any big wave surfer could have."

Bibulous Bibliophiles

We went downtown. Wren sparked a pinner on the way over, and the sweet smoke kept me at ease, the pungency of the world dulled to an amicable ambiance. I was getting used to her jerking my chain, and, if I'm being honest with myself, it was one of the things I liked most about her; she kept me guessing. There's something to be said for making a game of it all, me playing the fool and her deliberately but playfully fucking with me. Although at times my pride was stung, I relished those conversational opportunities to turn the tables. Wren was running alpha to my beta, but I didn't mind.

We descended a dim stairwell off of Fifth Avenue. This in itself was odd, because very few places in San Diego are below ground. Basements are unheard of in residences, and businesses inhabit the street level and above. There are no tornadoes, drainage is not equipped to handle large rain events, and granite chunks are common just feet below the topsoil, meaning that you need dynamite to install a swimming pool, much less a downtown bar.

I saw no signage above ground or upon descending the stairs. Instead I saw two metal handled fire doors, one in front of me and one to my right. I tried both and found them locked. I turned at the sound of Wren's laughter. "Everyone does that the first time." She turned a well-concealed handle on the left. The door was not visible until it opened, the entire face and wall around it being covered with lovely, pale green, faux vines.

"What is this place?" I asked as we entered. The room was dimly lit and extended back farther than I could see. On one side of the room a polished granite bar with cushioned low-backed barstools dominated, a narrow mirror ran across the top and more faux vines hung down around expensive looking wine bottles and top shelf liquor. Across an aisle sat two verdant circular chairs each large enough to seat four people in full recline. Behind them was the dining area. Massive candles, each at least a foot tall, flickered shadow-dancers across the polished granite surfaces of the tabletops. The dining area extended to the far wall, a combination of exposed brick, framed black and white photographs, and more faux vines.

The circular chairs drew my eyes back to them. "This isn't some kind of Alice and Wonderland themed swinger's club is it?"

Wren laughed again. "Most days it's a wine lounge. But we've got it to ourselves tonight."

"And who exactly is we?"

"Look around."

I did. The crowd was sparse. Two white-haired men in herringbone jackets sat at the bar drinking Chardonnay. The bartender serving them looked to be my age, bearded, with a purple top hat, short-sleeved button down and a green bow tie, perhaps my subconscious tie in to Alice. Toward the back I saw a pretty goth chick with a pixie haircut and enough metal in her face to set off airport detectors at ten paces. She was talking to a man decked out in California business attire, blue button-down, blue sport-coat and slacks; he looked like he should be selling houses not chatting up pixie-Elvira. Two heavily tatted dudes sat at one of the dining tables with two pretty girls, and toward the back of the room, someone appeared to be setting up a pair of turntables and some speakers larger than the ones Wren put in my house. I didn't see any connection between any of them except that they all looked out of place here, but who wouldn't.

"There're a few more people coming," Wren said "but these are the Bibulous Bibliophiles." We sat down at the bar. I was puzzled and stoned and kept my mouth shut as I took it all in. "Just don't order light beer or blended whiskey. "You'll make me look bad."

Wren ordered some fancy Syrah and an Arrogant Bastard on draft. The bartender knew her by name as did the two white-haired gentleman seated a few seats down from us.

"Who's your friend Wren?"

"This is Riley. Riley meet Herzog and Bellow." I raised an eyebrow. *Herzog and Bellow, really?* "They joined back when you had to have a moniker, a *nom de club* if you will, it had to be either a character or an author. The rules are a little more relaxed now."

"Oh. Well it's nice to meet you. Call me Ishmael."

They both chuckled. "Shit don't say that to Hemmingway. We'll never get that lush to shut up."

"Where is he anyway?" asked Wren.

"He's in the back setting up. Hey we saw your new pieces back there. Really cool stuff."

"Oh shoot. No one was supposed to see those yet. The music has to be playing to get the full effect. I'd better go have a chat with Hemmingway."

"Good luck. He's back there with Hunter S. and Duke Leto. They've been at it for a while." Herzog raised his fingers and took an imaginary shot.

"Surprise surprise. Mikey this is Riley," she said to the bartender. "Take care of him until I get back, okay?"

"You got it tweety bird." He tipped his purple hat to me. "You already got the beer back, you want a shot of Black Label to wash that down with."

I declined and ordered a Talisker 10. A wink from Mikey let me know I had correctly answered the trick question and I soon felt the warm buzz of whiskey in my chest. My high was wearing thin, but the drink came on quick and to my surprise I felt at ease, not the least bit anxious, just piquant curiosity and a thin film of paste at my disorienting evening. I sipped my pint of Arrogant and chatted up Herzog and Bellow.

"Bibulous Bibliophiles, eh? What is this some sort of book club with beers?"

Herzog was delighted. He slapped Bellow on the arm. "She brought in one with a vocabulary. It's more of a drinking club with books. At least it used to be."

"Now all sorts of art and music are part of the group," added Bellow. "It used to just be literary academics and failed novelists."

"One and the same," chuckled Herzog.

"So, Herzog? Bellow?" I grinned. "Did one create the other?"

Herzog scowled, an old man's scowl, which is always better and far more humorous than a young man's scowl, which either looks too angry or too petty. Herzog's scowl was too funny. "I invited him. 1973. I was a junior professor of literature and he was a grad student. So, you see, I created him. I brought him along and we let him in and then he picked that damn name." He turned to Bellow, "Self-appointed, self-important asshole."

Bellow couldn't help himself from laughing. Herzog continued, "For the record I am neither a Jew nor a cuckold. Shit, I'm not even from the northeast or Chicago. Although I have been divorced twice and I might be crazy. But I only picked Herzog because I liked how the name sounded.

Her-zog," he sounded it out. "Manly, melodious, and the –og makes it sound a little dirty. That's how we picked 'em back in the day, dirty melodious manly men. Although letting in the ladies turned out to be a good thing. Especially that little firecracker you came in with."

"Yeah Wren's something alright."

Wren's voice rang out through the lounge. "Wine is sunlight, held together by water.*"

"Here, here!" yelled Herzog and everyone drank. I picked up my Stone and took a slug along with the crowd.

Bellow jumped in and boomed out "Wine gives courage and makes men more apt for passion.*" More cheers and drinks.

The petite goth chick squeaked with exceptional volume: "Wine is bottled poetry."*

Again a cheer went up and everyone drank. And so it went, around and around:

"When men drink, then they are rich and successful and win lawsuits and are happy and help their friends. Quickly, bring me a beaker of wine, so that I may wet my mind and say something clever.*"

"Of the demonstrably wise there are but two: those who commit suicide, and those who keep their reasoning faculties atrophied by drink.*"

"It is most absurdly said, in popular language, of any man, that he is disguised in liquor; for, on the contrary, most men are disguised by sobriety.*"

From all corners of the room it came, one alcoholic quote after another, the universal thread that tied all of these strange and disparate people together, drink. Half way through the toasts my glass was nearly empty, but before I could even ask for another one, there was Mikey, pint in hand, clinking to a quote with me and throwing back a pint of his own.

A familiar voice called out from behind Wren, near the back room, "Always do sober what you said you'd do drunk. That will teach you to

---

* ORIGIN: Galileo Galilei

* ORIGIN: Galileo Galilei

* ORIGIN: Robert Louis Stevenson

* ORIGIN: Aristophanes

* ORIGIN Mark Twain

* ORIGIN: Thomas de Quincy

keep your mouth shut." Again we drank, and I thought, where do I know that voice from? I couldn't place it, in large part because I was spinning from the rapid ingestion of booze

"That's Hemmingway," whispered Herzog. "The quote and the quoter."

I was feeling it now, the liquor and the room. Saffron-tongued I shouted out:

Here's to a long life and a merry one
A quick death and an easy one
A pretty girl and an honest one
A cold beer and another one!

I didn't know who'd said that but it was on the wall at this Irish pub I used to drink at. It got a chorus of hoots and cheers and it was bottom's up again.

Then came the voice that I recognized again, Hemmingway, they called him, "Beer is proof that God loves us and wants us to be happy.[*]" This got the biggest cheer of all and everyone finished off their glasses in merriment. Then the speaker stepped from the back room into the light and my merriment didn't fade, it jumped back into my pint glass. Standing there, his arm around Wren, was the Professor.

****

Despite myself I wound up having a pretty good time that evening. The booze flowed and the vibe bounced, the DJ started spinning some mellow acid-jazz at a volume that allowed for conversation (the speakers evidently were a ruse), and I spent most of the night at the bar with Herzog, who despite being thirty years my senior was fascinating and dare I say, hip. We talked about books and to my surprise he wasn't stuck in the classics, or mid-twentieth century American authors the way you might expect a literature professor to be. He was knowledgeable in that way, but he also was a fan of David Foster Wallace, Vonnegut, Tom Robbins and even pulp sci-fi and modern fantasy. We must have been drinking for an hour and a half when Mikey came over and set six dark-tinted wine glasses

---

[*] ORIGIN: Benjamin Franklin

down in front of Herzog. "You ready to play?" he asked, then he hollered to the room, "Herzog's gonna play what's that wine."

The crowd around us was small, I guess most of the club had seen this before, but a few people moved in close, including the goth chick, who'd introduced herself as Erin, and Bellow. Mikey produced six bottles, each with the label taped over, and poured a taste of each one. He handed Herzog a lime wedge and a glass of water. Herzog bit the lime, swished the water around, gargled for thirty seconds and then spit into a pint glass. He then took up the first wine.

He closed his eyes and took a slow, tiny sip and you could see him swish it in his mouth from side to side, each cheek puffing ever so slightly. As he tasted, he waved his hand slowly above the bar top, his fingers bending ever so slightly as though yielding to some unseen object. He slid his hand down toward the bar then slowly back up. Finally, he swallowed and opened his eyes. He repeated the process for the remaining wines, each time cleansing his palette before moving on. He set down the final glass and cleared his throat. He pointed at each bottle, moving in the order in which he did the tasting, and called out the winery the grape and the vintage. After he called each name, Mikey removed the tape to reveal the label. He correctly identified four and missed only the vintage on the other two.

"Pretty impressive, huh?" Wren plopped down next to Herzog. "Zoggy tell you what he's doing with his hand."

"Oh that's our little secret dear," said Herzog.

Wren slapped his hand away from her thigh. "Not that you old perv. For real, did you tell him?"

"He didn't ask."

"Well I'm asking so tell him."

"You know. Why don't you tell him?"

"Fine. Riley, Herzog feels the shape of the wine as he tastes it."

Herzog interjected, "Every wine has a slightly different shape. The sweeter fruitier wines are more round whereas the sharper wines are just that, sharper, more angular."

"So you're a synesthete?" I asked, too curious to be pissed at Wren.

"Ha. I knew you had a vocabulary but I'm surprised you know that word. Yes, I'm synesthetic. My little talent works for food too."

"So you can tell the wines apart by touch?"

124

"And by taste. I mean they're the same thing, to me anyway. If something has a taste it also has a shape, there is no separating the two."

"So if you touch something do you also taste it?"

"No it only works one way. Thank God! If I tasted everything I touched I'd probably go crazy... although." He reached at Wren's skirt and again she slapped his hand away. He gave a lecherous grin and shrugged, "It's for the best. You only eat so often, but you're constantly touching things. Were it otherwise I'd probably run around with oven mitts on."

"That's amazing your taste, or touch, is that refined."

"Well it's a practiced skill, I didn't become a sommelier overnight. I had to work at it like anyone else, although I do believe my shared sense makes it easier. Some of the differences are obvious, like a Riesling ick! Compare it to a Chianti. One is oblong and squishy, like a deflated football, the Chianti is more of a firm pyramid, very pointy at the top. Other wines are closer in taste and hence closer in shape, which makes it a little tougher, but the most difficult part is remembering what wine has what shape."

"Herzog has an excellent memory," Wren interjected, "for quotes and for wines."

"Yes, well the problem is my shared sense gets stronger when I'm drinking. The objects I feel become much more defined, much more concrete. If I'm really blasted I'll even feel multiple copies of the same object. The problem is the more smashed I get the worse my memory gets. For that little game Mikey likes to make me play I try to find a happy medium where much touch is sensitized but I can remember my name, and the names of wines. Excuse me. All this drink is flowing through my aged body."

Herzog got up and Wren slid over next to me. "You having fun?" The answer was yes, and I was drunk off my ass, but that isn't what I said.

"So is this some kind of setup?"

"What?"

"Herzog just happens to be a synesthete? The Professor's here? Do you even want to go out with me or was this all just an excuse to get me here?"

She reeled back like I slapped her in the face. "No." She stared at me, all the sylvan cheer subsumed in the cold jade of her iris. I felt like I might be sick.

"So is everyone in the club a synesthete?"

"Not everyone, but Herzog is, and Erin and me."

"So what is this anyway?"

"You still don't know?" I shrugged and shook my head. I didn't trust my mouth to answer. "It's a drinking club, nothing more nothing less. It started out with a literary bent, literature professors and wanna-be writers, but that was way before my time. Now it's just a collection of intellectual oddballs. The only requirements are that you're invited by a member, you're smart, interested in arts or other creative activities, and like to drink. Sorry if I offended you with this *setup*. I thought you'd fit in, you seem like you could use some friends."

Now it was my turn to reel like I'd been slapped in the face. I couldn't tell if the sick taste in the back of my throat was from the drinks or from anger. "I don't need your pity."

"This is what friends do. They invite their friends to meet their other friends. The only person feeling any pity for you is you."

"And the Professor?"

"What about him?"

"You know he set me up. Tried to force me into some study."

"I didn't know that."

"So you didn't tell him? He's just in the club? He just guessed that I was a synesthete and you just happen to know each other? He had a hunch so he pulled me out of the study I signed up for and devised a whole questionnaire just for me? You had nothing to do with that?"

"He told me you were a synsesthete. And I don't know anything about him pulling you out of another study."

"Another—"

"Why? Is it some big secret? I mean I get it if you don't want to tell people because they won't understand or because you're worried they'll think you're weird or crazy or something, but he understands."

"You have no right," I said losing conviction as I said it.

"I'm in the study too. And it isn't a bad thing. It's a good thing. And if you would stop feeling sorry for yourself and hiding in your past sucking on your bong you might realize that."

126

"You're one to talk."

"What's that supposed to mean?"

"I mean, you rip bongs with the best of 'em."

"Yeah. And then I go out and live my life. I paint. I teach. I ride my Vespa. I surf. I don't hide in my family's factory, ruminating on poor poor me, and how life is so unfair."

"Some of us can't do those things anymore."

"Fine. Go ahead and wallow. Be pissed off. But you should know that the Professor helped me, and he could help you too if you'd let him."

"I don't need help."

"Everybody needs help. No one gets through life alone. This study, this thing that we are, this synesthesia, it's personal to every one of us, but it's bigger than any individual. So if you won't think about yourself because of pride or pity or whatever, at least try to see the big picture. Seriously, how can it hurt to go talk to him before you blow off everybody, including me?"

Herzog reached for his wine glass on the bar. "Pardon me," he said to Wren as he reached around her. I hadn't noticed him come back.

"Don't worry. I was just getting up." She stormed off and left me there choking back the fury that fouled the back of my mouth. She was angry with me? No. She didn't get to be angry with me. I was angry with her. She broke my trust, not the other way around. I couldn't believe she turned it around like this was my fault.

"You were talking about Hemmingway?" Herzog asked. "Are you synesthetic too?"

"Yeah," I admitted grudgingly, still too queasy to speak in complete sentences.

"How? You see colored letters? You see sounds, like Wren?"

"Colored letters." I suppressed a gag and swallowed back a throatful of puke. I took a deep breath through my nose. "And I taste feelings."

"Taste feelings? You mean like touch? Or like emotions?"

"Emotions," I gagged.

"Trippy. I never heard of that. No wonder ol' Hemmingway's interested. Look Riley, I only know you from our conversation tonight, but I'm going to give you a piece of advice. I've known Wren for a couple of years now, and she's a rare bird indeed. And in the time I've known her you're the first person she's ever brought to this club." He raised an eyebrow at me, and let that nugget sink in. "Look, if you meet a woman like that once in your lifetime you're a lucky man, most men never do. Shoot, she makes me wish I were thirty years younger. So if helping out that crazy professor's the only way to keep seeing that sweet little songbird, you'd better get on board with Hemmingway. Besides, he's got friends in high places, you never know where a man like that might take you." He got up and slapped me on the back. I choked back another surge of bile and beer. "Well my cab should be here by now. You think about what I said. It was a pleasure to meet you Ishmael."

I went to the bathroom and puked my guts out.

I staggered to the back room and found him staring at a painting, his back to me. "So Hemmingway huh? You planning on blowing your brains out?"

The Professor rocked unsteadily on his feet as he turned, a mad grin stretched across his face. "Don't play mind games with a psychology professor. I can turn you inside out. Even if I am shit-faced."

The garlic chicken wrap had been regrettable in reverse, but that and a little water splashed on my face had me feeling prepared to face the Professor. Now I was feeling sick again, but not queasy, the Professor's words put metal in me, like I got too much mouth on an aluminum can.

"Relax Riley. I'm only kidding. Profess if you want. Better yet, observe. Let's look at your girlfriend's paintings shall we." He flipped a switch and music came on, not the classical I expected to accompany her work, but some hard, angry, driving house, Ba-Bomp-bomp-bomp-bum-Ba-Bomp-bomp-bomp. A flock of blood-sparrows dive-bombed a sea of yellow and green octagons and shattered into metallic sparkled blackness that frothed and bubbled into midnight blue anger. The use of the blue was jarring to my senses. I could never have imagined that color to convey the fury that it did. It was all wrong, yet perfectly right. The flashing strobe aimed directly at the canvas and the pounding bass amplified the ferocity of the motion.

"It's genius," I said.

"Yes. It is. She is. This is how she professes. But it takes a keen eye to learn the language she uses."

"Her art moves. It screams. It's alive."

"I think you have an eye for this. You hear in color Riley?"

There it was. Drunk or not he was working toward his aims. First to study, then to profess, at least he was straightforward about his objectives, if not his methods. "No," I answered him, "but that's why I came back here. I'll finish my six hours with you." I paused awaiting a response, but none came. "Dr. Herriman wouldn't let me back into his study. I don't suppose you know anything about that."

"Of course not."

"Right. I'll see you at school."

I came out and looked for Wren. It took me a minute to spot her near the front door. She was talking to a dark-haired man. I had seen him before but I couldn't recall where. He was good looking. His tight t-shirt bore a dazzling metallic dragon design and emphasized his muscled physique. He walked away before I managed to limp over. I turned and watched him head to the back where the Professor was.

Wren smiled at me. *All was forgiven?* I wasn't sure, on her end or mine, but I was relieved not to be fighting and too drunk to care. "Who was that?" I asked.

"Oh. He's just a dealer."

"A drug dealer?"

"An art dealer. He's going to check out my pieces in the back room. He said if he likes them he might be able to get me a show in Portland."

"He'll like them. They're amazing."

"Thanks." She played with her hair, wrapping it around her fingers like a fistful of flames. She tucked the fire behind her ear. "I hope he does. But we should go, it's late."

"I can't drive!" I moaned. "I don't know what to do about my car, it's gonna get towed."

She rolled her eyes. "I'll drive. Give me the keys."

"But you're drunk."

"Baby I stopped drinking hours ago. You were just too drunk to notice."

A Proposition

Argument doesn't change minds; not often, not on matters of importance, core matters, the things people believe, the premises that govern where their logic can take them. You believe what you need to believe to hold your feelings together. People change their minds when they change the way they feel. People change their minds when they change their premises. The best way to convince someone, to truly change the way they think about an issue, is not to pound them down with rhetoric or win them over with clever arguments. The way to change minds is with information and opportunity: information that contradicts their current thinking on a subject and opportunity to view the subject from a different perspective. You don't change minds; minds change themselves.

I am talking meta here, big picture, religious faith, political leanings, all that bullshit that people think matters, that they build their identities around, but the thing is argument doesn't get you far on the practical stuff either, on choices, the decisions that lead to action. Argument doesn't move a man to act one way or another. You know what does? Two things: threats and incentives. In my experience incentives work better. Better still are incentives backed by threats.[*]

"I'd like you to spend a year with me," said the Professor the second I set foot in his office. The semester was over and he had called me in. "I would like us to work together exploring the nature of your synesthesias."

"You want me to be your guinea pig?"

He scoffed, "Guinea pig. Rhesus monkeys make better experimental subjects, but our relationship would be more interactive, more egalitarian. I can't sit and talk with a monkey: there can be no crosscurrents of information exchanged, no theoretical input from the subject. Whereas your subjective account is invaluable. I need your input if this research is to prove fruitful. Technically you would be my undergraduate assistant, but I prefer that you think of it as an opportunity."

"Opportunity? For me? Or you?"

---

[*] TANGENT: In this regard the Abrahamic religions are the most convincing philosophies in the world, as is born out by their success in recruiting converts. Follow the rules and society will be moral, break the rules and God will smite you. Follow the rule and go to heaven, disobey and you go to hell. The Abrahamic God is the greatest motivational speaker in history.

"For both of us."

"So now you're working *with* me. I did my ten hours. Because I had to. Go ahead and fail me if that's your threat."

"Riley, I am not threatening you. Your decision will in no way affect your marks. You have completed your course requirement. I have no intention of extorting your cooperation, but I do want you to cooperate. There are benefits to be had. You will receive academic credit sufficient to complete your degree in one year. If all goes well my recommendations and backing could advance you into excellent graduate schools or good jobs. And by participating you'll be at the forefront of an emerging specialty in the field of neuroscience, with a personal understanding of the subject matter that few can match."

"I'm not a scientist."

"So you say. The opportunity is a good one. I offer a carrot, not a stick."

"No thanks."

"Don't be hasty. I have a location available: a Rancho to the east, a magnificent property. You'll have free housing there, and we'll both have access to the best equipment."

"Why should I care what tools you use to poke me?"

"No one's going to poke you or make you submit to procedures without your consent. This is a collaborative opportunity. Don't you care to learn about yourself?"

"I can do that myself. Why do I need your help?"

"Because outside eyes add a fresh perspective. Besides, this is also an opportunity to learn about others like you."

"Like me how?"

"Other synesthetes."

"So?"

"Don't you want to impart some understanding of this phenomenon to the few others who also experience it? Wouldn't a greater understanding of what it is that you experience and experienced growing up have been a benefit to you? Wouldn't you have liked for someone to tell you why it is that you were different? And failing that wouldn't you have liked someone to tell you that you weren't alone? That you weren't crazy? That you weren't a freak?"

He played on my old fears. He was no mind reader, but he was pushing the right buttons. "Aren't I?" I asked.

"You know that's not the case. You deflect because you must. The truth is you just don't want to agree with me. You're scared of becoming my *guinea pig.*"

"I'm not scared," I lied. "I just don't see why I should cooperate."

"I've given you many reasons already: Free education, free housing, expedited degree, letters of recommendation, my connections."

"I already have a house. And I don't need your help."

"Fine. You can have the opportunity to learn more about yourself, about your own unique condition. You can help other synesthetes to learn about themselves. You can help others with the simple knowledge that there are others like them, that they are unique, not crazy, that they are special, not freaks."

"Semantics."

"Contrarian! Damn it Riley! Can't you see this is your opportunity to profess?"

"I'm not a professor. I'm not you."

"This is your calling man. I'm handing it to you. We all need a mission, something to drive us. You are in a unique position to make a unique contribution, to science, to synesthetes, to the world."

"To your research."

"Yes to my research. But why are you hung up on the benefit I might receive? Look at benefits offered to you."

"I'm not sure they're benefits. Why me anyway? Why I am I so important? You said yourself there are other synesthetes out there."

"There are others out there. But *you* are here. Also, I don't know that there are others out there quite like you."

"What do you mean? You said there were other synesthetes. Helping them is part of the benefit to me, right?"

"Yes other synesthetes, but not like you, not that I know of. I didn't want to get into this for fear it might corrupt the data, but I see I have no choice if I want to convince you." The Professor sighed and tapped his long fingers on the desk. "You are unusual even among the portion of the population that is synesthetic. A majority of synesthetes have one form of synesthesia. They may have colored letters or number forms. They may see sounds as colors. They may experience tastes as having shapes. A substantial minority, however, are like you in that they have more than one form of synesthesia, but even among these polymodal synesthetes, I have never encountered or read of one who was empathically synesthetic. Many synesthetes have strong feelings, often positive ones, but not always, that are associated with the synesthetic experience. However, you experience feelings themselves as synesthetic percepts. You taste and touch emotion."

"Okay. It's an odd form. Is it really that important?"

"I don't know. That's what I want to find out. I suspect that it may be."

"What exactly do you suspect?"

"Riley I do not want to reveal my hypothesis. You are the subject. In a sense you will be a guinea pig. There is simply no way around it. You are the synesthete. If I could test myself I would. You understand experimental protocol. I can't give you information that may affect the outcome of the experiment."

"You called this an opportunity, a collaboration. You say you can't do this without me. I won't do it blind. Decide. If you want my help, you tell me everything, every step of the way. Your choice, you can stick to your protocol and try to set up a double blind study, but you won't have me in it. Or, you can treat me as a partner in this collaboration like you said you would."

"So if I tell you my hypothesis you'll agree to participate."

"If you don't tell me everything, I refuse to participate."

The Professor sat silent a moment, close-mouthed, his lips moving slightly as he thought through my demand. "Very well. My hypotheses. Synesthesia is an increasing phenomenon. More and more people will have it and we will see more and more forms in years to come. A strong connection exists between emotion and synesthesia.

"That's it? That's not much of a hypothesis. And you don't need me to test it."

"That's part, but evidently not enough. So here it is: I suspect that synesthetes are the next step in human evolution."

The paste on my palette turned thin then sweetened and soured with excitement, the back of my knees tickled, as a cloud of cinnamon enveloped me lessening my judgment. Good that I was aware, better if I had heeded that awareness. "So, where exactly is this place?"

"It's fifty miles east in the Anza-Borrego Desert."

"That's awfully far from the ocean."

"The desert is beautiful and immense and the Rancho is quite spectacular. You may find the desert environment more appealing than you think. Besides, how often do you surf these days?"

It was a low blow. Salt hit my palette before the flavor folded in a foul direction, stomach juice at the back of my throat. I nearly walked out, but the tickle at the back of my knees and the cinnamon, slow to fade, stayed me from grabbing my cane, for walking or bludgeoning. "I still like the water. Even if I can't surf."

"And what if you could? Would that sweeten the pot?"

The mélange was heady. He offered miracles. I don't believe in miracles, but I wanted to. "My shoulder's fucked. I can't paddle. And my legs are too weak. I can't crouch, can't shift my weight."

"Let me worry about that."

"Don't bullshit me."

"No guarantees. But I will try. I have friends, connections. Bio-engineers, mechanical engineers, some are working on prototypes. I've seen a few. Defense applications mostly, but hydraulic or pneumatic supports that can be fitted to human anatomy do exist."

"Like some iron man shit?"

"Sort of, like I said, let me worry about that. I promise only that I will try to help get you back in the water."

"Fine. But I don't put much stock in that promise."

"Don't then, but I will do my best. Do we have a deal?"

"I'll think about it."

"Do so. Take your time, but I need a response by the end of the year.

"I said I'll think about it.'

"There is one more thing you should know. The Rancho in addition to being fantastic housing and having top-flight equipment, it's also something of an artist's colony."

An Unceremonious Goodbye

I didn't intend to, but an hour later I made my decision. I returned home and Wren's speakers were gone. I thought I'd been robbed. Then I realized my stereo was still there, and my tools. But her paintings were gone. I went in my room and verified that an ounce of marijuana and several hundred dollars were untouched. Sitting on my crappy little table was a note:

Riley,

I'm sorry. I was invited to join a prestigious art collective and I couldn't pass up the opportunity. I have a chance to show my art in Portland. With any luck I'll be able to show an entire collection. I know our two weeks were up and I wanted to see where things went. I hope you'll still want to see me when I get back, but I'll understand if you don't.

I know you can strut like a peacock. You don't have to let go of your cane, but you have to let go of the rope. You know what I mean.

Wren

P.S. You got an 'A' in my class. I didn't give it you earned it. Your final project was like a piece of your soul.

I looked behind the sheets and saw her still life lying against the bricks. I tasted tears before I fell down sobbing.

El Rancho

Two weeks after Wren left I boarded up the old Sparx factory and rode into the desert in the Professor's Jaguar. I brought a large duffel bag stuffed with a blanket, all of my clothes, my haggard copy of Moby Dick, two family sized bottles of shampoo and conditioner, two giant tubes of toothpaste, three toothbrushes, my water pipe wrapped in a towel, a sneak-a-toke, my thermometer, and four vacuum-sealed bags of marijuana each weighing precisely one ounce.

"This is it." The Professor motioned out the driver's side window. "El Rancho." All I saw was wind-swept dirt dotted with cacti and creosote. In the distance lay a rounded mound too small to be a hill but larger than the building to its right which looked like a dilapidated church with a crooked steeple.

"I thought you said this place was nice."

"This is the far edge of the property. We're still a few minutes from the main house."

We proceeded to the east and out the driver's window I saw what looked like an enormous honeycomb, further in the distance I caught glints of metal but couldn't make out any shapes. The Professor made an abrupt left onto a cement drive. We headed up a very steep slope. King palms, more fitting with what I'd been promised, lined both sides of the driveway. My knees burned with anticipation. Then I remembered I'd run away as much as I'd ventured out. I remembered Wren and tasted salt. I forced myself to focus on my excitement.

We reached the top of the drive and before me stood a villa fit for a Colombian drug lord. Red-tile and stucco extended so far that I could not see past the front gate and the wings of the home that extended to either side. We pulled into a curved drive that looped all the way around the villa judging by the circle of queen palms that reached eighty feet into the sky.

"This is where you get off." The Professor popped the trunk.

I got out and grabbed my duffel. "You're not coming?" I asked him through his rolled down window.

"No. I have business to attend to back at the University. We'll begin our collaboration in a couple of weeks. That should give you some time to get acclimated."

The front gate opened and a big-breasted redhead came bounding out. The Professor beamed and made a few quick hand gestures out the window as he spoke. "Shelly. This is Riley. Would you show him to his room and give him the tour."

She made a knocking gesture at the Professor. "Yes," she spoke in a low voice that flattened the 's' at the end of the word into an 'f.'

He extended the back of his hand toward her from his chin. "Thank you." He looked at me with his mad professor grin. "Get to know your way around. I'll be back in a couple weeks. Oh, Shelly's deaf so try to look right at her when you talk. You'd do well to pick up signs. Gotta go." He dropped the Jag into reverse. I limped back to avoid him. He spun the tires before shifting again and zipping down the hill, leaving me standing dumb next to a deaf girl as I watched his taillights disappear.

Shelly

Having no other options I did the polite thing. I extended my hand and said, "I'm Riley."

"Shelly."

"Nice to meet you Shelly. Please forgive me, I don't know signs."

"No problem. I read lips."

It was nice to meet Shelly. Her name gave a wonderful first impression, a well-utilized 'e' plugged between a red 'h' and a golden double 'l'. It blended, the 'e' in the middle, but the colors around it made sense, red-pink-orange-yellow-gold so the whole name flowed and then vanished in silver slide on the coattails of 'y'. The 'S' up front was a deep red, almost maroon, which was nice, although somewhat lost as her name ran away.

Shelly is a pleasant name, but the –lly, gold chasing silver, reminded me of Billy, which put a bad taste in my mouth, but that wasn't Shelly's fault and on pure aesthetics it was a pretty name.

Shelly led me through the metal gate that opened onto the courtyard. The courtyard was the entrance to the house, the central point from which all wings could be reached. We stepped down off a raised tile veranda onto a long path of crushed gravel that wound through the enormous walls of the perfect square. The courtyard was replete with barrel cactus and teddy bear cholla, there were countless succulents for which I do not know the names, and three fan palms near the center; it was a desert garden of the highest caliber. In the center of the garden was a circular fountain tiled in blue and white. Water flowed from the snout of an ornate dragon's head that seemed incongruous with the rest of the Roman/Mission layout. From the fountain the path snaked out in all four directions running to verandas that extended the length of each edge of the courtyard. At each corner of the courtyard hallways extended into darkness.

Shelly led me to one of the corners and I followed her, clack-clacking down an 'L' shaped hall, unable to keep my eyes off her ass. I didn't mean to leer, but I couldn't help it. She had a large butt. She was pretty and her hair was beautiful, but she was thicker than the petite, athletic type of girl I usually go for. Anyhow I don't think she noticed, I mean how could she without eyes in the back of her head, and she showed me to a long room just off the right angle of the 'L'.

138

"This is your room."

It was a big room, oppressively white, but at least it was plain and neat. Along each of the long walls were military cots, metal, low to the ground, dressed in thin sheets with a grey blanket. A waist-high, unadorned, three-drawer dresser sat next to each bed. Based on the few trinkets that sat atop some of the dressers: a couple mirrors, candles, a pack of cigarettes and a lighter, I gathered that five of the eight cots were occupied.

"Where is everybody?" I asked Shelly.

She shrugged. "Out. Making stuff probably."

"Looks like fucking barracks," I muttered to myself. Shelly must've been watching my lips because she laughed. She sounded like a donkey braying.

"Thas what the boys call them. The Barracks."

I found this much less amusing than her. This must've shown because she stopped laughing and looked a little hurt. It dawned on me that she was probably better at reading body language than most people.

"Relax and unpack," she said. It sounded like 'relats and unpad' but I got the gist. "I'll be back soon to show you around." I watched her wide hips sway as she walked out of the room.

I unpacked. I selected a cot and dresser toward the back of the room. I set my toiletries on the dresser. Clothes went in the dresser. There were no hangers and no closet, not that I cared about wrinkles. Out of an abundance of caution I left all the contraband in my duffel under my blanket and towels, and stowed it beneath the cot. Unsure what to do next I paced about the room.

I was fingering the pack of Marlboro's atop one of the dressers when a voice startled me: "Who are you?"

A short chubby man with a receding hairline stood clenching his fists in the doorway. His shirt was stained with what looked to be mud. His eyes flashed on the pack of smokes in my hand. "That's mine!" He yelled and charged at me. He covered the distance with astonishing speed. His loud choppy steps pounded like hooves across the tile. I dropped the cigarettes and stepped aside. He snatched up the pack. "Mine! "Mine!"

"Easy!" The cold washed over my tongue as I stepped back further and wielded my cane like a short sword, pointing the tip in front of me, my other hand half-raised in a gesture of peace. "I was just looking."

"These are mine!" He bared his teeth like an enraged primate and took a hard stomp in my direction. I flinched back. "Mine!"

"Okay," I said in as conciliatory a voice as I could muster, "Okay. They're yours." I heard the tremor in my voice. "I wasn't going to take them." I lowered my cane, slowly. "I'm Riley. I'm new here."

His eyes bounced furtively from side to side. They were tiny and full of fear. I cautiously extended my free hand, a bit like you would to let a strange dog sniff, palm outward for a handshake. He twitched. "It's okay," I said. "I'm sorry I startled you. I got bored is all. I'm just waiting for Shelly to get back."

He looked away then he grasped my hand and pumped it up and down. He reeked of tobacco smoke and body odor. "I'm Bob." He shuffled his feet and stared at the floor, his head rocking back and forward almost imperceptibly.

"Nice to meet you Bob." He ignored me and sat down on the bed muttering to himself. I studied him, still a little frightened at the way he charged me like a bull. Fragmented, was my first impression of him. His shirt was dirty and too big, his cutoffs too tight, he wore black dress socks, one pulled to his knee the other pushed down around the ankle, and work boots with residues of mud and cement. He kept darting glances at different parts of the floor. His head stayed down but couldn't stay still. He had a weak chin, a huge squished up nose, and tiny black dots for eyes. Nothing fit and everything moved and he just kept muttering to himself.

Another man walked into the room. He paid no attention to me at all. There was something wrong with the way he walked, and coming from a man with a cane that's saying something. His arms moved, but not with his legs. A pop of the shoulder and an outward turn of the elbow, it was more like an afterthought, a tic, than a part of his gait.

He stood in front of a dresser and stared. For at least a minute he didn't move except for the occasional forward thrust of the shoulders and turning of the elbows, the same motion he made when walking, only with both arms simultaneously.

"Hey," I said, the way you might speak to a sleepwalker you are afraid to wake. "I'm Riley."

His eyes weren't vacant; it was more like he was seeing somewhere else, like he was looking through me instead of at me. He popped his shoulders again. "Hey," he said in a croaking frog voice. "I'm Gary." He patted his pockets and pulled out a pack of smokes. He walked past me with that same awkward hitch and left the room without another word. He nearly walked into Shelly as he left.

Shelly was cheerful and ready to give me the grand tour but I told her I wanted to get cleaned up first. I grabbed my toiletries and thermometer and followed her back down the hall and around the turn in the 'L'. Through a small door on my left was a good-sized bathroom with a shower.

I made a flat gesture with my palm facing downward. It felt like I was saying 'No!' with emphasis, but I couldn't know for sure. "This won't do. I need a bath," I spoke out the word 'bath' with big emphatic lips in the hope that she would read them.

"Baf," she said. I wondered what she heard in her head when she spoke.

"Yes. Bath."

She smiled and waved for me to follow her. I wondered if her lack of hearing gave her balance difficulty. It was like her positional awareness was off, or maybe she was just a bit clumsy. She was cute in an awkward sort of way.

We walked back around on the veranda to a hall at another corner of the courtyard. At the end of the hall we entered the bathroom, which was more like a bathhouse in the Roman sense. Six tubs surrounded a large pool the shape of a kidney bean. Jets bubbled in some of the smaller tubs, the rest sat flat, all were bordered in red rounded bricks. I took a few steps forward and looked around a short corner to my right. On the far side of the room, steam poured out from the top of a squat wooden box, which I assumed was a sauna. Shelly walked past the sauna and turned the corner. She didn't return immediately so I surveyed the room. The floors were Spanish tile, plain and geometric like the hallways, but the walls were tiled in a blue diamond pattern and inlaid with gold that glittered when it caught the natural light that poured in through the windows spaced evenly high upon the walls. The roof was domed in clear glass above the pool, and then angled down in all directions. The ceiling bore the flat white finish typical of Mission architecture. A row of sleek padded lounge chairs in varying states of incline occupied one side of the pool. The whole room had opulence in stark contrast to the sparse furnishings in the barracks.

I set my things on a lounger. Shelly returned wearing a white terry-cloth robe and set down a pair of towels next to a spa that let off faint trails of steam but had no bubbles. I grabbed my thermometer and when I turned back to the tub I experienced a rare sensation, the discrete yet simultaneous tastes of bland boiled chicken breast and red hot peppers.

Shelly was completely nude. Her robe lay around her feet. Rosy areolas the size of half-dollars entrapped my eyes like Mesmer spirals spinning toward vertigo. Her prodigious bush burned like a forest fire. Her frame, more like Venus than a modern-day model, jiggled as she took a seductive step down into the tub, then another and another, calm sexy strides until she fully entered the tub and stood in its center, her heaving breasts floating atop the water like buoys in the ocean. "Baf." She wiggled her finger at me to join her.

I froze. The shock wore off. The lust remained, and fear and anxiety rushed in cold and heavy. Struck dumb by the deaf girl I stared, mouth open, as time zipped onward. Before I could process it Shelly slinked out of the tub. My eyes locked on her dripping mound of pubis, forest fire turned to rainforest, and with three long, curvy-hipped strides she was right in front of me, her hands undoing my belt.

I don't know what I said except it was loud and unintelligible, neither of which mattered or were noticed by Shelly. She did notice when I slapped her hands away and snatched up my cane. Once more I defended myself like a fencer. I thought for an instant that I really must stop waving my cane at my new roommates, but I did not put the cane away. Instead I gathered my belongings and scampered out, the clackety-clack of my cane drowned out only by Shelly's braying laughter. It rang in my ears just as surely as it didn't ring in hers.

Escorted

Cold, pasty, pressured, spicy and unfortunately erect I rushed out in a frenzy. I turned down a hallway and reached a locked door at the end when I realized I had made a wrong turn somewhere on the veranda. I backtracked down the hall and out of curiosity and a desire to hide from Shelly tried another door on my right only to find it locked as well.

"You cannot be here!" A large silhouette stood at the end of the hall, backlit by the sunny courtyard. The voice was deep and accented African.

"Sorry," I said meekly. I sure had apologized a lot since arriving. "I'm afraid I'm lost."

"Come. You cannot be here."

I limped down the hall and the shadowed figure came into view. His features were as light as his silhouette, black as night, except for the whites of his eyes. His countenance was firm and fierce, his face all angles and hard as onyx. He was imposing, clad only in sandals and a pair of baggy shorts he towered over me, taller even than my father, and his muscled physique looked as though it had been chiseled from the Black Rock that sits in Mecca. He jerked his head for me to move. I did. "No one can go there but Colin," he said firmly as we stepped onto the veranda.

"Who's Colin?" He looked at me with a mixture of puzzlement and disdain. "I'm sorry." Apologizing again. "Where are my manners? I'm Riley." I leaned my cane against my hip and extended my hand to him. He took it with a surprisingly delicate grip; perhaps he just didn't want to break my fingers. "Ndukwe," he said. I hated him at once.

Now don't go thinking that I'm racist. The truth is I couldn't have cared less about the color of his skin. I hated him for the color of his name. It was spectrally out of order, green-grey-pink, with a filthy 'k' right in the middle spoiling the beauty of its neighbor 'w', and an 'e' on the end muddling and blurring the whole damn thing in a pornographic sunset.

Our conversation ended with his name. He escorted me across the courtyard, and back to my room. We walked down the hall and he pointed out the library on the left, and then grunted "my room" as we passed it on the right. Just up from his room was the shower Shelly had showed me earlier. And then I was back. He left me without further comment.

Hot-Tubbing

I sat on my cot for a couple of minutes with my eyes closed trying to compose myself. I was too anxious to sleep so I snuck back to the bathhouse hoping for some privacy. I was relieved to find myself alone, although the possibility of unexpected company kept the weight from fading away entirely.

I pulled out my thermometer and checked the tub Shelly had tried to get me into, 104° F. Acceptable. Then I saw a slight disturbance under the water, the telltale sign of water flowing in through a whirlpool jet. I couldn't trust that the temperature wouldn't fluctuate. I checked the temperature in the pool, 80° on the dot. It would take a lot of water to move that number substantially so I decided to play it safe. I stripped down to my shorts and jumped in.

I just finished shampooing my hair and was wishing for warmer water and reaching for my soap when a voice I hadn't heard before hollered out: "What the fuck?" I looked up and saw two dudes in swim trunks at the edge of the pool. One of them, the one that had yelled, looked incredulous. "You ever heard of a shower?"

"I don't shower," I said and got out dripping.

"Holy shit. What happened to you?"

Still soaked, I pulled a t-shirt on and quickly wrapped a towel around my waist. "What's it look like?" I snapped.

"It looks like you laid down on a hot plate."

"Yeah," I said with a sick taste in my mouth, "that's about the size of it."

"Sorry," he said. "I didn't mean to be a dick. You just caught me by surprise is all." Finally, someone besides me apologized. "I'm Midas. This is Taggart."

"You guys in the barracks too?"

"Yeah. You must be the new guy."

"Riley."

"So your scars, that why you're all scrub-a-dub-dub in the pool?"

"Basically."

"Fair enough." Midas turned to Taggart, "Guess we're not going swimming. Hot tub it?" Taggart shrugged. "Go get the bitches." Taggart left. I put my jeans and t-shirt back on and immediately felt more comfortable with my scars covered. "So you meet the girls?" Midas asked.

"Just Shelly. Midas your real name?"

Midas laughed, because of my question or because of Shelly I couldn't tell. He flipped back his long blond hair. "Real as it gets. Around here anyway. Everything I touch turns to gold. Best selling artist here. You meet the other guys?"

"Bob and Gary. Oh and Ndukwe."

Midas snorted. "Colin's muscle. Fuck that ni— n'dukwe!" Midas caught himself, maybe because of the look on my face but he just laughed it off. "Yo I didn't mean it like that, I'm not racist or anything, it's just, well, Ndukwe, I mean Ndukwe man, like I said, fuck him."

"So what's up with Gary? And Bob too. But Gary especially."

"Yeah. How should I put this? Bob's crazy. But Gary, see he's what we call, fucked up... broken... cracked."

"I got that vibe."

"He's actually pretty cool. But a couple weeks back he took like forty blue smurfs. He hasn't been the same since then."

"Blue smurfs?"

"Ecstasy. I took two and I was rolling balls for like seven hours. That kid's cracked yo."

"Forty hits? All at once?"

"No it was over like three days, but he was rolling for like a week. Then he crashed out for three days and ever since he's like a zombie. You talk to him at all?"

"Not much."

"Yeah. He's been in like another dimension lately. When you talk to him he doesn't really make sense. It's like you're having one conversation and he's having another. Tripped out man. Taggart says it's probably a serotonin deficiency."

"Taggart?"

"He don't talk much but he's smart as shit. He used to study neuroscience. Can you believe that?" I shrugged. "That reminds me, where the fuck is Taggart? I told him to bring the girls back. I mean what fun's hot tubbing with no girls? We better go find him, come on."

Just then Taggart came back. He had a girl with him. I instantly recognized her, Erin, the goth chick from the Bibulous Bibliophiles. She

145

wore a black two-piece, was hard-bodied and heavily tatted, with full sleeves and chest work that looked like a suit of armor.

"Hey Erin," I said. "I didn't know you lived here. It's nice to see a familiar face."

"Hi Riley," she said with a little girl voice that seemed incongruous with the dark ink, but fit perfectly with the sunset start of her name. The contradictions in that one intrigued me.

"You two know each other?" asked Midas.

"Yeah," I said. "We met at a Bib—"

"Shut up!" Erin glared at me. "That's not for everyone to know."

My mouth burned and I felt my face turn red. "Oh come on," said Midas, unhappy at being on the outside of a secret. "Whatever. Fuck you both."

Erin seemed pleased both at my silence and Midas's displeasure. "So have you met everyone?" She smirked. "I heard you already met Shelly."

It felt like someone pressed a hot iron to my tongue. I was mortified. Fortunately Midas either chose to ignore Erin's smirk, or he was just obtuse. "He still hasn't met Daphne or Pedro."

"You'll like Daphne," said Erin. "She's a sweetheart. Pedro..."

"Nobody likes Pedro," said Midas.

"'Cept Ndukwe."

"Fuck Ndukwe." No one took issue with Midas on that. Shelly walked in. I was relieved to see her wearing a bathing suit. Midas whistled loudly. "Check out those titties."

Erin slapped him on the arm. "Don't be an asshole."

"What? It's not like she heard me."

"Well I heard you. And you're being an asshole."

So I sat there on a lounge chair, fully clothed while my four housemates enjoyed the hot tub. I stuck around even though I couldn't bring myself to make eye contact with Shelly. Where else was I gonna go? Then Midas said the magic words, "I wish we had some weed."

There is a book called "How to Make Friends and Influence People." Had I written this book it would have been one sentence long: Carry with you a large bag of chronic and the means to smoke it.

Midas and Taggart came back to help me carry the bong. They were astonished when I pulled out a vacuum packed zip. "Damn. And we've been dry for like a week. We were waiting for Colin to get back. Can I buy some off you?"

"Sure. But I gotta eyeball it. I don't have a scale," I said, quickly zipping up my duffel before they saw that I had not just an ounce but a q.p.

"This is a personal stash?"

"I didn't know when I'd have the chance to re-up."

"Dude, you are gonna fit right in."

Ten minutes later my bong had been thoroughly admired and there were five very stoned people in the bathhouse. Tastes dulled, weight lifted off my shoulders, I felt comfortable although I still looked away every time I caught Shelly's eye. Maybe I was just being paranoid, but I felt like she was giggling at me. I took the good vibe brought on by my good herb to ask a question that had been on my mind: "So who is this Colin everybody's talking about?"

They all looked at me like I was crazy. "How'd you come here and not meet Colin?" asked Midas.

"The Professor brought me."

"Colin owns this place," said Midas. "He pretty much runs the show. But...well you'll meet him. He's gone on business, but he should be back next week."

There was an uncomfortable silence. No one volunteered more information and being the new guy I didn't press for it. But it felt like I was missing a piece.

"So where is Daphne?" Erin asked. "Riley should meet her." Truthfully I wasn't looking forward to meeting anyone whose name ended in 'ne', but the others seemed to like her, so I figured I should give her a chance.

"She was touching up the red stones." It was the first thing I'd heard Taggart say.

"Yeah," added Midas, "they were pretty worn. Me and Taggart took like four hours to do the blue stones and they weren't nearly as bad, and Daphne was by herself."

"Fucking Ndukwe," said Erin. "Colin's gone and he's picking on Daphne again."

"'Cause she won't fuck him," said Midas.

"Neither will I."

"But you're too small." Erin scowled at Midas. "No offense. I meant too small for Ndukwe. I'd totally fuck you."

She flipped Midas off. "I'm getting out." As she turned to towel off I noticed her tight butt, but I also noticed yet another tattoo, a large interlocking CK similar to the Calvin Klein logo, but with a mail-like pattern throughout the letters, the same pattern she had on the armor on her chest. The weed kept the 'K' from bugging me too much. I almost made a comment, but the weed made me a little introspective so I kept it a thought and pondered its significance. Meanwhile my mind ran to what other piercings and tats she might have that weren't visible.

Erin

Erin offered to show me around the house, since I hadn't finished the tour before. I thought I caught her and Shelly exchanging a knowing look and a smirk at my expense, but I followed Erin anyway. Out in the hall she showed me another bathroom and the kitchen to my left, and then she showed me the girls' room on the other side of the hall. It was different than the barracks. Instead of cots there were four, four-post canopy beds, each with privacy screen and a vanity and a large wardrobe where clothing could be hung.

"I'm guessing yours is the one with the black drapery."

"How'd you know?"

"How come there's no art on the walls if everyone here is an artist?"

"All the art is in the art wing."

"Well let's go see it."

"You really need to wait for Colin. He'll show you everything. I could show you part of it, but you need a key for the rest, and you should really see it all at once. He'll explain it when he's back."

"Jeez. It's like waiting for Godot."

"Except Colin's actually coming. No one's trying to mess with you, but you need to wait for Colin. No one wants to cross him and frankly... look you saw how Midas and Shelly and Taggart looked when you asked who Colin was. No one understands how you're here without having met Colin."

"I told you the Professor brought me here. I'm supposed to take part in a synesthesia study. I figured that's why you were here too."

"I am part of the study. But I've met Colin." She wrung her hair out and flipped it over her shoulder. "The Professor may hold some sway here, but it's Colin's house. It's Colin's collective. It's Colin's rules."

"You make him sound like a dictator."

She pulled a pair of black jeans out of the wardrobe and put them on over her bikini bottoms. "He is. But this is a pretty sweet deal. We live in a mansion, rent free, and spend all day making art and doing drugs. Living by Colin's rules is a pretty small price to pay."

"I guess. You know I'm not really an artist."

"Well when Colin comes back you might want to fake it."

"I thought you were giving me a tour."

149

"I just said that to give you an excuse to leave. You were looking pretty nervous around Shelly." She pulled back the drapery over the bed. Neckties were tied around the two posts at the headboard. She picked a black shirt from atop her black sheets and sniffed it. "So what's up with you and Wren? She your girlfriend?"

Her question caught me off guard. "No. I don't know. I mean... she's gone."

"I know. Portland. But she'll be back." She tossed the shirt in a black wicker hamper.

"I guess."

She crossed to her vanity and put on black lipstick. She made eye contact with me in the mirror. "You like my tats?"

"Yeah." I looked her over as she held out her arms. Then she turned to face me and I stared at her chest. "Is that armor?"

"Sort of." She ran her index finger across her breastplate and licked her lips. "Dragon scales."

I gulped. "Same with the CK?" I felt picante on my palette despite the weed.

"Same." She turned again to show the tats on her back.

"What's that stand for?"

She turned again and ran her fingers across her dragon scales. "So? You and Wren?"

"I don't know. I like her. But she split and left me a note. No conversation. No kiss goodbye."

"I've got more tats and piercings." She stuck out her tongue revealing a huge silver stud. "Eight gauge."

"Wow. Did it hurt?"

She raised her eyebrows. "You have no idea."

I knew more about pain than she could guess, but I didn't say so. We could talk about her tats but I had no desire to talk about my scars.

"Too bad about Wren," she said. "She's a great girl. Synesthete. Did you know?"

"Yeah."

"So you are too. What type? You see music like Wren?"

"No. I taste feelings. How 'bout you?"

"Grapheme-color. Pretty boring. But tasting feelings? That's fucking weird. I never heard of that before. What's that like?"

150

"It's kind of hard to describe."

She nodded, "Yeah. I get that."

"Grapheme-color that's like colored alphabet right?" She nodded yes. "Me too," I said.

"So you're polymodal? Wow. And you taste feelings. No wonder the Professor's interested. It's making a little more sense how you got here." She went back to her wardrobe and flipped through the hangers, black shirts, black skirts, one after another. "So Shelly says you won't use the shower. That got something to do with those scars on your arm?"

My hand reached instinctively to cover my elbow below the cuff. "I don't like to talk about it."

"Okay. So, you and Wren, did you...?"

"Did we...? Uh. Did we...what?"

"I'm sorry Riley are my questions making you uncomfortable?" I stammered some more. "That's okay sweetie I've only got one more for you." She turned back from the wardrobe and pouted her black lips at me. "Wanna fuck?"

By Way of Explanation

I didn't fuck Erin.

Now before all you Neanderthals hopped up on testosterone and vaginal secretions start calling me a pussy, and before all you hopeless romantics start waxing poetic about the power of love, and before all you prudes, moralists, teetotalers and bible-bangers start praising my sudden, previously untold, strand of moral fiber with the tension of steel ribbon, let me clarify a few things. First, given the way things ultimately turned out, I sincerely regret not bending Erin's sweet ass over and trying my best to bang the ink off her back. But as they say, hindsight is 20/20. Second, motives are often unclear even to the one motivated, and pride and shame are forces just as powerful as love and moral character. When multiple forces and motives are at play, who can say which one is responsible for the ultimate choice? All I can say is that I chose, and that my scars run deeper than you can know. Finally, it is possible, that despite the high levels of THC metabolizing in my system at that moment, that I felt a tinge on my tongue of an unknown yet recognized flavor, and that I may, in that moment, have deemed said unnamed and complex flavor to be a flavor worth savoring, and thus I passed up other flavors in the hopes that I might experience a fuller serving of said taste.

Getting to Know Me: Art, Poetry and Music

That next week was one of the best I spent at El Rancho. I enjoy the company of eccentrics, oddballs and stoners, and I was in the company of all three, with an angry African and a couple of crazy people to boot.

I finally met Pedro who, although a bit taciturn, was nice enough to me that I didn't understand why Midas hated him, except that he was clearly on better terms with Ndukwe than anyone else in the house. In fact it was Pedro who convinced Ndukwe to open one of the rooms in the art wing so that I could see some of the works on display.

The art wing consisted of three rooms, each room accessed through a single labeled door. The largest room at the end of the hall was the 'Chill Room.' The other two rooms were on either side of the hall and labeled, respectively, 'Greaters' and 'Lessers'. I was permitted to view the 'Lessers'.

This room, which was at least twenty meters in length, even longer than the barracks, held a stunning array of artistic treasures, all of which had been produced at El Rancho. Several of Shelly's sculptures were included. She worked in metals, rusted scrap metals to be specific, and so the tones of her sculptures ranged from bronze, to rusted orange, to the greenish tones of aged and weathered copper. Her works were all variations on two consistent and distinct themes. One group consisted of stick figures; angular forms in recline, all with legs spread wide. Pedro informed me that a larger scale piece of this category was on display in the Sculpture Garden, which I would tour with Colin when he arrived, and that he and Shelly were working together on another large-scale piece. The other group was curvy, consisting of bent copper pieces layered around gaping apertures and strongly suggestive of the female labia.

Also prominently displayed were several carved wooden anthropomorphic figurines made by Ndukwe. Labeled 'N'kissi', these were intricately carved with exquisite detail particularly the oversized facial features, including, not only the eyes, nose, and mouth, but clearly defined ears as well. These 'N'kissi' looked even more ferocious than Ndukwe, if that is possible, and some bore spears and other pointed weaponry suggestive of an ancestral warrior tradition. They were adorned with colorful patterned cloths on the heads and on rectangular openings carved into the midriffs. The cloths in the center were stuck full of nails

153

and were reminiscent of voodoo dolls, although culturally distinct and serving an entirely different purpose which was never made clear to me as Ndukwe was reluctant to speak to me in any setting and steadfastly refused to discuss or explain his art to anyone.[*]

The 'Lessers' collection was rounded out by all manner of paintings, carvings and small sculptures. Most of the art could be categorized as ethnic, ethereal, abstract, violent or grotesque. Conspicuous for their absence were portraits, landscapes, and religious works, unless gothic and daemonic renderings of torture and death, gallows and guillotines, can be classified as religious.

Much of the art that week was participatory. Each evening Midas would break out his acoustic guitar and Taggart would bang on the bongos or occasionally some pots from the kitchen, and we'd have an impromptu jam session lasting several hours. Pedro was indispensable, whatever Midas said I was actually starting to like the guy. Not only did Pedro convince Ndukwe to take the jeep, the sole mode of transport off of El Rancho, the 28.3 miles into Jacumba on an epic, ten case beer run with a couple bottles of Jack to boot, but he was also the primary lyricist kicking freestyles without end. Erin sang a bit too. I contributed some back up vocals, a few weak freestyles and a couple spoken word poems I'd written over the years. The only one the group cared for was a disgusting, semi-sensical rhyme I don't even remember writing. I found it on my post-accident return from the hospital on a crumpled up scrap of paper at the bottom of the plastic sack that held my belongings. It was clearly written in my own hand, and I can only assume it was produced in a morphine-induced delirium while laid up in the hospital.

Fairy dust and spinster tales
Fibonacci's spiral snail
Darkened staircase spermy whale
Baleen cracks on lobster tails

---

[*] TANGENT: I should say that on this matter I was and am entirely sympathetic to, and in agreement with, Ndukwe. No artist should ever be forced to explicate his/her aims, manifestations or techniques to anyone. Either the art speaks for itself or it speaks not at all, and if you can't hear what it's saying it is not the job of the artist to act as a microphone for his/her work.

Spiny circus pointy clowns
Tiny cars and marshy downs
Hackneyed speakers in the round
Netless death in unmarked ground

Open sores and posey pox
Lockjaw, pores the smell of lox
Sickly whores with itchy spots
Syphilitic brainstem rot

Hobo's boxcar sealed to fate
Dildo double penetrate
Scrotum in the press for grapes
Totem poled, anal rape

I recited that doggerel four times that week. The group thought it was hilarious. Perhaps an indication of things to come, but I chalked it up to weirdo artists with a sick sense of humor, and I was happy to fit in however I could, pornographic rhymes included.

The girls continued to make their availability known. Whether they were, or whether they just enjoyed making me uncomfortable, I didn't know, but it was less aggressive, more flirtatious and the attention was a steady ego stroke.

The exception to the come-ons was Daphne. She was aloof in the extreme and spoke to me only when necessary and with the haughty bearing of royalty or, in America, of women who know they are beautiful. A true Grecian beauty, long-legged, with olive skin, thick dark hair and hazel eyes, even if she had been into me I didn't care for her name; 'e' works better up front than on the end. We were pleasant to one another if not particularly close and she was uninterested in our nightly jam sessions and drinking binges, so I didn't have to see much of her. Although when I did see her it didn't hurt my eyes.

The group defied easy classification and my expectations at every turn. For instance, Ndukwe was not a mean drunk. In fact he was prone to bellicose laughter and broad toothy smiles that shone brightly against his dark countenance. Gary seemed to be getting better with the consistent aid of my marijuana, although his hands still twitched and he popped his shoulders inward in involuntary spasms. He and Bob chain-smoked incessantly. According to Taggart, Gary was the most gifted musician at El Rancho, but since his extended roll he lacked the coordination to play guitar, keyboard or even the recorder. Sad, but as I said he seemed to be getting better and Midas in particular was holding out hope. He told me often: "Gary'll be okay. He'll master his high."

Bob was paranoid, and wary of me, but he was gentle and did many favors for the group, including the bulk of the cooking. Erin and Taggart were both vegetarians and Bob always made a veggie option, although the grill was frequently fired, and there was a freezer filled with meats in the kitchen. We ate well every night and by the end of the first week I was beginning to feel comfortable with everyone except Ndukwe. I couldn't get past his name, and even if I could have he didn't smoke bud with the rest of us, was surly and belligerent whenever he wasn't drunk, and was far too enamored with his authority in Colin's absence. Everyone hated him, except Pedro, but everyone followed his orders, which consisted mostly of chores for upkeep of El Rancho. I sucked it up and washed the floors in the barracks and hallway when he told me to. I was not permitted to roam the grounds, so it was a bit like house arrest, albeit in a very large house, the consensus being that it was the sole right and privilege of the mysterious Colin to give me the grand tour.

The day before Colin was to arrive the mood changed. The freewheeling, artistic joviality vanished. Smiles were erased, replaced with straight faces and tightlipped frowns, like everyone had suddenly donned pensive masks. Only Bob and Gary remained unchanged, inaccessible and a bit off. Ndukwe acted like a harried bird being chased about El Rancho. He sped out in the Jeep to check the progress of projects throughout the grounds. He returned and barked orders. The villa and grounds transformed into a hive of activity, artists turned worker bees verily buzzing about. It was spring cleaning on steroids.

That last night there was no jam session and dinner consisted of a one-pot lentil stew that suffered from a poverty of seasoning that lacked the panache and culinary technique I had grown accustomed to in Bob's cooking. We worked into the wee hours cleaning every corner of the house and pretending not to notice each other's lentil gasses.

156

Colin

I awoke the next morning to find the barracks empty. I found a note from Midas on my dresser: *Moon's phase: Waxing gibbous. Full in four days.* I didn't know what to make of that, but no one was around for me to ask. I eventually encountered Ndukwe who told me everyone else was working on art projects, either out in the gardens or off in the studio. No one had mentioned a studio to me and when I inquired about it Ndukwe told me that Colin would show me if he wanted me to see it.

Ndukwe took off somewhere in the Jeep, so I sat alone in the Library and read. The Library's collection was spectacular. Virtually every great work from Homer to Hemmingway was available, many had hand-stitched bindings and I came across several first editions. I had only an inkling of the collection's total value, but guessed it to be worth several hundred thousand dollars. I had a difficult time deciding what to read; I had been working my way through Anna Karenina, but I shelved it. I find the Russian novelists to be rather inaccessible and prefer Dostoevsky to Tolstoy.

My scars and bad hip ached from the awful cots in the barracks and previous nights' chores. My attention wandered as I scanned the titles scarcely acknowledging one before moving to the next, my mind unable to flee the unyielding spiral of synesthetic torment: a feather at the back of my knees, an iron shackle round my neck, my mouth full of sage and thyme and rosewater.

As my emotions spiraled my mind mimicked the motion and every title, every author, Cormac, Christensen, Chuck, Coward, Cribbage, came shot through with fleeting colors, even 'e' and 'k' blurring past without import, all thoughts circling back round the same name, Colin, Colin, Colin, when suddenly my eye stopped short on a remarkable book. The brilliant yellow cover caught my eye before the word on the binding: 'Synesthesia'. The author's name flashed by, brown whizzing silver to midnight blue and a brown finish: Cytowic. I liked him instantly, a 'y' a 'w' and a hard 'c' finish instead of a putrid 'k'. A closer inspection revealed it was a thin textbook: 'Synesthesia: A Union of Senses, Second Edition.' I was fascinated and sat down to read it, but I couldn't focus. I shelved it with plans to return to it later and walked back to the barracks.

I had to take the edge off. I didn't know when Colin would arrive and I wanted to be sober but we were out of coffee beans. As soon as I smoked a bowl I heard the footsteps approach.

"So you won't use the baths, or the showers." He stood in doorway of the barracks, his hands pressed firm against the frame. A yellow tank top revealed the definition in his triceps. I recognized him immediately. He was the art dealer Wren was talking to at the Bibulous Bibliophiles meeting. Again I had the sense that I knew him from somewhere else, but couldn't recall where.

"I don't shower," I said.

"And the baths?"

"I've been using the pool."

He walked toward me. Eyes the empty blue of glacial ice looked upon me like a doctor surveying a patient prepped for surgery, anesthetized and helpless on the table, eyes that thought only of where to place the markers, where to cut the meat. The eyes paused on my shoulder, on my cane, on the barely visible scars below the right cuff of my tee shirt. Colin looked upon me like you might look at a hammer, or a hamburger, or a work of art, his gaze conveyed a purity of assessment, a look that studied for utility or taste. I had the awful sensation of prey meeting the gaze of a predator. He sniffed deeply but didn't comment on the marijuana smoke that lingered in the room. "The pool," he scoffed. "Shorts on no doubt. I heard you were rather inhibited."

"Heard from who?" I asked. Never mind that it had less to do with inhibition and more to do with the ability to control the temperature.

"Shelly. Mind you she's not inhibited at all. I'm surprised you didn't take her for a tumble though." He moved close, less than a foot away, and put a hand on my shoulder his eyes locked on mine. I felt his warm breath and smelled the mint of his toothpaste as he leaned in even closer to whisper in my ear, "Trust me, you're missing out. You ever fucked a deaf girl? The noises she makes! She can't hear herself so she's totally wild. It's *animalistic.*"

Shelly was deaf but Colin's words rendered me mute. I could have given some macho locker room answer in an effort to defend my masculinity, but in truth I'd never had that kind of conversation. Colin's words and demeanor disturbed me. The casual way he touched me, the casual mention of having sex, or not having sex, the way he described

Shelly; it was all too close and it gave me the creeps, like he just presumed to be on intimate terms, or, maybe lack of intimacy is a more accurate description, that he didn't consider the topics to be intimate, just ho-hum, matter of fact, 'can't believe you didn't fuck the deaf girl.'

And again, as he pulled back, that cold, clinical stare. Meeting a man's eye is a sign of seriousness and respect when speaking or listening. But we have a built-in function, a habit, a social understanding that there is a limit to how long eye contact may be held. Scenario dictates as in all things social. It's okay to hold your lover's eye, especially as you lean in close, there it expresses intimacy. To hold eye contact overlong is to express intimacy and in most circumstances intimacy is unwelcome. Often it is interpreted as menacing or hostile. It is an intrusion on one's personal space that can be as intrusive as an unwanted touch.

And therein lies the built-in function, to avoid establishing unwanted or accidental intimacy we break eye contact and then reestablish. Usually eye contact cycles anywhere from one to four seconds, depending on the confidence of speaker and the status of the persons involved. When a boss speaks to a subordinate they essentially have the choice, no eye contact is as much an expression of social power as prolonged eye contact. To put the subordinate on a more equal footing a more moderated approach is taken, cycling eye contact at brief interval, one to two seconds.

Colin did not take a moderated approach. His eye contact was consistent and unwavering. He controlled situations with his eyes. I tried to fight this control, but no amount of self-discipline proved sufficient. I hated it. It made me feel less. The way no dog can meet the stare of a human, that's how I felt around Colin.

"You're not like the others," Colin said. "You're not just here to heal, to make peace with your deficiencies. No, you're here to advance."

I felt my saliva thicken, as cottonmouth set in. I had no idea what he was talking about. "Well, thank you, I must say that everyone here speaks quite highly of you."

"Were they talking about me?" His eye contact remained unnerving, intense, but now there was a glimmer that wasn't there before, a flash of heat behind his icy eyes. "Who was talking about me while I was gone?"

I looked for the door; the tin in my mouth so pronounced my tongue would have clinked if you tapped it with a spoon. I forced as calm a response as I could. "Oh no one in particular. Just small talk really." I ventured a glance at him but his gaze remained steady. Making eye contact was uncomfortable, but so was breaking it. I held his eye and pressed on, "That you own the Rancho and that you're sort of the leader here, of the arts..." I gestured with my hands. I can only imagine how silly I must've looked, groping for a word with my hands as though I could pull it out of the air. "Um... movement."

I immediately regretted my choice of words, but to my relief Colin smiled, the intensity gone from his eyes. "Is that what they're calling us these days? A 'movement.' I suppose that's to be expected."

The most basic of all tastes, moisture, wet and cold, relieved the pasty metallic brack. The fear faded and my eyes glassed over, the weed working with delayed effect.

"So how much of the art have you seen?" He asked the question casually, but I was instantly cautious, aroused by a faint hint of metal, as though a coin lay at the back of my mouth. It was less pronounced than earlier, but strong enough that my feelings overrode the weed. I tried to dismiss it, to chalk it up to my heightened anticipation for Colin's arrival, but there was something about his questions that put me on guard. The content was innocuous enough, but I sensed another meaning or motive lay beneath.

"I've seen some, but not all." A non-answer.

Colin smiled again. He is a consummate smiler. If you ever see Colin with an expression other than a smile you can be sure it is deliberate. "I doubt that you could have seen all of the art here. You might, *might*, have been able to look at it all, but not see it, not appreciate it. Besides it changes often, everything changes here. Let's take a walk."

We began down a long dirt path at the back of the villa moving beyond the circular drive. We passed between landscaped portions of the grounds, out toward the desert expanse, toward rock outcroppings and mesas that surrounded the Rancho.

"What counts?" he asked.

"Huh?"

"What counts? You said you've seen some of the artwork. What counts? What out here counts as art?"

"All of it I guess. I like some people's work better than others. Shelly, don't get me wrong I like Shelly, she seems really nice, it's just... Shelly's sculptures, all of those lady parts... that's not really my thing.

160

"What? Are you into guys?"

"No. I just mean… it's not really my aesthetic, you know?"

"No." He stared me down. His eyes were off-kilter, the right eye opened more than the left, not so much that you'd say he had a lazy eye, it was just… unbalanced, but his stare was so fixed and steady that the imbalance made me feel like I was tipping, like the ground under my feet wasn't quite level, like nothing caught in that gaze could ever be on the level. "What's not to like about spread legs and vaginas?"

I didn't have an answer for that. "I haven't seen any of your pieces," I said, eager to change the subject.

"What do you expect to see? Some oils? Landscapes maybe? Desert sunsets?" He laughed. "Maybe you think I build skyscrapers in the desert, or that I weld together monstrosities like Shelly's rusted virgins."

"I thought you liked her work?"

"I said I like vaginas. Doesn't mean I like those hunks of metal. Sure as hell doesn't mean I make crap like that."

"Sorry I just figured you were some kind of artist."

"Never said I wasn't. And so we're back to it. Same question I asked you before. What counts?"

"Show me something and I'll tell you if it counts."

"Okay. Keep your eyes open." He walked ahead about twenty yards without saying a word, then turned back to me. "You coming or what?"

"Coming to where? It's fucking hot out here."

"Wait 'til summer rolls around. Then you'll know hot. You asked me to show you something. I'm showing you something."

I limped over to where he was standing. Before us the desert sloped gently down to a steeper declivity and then down again to the basin floor. Barrel cacti and cholla were scattered about, along with brushy stands of creosote and spindly armed ocotillo dotted with red ribbons at the wrists and fingertips, but the overwhelming color was brown, the different shades of dirt and rock: darker browns lighter browns oranger browns yellower browns; browns broken up only by the few shrubs that made the desert home. Colin pointed into the distance. "You see that?" I squinted into the valley, shielding my eyes with a hand. I wished I had my sunglasses. "Out toward the rocks, about two-thirds of the way across."

"You mean that squiggle?" I asked. It was a spot where one small sliver appeared a lighter shade of brown, almost white, compared to the land on either side.

"Yes. That squiggle is a wash. It's also the property line."

"That's quite a lot of land."

"I figured you knew. Most people ask right away how big the Rancho is. You didn't ask me so I guessed you had asked someone else while I was gone."

"Nope."

"You really weren't curious?" Again I got that tin flavor. "It's actually about twenty feet across," said Colin, referring again to the wash. From where we stood I never would have guessed it that wide. "It marks the boundary between the Rancho and government lands, everything that you can see past that wash is BLM lands until you reach the edge of the artillery zone, on the other side of those rocks, then the military takes over. We're a long way from anyone who cares."

"Who cares about what?"

"Anything other than art. So?" I didn't understand. "So?" he said again gesturing to the wash.

"The wash? You want to know if I think the wash is art?"

"You say it like you think it's a stupid question. But I want to know. Does it count?"

"No. It doesn't count, it's nature it's not art."

"So nature's not beautiful."

"Of course nature can be beautiful, but that doesn't make it art."

Colin smiled. "You might not be as daft as I thought. So where's the boundary?"

"Out there." I pointed to the wash this time, gesturing more forcefully than was polite. "The wash, remember."

"No. I mean the *boundary*. Where does nature end and art begin?"

"Nature is the antithesis of art. Art is man-made."

"You think that wash is natural?" And he was off again. It was hot, mid-morning in the desert. It was winter but it was still a warm day. I dreaded the thought of summer. We were both sweating but Colin showed no signs of fatigue. His calves rippled with every step. I remembered when my calves used to do that and felt an unsettling sweetness upon my tongue.

162

First Colin was yards ahead, then fractions of a mile. I quickened my pace, but soon he was so far ahead that I was following a yellow dot across the landscape. The yellow dot advanced uphill over a well-worn trail that ran straight as an arrow, and then vanished downhill. I continued to climb, pressing my cane into a dirt slope as solid as stone and the shear exertion of it pushed me further into my mood. Exasperation bred fatigue, and fatigue bred impatience, and more exasperation.

Finally, I arrived. Colin came back up the hill like he was doing an extra lap. We stood together under a permanent awning that someone had built atop the hill. Trails ran angled into the distance, crisscrossing other trails, all straight as rulers.

Below, out in a cleared circular space devoid even of desert scrub and cacti, stood a massive gilded figure. The base was rigid with a copper sheen. It bent and narrowed the higher it rose from the ground. It could be the trunk of a tree bent by the wind, or the torso of a man reaching, leaning out that his arms might extend a bit further. From the gleaning, spire-like base, flat rods extended in three directions and from each hung a length of rope, dun and flat in comparison to the rest of the sculpture, each hung to a different height with a different sized sphere suspended at the end. The spheres swayed with the wind, occasionally brought to a bounce as the ropes stiffened and slackened against the breeze.

The spheres were colored. No, they only appeared colored. They were mirrored. With their every motion light was thrown about, and every so often I was blinded for an instant when a beam happened to flash my way. It was striking. He was striking. I now saw it as a man, a desperate man, reaching and flailing and signaling for someone with his balls of light. Or an angry man, armed with his mirrored maces to blind and crush his foes. The largest sphere was particularly mesmerizing and my eye was drawn to it. I followed its glowing motion until my eyes burned so fiercely that I became aware of the rosewater seeping in.

"Shelly?" I asked, but as soon I said it I knew that Shelly didn't make this.

"You see a vagina anywhere?"

Other than being big and metallic there was nothing of Shelly in it. It wasn't rusted, just the opposite, it was so polished it gleaned in the sunlight, the rivets where curved metal was held together sparkled like stars and the spheres were dazzling and pure.

"Yours then?" I asked, excited. "This is one of yours."

"Who do you suppose put this awning here?"

"Come on man tell me. Is it yours?"

"Tell me about the awning. Who do you think put it here?" He gestured to our shade. Four tall sticks with two by eights laid flat across the top. Worn, but standing. It was as rudimentary a structure as you could build with lumber.

"Who cares about the awning? Tell me. I want to know. All week I've been waiting to see you. All morning I've been waiting to see your artwork and you haven't shown me anything. All you've done is ask me weird questions. Have I seen anything you made? Come on man give me something."

"You think I owe you something."

"No. I didn't mean it like that."

"Fine. This isn't mine. But you have seen some of my art. Happy? Now, who put this awning here?"

"I don't know, you?" He didn't answer. Didn't shift his posture. He just stared, like he was waiting for me. "I don't know man. The artist, maybe. What does it matter with that awesome sculpture down there?"

"So it counts then, the sculpture?"

"Of course it counts. It's amazing. It makes you think. At first it reminded me a bit of a tree, but now I see, it's a man."

"Is it? And the awning?"

"What about the awning?"

"Does it count?"

"It's an awning."

"And we've been sitting under it."

"Yeah."

"And that doesn't strike you as important? You move like an old man. It probably saved your life, the way you're sweating and panting. But fuck it. Tell me this, is this sculpture better than the ones that Shelly makes?"

"Well I don't know if I'd say better."

"You fucking pussy. Take a stand. If it's art then take a stand. You know what you like. You know what you don't like. If you don't know that then I'm a real fucking idiot for asking you what's art."

"Fine. This is better. It moves. It's alive. It's shiny. Happy."

164

"Not hardly. Who are you to judge which one is better? Who are you to judge someone else's art?"

"But you just asked me to?"

"So? What gives me the right then?" He didn't wait for an answer. He pointed down the long straight paths to the left and right of the Man with the Mirrored Balls. "You see those?"

Off in the distance I could make out vague indistinct shapes, but no more.

"Two more sculptures. Off to our right." He pointed down a straight-line path leading downhill away from the awning. "And our left." He pointed the other way down an identical but opposite path. "Two more sculptures."

I squinted down the path to the left and I could make barely make out two thin lines joined together at an obtuse angle high above the earth.

"I should have brought some binoculars," Colin said. "That point you see, the angle where it comes together, that's fifty feet above the ground. Those lines that make the point, those are steel girders, cut to size on site. Does that give you an idea of the scope of this place?"

"And there are five sculptures in the garden?"

"Not all of them are that huge."

"Is that one Shelly's?"

"Yeah. The Rusted Virgin." He grinned at me, his eyes ever askew. "There's a lot to see, but we'd better call it a day."

"Hold up. Which ones are yours?"

"Mine? Oh, none of these."

"But I thought you said I'd seen some of your art."

"I didn't say when. If you can't recognize my art I'm not going to fill you in. I'll drive you around tomorrow, but you look like you should rest. Last thing I need is another death out here."

A Subjective Theory of Art

Colin awaited me in the courtyard when I returned from our hike. I had questions for him, but I didn't get a chance to ask. I didn't even have a chance to catch my breath before he took me to the art wing.

We walked past the 'Greaters' and 'Lessers' and he unlocked the 'Chill Room' at the end of the hall. "I've seen the 'Lessers,'" I said.

"I know. It remains to be seen if you'll get to see the 'Greaters.'" He opened the door and ushered me in. "The Chill Room." Frigid bliss met my sweat-soaked skin. The room was chill, literally, the A/C cranking, the only sound the hum of massive fans hidden somewhere above. "A constant sixty-eight degrees. All year. Come summer it's the most comfortable place for fifty miles in every direction."

The Chill Room was three times the size of any other I had been in at the Rancho. The walls, floor and ceiling were a uniform matte black. Large canvases and framed photographs of tortured faces adorned the walls at random, shelves bore welded geometric sculptures and jutted out at odd heights and angles. Clay pots etched with strange markings and hieroglyphs sat in the corners. I nearly banged my head as I turned to my right, confronted by a pair of wooden figurines on a thick black shelf, chipmunks in life-like verisimilitude, their faces contorted in expressions of anguish and pain. I recoiled and staggered back on my heels fortunate to catch myself with my cane, my reaction so visceral that the fungal wood-rot taste didn't register until after I had ceased reeling and stood doubled-over my cane with my good arm somehow holding me up atop the only working leg, the one made of wood and metal.

A bead of sweat emerged on my forehead despite the cool air and I began to compose myself and take up a broader view of the room. Blacklights shone in the far reaches of the darkened room illuminating demonic velvet posters. Black suede chaise lounges and backless white couches, plush benches wide enough to sit several across, were strewn about the room at haphazard angles.

"Have a look around Riley." Colin smiled and took up a seat on a nearby sofa then threw his feet up, stretched back, and stared with characteristic intensity at the ceiling.

I realized he was looking at a canvas tacked to the ceiling. From my vantage point I could see only blue and red stripes. Suddenly the

166

placement of the couches was not so haphazard. Each was positioned underneath an object of interest: a chair bolted upside down, a formation of stalactites, a plaster mold of a nude male, and a glaring dragon with crab-claws, wings and spiraling horns. The room was made all the more eerie by dim echoes modulated by the omnipresent white noise created by the whirring fans. I felt there should have been a thumping, jarring house track playing auditory backdrop like a macabre nightclub.

"Come sit here and have a look."

I took up the position Colin had occupied and lay in full recline to view the piece on the ceiling. I felt the cold wash of fear. Depicted on the ceiling was a banner. Stripes of red and blue and white and black both defined the edges and gave the impression that the flag blew in the breeze. The bottom of the flag bore symbols from left to right: a black equilateral triangle, a red pentagram inscribed in a brown pentagon circumscribed by a brown circle, and finally a black circle atop a vertical line, a lollipop shape, with a massive red swastika in the center.

I lay very still, breath held in my lungs, heart racing, sleet-like wash expanding inside out to my entire body, gagging on a spear point, but prepared to run or swing, or scratch or claw.

My thoughts raced: *Nazis! Satanists? Had I seen too much already? Would Colin simply let me leave?* I tightened my grip on my cane. *Why had the Professor sent me here? Was he some closet Aryan leader? But, Ndukwe? How? And why me? What use did he have for me? Ritual torture? Some horrible rite of the occult?*

Then I heard Colin cackle. "You should see the look on your face," Colin said. Suddenly a red dot appeared upon the banner. Laser-sight. "Don't get up."

Little good my cane would do me against a gun. And there was no chance of fleeing with my crippled leg. I slowly turned my head, only my head, careful to make no sudden moves. Colin nearly fell to the ground. His body shook convulsively and he howled with laughter, "Oh! Oh God!" Tears streamed down his face so fully engulfed in his own mirth that he could scarcely keep his feet. He raised his arm and the red dot rose with it and settled on my chest. I flinched as it bounced up and down with every guffaw. I looked to his hand.

It wasn't a gun. It was a laser pointer. He pulled it up, still laughing, and pointed it at the banner. "Ha! Ho man." He managed to compose himself. He flicked his head upward at the banner, "You recognize that white line?"

I followed the red dot with my eyes as it traced the snaking white line that formed the top of the banner. I squinted at it, but still saw nothing but a white line.

"How bout this black one?" He moved the pointer to the line that formed the bottom edge of the flag. "Still no? Okay look at the white one again." I squinted harder. "No, no. Don't look closer. Look like you're further away."

And suddenly the entire image changed. I wasn't looking at a banner. I was looking at a photograph. "The wash," I said. Comprehension shed the fear so quickly I actually felt a surge of warmth at its absence.

"Now you see," Colin said, "shot from an airplane at ten thousand feet." He moved the pointer to the bottom of the shot. "This black line is the road you drove in on." He snapped the pointer back up. "These other red lines are striations across the desert floor, clay and mineral deposits, or just sudden changes in elevation." He snapped the pointer again the movement becoming quicker. "Bluestones. Redstones." He moved the dot to the triangle hitting each point. "Bunker. Old Church. Studio. The shadow just below that is Morty's Mound."[*]

I jumped in. "The pentagram is the Sculpture Garden. The top point is where we were standing today, under that awning."

"Now you got it. And this," he moved the pointer to the swastika, "is the house. And you, are sitting right about here." He moved the pointer to a spot just past the right angle of the upper left 'L' shaped arm.

"That's still pretty fucked up," I said, "building a house in the shape of a swastika."

"Really? You feel the same way about military hospitals? Is the U.S. Navy *fucked up*, as you put it?" I took that question as rhetorical. "It's actually a fairly common architectural design. It uses space efficiently. It has a central access hub, the courtyard in our case. It provides distinct wings that can be sealed off from each other. Good idea for a hospital right? Maybe you want to keep some patients, some bugs, away from the rest of the patients. Or maybe there are certain activities of clandestine

---

[*] MAP: The photographic art in the 'Chill Room' is not reproduced herein. However, a map of the grounds of El Rancho is provided in Appendix A. A map of the villa (ranch house) and its various rooms is provided in Appendix B.

168

nature that you'd like to keep separate, like at a military installation. Separate wings make it easier to limit access to restricted areas. It can be efficiently cooled, particularly if you limit A/C to a single wing. And with correctly placed windows or overlooks you have 360° views."

"Okay. I get it. But still…"

"Riley do you even know the origins of this symbol?"

"Yeah the fucking Nazis used it."

"The fucking Nazis? Jesus Christ! I swear half this fucking country thinks that time immemorial started with World War II. That symbol predates the Third Reich by millennia. The Nazis appropriated that symbol, from Sanskrit, in part because of Hitler's fascination with dark forces and occult powers. Nearly every pre-Christian society used some form of it. It is used by the Falun Gong in China. In Sanskrit it means 'that which is associated with well-being', it's a lucky symbol. Tantric rituals use it to evoke 'Shakti.' It's a Hindu symbol for Ganesha. It's so prolific in the archaeological record among so many far-flung unrelated cultures that Jung ascribed its significance as a manifestation of the collective unconscious. *Nazis!*"

"So you're not Nazis?"

"Are you kidding? Have you checked the lineup around here? We got a black African, a Mexican, a Greek, a ginger, two homosexuals and fucking Gary is a Jew. That sound like a white power convention to you?"

"I didn't know Gary was Jewish."

"Well, culturally, or ethnically, anyway. Religious affiliations are a bit fuzzy around here. But it's hard to know much about Gary. I'm not sure Gary knows much about Gary anymore, he's been on a different plane of late."

"The smurfs," I said. Colin nodded. "So who's gay?" I asked.

Colin's look was incredulous. "Wow. I take back what I said earlier." I gave Colin a puzzled look. "You are as daft as I worried," he said, and then opened a cabinet built into the wall. I hadn't even known it was there. The hinges were hidden on the inside. He pulled out a thick water pipe about three feet tall.

He turned it over in his hands admiring the whorls of color and the glass shapes blown inside the knobs. "You see this. It belonged to a master glassblower, it was his personal piece." He pulled a small jar from the cabinet and pinched off of a bud that weighed at least seven grams. He stuffed the nug into the large glass bowl and held up the bong to examine water level in the base. Satisfied, he handed me the piece, holding it tightly with both hands.

I received it in kind, gripping high on the pipe with one hand with the other beneath the base. The colors were fantastic. A deep blue permeated the entire base and blended into lighter shades and flecks of silver higher on the pipe that gave the impression of flowing water. Knobs and thumb handles, round protrusions of glass, stood out against the blues. Each was filled with a glass shape: a small red pyramid was set a few centimeters up from the base on the left side of the pipe, another opposite that was filled with a yellow cube. Metallic whorls and sparkles throughout the blues disoriented the up-down left-right perspective, and brought to mind a juxtaposition of locales: the open ocean and the spinning stars, whirlpools pulling at each other in a bubbling froth. Most impressive of all was a massive hand knob halfway up the pipe that housed a tiny ship, an old sailing vessel, in its center.

Plub-pl-pl-pl-plub-sheeee. I cleared the hit. I coughed. I handed the bong back to Colin but he refused, "No that's a personal man." It took two more hits and three more hacking fits to finish the bowl. My tastes slipped away. I thought of where I was and I knew that I was sitting there with Colin at the Rancho, but I didn't feel it, my sense of time and place turned down until it faded away entirely.

The cannabis chain of asocial introspection began: *Finally Colin man, people been talking about him and now I finally get to meet him and what do I think, I mean he's a hard dude to figure right? One minute he's creeping me out. The next minute he's talking about ancient Sanskrit symbols and stacking fat bowls. He's a hard dude to figure.*

I looked at the bong and got caught up on that ocean as I pondered the starry sky or shimmering seas in the glass and wondered if there was someone on that ship to nowhere, its own little universe moved about by a giant too large to be seen from the deck of the ship and I wondered if maybe we were just sitting on some desert house on some giant's bong and if so what that meant about our world and that all you saw and could see and could know was limited by where you sat and that even if we were just sitting in the handhold of some giant's bong it didn't really matter because we'd never know and we'd still just live out our lives here seeing what we saw and doing what we did and that the same was true of the tiny man

170

swabbing the deck of the ship in the knob of the bong I held in my hand and to him I was a giant even if some giant was actually holding me.

I was really moved and then Colin brought me back from my meditation on here and nowhere.

"She's beautiful right? Hits nice too man."

And then I realized that I was done smoking. Colin took the bong back. "She hits, man." He packed one up for himself. Ripped it. Snapped it. Cleared it. Blew out a fat stream of smoke.

"Have we met before?" I asked, finally voicing the question that had been on my mind since I first saw him at that meeting with Wren.

"I don't know. Have we?" I shrugged in response. "Well," he said, "if we have I'm sure it'll come to you. I'm a tough guy to forget." Colin put the bong away then came back and sat down next to me on the couch. "Now you see. I had you look at that photo for a reason. Everything here is art, man. No. I take that back. Some of it's history, man. Everything here is either art or history."

"Then you should study art-history." I laughed. Colin didn't.

"Do you think this is a joke?" he asked. "Did you come here to become an artist?"

"No," I said.

"No?"

"No. I came here for the study."

"What study?"

"The Professor's study."

"Goddammit! He thinks he can just order up a study on my time on my land. That rat bastard! I told him we're not going back to those days."

"What days?"

"Not a chance. Fuck. So you're not an artist at all?"

"I'm sort of an artist, but not really. See I'm thinking I should write a book."

"A book?"

"Yeah, like a novel."

"Great. Just what we need, a *novelist*." I got the distinct impression that he was talking to himself. "He sends us a novelist, fucking lowest form of art. Well, except for fashion."

"I thought they call it high fashion?"

"Yeah. They have to because it's a low form. Art, *true* art, reveals. Fashion doesn't reveal; it hides. No matter how revealing the outfit it conceals the human form. There's a reason the greats sculpted nudes, painted nudes. They revealed the perfection and imperfections inherent in the human form. Only wacko Christians and fucking prudes would want to put a pair of Dockers on David, or drape Venus in Chanel." He looked at me with unveiled contempt. "A *novelist*, he could have at least sent us a poet."

"I'm not really a novelist. I haven't actually written anything."

"No. Then what are you?"

"I'm a surfer."

"Really? Aren't you kinda gimpy to be a surfer? That cane double as a paddle?"

"I haven't surfed since my accident."

"What accident? Car wreck? Bad relationship?"

I didn't respond. I was really high. I had no comeback. And I was not about to talk about my accident.

"See what's funny Riley is I asked you what you are. Not what you do and sure as hell not what you were. So instead answer me the one question I've been asking you all day: what counts?"

Again I had no response. I was there but not, more watching than participating. To call it an out of body experience would be a copout. It was a chicken shit moment, consummate cowardice. Somehow, some part of me mustered the motivation for a response, "Why do you care if I'm not an artist anyway?"

"And why would I want your opinion on art when you're not even an artist?"

I nodded.

"That wasn't a rhetorical question. I have a perfectly legitimate reason for wanting your opinion. Now what counts?"

Silence.

"Fine," Colin said. "Where's the moon?"

"Waxing gibbous. Full in four days."

"All right," he said, still smiling that smile that wasn't happy and never left his face. "It's a good phase, things on the up swing until it's fully full. I see you got a cheat sheet from someone. Good that you remembered."

"What's with that anyway? The moon stuff?"

"Part of the house rules. You want to stay you have to follow them like everybody else."

"The Professor didn't say anything about that."

"Whether you stay or go, that's my call not the Professor's. You'd do well to remember that."

"I didn't realize this was a tryout."

"Rule one: Watch the moon, know the phase at all times. I'm a Cancer. Born on the Fourth of July."

"Really?" I asked.

"When's your birthday?

"October 31. Why?"

"Cancer's are ruled by the moon. We all are to some extent. I just feel it more than most. You are a Scorpio, also a water sign and thus susceptible to lunar pull, tides and such. It'll be of great benefit to you to watch the moon." I shrugged. I don't go in for superstition. I saw how much that helped my mom. "Rule two: Court is every other lunar month on the evening of the fullest full moon. You must participate in Court with everyone else."

"What exactly is Court?"

"Well what have you heard?"

Pedro had started to tell me a little bit about Court at one of our jam sessions, but Ndukwe stopped him before he said much. "Not much. Pedro said we'll eat, like it's kind of a feast."

"Usually. You'll see soon enough. Court's in five days. I'll get you your part tomorrow. Rule three: You must have an art project in progress at all times. I expect you will begin your novel tomorrow." He said the word 'novel' like he wanted to spit. "Rule four, and this is an especially important one: All art must have a subject. And I don't mean a topic."

"What does that mean?"

"It's why I showed you that photo, because the art is between your ears. That is my fundamental theory of art. That is what every artist at El Rancho must accept and work with. What's on the canvas, what's sculpted or painted or shot, that's just the stimulus. The art takes place between your ears. The artist merely provides a stimulus for the subject: the viewer, the participant, the locale. The subject's mind is where the art resides. Whatever art you make, you must make with a subject in mind.

There is only one significant concept in art, subjectivity. Art reveals what the world wants us to ignore. The world talks about objective viewpoints. Art reminds us there is no such thing. When you first looked at that photo, you didn't see a photo did you?"

"I saw a flag."

"Most people do. The photo has been augmented a bit to create that effect. The important thing is that once your point of view shifted, that flag became something else entirely, but nothing about the photo changed, only your perception of it. Even a photo is not objective. The camera reveals not *the* viewpoint, but *a* viewpoint, one spot amongst infinite possibilities.

"Then when I look at the photos, my mind chooses which aspects of the photo matter and constructs a whole from parts and attaches meaning. Only then can I process in my mind the image. Only then do I decide what is significant, decipher what it is I'm seeing. I. I. I. At every step past the subject's mind there is an 'I.' The artist's task is to intervene at the level of the subject's mind, the initial impression, the construct and meaning beyond the control of 'I,' and by doing so alter every perception 'I' has going forward.

"You are required to create a stimulus with a specific 'I' in mind. The only limitation is that you cannot be the subject for your own work. And this theory brings us to the fifth and final rule: If you are the subject of a work you must do your best to explain the art to us. That's it. Five rules. Other than that it's pretty much anarchy."

Self-Inflicted, Self-Medicated, Self-Abused, Medicated, Diagnosed, Cast

I awoke with the distinct impression I had dreamt of tanks, huge machines rolling through the streets. I couldn't be sure because I didn't remember. I never remember my dreams.

There was a sudden stillness, silence, like some noise I hadn't even been aware of had abruptly shut off. I was alone in the barracks, the start of day two under Colin's reign. His rules rubbed me the wrong way. I felt duped, which was unfair to Colin. It was the Professor's fault. For the first time since arriving in the desert I felt the mood creeping in: the fructose tinged rot and heavy chest of oppressive melancholy. If you have never been depressed count yourself lucky. I hate the taste of it, but equally awful is the effort that even mundane matters, like getting out of bed or performing your morning toilet, suddenly require. Life becomes like a boring video game on which some nefarious deity has, without warning, raised the difficulty level. It used to be fun, but now it's too damn hard and you just keep dying and starting the same level over again. Only for this system you can't just set the controller down, walk away, and take a break. And you can't quit, not unless you're going to play it the Skip Sparx way.

So there it was, melancholy in its well-known form and flavor, all be it subdued and in its infant stages, so there was still hope to cut it off before it overwhelmed me. I feared a dearth of anti-depressants. Anxious to be rid of the taste I smoked a bowl before brushing my teeth providing temporary relief.

I had a bowl of oatmeal in the kitchen. Coffeeless, I smoked yet another bowl. I decided to work in the library, in theory to begin my novel, though in earnest I planned to pretend to do so, lay low and read a few classics. I was met at the library door by loud shouts from inside.

I recognized Colin's voice. He and the Professor were arguing about me. While much of their fight was unintelligible through the door, I gathered that Colin wanted me out, the Professor insisted that I stay and that little progress was being made by either to convince the other. At one point the voices became very low, almost muted, and I pressed my ear to the door, but could only hear murmurs. It sounded as though the Professor was the only one speaking and then I heard Colin shout a single word.

"Brother!" The Professor shushed him loudly and then murmurs returned along with a steady rumble of laughter that Colin evidently could not suppress. Unable to hear more and not wanting to be caught eavesdropping I returned to the barracks to await my fate.

I didn't care if I got sent home. Yet I swore I felt the subtle drying of the mouth and rounded pressure I associate with disappointment. Disappointment cannot occur in the absence of expectation. So I was confronted with a question: *How was this experiment failing to live up to my expectations?*

I thought I came to the desert with few expectations. The Professor's carrot, my possible evolutionary importance, was yet to be determined. My disappointment seemed unfounded.

It is easier to lie to yourself than to keep a secret from yourself, although I have proved capable of both, but once you start searching it is hard not to stumble on the truth. And I did. I couldn't lie about it anymore. I had come here with a hope. A foolish hope, implanted in my mind by the Professor, manipulative bastard that he is, this hope being that a certain female artist, who had just joined a new collective when she left my company, would be a part of the 'artist's colony' to which I traveled. I had no evidence that the 'artist's colony' mentioned by the Professor was at all connected to the 'collective' Wren had set out to join, but this hope was there, rational or not, and now, with the return of the Professor, this hope was dashed. I had been there a week and a day. The study was set to begin and I was faced with the reality that Wren had gone to Portland and was not coming here. Why I should have thought that the Professor's colony and Wren's collective were connected is beyond me, foolish in retrospect. I hadn't even read her goodbye letter when the Professor sent me away with his final vague comment about an 'artist's colony.' Yet that is what I did, I took this comment designed, no doubt, to play upon my perceived interest in the arts, and twisted it into something more, some illogical far flung hope at reunion and the avoidance of unrequited love.

Oh damn it! So I said it. So I say it. You can believe that I'm a silly sad cripple who placed the idea of a woman on a wren's high perch and confused my inability to touch its loft for standing in a hole shouting up my professions of love. But love her I did! And I say it now despite the way things turned out.

And so at this rare moment of honest self-appraisal leading to the discovery of self-deceit I was, of course, in a better position to face my disappointment and move on to a new chapter of healthy self-discovery.

True...if I were a reasonable man of intellect looking forward to the opportunities and challenges of the future. I was not. I was a stoned cripple, a borderline alcoholic frightened of what the next day might bring and mired in the beginning stages of a depression much like the one I had emerged from years earlier to find my former self dead and buried and the man that remained a hideous doppelganger, a fractional me housed in a scarred casing that bore my name and face to the world, not empty but not full, a diminished homunculus that occupied the shell of what used to be Riley Sparx.

I flipped. I took my cane to my dresser and watched the wood splinter as bits of pine and particleboard backing flew about the room. But that wasn't enough. I pounded my cot. I bent that flimsy spread of metal and coil into a vee. I bashed its rounded flip-out legs from the hinges and still not satisfied I hit Gary's cot, and Bob's, and Taggart's and Midas's until the barracks were strewn with cheap aluminum wreckage and wadded blankets. I did it all with one arm. It's amazing the damage my cane can do. A solid rod of steel runs through its center and the wood is pure cherry sealed with an epoxy resin. A single scratch was all the damage it bore following the rampage.

I fell into the corner sobbing with rage, but so stoned my taste buds lay dead and dull. I needed to taste. I needed to feel. And so I threw a punch. My right hand balled into a fist and bashed into my temple sending showers of sparks flying before my eyeballs. Again and again I blasted my head. Again and again I rained shots upon my temple. There is a sick satisfaction in delivering and receiving the same blow. The exquisite control, the exquisite pain, the mastery of rage as it flows from head to fist to head and back again, there is no sensation like it, the sheer desperation is as close as you can come to suicide without an actual attempt.

They stood in the doorway as I delivered the last blow. The Professor bore a look of horror. Colin was, dare I say, giddy. "Wow." Colin surveyed the damage. "I was wrong about you. You can definitely stay. But you have to follow the rules." He kicked what used to be the leg-stand of a mangled cot. "Looks like everybody's gotta sleep with Shelly tonight."

177

No blood was shed, but I jammed my wrist, bruised my knuckles, and a large knot swelled on the side of my head. I smiled as the rosewater trickled in.

****

The Professor bade me to follow him outside. Parked round the back of the drive was a recreational vehicle some forty feet in length. Paint it black, stuff a band in it, and you'd call it tour bus. "Wait here." The Professor climbed up the steps into the R.V. He emerged with an unmarked bottle of pills. "Sertraline," he said. "Take one a day in the morning. Take one now." When I started to protest he cut me off, "The way you were striking yourself is akin to the behavior of 'cutters,' people who deliberately cut their skin. It stems from a combination of self-hate and a perceived lack of control over one's choices and environment. The endorphins released by cutting, or in your case bashing your head in, have both a stimulating and anesthetic effect. Bottom line, you're depressed and you have impulse control issues. These pills will help."

"I used to take Prozac."

"My professional judgment is that this will work better." He sighed. "I owe you an apology. I'm sorry that I dropped you in such an unfamiliar environment. This place would give the most well adjusted of us a healthy dose of culture shock. I can only imagine what a confusing week you've had and how out of control you must feel."

I didn't respond. The apology surprised me. He didn't seem the type to admit mistakes and it made me feel better to have someone acknowledge my pain. I didn't think he cared. I popped a pill.

"I only hope the medication won't affect your synesthesias," said the Professor. "I have no reason to believe it will, but if it does, inform me at once. We'll have to try something else."

There was the Professor I expected. He'd let me beat myself to pulp if it put his precious study at risk. I stared up at the monstrous R.V. "You staying in here?"

"Yes, it serves as both a work space and a makeshift home. I've lots of water and canned food. I'm a bit of a junkie for franks and beans, something I picked up in my college days. Old habits die hard, as they say. If they don't kill you first."

****

178

We spent the day in the library cataloging my Yangs,[*] as we would spend each day for those first several weeks. The process was tedious, for me it was a matter of rote and repetition, as I described the color of each letter and number. Several times the Professor admonished me to use only specific color terms and concrete comparisons. My tendency was to wax poetic about my livelier colors. He emphasized the need to establish a common frame of reference and to describe my synesthesias in the simplest possible terms so as to profess them to the widest possible audience. Already he began to affect my vocabulary and thus my understanding of my own experiences.

I did manage to break him away from his dogged attention to the catalogue with a few questions about the original questionnaire he had presented to me at the University. In particular I wanted to know why he thought I might be autistic, and whether he thought I was. He explained that the autism question arose after the test of my ability to distinguish a larger letter comprised of many smaller letters.

"Autistic persons have a tendency to focus on the specific." He said. "Attention to detail, to the parts that comprise the whole as opposed to the whole object, is one of the defining characteristics of autism. An inability to deal in generalities is one of the things that make navigating life and social situations difficult for autistic people. When presented with the letter cards most people recognize the larger form before they recognize the smaller individual letters that comprise it."

"Whereas autistic people see the small 'E's that make up the big 'A'."

"Precisely. There is a measurable difference in response times that is inverted when autistics are compared to normal people."

"And my response times suggested I was autistic."

"Yes, but there was another possible explanation, your synesthesias. If certain colors were jumping out at you, this could cause you to favor the specific over the general. So, I devised that questionnaire in part to test other variables symptomatic of persons on the autistic spectrum."

"And?"

"And you tore up the questionnaire before I could make an assessment." I was disappointed. I wanted to know. The Professor must

---

[*] CHART: My various synesthesias are charted in Appendix C. These charts are substantially similar to those created by the Professor during the cataloging process, but were created, *ex post facto*, by me.

have seen my forlorn look because he provided an answer. "Nonetheless, I have concluded you are not autistic."

"How?"

"Frankly you are too glib, too extroverted and too adept at reading social cues. You've mouthed off to me on more than one occasion. You've made friends with nearly everyone here. You make eye contact when you speak. For all your synesthetic qualities you are oriented outwards, into the world, as opposed to inwards upon yourself. Your little tantrum notwithstanding I'm inclined to attribute any social difficulties you may have to depression, anger, excessive use of cannabis and self-consciousness resulting from your injuries, not autism. That's my observation anyway." Such was the nature of his professions; never give a spoonful of sugar without a bitter elixir to wash it down.

****

I was relieved to find a row of new cots and no signs of destruction when I returned to the barracks. All of my clothes were on the floor, no new dresser. However, word of my outburst had reached my roommates. I endured mostly harmless jokes, but Midas was pissed. "It's bullshit. This new cot is like a rock. My back's gonna be all jacked-up. He could've at least given us new pads, something to cover these springs. Just wait, my back's gonna be covered with little circles tomorrow. It'll look like cupping therapy and acupuncture, but without the benefit to my Chi."

He turned his focus on me, the volume on his rant rising with every word, "And you! You did it, fucked my back, and now I get stuck with the porter's role while you play a prince!" I had no idea what he was talking about until he thrust a piece of paper in my face. It listed everyone in the house and their roles for Court. Evidently it was a royal court, with Colin playing the King. I was a visiting prince and Midas was a porter. "I bet you knew. You did it on purpose right? Went all crazy knowing Colin would love that. My name's Midas and he makes me a fucking porter! Maybe if I bash your face in he'll give me your part."

I muttered an apology and told him I had no idea what Court was about. He stalked off, probably to go bitch to the girls. Meanwhile I looked over the rest of the cast: Daphne was the queen, Ndukwe and Pedro were soldiers in the King's Guard, Taggart was another porter, Shelly was a princess and Colin's daughter and only heir, Erin was a peasant woman married to Bob's character, the village idiot, and Gary rounded out the cast

180

as jester. I didn't know what to make of it. It read like the cast of a play, but no script was provided. I figured I'd learn more as Court drew closer. And I did.

Building the Catalogue

Half-day sessions with the Professor dominated my time in the days leading up to Court. We started with attempts to catalog my emotional flavors, but an innocuous comment I made led to an entirely different line of inquiry. It began with a simple exchange of pleasantries, the Professor asked how I was doing, and I responded that I was looking forward to tomorrow. When he inquired why, I told him that I was tired of all the green days.

"Your days have color?" he asked suddenly very alert and interested.

"Just my months. Well and years too, but that's different, that's just if I'm trying to remember a date."

"Tell me everything you can," he said. "Be as specific as possible."

I explained that January was green, a chartreuse shade, or a pale lime, not so obnoxious as the letter 'k', but hardly my favorite. The Professor was astounded, but became even more shocked when I explained that January was also located directly in front of me, close to my belly button. He queried me about every month of the year until I grew weary of his questions and told him to let me explain it my own way:

"The best way to visualize my experience of time is as a thick hula-hoop round my waist. The hoop is frozen in mid-swing, so that one edge of the hoop is up against my left hip, and the other edge is swung out several feet behind me and to the right." I drew him a crude diagram.* "The months circle around me counter-clockwise, with January directly in front of me, April on my left hip, July behind me, and October far to my right. As you can see, some months occupy a larger space than others; October is my biggest month and February is my smallest. Each month also has a color, which is consistent and doesn't change."

"How about days? And years?"

"Days affect where within the space of a month the time is located. For instance, my birthday is October 31, so my birthdays are always right at the forward edge of October, directly to my right, where it borders November. October 1 is more behind me and to my right, where it borders September, but both days are brown."

---

* PICTURE: See Appendix C.

"So you must have developed this after you learned the months. Or else superimposed months on your existing conception after learning them."

"To be honest I don't remember when it started. This isn't something I try to do, it just is. Is this synesthesia too?"

"Absolutely! Time-space synesthesia is how I would classify it, with a color aspect as well. But what about years."

"My hoop is built up, every year it increases in thickness, my earliest memories are down around my waist, more recent memories are higher up." I held my hand up flat just in front of my chest. "Today is sitting right about here, where my sternum is, maybe six inches in front of me."

"So if I told you that the Spanish Armada was August 7, 1588, where would that be?"

"That doesn't have a place."

"Why not? It's a time, a date."

"Yeah but only times in my life have a place. The Spanish Armada was actually August 8, 1588, although that was the battle, not the launch of the fleet."

"And how do remember that?"

"I see it, like on a number line."

"Describe it to me."

"I see the progression of years queued up for my eyes. It's a bit like viewing an IMAX only the screen is closer, about a foot to eighteen inches in front of my face. I start at eye level and look up about six inches. It's like looking at a screen that bends up and around like I'm looking at the inside of a dome, a black dome. It occupies an area greater than my field of vision, close to one hundred eighty degrees around both sides of my head."

"Do you see all of it at once?"

"I can kind of take it in at a glance, but I usually know roughly where I need to look, so I scan a specific section."

"And where do the numbers start?"

"One foot in front of my face, dead center, about six inches above my head, I see 1974, the year I was born."

"Are the years colored like your months?"

"Yeah. The years move past to present from left to right, but the color depends on the decade, except the 70's, 1974 to 1979 is grey and really hard to see. 1980 and every year in the eighties are purple, but a really light purple, lavender I guess."

"Wait, wait. You have this number line for dates that occurred during your life? I thought they were organized around you, your time-space synesthesia."

"My hula-hoop is just for my life. Every moment of life, my experience, has a place. But if you ask me a historical question, like what date the terrorists struck the World Trade Center I see two dates on my number line, February 26, 1993, that's green like all of the 90's, and further to the right I see September 11, 2001, which is pink like the rest of that decade."

"What if I ask you where you were on September 11, 2001?"

"That's behind me, to my right, and glacial blue. I was in the hospital."

"Fascinating. How far back does your number line go?"

"The decades go back to 1900. 1973-1970 is beige and hazy, after that each decade has the color of the decade's first numeral, like the colors we charted the other day. 6 is brown so the 60's are brown. Same for all the rest back to 1917. 1917 and 1918 are both red. This is consistent with the first digit controlling, because one is red, but 1919 is orange, because the yellow 9 blends with the red 1. I think it may have something to do with the doubling of the 19 because I ordinarily see 19 as red, just like every other 'teen' above 15. But 1910-1915 are black. They are almost impossible to see against the black background. 1916 is clear like I can see through it. I don't know what's special about 1916. You think it could be the year of my birth in my most recent past life? For some reason I had that thought once in college and it's kind of stuck with me."

"This is the most incredible manifestation of synesthesia I've ever encountered."

"Why do you call this synesthesia? There's no blending of senses, I'm just keeping track of dates."

"Many synesthesias do not involve a literal blending of senses; many forms are categorical. Take for example your colored letters and numbers, they are not 'senses' per se, but symbols categorized by color. What is really incredible is that you have memory maps and time-space synesthesia! You are polymodal to an extent I had not fully appreciated.

184

We've been going about this all wrong. I need to figure out all of your different synesthetic manifestations before we continue cataloging.

"Now when you track years, historical dates, how far back do they go? You mentioned 1900 do they go back further?"

"Yeah, I mean the Jurassic is like 145 million years B.C. to about 199 million years B.C."

"And that's on your line?"

"Yeah. It's not by decade though. After 1900 it switches to centuries and anything B.C. curves downward away to my left and is kind of lumped together, the same way that my months bunch up for my… what'd you call it, time-space synesthesia, like how February and March are crunched up, same thing. The centuries bunch closer and closer together the further back I go."

"How about the colors of your centuries? Back to B.C.?"

"They have their own colors, totally unrelated to my numbers, 1800's are teal. Everything B.C. is grey, and the further back it goes the harder they are to see. The 1500's are white, which stands out really well against the black background. I'm really good at remembering dates in the 1500's, like the Spanish Armada, or that Cortez conquered the Aztecs in 1533. Did you know that?"

"Why are the 1800's teal and the 1500's white?"

"I don't know. They just are. I'm surprised you're so interested in this."

"Riley your gift is astounding."

"A gift? I don't get that. It's not terribly helpful except on history exams."

"All of these abilities are manifestations of a magnificent brain. I have been studying the phenomenon of synesthesia for decades. I've encountered hundreds of synesthetes, either personally, or through the literature. I have never encountered one with this many modalities. I have never encountered a synesthete whose manifestations were so idiosyncratic, of course all synesthesias are idiosyncratic to a degree, but your polymodal expression of the phenomenon is unparalleled. You alone are unique amongst a group of human beings defined by unique and distinct ways of interacting with and perceiving the world."

Stroke. Stroke. Pet my ego like an Angora cat. Stroke. Stroke. I'm soft and fragile. I desire your touch. Stroke. Stroke. Can you make me purr?

He believed at least part of what he told me. And he knew to string me along so I wouldn't bolt from El Rancho. He couldn't have known exactly what would go down those next few months, but he knew Colin. And since he knew Colin, he knew enough.

Photism, that's another Professor word. A photism is a visual impression triggered by a sound. They are rare for me. Only certain sharp noises trigger these. For the most part they are limited to flashes and pulses of color, a bit like seeing stars, if you'll forgive my cartoonish language. I'd mentioned them before, but now I've named them. And with that I've named them all, all of my Yangs, curses, gifts, or synesthesias, depending on how you look at them.* I take that back. They're not curses. It's unfair to call them that. The only curse was the interest the Professor took in them. I would not be the person I am without them and wouldn't wish them away. But I wish I never met him.

---

* RECAP: My synesthesias include the following types: grapheme-color, numerical-color, photisms, emotion-taste, emotion-tactile, time-space, and historical memory maps.

186

A Mental-Monty

It being established that I am special, unique even, we can move on to the other tactics used by the Professor to obtain my compliance and cooperation in his 'academic' endeavor. Give some knowledge, but withhold other knowledge. This is nothing but lying by omission, similar to mixing truth with lies to give a semblance of truth. Mystery. Misdirection. Manipulation. The moves of a mental three-card monty.

Something had bothered me ever since I had arrived, and I questioned the Professor about it. "Where are the machines? You said we'd have access to state of the art technology. That's why I had to come to the desert. All I've seen is a library and art."

"Yes. We have CAT scanners, an MRI, and an fMRI. Very expensive. As are the computers we need to run them and analyze the signals."

"But where are they."

"In the Bunker, of course." It was an answer that answered nothing, truth, but only part. *Manipulation.*

"What's the Bunker?"

"I surmise that Colin hasn't given you the full tour. That's not entirely unexpected. He made it clear that he didn't want you here. You know I fought for you Riley. We're together in this. I'll make sure you see the whole grounds. Tomorrow maybe." He makes promises to be fulfilled in the future. *Misdirection.*

"How did he get this place anyway? He must be filthy rich."

"That is a question you should ask of Colin. I don't think he would appreciate our discussing his affairs."

"Does he have to know? And since when do you care what people appreciate. Profess what you know *Professor.*"

"Riley, for better or worse, Colin is the owner of El Rancho. While I have experience here, and considerable sway with Colin I will not jeopardize our collaboration, nor will I jeopardize my access to these facilities in any way, and to discuss Colin while he is not present presents great jeopardy indeed. You must ask him." He hints at enigmatic danger. *Mystery.*

A Mental-Monty, that crafty bastard.

Gossipy Gents

Despite the Professor's prompt I wasn't about to ask Colin anything. I wanted to avoid him. It was weird that he enjoyed my outburst so much. Everything about El Rancho and Colin was weird. I decided to feel out the roommates and see if any of them knew more about Colin. I got my first chance with Midas, two nights before Court.

He came and sat next to me on my cot. "Sorry I said I'd punch you in the face."

"You didn't. You said "maybe if I." Besides, I did break your cot."

"Yeah. Dude it looked like a tornado hit this room when I came in. You must've gone fucking crazy. I can't believe you exploded that dresser man. I mean the cots were flimsy, but…damn."

"Yeah."

"Anyway, the cot's your fault but Court isn't."

"What's up with that anyway?"

"You'll see. It's basically performance art. That's sort of his thing."

We chatted for a while and I stacked a few bowls. I was glad to be back on good terms with Midas and I let him vent while we smoked. Whatever anger he had left was directed at Colin. He was furious at being made a porter. I didn't understand why he cared so much about the part, to me it seemed about as significant as getting a part in the school play that you hadn't even auditioned for.

I pointed out it could be worse, that he could have Bob's part. That got him to laugh. "So if you don't want to be a porter why play along?" I asked.

"It's one of the rules man. You participate in Court."

"Yeah but you said your art sells. Can't you just tell Colin to fuck off?"

"I guess I could, but nobody's here to sell. Everybody really cares about the art. If I'm serious about mine don't I owe it to him to be serious about his? Whether I like it or not is irrelevant. Whether it's fair or unfair is irrelevant. His art is what it is. He supports my art so I support his. I made thirty separate works last year. I work with metal and glass everyday. I couldn't do that, be that prolific, not anywhere else, this place is unique."

188

"I get it." I seized my opportunity and asked as casually as I could: "So, how'd Colin wind up owning this place anyway?"

Midas looked around then put a finger to his lips. He walked to the door and checked down the hall. He shut the door behind him and sat close to me on the cot. He spoke in hushed tones, "I don't know for sure, so don't repeat this. I'm just telling you what I heard. Colin was a pimp."

"No way." It sounded unbelievable. Not that Colin would have ever trafficked in flesh, but that he could have made enough money doing it to buy such a sprawling estate. Even in the desert land wasn't that cheap. This was still Southern California.

"You don't have to believe me. Like I said I don't know if it's true. But I heard—"

"Heard from who?"

"From someone who's known Colin a lot longer than I have. Anyways she said that Colin had harems in St. Louis, Chicago, Gary, you name it; he peddled pussy all over the Midwest. Said he bought his first girl off of her own daddy for a fat bag of crystal. Said she was only fourteen, then he used her to recruit other girls. Kept selling the ice too. I figure he was smart enough to get out of the game and took up residence as an art aficionado."

I didn't believe it. I could've spit up the catch of the day, sitting there sucking up shellfish and snapper. Either somebody lied to Midas, or more likely Midas was feeding me a line. I couldn't tell if he was messing with me for the fun of it or if there was some bad intent. I nodded in silence and tried not to make a face at the clambake going on in my mouth. Pedro walked in. Midas took one look at him, stood up, and walked out.

"That was subtle," Pedro said and crossed the room removing his dirty white t-shirt as he went. His torso was toned and hairless. He pulled a clean white t-shirt from his dresser. His attire was always that of the workman artist. His eccentricity lay in his work. I had yet to see any of it, but he told me his latest project involved lasers synched with music. Judging by his freestyles he was talented, I couldn't wait to see the lasers. "Midas doesn't like me."

"No he doesn't," I said. "He hates that you don't hate Ndukwe."

"Yeah that's part of it. I get along with everybody so he can't get along with me. He's just being contrary. Fucking cabròn."

"He hates Ndukwe more than he hates you."

"Ndukwe is just doing his job. Colin doesn't like dealing with all the details, the day-to-day shit. Ndukwe keeps this place running. Can you imagine if he didn't push and prod and boss every one around? Nothing would get done. We're a bunch a crazy artists. The only thing we work hard on is our art. If Ndukwe weren't here we'd sit around getting high, admiring each other's art and having orgies all day. It'd be anarchy. Midas can hate all he wants. Ndukwe holds this shit together." I guessed Pedro had a point, but the guy still had a foul name. "Besides Ndukwe's not the reason he hates me."

"Uh I think you're wrong about that bro."

"No I'm not. Hey I don't want to bad mouth Midas, but you shouldn't listen to what he told you."

I felt the anxiety roll across my neck. "What'd you hear?"

"Just some rumors about mid-western whores and methamphetamine. Pretty scandalous. Do I really need to tell you how ridiculous that is? I don't know where he got his info, but here's the real, Colin made his money in T.V. He had some national ad as a kid, maybe a couple, I don't know, but he got parts in T.V. shows too. I bet he's still getting fat residual checks."

"I don't know man. This place is huge. That's an awful lot of residuals."

"I bet you he bought it piecemeal, ten acres here, ten acres there, no developments, no electricity, no water. The land's cheap. The only question I have is how he got them to pump in water and power. We're connected along with that artillery range over the mountains."

I didn't speculate on that. I was already worried my conversations would get back to Colin. Pedro was too close with Ndukwe and Ndukwe was Colin's right hand man. Pedro's story sounded a little more plausible than what Midas told me, but all the talk got me was more information and less knowledge than I had before. I tried to change the subject, "So if it's not Ndukwe then why does Midas hate you so much?"

"You really don't know?"

A Tour of the Grounds

I walked into the library expecting to see the Professor, but found Colin waiting for me. "Morning sunshine. I'm your substitute teacher for the day." He pointed at the door. "Field trip."

We headed west down the road in a beige jeep with four-wheel drive. Colin pulled over to point out the Sculpture Garden on the right, some of which I had already seen. He handed me a pair of binoculars and pointed out three more sculptures. One was a stone form that bore curves and lines. I couldn't discern what it was except to say it was abstract. Another appeared to be a large stone altar adorned with tall white spires topped by red-orange flags that simulated candles flickering. The last was the honeycomb shape I had seen on the way in. It was through binoculars what it appeared to be at a distance, a massive plastic honeycomb.

We didn't dwell on the sculptures and to my relief Colin didn't bombard me with questions, but allowed me to see them and then moved on. We proceeded west along the south edge of El Rancho and turned right onto a dirt road headed north. The road was rocky and rutted and I felt every bounce of the jeep rattle through me. Rosewater settled upon my tongue and my hip and shoulder ached.

We traveled no more than a half a mile before a ramshackle building with a tilted cross atop it came into view. "We're coming up on the triangle," he said. We passed a mound of dirt twenty-five feet high. Roots and branches sprung out of it at random points like eels poking their heads out of a rock reef in search of prey. It felt unnatural and ugly, but this was unsurprising. Most of the art I'd seen was unnatural and ugly. This one seemed different because it managed to be unnatural despite being made of natural materials.

"Morty's Mound," Colin said as he swerved to avoid a particularly deep hole.

"Why Morty's?" I asked.

"Because Morty's the one inside it." I started to ask what that meant but Colin cut me off, "I'll explain some other time. Here's the church."

He stopped the jeep, sprang out, and jogged to the large wooden doors on the front of the church. I limped behind studying the building. He turned to me, his back to the church, his arms outstretched. "Ta-da!"

I stared, underwhelmed. "Ta-da!" he said again. It was little more than a derelict shack, squat, narrow but deep like a shotgun house, framed in rotted boards, the front doors half-caved in, empty windows, flat roofed with no steeple, and its cross askew in an unbalanced 'x'.

"What kind of art project is this?" I asked.

Colin looked at me like I was nuts. "Art? This isn't art. It's history."

"Is this some old settler church?"

"Sort of, but not the settler's you're thinking of. It's not that old. But it has been here since before I was born. It's part of the history of El Rancho." Colin stared at me expectantly and I looked away. The flush of heat was intense. "Go ahead and ask," he said as I struggled to recover, still unwilling to meet his eye. "Ask me anything. What do you want to know?"

"So how old is it then?" I asked.

Colin scoffed. "The church or El Rancho?"

"Both."

"Well the land is as old as all the land in Southern California. Which is to say several billion years, or six thousand, depending on who you ask. El Rancho, in its current dimensions was formed in the 1950's. This church was built in the early sixties. It hasn't been used since 1973." Colin slapped the doors. They wobbled but didn't fall. "It stands as a reminder."

"Reminder of what?"

"Not what. Who. The ones that came before us." He was already headed back to the Jeep. "Three more things to see, then we can really start the field trip. And Riley, next time ask what you really want to know."

****

The church was the easternmost point on the triangle. Down the leg from the church to the south and west, the studio sat on the southernmost point. It lay in the shadow of Morty's Mound, giving some perspective of the enormity of that particular pile of dirt. It was a long building, with tall bay doors. It resembled a high-school multi-purpose building. Colin led me inside. Most of the artists of El Rancho were busy at work. Midas inflated a molten bubble of glass at the end of a thin metal blowpipe. Pedro and Shelly used blowtorches to weld together steel girders. Ndukwe molded a small lump of clay. Taggart wore headphones while he worked on an IMac. Daphne finger-painted from atop a ladder on a canvas the size of a box-car, while a stone's throw away, Erin flicked globs of paint onto a canvas, varying her distance and angle from the canvas with every throw, raining backsplatter and making her smock nearly as interesting as the painting. Only Gary and Bob were absent.

No one paid any attention to me, not so much as a hello. I felt the rush of heat that had become so common with Colin's arrival, but lied to myself and attributed it to the kilns and ovens. It wasn't. I didn't belong here. Everyone else maintained intense focus and continued to work as I surveyed the studio with Colin.

It was well stocked with paints, brushes, metals, beads, clays and glasses, there was a kiln for firing clay and a host of industrial tools for working with metals, there was a scissor-lift to work at heights along with a forklift and several articulated ladders, and there were two furnaces: a glory hole and an annealing oven specifically designed for glasswork.

I respected the atmosphere of creation and toured with Colin in silence and a bit of unspoken embarrassment. We left without saying a word or giving so much as a nod of acknowledgment and I felt a lifting of pressure from my back that I hadn't even noticed was there. Then Colin led me due north to the final point of the triangle, the bunker. I saw only the outside. We didn't go in through the riveted steel door. It wasn't impressive: one door centered in a façade of corrugated metal set beneath a concrete arch. It looked as though the uppermost aspect of an airplane hanger had been faced with a door and set into the side of the hill. Colin gave little information about it except to say it was older than the church and was the Professor's domain, "It's the only spot here that he runs."

Then Colin took me to the edge of the mesa where we looked down on lengthy curves of blue and red on the desert floor, the bluestones and the redstones, painted rocks stretching for a mile parallel to each other and the distant wash. "They require a lot of upkeep. Paint wears quickly between the sun, the sand, the wind and the occasional downpour. Fortunately I have both artists and free labor at my disposal."

We drove back to the main road in silence. Again I had gained information, seen more of my circumstance, and yet somehow knew less about El Rancho.

"You should ask," he said. "Now's the time for conversation. Once we leave the property we won't be able to hear each other in the jeep."

"What do you mean?"

"Don't play coy, just ask. I know you want to. You've probably got a million questions, but start with the one you really want to know. We're running out of time."

I don't know how he knew, the Professor, spies, Midas, Pedro, but I knew he knew, so I asked, "How'd you get this place?"

"Inheritance." Yet another answer that answered nothing.

"Your family owned all this?"

"Ownership is an amorphous concept, the law describes ownership of property as a bundle of rights. I have some rights acquired from my family."

"So you don't own it?"

"I didn't say that."

"So do you?"

"For most purposes yes."

"And you inherited from your family."

"Dad."

That struck me. I swallowed through a taste of mushy mealy corn. "Sorry. I lost my dad too." The words stuck in my throat, dry and granular, I wanted a glass of water.

"I know. We've got a lot more in common than you suspect, brother."

"Where are we headed now?" I asked, not wanting to ponder any similarities between us.

"Sight-seeing."

Borregos

We headed deeper into the desert on another dirt road. After several miles we left the dirt road and skidded into a dried out wash. I lost my bearings and all sense of direction, but Colin handled the Jeep like he knew exactly where he was going, we flew down the wash, dodging the occasional stone or hole, and bounding over whoops. Eventually we headed uphill out of the wash. At first the ascent was steady, but soon the terrain became steep and rugged. Colin navigated expertly over a series of boulders and set us on a trail as wide as the jeep.

"Old game trail," Colin said.

"What exactly are we looking for?"

"Borrego."

"Sheep?"

"Yeah. There's a watering hole that's pretty consistent year round about two clicks east. You can usually find some rams up in these hills. This is my favorite time of year to look for them, the mating season just ended."

"Why borrego?"

"It's a majestic animal. Sentinel of the desert. Powerful rams. Besides they're one of the symbols of El Rancho."

"I thought the dragon was your symbol."

"You figure that out on your own?" I realized I had without even knowing it, not consciously anyway, but the info was there. "You're partly right," Colin said, "but did you look closely at the dragon on the fountain in the courtyard? Did you look at any of the bas-reliefs on the base?"

I thought back to the fountain. All I recalled was the dragon spouting water, and I remembered the dragon design Colin sported on his shirt at the Bibulous Bibliophiles meeting.

"Think about the horns on the dragon," he said. "They remind you of anything?"

I thought about the dragon fountain. The dragon had huge curved horns, a full spiral, just like a mature borrego's. "Ram horns," I said.

"Exactly, now what else is the dragon made of? What about his feet?"

The hooves of a ram? No, that wasn't it at all, they weren't hooves, but they weren't paws either, more like claws, or pincers.

"Still can't get it huh? That's okay they're less obvious than the horns. They're crabs, eight legs including the pincers. The three symbols of El Rancho: the dragon, the borrego and the crab."

"But why? Why those three? Why not just the dragon?"

"The borrego is of the desert. He represents our connection to the earth. The crab, obviously, is of the ocean and represents our connection to the water. The dragon is our vitality, our breath, and our power. He breathes fires and he flies amongst the gods. The dragon is our connection to both fire and air. Three totems connect us to the four elementals. Three plus four is seven. On the seventh day God rested. There were seven cities of gold. Seven wonders in the ancient world. Seven is a very auspicious number, a lucky number. Then we have the pentagram and the pentagon. Ten points, plus the four arms of the swastika is fourteen. Fourteen plus seven is twenty-one. Three times seven. Lucky seven three times over. Blackjack baby, twenty-one. Out at the Rancho all the numbers add up.

He smacked my arm. "There they are. Reach in the glove box and grab the binoculars." I didn't have time to ponder the ramifications of Colin's weird number theory or symbologisms. Out on a flat outcropping just beyond the ridgeline, not two hundred yards away, stood a flock of borregos. Ten, maybe twelve, it was hard to tell.

"Ooh hoo hoo!" Colin howled. "You got to see this!"

He handed me the binoculars and I looked out adjusting the zoom, trying to bring them into focus. I locked on to a big male. His horns were a full curve, the thick rounded bone on the front showed scratches, scars from mating battles. The ram stared across the canyon, his pupils enormous black spheres. At first he seemed to be scanning the horizon, but then I got the distinct impression that his eyes were fixed upon me, like we were locked in some sort of staring contest, only I was cheating with magnified vision. "I think he sees us."

"He probably does. They have keen eyesight, it's their main defense against predators, well, that and the horns."

"What predators?"

"Mountain lions mostly, but coyotes too. They'll only chase the small ones and stragglers though."

Around the big ram the other borregos were stomping about, moving closer together, circling in. I kept the lenses focused on the big ram. He turned to his right and lowered his head. He ducked and twisted under the hindquarters of the borrego closest to him. "It looks like he's licking that other sheep's..."

"Probably is," Colin said, "keep watching."

The big ram pulled out his head and I saw his long red tongue flick back into his mouth. Then he turned even further and mounted the sheep he'd been licking. Forepaws on it's back he thrust several times and then retreated. He paused a moment then repeated the act. I pulled back on the zoom and saw several other rams lick and then mount their partners. It was a borrego orgy! There seemed to be a certain amount of swapping occurring, which was odd. I didn't know much about borregos, but I thought they used their horns to fight over females. Sharing didn't seem congruent with that sort of behavior.

"I thought you said mating season was over?"

"Oh it is." Colin cackled. "Those are all rams. It's a bachelor flock."

I stared with a mixture of amusement, amazement and horror. The taste I experienced was bizarre, primarily the sticky sour of glue, but tinged with fresh thyme and tarragon, near ripened berries, shrimp, and the earthy, wood rot taste of morels past their prime. I also felt a flush of heat.[*] I was shocked into silence. The only sounds were the slight breeze blowing through desert scrubs, Colin choking on suppressed howls of delight and, barely audible on the desert air, the distant bleating "baaa's" of the bighorn orgy.

I'm not homophobic, but I was taken aback at the sight. And then things took a foul turn and the orgy became far more disturbing. I noticed, still looking through the binoculars, that one of the smaller males had moved to the far edge of the group. He was probably three or four years old, based on what I now know of bighorn maturation, and had a mid-sized set of horns, a half-curl. Two plodding rams pursued him. They were large beasts, each in the neighborhood of two hundred pounds, and each with a set of proud, full-curl horns. One of the big rams licked the little guy's genitalia and the little guy scampered away closer to the edge of the outcropping. Then the other mature ram charged forward and stopped. He

---

[*] CLARIFICATION: Caliente, not picante. I wasn't getting off on gay sheep sex.

197

waited a moment, then thrust up his forepaws and attempted to mount the juvenile, who again scampered away. The other ram tried again only to have the juvenile evade him. The juvenile came perilously close to the edge of a steep descent, a veritable cliff face. Nowhere to run he turned to face his assailants as I watched in mute horror. The first of the big rams lowered his head and the juvenile met him with his half-curl. A thunderclap rang across the canyon as the juvenile staggered at the blow.

"They're trying to rape him!" This nature documentary had become far too real and sinister for my tastes. These weren't merely horny rams having fun but brutish monsters victimizing the weak among them, not even to spread their genes as animals sometimes do, but for the sheer satisfaction of their sick urges.

"No they're not." Colin's laughter ceased and he sat unmoved by the scene before him. "They won't force him. This isn't really about sex."

"Isn't about sex?"

"Nope. Keep watching."

The juvenile stood his ground. I feared for him, but admired his bravery as he faced down two enemies twice his size. Again he withstood a powerful charge and nearly buckled to the ground. Before he could recover the other ram nudged him in his side, the two big rams now pressing in against him, the juvenile's position even more precarious as he teetered on the edge of the precipice.

"They won't force him? They're going to kill him!"

Again Colin was unmoved. "No they're not. Keep watching."

A standoff ensued. Neither of the bullies gave ground, but neither made a move against the juvenile. The juvenile tried to press forward but they blocked his advance with their massive horns and bodies.

"What a proud, brave borrego," I muttered.

"Not brave. Foolish."

"For resisting rape?"

"Like I said it isn't about sex. Keep watching. It's almost over."

Neither the bullies nor the juvenile yielded. I strained to hear the nearly inaudible bleats of the juvenile, the desperate, sad 'baa's' as he begged his tormentors for mercy. I felt a wave of frigid saltwater crest upon my palette at the brave ram's inevitable demise. The big rams advanced on him slowly, inching toward him one tiny step at a time. The juvenile's hooves were now all beneath him, four hooves, pressed into a space no wider than a Frisbee, his poor legs trembling beneath him, whether from fright or stress I could not tell. And then he slipped.

I cried out in horror. Colin laughed. I cannot express the depth of the hatred I felt for him at that moment.

But then the slide stopped. The brave borrego caught on a ledge imperceptible to my eye even with the aid of binoculars. Colin laughed again. "They can balance on a ledge as narrow as two inches. Olympic gymnasts, their balance beam is twice as wide as that. Pretty impressive right?"

It was. The little borrego stared up the cliff at the rams, but they refused to allow him back up. After a couple of minutes that dragged on and on, the juvenile finally turned and headed down the cliff on unseen footholds until he vanished from sight. The orgy complete, the rest of the bighorns turned and headed off in the opposite direction.

"I told you it wasn't about sex," said Colin. "That was a lesson in group dynamics. Those two big rams weren't trying to rape. They weren't trying to dominate him. They were enforcing a group code. If you want to belong to a group you must participate in it's rites, in it's rituals, and in it's behavior *as a group*. What we just saw, that behavior, the sodomy, it's not at all unusual for bachelor herds. It's a form of bonding, of solidifying the group. That little one wasn't going along with the group, they gave him a chance to join in, he didn't, so they ostracized him."

"So what will happen to the little one?"

Colin shrugged. "Who knows? He'll probably die, but maybe not."

"So they did kill him?"

"No. Borregos form these bachelor flocks for protection. The desert is a harsh place. Water is scarce, food is scarce and even an animal as powerful as a bighorn has predators. The herd provides protection, multiple lookouts and many pairs of horns." He lowered his shades and I met the cold eyes of a predator, the only honest look Colin possesses, and shivered at the wet copper ice cube suddenly upon my palette.

Colin continued, "Out here in the desert, that juvenile needed the group, probably more than any other male in that group, and certainly more than the group or those big males needed him. That's a lesson you'd do well to remember." Colin let out a hollow laugh and slapped me on the shoulder. He smiled and said, "I'm just kidding with you man, relax."

We returned to El Rancho in relative silence. Colin was goofy and high and answered all queries with nonsense. He had his moment on the mesa and was in no mood for a Q&A session.

The last thing he did before we parted ways was hand me an envelope. "A description of your role. Slight change you're no longer a prince. You're an earl."

Court

Two things were clear from my role assignment. One: Court was not a scripted affair. Two: Colin, or someone close to him, had obtained a certain unflattering quote from back issues of various surf publications.

My new role card consisted of the following brief description: *Riley Sparx Earl of Segund, half-brother to the King, crippled in war at the Battle of Borrego, he is jealous, desirous of power and influence, but a hero and champion of the common folk who see in him something of themselves. Stay in character at all times. And remember that even nobility kneels before the King.*

To understand the slight that my position represented you need to understand the ethos of professional surfers. There are two contradictory impulses that exist simultaneously within every professional surfer. One arises from the communitarian nature of the sport, the shared sense of belonging, oneness with the ocean and zest for life, the joie de vivre characteristic of those whose pastime has no point except the sheer joy of it. The other impulse is the competitive spirit, the desire to be better than the next guy. This is the impulse my father tried to steer me away from, because he knew how quickly a healthy competitive spirit could turn to narcissism and self-aggrandizement when met with success.

When I began my career as a professional Sparx Surfboards sponsored me, but my father didn't support me. However, the rest of the pros on tour, excepting Nehud, didn't know this. And so after a couple of poor finishes following a couple of magazine covers, I found myself the target of scorn and derision from other surfers who felt I hadn't earned my place. In particular, surfers sponsored by other companies used my failures as opportunities to attack the Sparx brand as well as me personally. No surfer epitomized this tactic more so than Chad Doering, who at the time was the number one ranked surfer on the planet, and whose primary sponsor was Surf Company 'X'. The most damning and derisive quote was one that followed me for my entire career.

The first article to feature the quote came out after Chad won his third straight championship and was titled: 'Chad Doering: King of the Waves.' It wasn't long before the quote was picked up by every other major surf publication:

"Riley Sparx is surf royalty. I mean he's the son of Skip Sparx. No one's disputing that Skip and Sparx Surfboards have been great for the sport. Back in his day, Skip was the King. But everyone else on the tour had to earn his spot. That's why we call him 'the Earl.' He's like the bastard son of the former monarch. He enjoys the privileges of royalty but he'll never wear the crown. He has to settle for the fiefdom of a lesser noble."

That last line reeked of Maxwell. The whole quote did. If you've ever heard Doering speak you know he doesn't use phrases like 'bastard son of the former monarch.' He doesn't speak complete sentences or any phrase that doesn't end with the word 'dude.' Maxwell's fingerprints were all over it, especially the way it kept popping up in new articles for the next six months. It was a hit piece because my dad pulled my contract with Surf Company 'X' all those years ago, and it was unfair. I had to qualify like everyone else, but that didn't stop the others from treating me, not like royalty, but like a second-class citizen.

And Colin made me relive it. I should have taken my own advice and told him to fuck off, but I was the new guy.

****

I awoke the morning of Court to Ndukwe wheeling in a wardrobe full of costumes: a red, blue and yellow jester's motley complete with hat, a set of torn rags, four fine sets of scarlet livery that bore a custom crest of a dragon with ram's horns and crab's claws, and my noble's outfit. My raiment consisted of a burgundy tunic with gold embroidery hand stitched from sturdy hemp, a vest studded with rubies and sparkly beads, costume jewelry, but at a distance it could pass for the real thing, a cape that bore the dragon crest, a felt hat with a feather, scarlet tights and leather shoes. Sweet vanilla touched my tongue at the authentic beauty of my costume. A tickle, a weight and a spike of aromatic herbs forced me to admit my intrigue at playing this role. I had never acted before and had no training, but I was thrust into it and thought to my astonishment that I might actually enjoy it.

The day dragged on and no one else seemed to have the least bit of enthusiasm for it. Sullen, distant faces passed like ghosts in the 'L' shaped hallways and the usual bustle of artistic progress was conspicuously absent.

202

I arrived at the Art Wing, in costume, at the appointed time, four-thirty p.m. I took the role seriously. Chin aloft, shoulders back, I carried myself with royal bearing so far as my limp and cane would allow. A young man who I had never seen before knelt and genuflected at my arrival, "My lord," he said, and once I passed he rose and bellowed, "Make way for Lord Sparx, Earl of Segund!"

Fifty plus men, women and children lined the hall of the art wing clad in raggedy peasant garb and merchant tunics. All parted and knelt as I clacked past them with an unwitting taste of cinnamon, as I discovered I was not immune to the trappings of nobility, albeit a false one.

Pedro, dressed in the scarlet livery of the guard, announced my entrance to the Chill Room, "Lord Sparx, Earl of Segund!" The Chill Room was transformed, all the artwork removed, replaced with tapestries that covered the side walls in scenes of dragons breathing fire, knights clashing upon the field of battle under the constellation of Cancer, and rams butting heads. Even the floor had been replaced with worn wooden boards.

At the head of the room five regal and imposing chairs sat atop a dais that stretched from wall-to-wall. At the far left, from my point of view, Shelly occupied a hand carved but plain throne with plush burgundy cushions. She wore a scarlet dress and the emeralds hung round her neck were breathtaking accents against her flowing red hair. Next to her sat Daphne, clad in an understated off-white gown with silver Grecian sandals that suited her. The understatement of her gown stood in sharp contrast to the sapphires that shimmered on her fingers, tight round her throat, and atop her slim silver tiara. Her throne was the color and sheen of ivory, its arms and legs inlaid with the pitch black of onyx, and the forward edges were studded with rubies.

In the center Colin towered upon a throne of gold. The lines of the legs were straight and sharp as though running a finger across one would draw blood. The legs ended seamlessly at the seat where two gold bars rose straight above the back legs, then extended forward into a pair of curved gold arms cut with the single joint of crab legs and terminating in claws atop which Colin's bejeweled fingers lay draped. The throne back was straight, oval shaped and padded with more of the scarlet felt that abounded in the scene. Above Colin's head was the horned dragon, fearsome and fantastic, with polished opal horns, glittering green scales of emerald, and ruby fire breath.

Colin looked all too comfortable in the role of the King, with the icy eyes of command, unfeeling and unblinking. His vestments were deepest burgundy, fringed with gold. He wore a heavy cape, and rings on each finger of varied precious stones and metals. His crown was a gold circle with ruby points all round like the rooks on a castle and it too bore the crest of the horned dragon crab.

The production value was suitable for a Hollywood blockbuster and only this thought kept me in character, as it was too real to comprehend. I knelt in the center of the hall. "Your Grace."

Colin's teeth flashed in a cruel smile and he beckoned me to the dais and the ornately carved wooden throne to his left. "Come join our Court dear brother."

I did as commanded and took my place upon his left. Colin clapped his hands. "Send in the rabble!" Pedro hopped to it and ran to the hall. I looked at the empty seat beside me and wondered who would fill it. Ndukwe moved in from my left and came before the dais, directly in front of Colin. I hadn't even seen him off against the wall, he was invisible as a good guard should be, unseen until called for and then ready for action at a moment's notice. For a moment I worried that he would sit next to me, but he knelt briefly before Colin and then turned to face the doors. His muscles bulged and rippled underneath his tunic as he stood at attention, the epitome of a soldier of the Court, leader of the King's personal guard.

As I watched the 'rabble' file in without so much as a murmur I had to admit I was impressed. It was quite a production, especially for an improvisation. The 'rabble,' (I assumed hired actors), fanned out to fill the room and knelt facing Colin. I knew it was an act, but the cold wash of fear crept over me and brought upon a familiar weight and a pain in my stomach. I felt danger, but not for myself. It was the creepiness of the act, the ease with which Colin assumed this role of absolute authority, the way he commanded fealty without a second thought, as though the bowing of subordinates were his due. Once the 'rabble' were down, Ndukwe turned and knelt. I followed Shelly's lead and did the same, and soon the entire room was down before Colin and his queen.

"Rise!" He commanded. I resumed my seat. I remembered to play my role and kept my chin up. At first it had been cool, when they bowed as I walked down the hall, but now it was uncomfortable. Humanity had been removed, but the more disturbing aspect was that I wasn't sure whose humanity had been taken, theirs or mine.

"Call the case!" Colin commanded from the throne. From the back of the room came Taggart's meek voice as loud as I had ever heard it: "Hear ye! Hear ye! All are called to order in the Court of Equity, King Colin, Presideth, Ruleth, and Dispenseth Justice! Now stand forth Erin Shire! Stand forth to answer the charge of larceny of the King's property!"

Pedro pushed Erin toward the throne. She stumbled forward through the parting crowd, hands bound in front of her, clad only in filthy tattered rags. Vengeance filled the air, the mob so convincing in their portrayal that I felt the chill of fear and the taint of iron and suppressed an urge to flee. Danger mounted as the mob smelled blood; truly now they became the rabble, anticipating punishment and pain to come for their edification and entertainment. The jeers rained upon Erin: 'Harlot!' 'The axe!' 'Whore!' 'Thief!' Even as an act the words wounded. She could not have faked the fear on her face, nor the tears welling in her eyes, not behind cheeks smudged with dirt and soot— and a bruise upon her cheek! A swelling under the eye! It looked far too real for my tastes and again the foul slime of anger crept unbidden in my throat and I glared at Pedro behind her, and then at Colin, the *King*! Filthy green word! I saw no art in this whatever it was.

Pedro gave a final push and knocked Erin to her knees before the dais. "She was found stealing produce from the King's garden!"

"How plead you?" asked Colin.

"My liege, I beg your mercy. My family. My children were starved." She gestured to the edge of the crowd where two dirty young boys stood, thin with sallow faces and eyes that bore a look of shock, like children grown up in war-torn lands. I couldn't help but feel a burn of embarrassment that they were forced to witness this *art*, and that I was a part of it and had no power to stop it.

"So you do not deny the charge against you?"

"My Lord I took only the meagerest of portions, roots and bulbs half-rotted, leaves blighted by the passing of snails and slugs, fruit over-ripe that it had fallen and was wasting. I took none that were fit for a King."

"And a better use it were to feed your children than to rot in my garden? Lazy! Indolent wench! You are the slug that blighteth my garden! Your children are parasites upon my crop, locusts and fleas! What? Are ye feeble? Can ye not work? Set up shop in a back alley? Doth not your body fetch a shilling in the square?" He looked Erin over, head to toe, as though inspecting stock for fitness. "No. I suppose not. But perhaps a pence." He laughed, a mean laugh full of pride and scorn, it rang hollow through the hall. The crowd echoed his laugh back to him and the jeers of whore and thief rang down once more.

"Silence!" Colin roared and the room became still and Colin's voice seemed to fill the space as it returned from the back walls.

"My Lord, I could not dishonor my husband so."

"A husband! You have a husband? I assumed your urchins were illegitimate beggars. Come forth husband! Come forth and answer for ye poverty!"

Ndukwe's big hands tossed Bob to the floor next to Erin who was now sobbing. Bob stood up and spun in a circle, arms outstretched as if to protect himself. He spun again. He looked more confused than usual, more panicked. His fear was not an act. He spun and spun looking furtively for an escape, but found himself surrounded at each turn.

"Of course!" Colin cried. "Who else would marry you but the village idiot?" More cruel laughter and jeers came from the crowd. I burned from head to toe. I stole a glance at Colin, who was fixated on his victims, then stole one at Shelly and found her staring intently at me. She jerked her head at Colin as though to signal me. To what? Tackle him? Not likely in my crippled state. Besides this wasn't my show.

"My Lord!" Erin inched toward the dais on her knees, her hands clasped before her in entreaty. "My Lord please! Please show us mercy!"

"Idiot!" Colin roared at Bob. "Idiot! Are ye so weak and stupid that your woman must intercede? Must your woman earn ye bread and feed ye children?"

Erin's chest heaved. Her breathing went shallow and rapid, gasping, gasping for air in between sobs and pleas. "My Lord show us mercy! Never again shall we take from your gardens! Please my Lord, I beg for mercy! Our children! Our children!"

"Your children starve with you. What matter if they starve without you? Better that your line of imbeciles should die out than propagate and fill my kingdom with fools. The penalty for larceny of the King's property is death. The axe for them both." The crowd roared its approval. Over

206

the din I heard Shelly, a faint sound, but audible and tortured, the wordless cry of a mute, as though she had reverted to her pre-speech days. Colin heard it too and looked to her, then to me, because she was glaring at me with hatred.

Pedro came forth with the block, and Ndukwe with the axe. Still Shelly stared me down and Colin looked on with amusement. I remembered my role, the favored noble of the common folk.

I swallowed down my anger and confusion. "My Lord!" I said above the noise of the mob. "My Lord!" The crowd quieted. "I wish to intercede on behalf of these foolish peasants. Knowing as I do of your infinite wisdom I see clearly the need to uphold the law and none could doubt that your sentence is just. But also do I know of your infinite mercy and beg for it now. My King, I entreat you, your brother hath not the stomach to see bloodshed this eve, grant them pardon as a boon to me."

There were a few murmurs in the mob, but none dared to question a noble, or at any rate none broke character. "Well spoken brother. Your mouth works better than your legs." Colin stood and addressed the crowd, "The Earl's stomach is queasy. Fitting that my *half*-brother should intercede for this *half*-wit!" This drew a couple of nervous chuckles from the rabble. "Indeed a King is called to rule and must make the difficult decisions, decisions of life and death, decisions often shirked by *lesser-nobles*." It was a low blow, and the memory came up again hot and bilious and raw, like a scab torn from my flesh. Colin continued, "How alike. How common. An Earl and an idiot: one broken of body, one broken of mind, and both weak in stomach, and spirit, and the will to rule. Alas, I grant your boon Earl. Remember my strength. Remember my mercy. Remember my justice. Remove the axe! Bring forth the stocks!" The crowd roared its approval as the execution halted for more interactive sport.

Ndukwe and Pedro led the prisoners to a back corner. Midas and Taggart carried in a pole on each shoulder. I was stunned bland, utterly void of spice, as the sturdy poles were placed into postholes that had been bored through the floor. It dawned on me that this had been the plan all along. But what if I hadn't spoken up, what would Ndukwe have done with that axe? Midas and Taggart made a return trip and came back with the hinged boards cut with three holes, two for wrists and one for the neck. Erin willingly allowed the pillory to be clamped down upon her neck and hands. Red-faced and fighting back sobs, she stood with what pride she could muster and faced her humiliation. Bob tried to break free. He flailed and screamed like a caged animal, cries of rage and fear. He was horrible to hear. For the first time some in the crowd broke character, unable to conceal their concern. Others carried on, even cheered, when Ndukwe smashed Bob's nose and stuffed him into the stocks. Bob continued to cry and scream until he finally gave up and went limp. Through it all Colin sat and smiled, and Daphne sat next to him, stoic, as much a prop as an actress.

Midas and Taggart left again only to return with baskets full of rotten fruit and eggs and now a renewed spirit surged through the mob, and even those previously disgusted were once again caught up in the act as they pelted Erin and Bob mercilessly and taunted them from a distance.

Heat. Throughout the whole display I was consumed by heat, no amount of surprise or confusion or anger, no amount of fear or concern, could displace the unyielding sense of shame at my participation in this exercise. Heat. I burned upon that dais in my own personal hell, impotent and shamed.

We are captives of our emotions, all who are human. I believe this. I taste this. Everything we think we know about ourselves, every impulse to decency, any code by which we try to live, all can be subverted if the right switch is thrown and the right emotion called forth. Empathy, that distinguishing characteristic of humanity, can be turned off or forgotten if the right emotion is called forth. That crowd, that mob, lost their empathy in the frenzy of the pillory. The loss of empathy is the failure of shame. The exhilaration of giving over control, the will to power over others, be they worthy enemies or pitiful defenseless creatures staked to the ground, and the amusement that comes when someone else hurts, the knowledge that it's not your pain, all of these can cause empathy to be set aside, all of these can cause shame to fail. But so too can something internal, a sensation that depends not on objectifying the other, but on being so caught up in your own emotion that nothing else can matter. That is what happened to me. For the heat was soon quenched by the flavor of my own personal joy.

A trumpet blared. Midas called the rabble to attention. "Welcome with the respect due nobility, a guest to the Court of King Colin, the appointed emissary from the Court of Saint James, Wren, Duchess of Logan."

The rest of Court was steeped in saffron. Oh the humiliations continued: Erin and Bob were banished, and I last saw them exit together, Erin doing her best to comfort Bob despite being in need of her own consolation. Colin shattered glasses and tossed plates full of food upon the floor then made Midas and Taggart clean it up while he called them dogs. Gary was called out. Decked in full motley, face painted, Colin made him sing and dance and juggle and yodel, but he took to his role better than any other. He relished the chance to play the clown and thus could not be humiliated.[*] He took unordered pratfalls and told bawdy jokes and limericks about men from Dublin and Nantucket. Best of all he played an eight-string lute, an instrument I had never seen before, and sang lewd songs:

> *Now show me a man who knows of the lute*
> *And I'll show you a brute and a lout.*
> *But show me a lass who plays her the flute*
> *And I'll show you a girl most devout.*
>
> *Now how, you declare, by an instrument fair*
> *Could I know that her soul is pristine?*
> *She's a flautist in prayer, though her shoulders lay bare*
> *Why else was she down on her knees?*

Self-deprecating, female degrading, utterly ridiculous, needless to say, that song won over King Colin and in the end Gary ate the same food as the nobles. Gary was an impressive lutenist and it was good to see him regaining his dexterity and his wit. Nevertheless, he seemed the only one, aside from Colin and perhaps the inscrutable Ndukwe, who was comfortable playing his role.

---

[*] It is impossible to humiliate a man who willingly plays the fool. This is an easy enough lesson to understand intellectually, but is a much harder lesson to apply. The wisdom Gary displayed was that of a man who does not take himself too seriously. Pride and anxiety color (or rather, flavor) my existence. To not take myself seriously is to change my character. Not impossible, but difficult, and a charge with which I continue to struggle and continue to sit.

So, the humiliations continued, yet none of it could budge me from my joy. No despicable act, save one committed against Wren could have broken through my saffron shield. Wren sat in the throne upon my left and though we barely spoke as we continued to play our parts, my disgust and horror at the evening's grotesque play, my shame at having joined in it, all were gone, banished by her beauty. The prisoners were freed at Wren's gracious request, the rabble sent home, and we feasted on roasted quail with our bare hands. The night took on the illusion of fairy-tale, me a noble and my princess beside me. I wanted to stare at her in her gown of midnight blue. I wanted to stare into those glimmering green eyes. I wanted to take her hand and lead her through the garden. I wanted to ask her about Portland, about art, about school, and about love, but instead we played our roles to the end and I basked in the joy of my wish fulfillment. That wish granted, which denied had sent me into depression, now sent me to the heights of ecstasy and all the rest of that awful evening was washed away by the richness of saffron and that ineffable flavor that was Wren and love.

Evolution

The afterglow of Wren's arrival lasted two days. It was replaced by a stabbing in my chest and the sickening flavor of decomposing mango meat.

The Professor was equally cheery. I was useless to him, every stimulus he presented yielded the same response: pressure over the sternum, mouthful of rotted fruit.

"Have you been taking the medication I gave you?"

"Yes."

"Hmmm. Perhaps we'll have to adjust, although it seemed to have been working. Why so glum?"

I shrugged. I didn't want to discuss it with him. She was back, but she wasn't. I hadn't seen her, hadn't spoken to her, since the night of Court. She lived in the studio; day and night she was there. I waited up for her the first night, but she never returned. I rose early only to find she had come for a few hours sleep and then left again. She returned to my life, but only as an act, and now that she was so near it hurt me all the more. It was easier when she was off in Portland, absence makes the heart grow fonder, but proximity makes separation all the more painful.

"We need to bring you out of this," said the Professor, "no charting today. It's fruitless anyway with you in this state. Besides, it's time we had a chat. Evolution?"

"What about it? You going to explain to me how evolved I am?"

"I don't intend to explain anything...yet. To begin, I'm curious what you know. You've taken some science courses I presume. What is evolution?"

"It's how new species are formed."

"Sort of, yes, but how? What is the process of evolution?"

"Process? You mean like natural selection?"

"Yes. And no. That's only part of the picture. Evolution is fundamentally a negative process. It is a culling. Random genetic mutations occur all the time within individuals. Most often these mutations are insignificant, other times they produce traits that are harmful in which case the individual dies without reproducing and thus the mutation is not passed on. But, on those rare occasions where the mutation results in a trait that is both novel and useful, that individual is able to pass on the mutation to his or her offspring. This is where natural selection comes in. Natural selection defines whether or not a mutation is useful. A mutation is useful if it provides a reproductive advantage over other members of the species. This needn't be a direct advantage like more potent, faster swimming sperm, rather it can be any advantage that increases the likelihood of reproductive success. This includes the ability to access a food source unavailable to other members of the species, or enhanced ability to evade predators through camouflage or better venom, as these abilities increase the likelihood that the individual will survive to reproductive maturity, a necessary condition precedent for passing along those genes. This is the role that selection plays, because an advantage conferred to one individual is also a disadvantage to any similarly situated individual lacking the new, useful trait. Sometimes the advantage is so potent that the original form of the species, the one lacking the new trait, cannot compete at all and goes extinct, leaving only individuals that possess the new trait. Other times, the advantage may apply only within a limited environment, Darwin's finches are an example of this, where a different species of finch thrived on each different island, because their beak and body structures allowed them to access food sources available on one island but not on the others, in a case like this, extinction does not occur, but rather differentiation within specific ecological niches. However, it is important to remember that the process of evolution is fundamentally negative, advantaged individuals succeed because disadvantaged individuals fail."

"And you think that synesthesia confers an evolutionary advantage? I don't see how. I think you're just trying to get me interested so you can study what you want."

"Ah, you always doubt my motives even though I wear them on my sleeves. But you are right. I don't think synesthesia confers an evolutionary advantage."

"So you're full of shit."

"Don't insult me. I am no false Professor. I think that selection will no longer be the mechanism by which evolution occurs."

"Dumping five billion years of evolutionary history? That's a bold statement."

"Of what use are timid professions? Of course it's a bold statement, were it not I wouldn't bother to profess it. What do you think of when I say the word 'brain'?"

"I don't know, uh, mind, I guess."

"You aspire to be a wordsmith of sorts, so how about we deal in metaphors instead. You've heard the brain compared to a computer, right? How does that strike you, as a metaphor?"

"Okay I guess. Computer is like an information processor and a controller. I guess that's more or less what the brain does, processes info and controls the body."

"It's a crude metaphor, but understandable for the reasons you just gave. Now how about sponge? Have you ever heard the brain referred to as a sponge or as spongy?"

"Yeah. Or kids anyway. They say they soak things up like a sponge. You know because little kids learn really fast, or because you're not supposed to swear around them so they don't pick up bad words. Not really talking about the brain I guess, but sort of."

"Yes that's the kind of metaphor I had in mind. Also, the appearance of the brain, squishy grey matter, it looks a bit like a sponge, and so sponge-like qualities are often attributed to the brain, as in the example you gave of the amazing plasticity of young children's brains. We refer to them as 'soaking up knowledge' and we then comment on how they are 'sponges for information.' I don't know the etymology. Perhaps it can be entirely attributed to our materialist culture with ads for scrubbing bubbles dish soap and super-absorbent paper towels, or the availability of synthetic sponges in nearly every household kitchen, but people associate sponges with absorbent qualities, sponges soak, sponges sop. But sponges do much more. Sponges are ocean filters. Yet the brain is analyzed as a computer, metaphorized as a sopping sponge, and largely ignored as a filter. Given the brain's similarity to a sponge, are we not overlooking a potentially obvious function?

"Let's run with this metaphor a bit further: The brain functions as a computer, and as a sopping sponge, but also as a spongy filter. The brain, in conjunction with the sense organs, causes us to experience sensation. What is sensation? A short definition is the perception of a condition of the body or external reality. We trust our perceptions, our sense, to tell us what exists in the world outside our bodies and minds. But this definition betrays the disconnect, the flaw inherent in our use of metaphor and language, because sense is linked to perception and perception to sense. It is circular. The two terms are interchangeable.

"We need an additional level of differentiation. Sense organs reach the world external and send an electrical signal to the brain, which the brain interprets and we experience as the touch, smell, taste, sight, or sound of the world external. The signal, the electricity, is sense and the interpretation is perception. Yet what we experience as sensation is determined by the brain, and not by our fingertips, nostrils or retinas. Our sense organs serve no function without the brain. The only true sense organ is the brain. It is the interpretive organ. And so the distinction between sensation and perception is again collapsed. The electrical signals and the nervous system are a means to an end, estimations and operating instructions for the body processed by the brain. Unless, something more is occurring, unless the brain is not merely interpreting the raw data provided by the so called sense organs, but is in fact doing something more!

"What is reality? What is *out there*? We know nothing of it except through the compilation of sensations. Assume that the brain is a filter. What does this suggest? This suggests that what we perceive and experience to be reality is in fact a reduced version of reality, it is reality filtered, sensations simplified and then reinterpreted, even recreated, by the brain. We know that the brain does this. How else can we describe abstract reasoning? Visualization?

"Humans, through cognitive activities are capable of creating mental constructs and reinterpreting sense perceptions, i.e. facts and memories in the context of those constructs. Based on this would it not be a rational assumption, or at least, a hypothesis worthy of exploring, that our entire perception of reality may in fact be nothing more than a construct. Maybe the brain filters a larger portion of reality than we expect. And maybe our perception of reality is distorted by this incompleteness. And maybe the next step in human evolution, the next limit to be tested, is our current perception of reality. Maybe the brain is a filter and the next step in human evolution a lessening of the filter."

"And synesthesia is that step?" I asked.

"Yes! The lessening of the filter! The brain and body allowing in more raw sensation! This is the next step, and the emotional aspects of

214

your synesthesia are the key. Emotional and sensory evolution as increased sensory experience yields the possibility of enhanced perception and/or the development of entirely new senses."

"New senses? What like ESP? You think I can learn to read minds?"

"ESP isn't mind reading. It is what it stands for: extra-sensory perception. And yes enhanced perception or new senses would fit the definition of ESP. In fact I would argue that synesthesia itself is an extra-sensory perception. You taste emotion, you feel time, that sounds extra-sensory to me."

The notion that I had ESP was intriguing. I've read *Matilda* and *The Girl With Silver Eyes*. I would love to read minds or do astral projection, but that stuff is ESP, my Yangs aren't. "ESP? Either you're crazy or you think I am. Besides, scientists don't usually theorize on the basis of metaphor. And that still doesn't explain why natural selection is or isn't at work. Isn't that what you started out saying?"

"That is owing to an entirely different feature of life. For most of life's history random genetic change occasionally caused traits that gave a reproductive advantage within local environments. Nature selected for those with the advantageous traits because they were better able to pass on their genes. With the arrival of modern man this ceases to be the case. Do you know why?"

"Condoms."

"Don't be flippant. The answer was imbedded in my statement of the problem, 'reproductive advantage within *local environments.*' Do you see now? Humans change the life process in two ways. First, our ability to travel the globe has effectively made all environments local, there are no more isles of the Galapagos, no isolated environs; humanity touches all."

"What about the oceans? There's two-thirds of the planet we don't inhabit."

"Yes. Which brings me to the second change. Humans are now so adept at tool usage that our ability to either mechanically adapt to environments, or alter them, has surpassed nature's ability to randomly mutate into adaptations that are then selected for. Nature is too slow and we are too fast. We haven't grown wings we've built airplanes. We haven't grown gills we've built submarines. Do you think it is more likely that we will evolve physical adaptations that allow us to withstand the pressure at a thousand fathoms and breathe underwater, or that we will construct livable environs on the ocean floor?"

"So we build stuff. We're good at science. Doesn't mean evolution stopped. Doesn't mean I've got ESP."

"No, evolution will not stop. I never said that. I said selection would cease to be the mechanism by which evolution occurs. Robotics, cybernetics, artificial intelligence, genetic engineering, any of these could lead to the creation of a new species, and hence 'evolution.' But the kind of evolution I foresee, the kind synesthetes represent, that kind of evolution is more organic. The era of evolution through selection for new overt physical characteristics is over, but there is one organ that continues to evolve, those metaphorical sponges inside our cranial cavities. We can't see it, so it isn't obvious, but in an era where intelligence is the trait that confers the greatest survival advantage—"

"It sounds like you're arguing that nature will select for intelligence."

"No. Because there will be no culling. Humanity's collective resources insure overall survival and reproduction rates far too high to allow a few mutations for intelligence to cause the large-scale die-off of competitors sufficient to permit the formation of a new species in the absence of geographic isolation."

"How then?"

"The same way we do it with dogs of course, selective breeding. Members of the fiscal aristocracy and intelligentsia already self-select, I see no reason why this shouldn't continue or even be aided by modern science, and perhaps as synesthetes are identified and more is learned about the condition they too will seek each other out. Meanwhile the brain evolves, unseen, unobvious, but evolving nonetheless."

"Sounds creepy."

"How's Wren?"

"What?"

"That is why you're in such a funk isn't it? She's back. She's here. And yet you never get to see her."

"I guess. I... It's not like she's my girlfriend or anything."

"But you'd like her to be. It doesn't take a psychiatrist to see that you're infatuated with her. Although it doesn't hurt that I am. How does infatuation taste?"

"I'm not infatuated."

"Fine, insist on your illusions. Denial as they say is more than just a river in Egypt. But surely you have been infatuated. Must have been some young woman that got more than spice going, it can't all be lust, some woman must've got her hooks in deeper, even if Wren hasn't. So you say. But how does infatuation taste?"

"It doesn't."

"Love?"

"Fuck off."

"Frustrated?"

"Sure."

"So then what does frustration taste like?"

"It doesn't taste like anything."

"What do you mean it doesn't taste like anything?"

"I mean there is no taste of frustration. When I'm 'frustrated' I might taste any number of things, the bile of anger, the cinnamon of pride, the salty of sadness."

"So frustration isn't an emotion?"

"I guess not."

"But pain is?"

"Pain has a taste. I told you that already, rosewater."

"And how did you come to identify that flavor?"

"Gelato. I had a gelato in Italy, cioccolato-acqua di rose. I tasted it and knew right away, it was chocolate flavored pain. It's a bummer none of my feelings are chocolate don't you think?"

"Riley do you realize the implicit assumption we have been proceeding under as we map your synesthesias? Like flavors equal like feelings."

"I guess. I hadn't really thought much about what we're recording, I've just been telling you what I taste and what I feel."

"I think the assumption is both valid and necessary. I think we both intuited the truth of it, and that's why it has remained until now an unspoken premise of my, our, research. That like flavors equal like feelings had led me to some preliminary conclusions, would you like to hear some of them?"

"Sure."

"First, I now conclude that frustration is not an emotion because you don't taste it as such." He tugged at his beard. "How to define frustration then? Oh I've got it. Frustration is thwarted will or desire; it is an action not an emotion. A frustrating act stimulates an emotional response but is not an emotion itself."

"Okay. Is that important?"

"This entire process is important. Riley I am as interested in what your synesthesias may tell us about the nature of emotions, as I am interested in the synesthesias themselves. Indeed it is your unique perception of emotion that leads me to believe that the possibility of human evolution lurks in the background of your mind. To wit, pain is an emotion. I would not have suspected this prior to our research, but now I accept it as empirical fact. Pain is both a physical response to unhealthy stimulation of nerve ending, and it also has an emotional component.

"What else can we conclude, oh yes, sadness is separate and distinct from depression. Dismay is distinct from both sadness and disgust, and is an anxious worry brought to fruition. Similarly relief is distinct from joy, and is the lifting of anxiety through the non-occurrence of a specific anxious worry. Shame and embarrassment are one and the same. Threat or danger, usually experienced concurrently with a fight or flight response, is separate and distinct from fear, and to my surprise, threat is an emotion, while frustration is not. Another non-emotion that I find surprising is envy, which as best as I can gather from your answers is a combinatory experience of pride, anxiety, disappointment, and in some instances lust. Perhaps this is better thought of as a composite emotion, or an emotion comprised of other emotions... Oh! Maybe frustration falls into this category too. You see Riley the implications for our understanding of human emotion are tremendous! Frankly these conclusions I'm drawing are surely premature and off the cuff. It will take me years and hopefully many more subjects to fully analyze the data. On a more personal note, you clearly experience anxiety more than any other emotion, and at this I worry for you. Also, you are prone to depression and seldom experience joy, and at this I am sad for you. But I do have a suggestion to help in this regard, meditation."

"Meditation?" Shellfish floated in my mouth. "You don't seem like the type to go in for a lot of mumbo-jumbo."

"It is no such thing. Meditation is practiced self-awareness. Meditation includes calming exercises that can move brain wave activity toward a more dream-like, theta-wave state, while still maintaining

218

concentration. There are learned scholars from the east who profess. Don't forget that knowledgeable profession is not limited to Western science, although it finds its highest precision there.

"I want you to try to meditate today and stick with it if you can. It may benefit your moods without you even knowing it. Oh yes, mood, I almost forgot, mood as distinct from feeling, we must discuss in greater depth your experience of adolescence, the taste you described as 'rotten' or 'stinky' and not like fruit but more like fetid meat. I am truly curious at the implications of feelings that last over time such that they may be considered moods. At least that is my tentative working definition. Oh tangent tangents, meditation is simple enough, find a seated position that is comfortable, if you like I have a round cushion in the RV called a zafu that you can use, but you could use a chair if you like. The important thing is to be comfortable with your airway unobstructed. Then focus your attention on your navel and breathe, experience the rising and falling of your stomach. To establish a rhythm softly chant under your breath. The Thai call this a mantra, a phrase you repeat over and over, you could say anything, but you may as well start with a common one. It goes like this, *om mani padme om*."

I felt a nagging sensation. It tugged at me, not as a feeling, but in my mind, like there was something I meant to say, or do, or remember, but couldn't quite put my finger on it. The anxious weight was there, but also that troubling feeling that you get when you can't remember what it is that you're supposed to remember. You can't remember because you forget, such is the nature of forgetting, but this was worse, because I hadn't forgot, I had kept it secret, although I didn't know it at the time. "What does that mean, *om mani padme om*?" I asked.

"All hail the jewel in the lotus."

V. CHOICES

Road Trip

I did not startle; I sprung awake pushed by the impetus of saffron stalk to sunlight for there she stood her finger drawn to her lips in a silent "shhh," her face in all its complexity and freckled beauty directly above mine, fine black hair drooping to one side one eye hidden behind a dark veil of lovely to reveal the singular emerald depth of the other. Saffron faded as I tasted her presence. She beckoned me to rise with haste. I dressed in the dark and followed her out in stealth. All the rest breathed heavy in the barracks and we stole away with only the faint click-clack of my cane upon the terra cotta.

I followed her as one might follow a ghost in a dream, though I was conscious of my flavors and knew they would not deceive me. The roar of eight cylinders shattered the thin illusion of unreality. The squeal of the Jeep's tires and the bounce on the shocks thrust me into a strange state of wish-fulfillment, my fondest hopes riding wordless beside me as we careened onto the highway and her hair, her natural color, whipped behind in the open air as if stretching back in freedom to mock the caged birds with our flight to freedom, me and my Wren.

She adjusted the mirrors as she drove. The early air of desert morning brought a numbing chill to my face as we speed down the highway and then turned to the north. "So are we stealing the jeep?" I yelled over the roar of the wind and the engine.

"Borrowing." She smirked and checked the rearview mirror. "Colin knows." She stepped on the gas and brought the Jeep up to eighty.

"Where are we headed?" I asked.

"Home."

"Home?"

"San Diego." She gave me a sideways look. "Where else is home?"

"I don't know where you're from."

"Now you know. Maybe you'll know even more after today." She checked the rearview again. "I had to take a break. I've been going non-stop for the past three months. No chance to breathe out at the Rancho."

"Yeah who knew desert air was so stifling?"

****

We made far more turns than necessary and ran stretches of rutted road I didn't even know existed. We saw a desert sunrise, and not a single car until we reached off-road alley out past Ocotillo Wells. A couple of sand-rails and dirt bikes were out early and broke up the monotony of the scenery.

We stopped at a greasy spoon in Julian for eggs and coffee and it was there that the glow of the morning's events started to wear off and I felt an uncomfortable weight upon my neck. I ignored it and tried to savor the complexity of the flavor on my palette, the pairing of saffron with my eggs, for my joy had not wholly left me, but the weight remained and I felt it growing.

Wren enjoyed the quaint mountain town aspect of Julian, with its main street semi-preserved to resemble its late nineteenth century heyday. To me it felt phony. Modernity might be sterile and without character or charm, but this sort of faux-preservation of the past was museum–like, mummified, I'd take Tokyo neon or San Diego strip mall over this any day. But I didn't offer my observations while Wren rambled on about the gold rush here and how it was once a mining town as thriving and bustling as San Diego at that time. I knew all that. Escondido was just down the hill. I'd been to Julian plenty of times. All you really needed to know was that the pies were the best in the state and that the Wagon Wheel had fried pickles, but I asked a few questions so she could show off her knowledge, which seemed to make her happy. Unfortunately the pie company was yet to open and it had started to rain, so we zipped the soft top closed on the Jeep and headed down toward Ramona and Escondido.

The closer we got to my childhood home the greater the weight became. Part of me wanted to show Wren where I grew up, especially the Lake and the neighborhood I grew up in, but part of me wanted to hide it, to steer clear of the memories and familiar faces that might be encountered if we ventured too close to home. Timidity won out, and when Wren blew through Escondido and continued toward the coast I let my hometown pass without comment. Wren did not. We were just through Escondido, still headed west on the 78 when she asked, "So you're not going to give me the tour? You're from around here right?"

"Yeah. But I grew up on the other side of town." I told her the half-truth, "I didn't want to take us out of the way."

"We've got all day. So will you show me later?"

"You want to come back? I thought we were going to San Diego?"

"This is San Diego."

"I mean like San Diego proper, over on the coast."

"We've got all day. We'll come back this way before we head south."

"So where are we going now?"

"Oceanside. I'm gonna drop in on a friend. I'd rather do it in the morning. I don't want to go there after dark. Besides, we got other things to do today."

Island Connection

We parked on a street in front of a ramshackle bungalow in a neighborhood north of Oceanside Boulevard. I understood why Wren didn't want to come at night. It was the kind of neighborhood that passes for ghetto in a sprawled out city like San Diego: too many cars and not enough driveways, houses small, close together, and of 1950's construction, mostly bungalows and Craftsmen, some kept up, others not, and on the occasional corner a three-story apartment building with faded and cracked pastel stucco.

The bungalow we parked in front of looked like every other house on the block, only more dilapidated. White siding and green trim peeled off in strips to reveal the wood beneath, the porch sagged like a hammock, and a waist-high chain-link fence enclosed the front yard, little more than a well-worn patch of dirt that the rain was slowly turning to mud. A lone tree sat naked in the center of the lawn, a chain wrapped around its base disappeared into a newly formed puddle on the other end. It was a thick chain, the kind that holds a thick dog. The tree would break long before the chain.

"I'll be back in a minute," said Wren as she hopped out of the Jeep.

"I'm not coming in?"

"No." She pursed her lips and shook her head. "This is just a quick errand. We'll get going in a minute."

I couldn't take my eyes off of her until she disappeared inside. She looked graceful tiptoeing around puddles in her mid-calf lambskin boots. She looked more urban than I remembered in a knee-length grey knit dress. It was close-fit but conservative by Wren's standards. I wondered if she picked up that outfit in Portland. I kicked myself for being so rude; I hadn't even asked her how it went up north. I made a mental note to strike up that conversation.

I sat in the car and surveyed the neighborhood as rain tapped gently on the soft top. A pair of faded blue Chuck Taylors hung from the power lines above the sidewalk. Who could she know in this neighborhood? The street was quiet; San Diegans tend not to venture unnecessarily into the rain. I got the tinny taste that sets me on edge. It was probably the neighborhood, probably nothing to be worried about in the a.m., but I know when I'm out of place.

Down the street an old Cadillac rolled slowly toward me. I slunk down a little in my seat, an irrational but undeniable wash of fear and metal swept over me. I got a horrible premonition that something was wrong with Wren. I looked at the clock. Wren had been gone five minutes. The Cadillac continued to creep. It was driving too slowly. My mind raced through movie scenes: drive-by, gangsters on a hit, that was who drove that slow, or they were looking for an address or looking for 'For Sale' signs, or any one of a million other logical, peaceful reasons for a slow roll. But still my mind chased the shadows.

Six minutes. Wren had been gone for six minutes. The Cadillac was almost to me. Could they be looking for whomever Wren was meeting? Was Wren in danger?

I glanced at the Caddy as it passed. Three black kids. I looked away. I could feel the eyes of the kid in the back seat on me, trailing on me as they moved away. I watched in the rearview until they turned the corner at the end of the block.

I realized I was holding my breath and let out a fierce exhalation. Enough of this, I thought, there was no sense in creeping myself out sitting alone in a 'borrowed' Jeep in a strange neighborhood.

My cane sunk into the soft ground as I worked my way to the porch. I rapped sharply on the door with my cane. My anxiety grew as I waited for a response, the tin at the back of my mouth growing sharper with every passing second.

The door opened. Six and a half feet of dark tan flesh housed in a red tank top and shorts occupied the entire width of the doorframe. I gathered my wits, none of my fear or anxiety subsiding, and sized him up. Dark green full sleeve tattoos wrapped around to meet at the neck and upper chest and along with his tattooed shins gave me the strong impression that the sleeves were part of a full suit. He glowered at me and I could feel myself blink like my eyelids moved in slow motion. "Who are you?" he asked in a deep pacific island accent.

I shouldn't have been caught off guard. I knew I would probably have to talk to a stranger at the door, but I was thrown by the sheer size of the man.

"Who are you?" he repeated.

I wondered if he might be Samoan. I didn't ask. I managed to spit out my name.

"Yo Mak!" the big man called back into the house, "Dea some *haole* named Riley hea."

"Riley?" Wren said in her singsong voice. "He's with me. He was *supposed* to wait in the car."

Another accented voice called out, "Let him in."

"Be sure fo hemo yo slippahz befo go in," said the man-mountain.

"What?"

"Take off yo shoes fool."

The big guy pushed me forward into a cramped kitchen. Wren sat at a table with her back to me. She frowned at me over her shoulder. "Sorry for my friend's intrusion. This is Riley. Riley this is Makaio." She gestured across the table, but I couldn't see around her.

I leaned hard on my cane as I entered the narrow space and stepped around Wren. The stove was close next to me and I focused on the floor, trying to find a footing for my cane. I looked up just in time to see a massive red-nose pit-bull lunge at me.

"Grrr-Arr!" The table jerked forward. My cane slipped and I fell backward knocking the wind out of me. Cold wet metal overwhelmed me and I scrambled backward across the floor like a sand crab. Makaio and the big guy standing behind me at the door both howled with laughter while the pit snapped its powerful jaws again and again inches from my feet.

"Oh braddah!" Makaio howled. "Oh he make 'a'. I think he go shi shi. Lola hea!" The pit snapped one more time. "Lola no act!" Makaio yanked back hard on her chain and slapped her on the head. "I said hea!" The dog ducked its head, tucked its short tail between its legs and returned to its master. The chain holding her was thick, but only a couple feet long. The table leg it attached to was scratched and scarred. Thankfully the dog hadn't been able to pull the table any farther.

I stood up with some difficulty using my cane, never taking my eyes off of the dog.

"Howzit Riley? Sorry bout Lola brah. She real sweet, but she don't know you, and you in her house. Come tink of it, I don't know you and you in my house." I tried not to flinch and didn't take my eyes off the dog. She barked again. And again. This time Makaio made no effort to stop her. She looked like she wanted to tear me to pieces, lunging at me, causing the chain to pop with every ferocious bark.

226

"Mak!" Wren intervened, "Das enuf!" Her pidgin had command.

Makaio smiled a big scary grin. "Fo sure." He pulled the dog back and made her sit. "Jus' joke braddah. Kale, bring chair fo Riley." I looked at Makaio for the first time, he looked short, especially compared to Kale, but he was buff, one of those short guys that spends a lot of time in the gym. But it wasn't his guns that caught my attention. It was his *guns*. As in firearms, spread across the table at least a dozen handguns, a couple of shotguns and what appeared to my untrained eye to be some kind of automatic weapon. Boxes of ammo rounded out the deadly array.

Kale returned, set down a stool for me and stood behind it with his beefy arms across his chest.

"Relax," said Makaio.

Not likely, I thought, as I stared at the arsenal. Makaio stopped smiling. He appraised me from across the table. I felt the body heat of the man-mountain behind me. Any confusion lingering on my palette washed out in a river of copper.

"Cop?" Makaio asked.

"No! No-No-No. Not a cop."

Makaio smiled but it didn't put me at ease. "No I don't tink you a cop. Kale, what you tink? He a cop?"

I couldn't help but look back over my shoulder. I saw nothing but red fabric over belly.

"Nah," said Kale, "he look familiar. I tink I know him from somewea."

"Fo realz? How he know you braddah?"

I had no idea how he knew me. I'd never met him before. But Wren guessed the connection right away. "You know surfing?" she asked.

"No shit!" said Kale. "Das Riley Sparx! Riley braddah, you know Apo?"

"Apo Kukui?"

"Yeah he's my cousin."

"Don't listen to Kale, braddah," Makaio said. "Dis buggah shtay mento. He tink all Hawaiian his cousins. Fucking moke from Molokai. Apo's from Oahu."

"Yeah I know Apo. Surfed with him plenty of times."

"So wot's wit da cane den? Get fo paddle?"

I didn't fully understand the pidgin, but I got the gist, he was clowning me. "Old injury. I'm retired now."

"How'd you get hurt?"

"Freak accident."

"Apo is my cousin," said Kale sullenly. "Auntie Tina's tutu, is cousin of Apo's tutukane."

"Okay cuz. You ohana. Whatevahz. Ainokea. Neither does Riley. So Riley you need a gun? Protect ya neck since you can't run nowea."

"We gotta bounce Mak," Wren said to my relief.

"Wot? You goin bag already? Stay and smoke, eh? Das why you hele, right?"

"We really gotta go Mak."

"Smoke, K? Fo me. And fo big moke Kale, he wanna smoke wit Riley Sparx. You smoke pakalolo right braddah?" Makaio pulled out a freezer size bag of purple buds that stunk up the whole room. He pulled out a single long bud and sniffed it, then handed it to me. "Eikaikau pakalolo. Strong bud."

We got ripped. Makaio rolled up a blunt and within a couple of minutes the room filled with smoke and my eyes were glazed like a donut. Everybody mellowed out and my flavors faded into oblivion. Even Lola mellowed out after Mak blew a few hits in her face. I signed a couple of surfboards for Kale, which made him very happy.

Then Mak loaded a pistol.

All that warm vibe sucked right out of the room. I could feel the pressure and taste the tin despite being stoned out of my gourd.

"You sure you don't need a gun Riley Sparx?" I nodded, unable to speak. "K. You and Wren go on your way, wiki wiki. And Riley, if you ever show up at my hale again, I'll let Lola eat your balls brah."

Back in the Jeep my mind spun circles, somehow sober and stoned at the same time I alternated between relief floating off my shoulders and pressure pounding my neck and shoulders. "What the fuck was that? You took me to a fucking arms dealer?"

She shrugged, "That's Mak."

"Do you think he's coming after us?"

She laughed. It trilled out like a schoolgirl's giggle and it really pissed me off. "No one is coming after us. Relax."

"He loaded a gun!"

228

"Like I said, that's Mak. Unlike his dog, his bark is actually worse than his bite."

"He's sells drugs and guns. People like that shoot people."

"Relax. He's my cousin. This is why I told you to stay in the car."

"Why'd we even come here?"

"*We* didn't. I did. I stopped to get some weed, what else?"

"Weed! For God's sake I could have called Sean. Weed? We almost got shot for some weed?"

"We didn't almost get shot. And if your haole ass hadn't barged in I'd have been out of there in ten minutes flat. Instead you crash the party while he's got his guns out and make him all nervous. That's why he got all crazy. He was just showing you that he's a tough guy. He can't help it, that's just how he is. It's 'cause he's hapa like me."

"Why are you making excuses for him? What's that even mean?"

"It means he overcompensates, especially when some haole shows up uninvited."

"Bullshit! Overcompensates for what?"

"For the white half. All that pidgin, das ovakill braddah! He speaks perfectly good English. He just wanted to make you feel dumb and prove how Hawaiian he is. He thinks it makes him sound more authentic."

"Doesn't it? Kind of?"

"I guess so."

"So why don't you have to prove your Hawaiianness too? You don't talk pidgin."

"How you figgah? No make l'dat. Cause I speak English mo better dan you? Dat mean I no like pidgin. Dat mean I get no oddah words. I walaau how I like. When I like. So dea!" She flipped her fingers at me across the bottom of her chin. "Wop yo jaw braddah!"

Sufficiently chastised I said, "Okay. You made your point. I'm sorry. You can speak pidgin. That still isn't an excuse for Mak, you said you're hapa too, and you don't act like that."

"Yeah, but I'm a girl. Plus he's hapa haole fo realz. I'm a mutt." She grinned at me, and that complex flavor only she could evoke fought its way through the haze for an instant then vanished.

"So you're not Hawaiian?"

"Do I look Hawaiian?"

"Kind of, I guess, but the freckles... What's a Hawaiian look like anyway?"

She laughed, "You're catching on, but you got no grasp. How should I get back to your hood?"

"Down the 5. We'll take Via de la Valle, it's a prettier drive."

Home Sweet Home

Lake Hodges was closed for the winter. We couldn't drive the road to the boat launch, so instead we took the footpath on the north shore. Wren walked. I limped.

Wren was lovely to be with and her flavor dominated my afternoon. Time spent in nature reveals two kinds of people: those with a knack for appreciating the outdoors, and those who can't wait to get back inside. Wren was the former kind of person and as a consequence we spent far more time at the lake than I had planned. Obviously it wasn't rugged outdoors or backcountry wilderness, but it was difficult for me to traverse. Wren was kind and patient with me. She listened to me describe how the lake was made by dredging the riverbed and damming the San Dieguito River. She let me ramble about Native American artifacts at the Harris site further down the river course, how they were preserved in layered strata and date back more than ten thousand years. She was curious about all the flora and fauna around the lake and asked me the names of plants and which trees were native and which were transplants.

"The live oaks are the main natural feature," I explained, "just a couple hundred years back they dominated the inland areas. Imagine the whole valley floor used to be covered with them. Some of these trees here in Del Dios are a hundred years old; they saw this lake when it was still a river. The tules are native and a lot of the brush, the coastal sagescrub, the black sage and white sage, the chapparal broom. But most all of the other plants are invaders, the palm trees and the eucalyptus. The eucalyptus is the worst of all. Its leaves are toxic. They poison the ground so other plants can't grow. Eventually it will take over everything if humans don't prevent it."

"It all looks so natural," said Wren, "but I guess that's how San Diego is. It's full of beauty but it's mostly transplants."

"You understand. You grew up here. Everyone you meet is from somewhere else, right? Plus everyone who's actually from here is running a casino nowadays."

She laughed. "I can relate. Coming and going, no place of my own, I'm a stranger even when I'm at home."

"You poet you."

"I dabble. Natural or not it feels like nature, doesn't it?"

"It feels like home."

"It must've been great growing up here," she said.

"It was." I thought of my mom. Then I thought of my dad. I choked back a saltwater swallow and blinked my eyes.

"You alright?"

"Yeah. Hey look at this." I pointed to a large cactus stand, "This is native."

"Nopales," Wren said and moved closer to the stand of large flat paddles.

"Very good."

"Prickly pear, right? But no fruit."

"Not the right season," I said. Then I heard the sound I was hoping to hear. "Shh. Listen." There was a low 'kek-kek-kek-kek-kek' call. It was rhythmic, but rough and progressing, becoming higher, louder and quicker as it went on. "Keep your eyes open, I bet we'll see her. She's in that cactus somewhere."

"Purple dots," Wren whispered.

"Purple dots?"

"That's what I see. Purple dots. It's barely musical, but it has colors."

The little bird popped out from under a paddle, it flitted quickly about, bounding with half-hopping flights in and out of the cacti. "There it is. Did you see it? Grey-brown with speckles and a white stripe over the eye."

"Yeah what is it?"

"It's you."

"What?"

"It's a wren, a cactus wren. I was hoping we'd see one."

Wren watched the little bird flit about. She seemed delighted and her rich flavor filled my palette. I touched her elbow. She turned to me, smiling, chin tilted ever so slightly down. I leaned in and kissed her.

That was the highlight of our walk. I pointed out some red-wing blackbirds and red-tailed hawks circling in the distance, but no bird could hope to top her namesake, and for me nothing could top that kiss.

"So will you show me your house?" Wren asked when we got back to the car.

"It's not my house anymore. When Dad died Billy got the house and I got the company."

"Can't we at least drive by? It's right here isn't it?"

I couldn't see a way out of it, so I acquiesced. I just hoped we didn't run into Billy. Sure enough, we rolled up the hill and who was standing out front watering plants with a garden hose? Billy. "Shit. Park over there," I grumbled.

"I thought we were just driving by."

"Yeah but Billy saw me. I should at least say hello. He is my brother."

I got out and click-clacked downhill toward Billy. The hill was steep and I was really working my good arm to brace myself against the cane. Rosewater was seeping in.

"Billy," I said.

"Riley." We shook hands.

"This is Wren."

He took Wren's hand. "Pleasure to meet you Wren."

"Likewise."

"So what brings you two out here?"

"Wren wanted to see where I grew up."

"Well this is it. Good old Del Dios. So are you like his girlfriend or something?"

Wren looked at me, gave a coy smile, then looked away. "Or something," she said in a singsong trill.

"So what are you up to these days Billy?" I asked.

"Same old. Veteran's benefits suck, but it's good enough for beers at Hernandez and some cheap food."

"How's the leg?"

"Hurts like hell. Doc down at the VA gave me some painkillers, but I don't like to take em," he grinned at me for the first time since we showed up, "unless I'm drinking. How about you?"

I lifted the cane. "Still limping." I didn't mention I was living at a bizarre artist's commune as part of a study on that weird thing about me. Didn't want to bring up any comparisons to mom. We stood staring at each other. Not two minutes and we were already out of things to talk about.

"Do you think we could look inside Billy?" Wren asked.

"Be my guest," Billy said. "Matter of fact that's probably a good idea. Might be your last chance.

"What?"

"I'm selling the place little brother. Guy offered me $900,000. Cash offer. I had to take it. It ain't worth close to that."

Whirlwind tour seems an appropriate expression. I couldn't wait to get out of that house. It was a bad idea going there. I'd have rather found out after the fact that Billy sold it. I wasn't mad at him. He needed the money. But I was choked up on rosewater and old memories. Part of me thought, good riddance the place died with Dad anyway, but another part of me held onto the memory of this place as a life preserver. Wren oohed and aaahed at the views of the lake. Nothing else was how I remembered it, different shabby furniture and some barren walls. It was a bachelor pad now. Who knew what it'd be in a few months. I showed Wren my old bedroom and we split.

"Are you okay?" she asked.

"Yeah. I will be. It's just… never mind."

"Look I was going to take you to my home. Where I grew up. But if that's too hard on you I totally understand."

I felt the heat flush over me. I didn't want her pity. "No it's fine. Just because my home is lost doesn't mean you should have to hide yours."

I was actually thrilled. All I wanted was more of her. This trip, that wren, that kiss, that made the episode with Billy worth it, made almost getting shot by her cousin worth it, but I wanted El Rancho to be worth it, and for that to happen we had to happen, Wren and me. I wasn't sold on being the next step in human evolution.

Oasis en un Jardín del Barrio Logan

We stopped near downtown, but south and east, on the other side of the Coronado Bridge, near the harbor. I could see a few battleships and destroyers in the distance at the Embarcadero. That was the closest I'd ever been to this neighborhood. This was Barrio Logan. White people didn't come here without a good reason.

The sun was setting as we rolled down 27th through a dense industrial zone. Manufacturing plants and warehouses with rusted bay doors sat squat behind chain link fences topped with razor wire and lined with green and black sheathing to obscure the inner workings from prying eyes and would-be thieves. Dotted in amidst the industrial landscape were houses and apartments. Their placement seemed haphazard at best, a cruel joke at worst. Overhead, power lines ran every which way crisscrossing the streets and linking up at a large tower, a transformer in the distance to the north. We made a left turn and the neighborhood abruptly switched to residential, the same sort of neighborhood where her cousin lived, cracked craftsmen, tiny bungalows and square blocks of weather-beaten stucco. Another turn led us down an alley and we parked in a small, unmarked spot.

"We'll go in the back." Thick green shrubbery covered the concrete walls to either side of a wrought iron gate with spear-tip points at head-height. We passed through the gate to a different world.

A small white fountain burbled next to a well-plotted garden. I recognized cilantro, mint, and what I thought were Anaheim chiles amidst a host of other plants. To the other side of the small yard was a planter of red and yellow roses. Next to the house hibiscus rose high up the wall. A true San Diego garden, few other places have a climate moderate enough to grow thriving varieties of so many different plants.

Wren opened the outer door and called out, "Mamá. Abuelita. Estamos en casa. We're here." The aromas of chiles and peppers and corn and something else, chocolate or cinnamon, maybe Mexican chocolate, floated to my nostrils, and a short thin woman in a green apron came running to the door and threw her arms around Wren.

"Oh mija. Oh mi pajarita. La canción de mi corazon. Oh mija, it's so good to see you. Te amo! Te amo! Beso, beso besame mucho."

Wren's mom kissed her again and again. "A mi amor, mi pajarita, Como estás? "

"Mamá. Te amo también. Pero inglés por favor. Tenemos un invitado. Mamá this is Riley."

"Of course where are my manners? Hello Riley welcome to our home." She hugged me and said to Wren, "Es tu novio?" She had the same shimmering emerald green eyes as her daughter.

"That remains to be seen," I said before Wren could answer, and flashed her my own coy smile as payback for earlier. "Mucho gusto Señora…"

"Morgan. Oh, but please call me Rosa. Hablas español?"

"Un poco. I grew up in Escondido so I picked up a little. I must say you have a lovely home. Your garden is spectacular." It was true. I had been deceived by the neighborhood, but the garden was immaculate, and the first thing I noticed upon entering the home was the terra cotta tile that was every bit the equal of the tile in El Rancho.

"Thank you, you are very kind. Wren you must give him the tour."

"It smells great in here," I said.

"Yes I hope you are hungry. I made Wren's favorito. If you'll excuse me I have to get back to the kitchen, I was pressing out the tortillas when you arrived. Wren, show him around. Mamá is in her room. Make sure to introduce her. Riley make yourself comfortable."

Wren showed me the house. It didn't take long, thankfully, because it was getting hard to ignore the rosewater that flowed slow and steady across my palette, and walking was only making it worse. A kitchen, a bedroom and bathroom were off of the main hallway, the living room was at the end of the hall and the other bedroom was next to the living room. The house was impeccable, not a speck of dust anywhere, and the same beautiful terra cotta tile throughout. It was a little cluttered, but in a good way. Except for a couch, two chairs, and a path to walk through, every square inch of the living room and its walls were filled with oil paintings: still-life, landscapes, three different portraits of Wren, paintings of the San Diego skyline, the warships in the harbor, the Coronado bridge lit up at night, and a hauntingly realistic depiction of twenty some people scrambling through traffic at the San Ysidro border crossing. I spent several minutes saying nothing, just looking at the paintings. I found myself especially drawn to two. They used streaks of bright color against

236

black backgrounds: one depicted ascending orange spheres, while the other featured green and pink patterns of latticework. "Did you paint these?" I asked Wren.

"I hoped you would catch that. No. I didn't. Every painting in this house was done by my mother."

"They're spectacular. But is she a... I mean is she one too?"

"A synesthete? Yes. But don't tell her that. She prefers to think of her colors as divine inspiration, a gift from God. She don't need no stinking science."

"I can relate to that," I said thinking of my mother. Although I realized Wren might have thought I was referring to my own tense relationship with the Professor I didn't bother to clarify. If only my mother had accepted a little bit of 'stinking science,' how different things might have been, for me and for her.

"Is anyone else in your family a synesthete?" Wren asked me.

"None confirmed."

"What's that mean?"

"I have suspicions about my mom. She was...she was odd. But it doesn't matter anyway there's no way to find out now."

"Have you told the Professor your suspicion?"

"No."

"You should. Ask him about genetic links. Is synesthesia inheritable?" I shrugged. I wasn't looking to volunteer anything to him. Wren saw my look and didn't let the issue go. "I know you're ambivalent about helping him, or maybe you're hostile, I hope you've forgiven me for telling him."

"I have."

"I'm glad, but you should want to learn about this... for yourself. We're different. Don't you want to know why? Sorry I'm not trying to be a bitch, I'm just saying that what he's studying matters. The genetic link matters to me. I want to know if I inherited this from my mom. I want to know if my daughter or my son can inherit it from me. So even if you don't want to do this for yourself, I'm asking you to do it for me."

"Okay."

"Enough said. I'll let it go now."

"Good. So is your mother a professional artist? Is that how you decided to become an artist too?"

"No. And no, although, my mom's paintings inspired me and she taught me a lot of technique. What you see here is a lifetime's work from painting in her spare time. This is what she accomplished on weekends and in the evenings. Can you imagine what she could have done if she painted full time?"

Abuelita

"Ay, mija!" A very short elderly woman stood at the end of the hall, her arms outstretched. "Besame, mija!"

"Abuelita!" Wren kissed her on both cheeks and hugged her close, and the loving greeting I watched between Wren and her mother was now repeated with her grandmother, with possibly even more kisses.

"Abuelita this is Riley. Riley, meet my grandmother."

"Mucho gusto, Señora."

She spoke in Spanish that was too fast for me to comprehend, then turned to Wren and said even more, just as fast, and gestured at me and pointed at her head. The only word I picked up was 'pelón'. Then she shuffled back down the hall toward her room. She moved with remarkable speed.

"She said you should call her Abuelita, too."

"Did she say something about hair?"

"She said you have the same hair as my grandfather."

Abuelita returned with a framed photograph and took me by the hand. She asked me to sit with her on the couch. I think. I couldn't understand what she said, but I let her lead me. I caught Wren watching us with a smirk. Abuelita showed me the photo, an old black and white of a young man with ruddy features. Even in the black and white you could see his red nose and cheeks.

"Mi esposo," she said.

Wren sat down on the other side of Abuelita. "That's my grandfather." Abuelita rattled off another string of Spanish phrases to Wren that I couldn't comprehend. She patted my hand and smiled at me, her face was lined with deep creases and her grayed hair was very thin, but her eyes were full of life, a deep chocolate, unlike the emeralds her daughter and granddaughter possessed, but just as vibrant, with a sheen like a chocolatier's glaze. The eyes of a young woman set in an old lady's face.

"Abuelita says you have the same hair." I looked closely at the man in the photo, his hair hung over his ears slightly and curled up at the ends. The color could have been brown, or sandy blond.

"Su pelón fue el color mismo?" I asked. Wren turned her head and opened her eyes wide, as if to say 'not bad'. Abuelita chuckled and said,

"Sí." Then she said something more, again too fast for me to comprehend. Wren got up and left the room, and I sat there, feeling the heat build on my tongue and the pressure on my back.

Being alone with old people always makes me nervous. They usually tell stories I don't care to hear and I am forced to nod politely and laugh at the right times even though I don't give a shit and just want to get away. Asking a question in Spanish gave Abuelita the wrong idea and she jabbered at me in español thinking that I could understand. This was worse than a typical old person conversation in so many ways. A perfectly kind grandma, a grandma to a girl I liked, might love, and definitely wanted to sleep with, was chattering away in a language I couldn't comprehend and all I could do was gape and smile, and make nervous eye contact while silently praying for Wren to return.

Mercifully she did return with yet another photograph of her grandfather, this one in color, standing on a porch with his arm around Abuelita. She showed it to me. "His hair's gray in this picture."

What I noticed in the photo was not his hair, but his eyes, the same single tone green that shined in the sockets of Wren and her mother. The other thing I noticed was the band of freckles across his bulbous nose.

Un Sabor Mágico

"Dinner is ready," Rosa called as she came into the living room. "Oh, is Abuelita showing pictures of dad again? Careful Riley, if you get her started she'll break out the photo albums." She said something to Abuelita in Spanish to which Abuelita responded with more Spanish and a dismissive wave of the hand.

Rosa directed us to take our plates and get some rice and chicken from the stove. I filled half my plate with rice seasoned with yellow and green chiles and took two chicken thighs with the skin on, cooked to a beautiful golden color. We sat down to dinner at a small table. The table settings were simple, but brightly colored and looked festive paired with our yellow plates. A large pot and ladle occupied the center of the table along with a tortilla warmer.

"Mmm. It smells delicious."

"Thank you Riley. It is Wren's favorite. Abuelita wants to say grace, okay?"

We held hands while Abuelita gave a blessing in Spanish. I managed to get in the 'amen' at the right time.

"Wren go ahead and serve our guest por favor."

"Oh no. Ladies first," I insisted. Wren rolled her eyes at me, but I thought I saw Rosa give a silent nod of approval to Abuelita.

Wren opened the pot and the kitchen was filled with aromatic layers of spice and chocolate. Wren scooped a ladle full of a deep red sauce onto her grandmother's plate, then another, then another. Clearly this sauce was the star of the show.

"What is that?" I asked.

"Molé," Rosa answered. "I got the recipe from my mother, who got it from her mother, who got it from her mother."

"I've heard of molé, but I've never tried it. I thought it was black?"

"No that's molé negro. They do that in another part of Mexico. My mom came here from Mexico D.F., Mexico City that is."

"It smells amazing. I can't wait to try it. What's in it?"

"Do you have a pen and paper handy? There are more than twenty ingredients and even more steps, I roast the chiles, I grind the spices, I boil, I simmer, I taste, I add. It takes two days to make right." She smiled at her daughter and touched her arm. "I made it because Wren is not home very often, so this is an especial occasion."

"The recipe is a family secret," Wren added. "Mom's waiting until I'm more grown up to bring me into the circle." I laughed and Wren took my plate to load me up with molé.

"She's right," said Rosa. "Maybe when you're thirty mija. So you see Riley I could tell you but then I'd have to kill you."

I took a big whiff of the aromas emanating from my plate. "That's okay Rosa I'm content to guess."

I watched Wren take a bite. Her eyes rolled back into her head in enjoyment. I tried to eat it the way everyone else did. I cut some chicken from the bone forked a little rice and ate it all together with a hearty helping of sauce.

For a moment, my heart stopped.

Not only was it delicious, not only was it rich and complex as a twenty-ingredient sauce should be, not only was the hint of chocolate the perfect note to finish the sauce, but the taste was familiar, like that rare pair of jeans that sit just right, familiar in the way a fir tree smells of Christmas, familiar as the sound of surf and the salt in the air, familiar like the sun and the moon, familiar like the drop-in on a right-hand barrel when the morning sea is glass and the world stretches before you in an endless moment.

It was the flavor of Wren.

After the first bite of molé Rosa must've seen something in my face, because she tentatively asked, "Do you like it?"

I assured her that I did and managed to guess one ingredient, chocolate.

"The chocolate goes in last," she said in the knowing tone of an expert.

I had seconds of the molé. I followed the lead of the three women and sopped up the sauce with the homemade tortillas. Rolling up food burrito-style is more of an American thing. We drank a bottle of vino and the conversation shifted from molé to me. I eventually declined, politely, to discuss my injuries, but did show off the fine craftsmanship of my cane. "Oh how did you get this scratch on it?" Rosa asked. At which point I made up a lie about falling in gravel rather than detail my cane wielding barracks rampage. Eventually I managed to shift the conversation to Wren and her family and I finally developed a more complete picture of her ethnicity, which was even more complex than I had imagined.

Coming to America

Wren and her mother took turns translating as Abuelita described in detail how she had met Bran[*] Morgan, Wren's grandfather. They met in Mexico D.F., in 1927, when she was twenty-one years old. She snuck out of the house and met up with some friends to go dancing in the city.

It was mostly Mexicans in the dance hall, but there was a small group of white-men at a table in the corner talking loudly and drinking excessively. She danced with one Mexican gentleman and politely declined another, but the whole night she was intrigued by the foreigners and could not keep from staring, they were so different, with strange accents. Abuelita had never traveled anywhere, and had only met a couple of gringos, an American businessman and visiting priest from Italy. The men in the dance hall were not American and they talked so funnily, like singing birds. Finally, after an hour of staring, one of the men, the shortest, palest one of the bunch, walked up to her and said in perfect, but strangely accented Spanish, "You are the most beautiful creature I have seen on either side of the Atlantic, you are a star and all others are candles, pale imitations of radiance. My name is Bran. May I have this dance?"

She laughed out loud, it was the most ridiculous thing she had ever heard, but she consented to a dance, all the while thinking this man was far too pale for her to ever fall in love with. They had one dance, and another, and another, and as the night wore on she decided that she liked his pale skin and his freckles, they suited his hair. He was exotic and the more she looked into his eyes the more she wanted to look into his eyes. By the end of the night she decided she loved him.

He asked if he could see her again and she said yes. They carried on a secret courtship, and she snuck out at night to see him. His Spanish was perfect and they talked for hours under the stars. He was Welsh and an artist. He survived a stint in the army during the First World War. When he returned home Wales was poor and becoming poorer, and he saw the writing on the wall. His friends worked in coalmines and even those jobs were disappearing. He wanted to paint something other than seascapes, and he would never sell enough paintings in Wales to support himself. Paris was devastated, Europe was broken, but he wanted to meet up again

---

[*] Pronounced - Brawn

244

with artists he had met in France after the war. They were fleeing Europe in droves then, the artists and anarchists and writers and radicals and most especially the poets and the painters, they all came to Mexico D.F., and when he arrived Bran found that they came not just from France and Spain, but from all over America and South America, and Bran was happy in this happening, dirt cheap city, with smart people, mucho sunshine, a new language, new ideas, and now, a new girlfriend.

Then her parents found out.

And things became dire. They locked her in her room. He called on her and her father cursed him and threatened him with a gun. She was a good catholic girl, and he was a protestant, and neither of them cared, but her parents did. So she snuck out for the last time. They knew they couldn't stay. Her family would find her, or call the police, or involve the church; they would never have peace. Bran knew a man, an oilman who had bought one of his paintings. He could get a job with him, so they went to Long Beach, to California, and there they were married and made their home. Eventually they moved to San Diego and left Mexico and oil behind.

It was a wonderful love story, and when she was done telling it she made a crack in Spanish that made Rosa roar with laughter. Wren blushed and put her hand to her face. "Abuelita!" she admonished her grandmother, who just roared along with Rosa.

"What?" I asked. "What did she say?"

"Don't tell him," Wren said

"She...ha she..." Rosa wiped the tears from her eyes, she was laughing so hard she couldn't speak, but finally she composed herself enough to say it, "She say, 'Wren has his eyes and you have his hair, so you should make little babies that look like him!'" She cracked up again. Wren hid her face, but I could see her blushing. I should have blushed to, maybe I did. I laughed along with Rosa. I couldn't help that, how else could I react? But I didn't feel the heat in my mouth. I didn't taste the embarrassment. All I tasted was Wren, and she was delicious.

The evening campaign was shock and charm. Only the charm was intentional, the shock was the molé, and I could not get over it. Nonetheless my charm strategy was excellent; unfailing politeness and genuine interest can charm even those whom you can't understand. Abuelita went to bed early, but not until after she pinched my cheeks and gave me a kiss. I wanted to ask Rosa about Wren's dad, but I thought it might be a sore subject since there was no evidence of his existence anywhere in the house. Besides, it might have invited questions about my dad, and the best answer I could give without lying would be a terse, 'he's dead,' and that tends to be a downer. So instead I complemented Rosa's art and her cooking, and soon it was time to go. Rosa gave me a warm hug at the door and told me to come back soon. She assaulted Wren with kisses and begged her to come by more often. Wren promised she would and we were on our way.

Guessing Games, Family Trees and Math Problems

I started up singing as soon as we headed out of the neighborhood, "Your mom likes me. Your mom likes me."

"Yes," she said. "I was surprised. You made a very good first impression. Unlike with me."

"Oh don't be grumpy. Just because your grandma wants you to have my babies."

"Shut up."

She was serious, so I backed off. "Oh come on I'm just teasing. You should probably be able to call me your boyfriend before we get you knocked up." She frowned and turned up the radio. We cruised up the 5 then headed east on the 8.

"So what's up with your dad?" I asked.

"Excuse me?"

"Come on. We didn't go to your cousin's just to get weed. You wanted me to see."

"I don't know what you're talking about."

"How exactly are you Hawaiian? It must be on your dad's side. And is your last name Morgan? Or is it Hawaiian? What is it?"

"You sure have a lot of questions."

Come to think of it, I did. I'd been stewing on them all day without knowing it. There was so much going on. "I think you want me to ask these questions. I think that's why we've been driving all over San Diego County. But you could have just told me."

"I like you Riley. So if you want to ask me questions go ahead. But if you want me to answer your questions then you have to answer one of mine."

"Okay."

"How'd you get hurt?"

"Wren, I don't talk about it. If I talk about it I remember it and if I remember it I relive it. Besides it really doesn't matter."

"It matters to me. You're right, okay? I've been driving around showing you branches on my convoluted family tree. It seemed easier than trying to explain it. Besides, if I did it wouldn't have meant anything. It would have been a list of facts. Meeting some people gives some context, so you can start to understand what it means to be a Welsh-Mexican-Japanese-Hawaiian-American."

"Japanese?" That explained the eye shape.

"Tell me about your injuries. I want to know what happened. I want to know why you stopped surfing.

"Fine. I will. But you go first."

"My last name is Keawe. But it used to be Morgan. Before that it was Keawe."

"What?"

"My mom changed my name when I was four, along with hers."

"Why?"

"I'm getting to it. Let me explain, okay? This is gonna take a minute."

"Sorry."

"I was born Wren 'Iolani Morgan Keawe. I was named for both of my grandfathers: Abuelo and Tutukane.

"I thought your Abuelo's name was Bran?"

"It was. Let me talk. 'Bran' is the Welsh word for Raven. Wren and 'Iolani are both bird names, Wren was a bird in Abuelo's new country, an American bird, and an American name. 'Iolani means 'bird of heaven' in Hawaiian and honored my father's side of the family, as did 'Keawe' which was his last name.

"Now, my dad's dad, Ka'aumoana Keawe, my Tutukane, was full-blooded Hawaiian. He was married to a Hawaiian woman, Ano, Mak's Tutu. But, he had an affair with my Tutu, Fujiko."

"Wow. That's one hell of a family history."

"Oh it gets better. Fujiko, my Tutu, she was half-Japanese, half-Hawaiian. Her dad, my great-grandfather, Suzuki Hideki, came from Japan to the Big Island to work on the sugar plantation. Eventually he married a Hawaiian woman, my great-grandmother, Mamo, and so my Tutu was born on Hawaii. From the affair between my Tutu and my Tutukane, my dad, Suzuki Holokai Keawe was born. It was a big scandal, but Tutukane was a good man, and even though the scandal shamed him, he always cared for his families, both of them."

"Hold up, let me see if I can get this. Your dad's dad was Japanese, no wait, your dad's dad was Hawaiian but his mom was half-Japanese half-Hawaiian. That makes him half-Hawaiian, no a quarter… wait, half-Japanese…but…"

"You're terrible at math. It's really not hard, third-grade fractions. My dad was three-quarters Hawaiian, one-quarter Japanese, my mom is half-Mexican, half-Welsh, which makes me one-quarter Welsh, one-quarter Mexican, three-eighths Hawaiian, and one-eighth Japanese."

I laughed. "Yeah it would've taken me an hour to get there. So your ancestry is more Hawaiian than anything?"

"Yeah by blood, but I was raised in California in a Mexican neighborhood."

"So do you consider yourself Hawaiian?"

"I consider myself an artist. But I do care about my Hawaiian roots. That's why I took back the name Keawe. My mom changed both our names to Morgan when my dad left. I changed it back when I turned eighteen."

"Wow. I'm sorry."

"Don't be. I'm not."

"So did you know your dad at all?"

"Not really. He was a fisherman like Tutukane. He would be gone for weeks at a time, one time he left for Seattle and he never came back. He sent an envelope with some money and a note that said he met someone else and wasn't coming home. I haven't talked to him since. Tutukane was still alive then, he was furious. He disowned my dad. Imagine after all those years with my dad a living reminder of that scandal, and then my dad runs out on his legitimate family. I was too young to understand then, but now I think it may have been what killed him."

"So after your dad left and Tutukane died what connection did you have to Hawaii?"

"I went to Hawaii every summer and stayed with my Tutu, and after she died I would stay with my Aunties, that's Mak's side of the family."

"So, your grandma was like, the other woman to that side of the family, but they treated you like family and let you stay summer's with them?"

"I think Tutukane made them promise. It's not something anyone talked about. My Tutu wasn't welcome of course, but I was still ohana. Plus I usually stayed with Mak's parents, they weren't prejudiced."

"Why not?"

"Because my Auntie Carrie is white. That's why Mak's hapa. By the way you shouldn't think all my family is like Mak."

"I don't."

"Good. He's the only one selling dope and guns. Speaking of which, there's a pipe in my purse. You should pack a bowl. Anyways, I only took you there because he's the only one on the mainland from that side of the family. My Tutukane wasn't like him at all. He was the nicest man. Big and strong, always laughing, I remember he used to give me mochi when I was a little girl. I still love the stuff. I miss him. I barely knew my dad, so I don't miss him at all, but I miss Tutukane."

Painful Memories

We pulled off the 8 in Jacumba, a tiny town on the U.S.-Mexico border. "We going hot tubbing?" I joked and passed the lit pipe to Wren.

"Oh, you know your local history.[*] But no," she said while half holding her breath and exhaled a cloud of smoke. "You'll see where we're going. And then you'll tell me your story. Don't think I forgot."

We drove southeast toward the border and the town, and then turned onto a paved but poorly maintained road called Old Highway 80. We passed under a set of large power lines and turned onto a dirt road. The road became bumpier and after another turn Wren dropped the Jeep into four-wheel drive. The trail, it ceased to be a road, was muddy from the day's rain and Wren used the high beams and caution as she navigated an incline with slippery rocks. The only signs of civilization were two large microwave towers we passed on our right. Soon the outlines of Jacumba Peak and Table Mountain could be made out in the near distance, and then we descended between them into a valley. I watched in silence, ignoring the anxious pressure at the thought of describing my injury, and glad for the dulling sensation of the weed. The pale efforts of the crescent moon illuminated only silhouettes in the desert valley. We took the left side of a fork in the trail and the high beams soon revealed our destination, a cluster of large lumps growing from the earth. As we came closer the lumps took greater form and revealed themselves as giant boulders. We drove into the cluster and turned off in a flat spot nestled between three of the largest rocks.

"Here we are," said Wren. "A nice private spot to watch the stars. You stay put." She hopped out to roll down the Jeep's soft cover. The rain clouds had cleared and the desert skyscape was clear and bright with stars. I could hear a soft trickle of running water nearby. "I've never been here when there was water in the creek," Wren called out from behind the Jeep."

"Have you been here often?"

---

[*] There is a natural hot springs here and in the 30's and 40's the Hotel Jacumba, with its public mineral baths, was popular with the celebrity set. Jacumba exists now as a cultural footnote and sleepy desert town.

"A few times." She hopped back into the front seat. "I think you owe me an answer."

"Wren we're having a good time. Why spoil it? You don't want to hear about it, trust me. It isn't a happy memory."

"You mean like my happy memory about my father's illegitimacy and how he ran out on me and my mom? I thought we were getting to know each other."

I sighed. "And you really want to know this? It's not just sad, it's gross." She nodded. "Okay. Let's smoke another bowl first." We did. And then I told her the story of how I got hurt, a story so painful no amount of weed could dull it completely:

When my dad died, his entire interest in Sparx Surfboards was transferred to me. Zak Beshev owned the other half and decisions needed to be made, decisions that I wasn't making. The factory had stopped producing boards, for one, and we either needed to start back up, or find a new location. I couldn't do either and Zak couldn't do anything without my consent. He was in a pickle and I was the jar.

To say I was grieving for my dad wouldn't be true. They say there are five stages of grief: denial, anger, bargaining, depression and acceptance. This might have been true when my mom died. I couldn't really tell. I went back to chasing waves right away. I just pretended it didn't happen and threw myself into the life. Maybe that was denial, and maybe I went straight from denial of that loss to the undeniable reality of my dad's death. For him my grieving process had one stage: rage.

The horrible flavor of rancid meat was like a ghost from my adolescence returned to haunt me. It lingered and hung about sometimes fading but never disappearing. It conjured memories of days best forgotten, when my father stood between my birthright and me. Now my father was ash on the water and I grasped my birthright by the rails.

Zak decided I needed to get away to clear my head so I could focus on the day-to-day aspects of running the business. So I went with Nehud for a three-week trip to Costa Rica to surf, relax, check out the rainforest, and shoot some much needed promo-footage. While I was gone Zak would look for an alternate location for shaping. This seemed best given the macabre incident in the old building.

We stayed near Puerto Viejo on the Caribbean side. Puerto Viejo is not typical of the rest of Costa Rica. It has a substantial Jamaican population and if you hang around town for a minute a ganja solicitation is inevitable. We came in the midst of the winter swells and the reef break at Salsa Brava, the heaviest wave in Costa Rica, was producing consistent tubes.

I would argue I was living as healthy a lifestyle as was possible at that time. I would surf sober in the morning to taste the bright sour rush of the powerful waves and remind myself I was still alive. Then I would return to our accommodations, a fancy home we rented from a French ex-pat, and spend the rest of the day lounging on the balcony watching the ocean and obliterating my senses with marijuana and Red Stripes.

Nehud was supportive at first. He kept the photographer and videographer at a distance and sent them back to the States after a week. We sat and smoked, sometimes talking, usually not. He tried to give me my space and be there for me. He was a good friend, but I was too caught up in my rage to notice that Nehud was going stir crazy. So on the last day of March, five months after my dad's death, we threw a party.

More accurately, Nehud threw a party. It was an orange day on my left hand side. Nehud left me at the house to go pick up some beers and returned with twenty heads, most of them tourists and a couple of locals. There was music and bud and girls and beer and cocaine…lots of it. At first I wanted no part of it, I was busy chewing my rage and smoking my weed and I sat on the balcony by myself. Then Nehud brought a couple of girls out, surfer chicks with grey names, I remember they both had grey names Melissa or Miley or something, and this local cat they called Polvo. He pulled out a bag of white and started cutting lines on the glass tabletop. Then the party started.

The rush I got from the coke was like dropping in on a wave. Only I didn't have to wait in the water for the coke. Just one hard sniff set me flying down the tangy face of exhilaration, the emotion I'd spent my whole life chasing.

But that was just the sweet and sour starter's pistol.

The music sounded good and the girls got prettier. Went from lemonade to cinnamon, as I got wittier. I grinned vanilla. I spy-eyed spice, as bikini tops and bottoms bounced through the night. I laughed blueberry jam and sang sugar serenades. I jumped and skipped and danced, and when it started to fade I took another bump and started up the lemonade.

I bade two pretty babes to skinny dip in the ocean knowing cocaine and vodka's a potent love potion. My face went numb and my confidence rose like a peppermint steamer with a hint of fresh clove. But the salt in the ocean was sadness and tears, and thoughts of cold death crept in with the fear. A kick to my stomach. The 'k' in his name. A foul shade of green and white-hot shame. Gritty self-pity dug up with a spade, 'fore I took another bump and started up the lemonade.

Crisis averted. I thought with a grin. Though my face couldn't feel it, my nose or my chin. Not dumb just numb just a cinnamon stain—and a peppermint twist, I was running my game. "Hey what's your name? Come sit on my leg." Spicy and dicey the party had changed when I took another bump and started up the lemonade.

She was cute and hot and smooth and caught. Then her friend took a hit of this coke I just bought. And for the first time in months and three thousand miles a saffron strand slipped into my smile. Felt joy like a child. I'd keep it the same. So we all took a bump and started up the lemonade.

I waded in the shallows. Depth held the pain. So I took another bump and started up the lemonade.

The party was a crutch. It presaged my cane. I took another bump and started up the lemonade.

I took another bump and started up the lemonade.

And another, and another, and another...

When I started to come down I smoked myself into a stupor. It wasn't hard. I was exhausted. See, the coke did the exact opposite of what the weed did, it didn't dull my synesthesias, it amplified them, but it also put me on a pleasure track. So as long as I didn't let my mind go to the anxiety and the rage and the sadness, I was okay, flying high, riding the rush, long-lined out on a perpetual upswing. But the second we ran out of white, I ripped bowl after bowl and the pendulum swung back so hard it knocked me flat.

I woke up naked the next morning in-between two grey-named girls.[*] For the first time since my father's death I didn't wake up with the foul taste of rotted meat on my tongue. My mouth was dry, but other than that

---

[*] When I told this story to Wren I may have left out certain details, like this one. There is a difference between honesty and tactlessness. It also rhymed less.

I didn't taste anything. Dopamine-dumped I felt disoriented, out of place; sometime during the night I missed the change from orange days to green days, and when I woke up the day was a colorless, placeless void. I smoked a bowl, more out of habit that anything else, and I went to the bathroom to take a shower in the hopes that it would wake me up.

The bathroom was well appointed, all be it in a European style, tiled in provincial French colors with a bidet next to the toilet. The highlight of the bathroom was the glass-enclosed steam shower. I turned on the shower then pressed the button for steam. I looked myself over in the mirror while I waited for the steam to build. My hair was shaggy and I looked a bit haggard from the night before and the last few months of agony, but I was fit and young and handsome. I will never forget how I looked that morning. The shower produced a tremendous amount of steam, and soon my reflection fogged over.

I opened the shower door. Steam billowed out so profusely that I couldn't see the other side of the shower. I reached my hand in to test the water. I distinctly remember doing this. It felt fine and I stepped in. The showerhead was angled down and slightly away from me. I wet the left side of my body first, purely by chance, splashed some water across my chest then turned to get my back.

I looked down and saw black wriggling worms across the entirety of my chest. My first thought was that it was some sort of cocaine-induced hallucination, I'd heard of something similar happening to Sigmund Freud. Then I realized those black worms were not worms at all, but hairs melted to my skin atop the blisters rising on my chest. I looked in horror at my left shoulder. It was red and raw. The water continued to pour over it from the back, but my shoulder was not blistered. Instead tissue sloughed off it like a molting snake then peeled away in strips and clumps.

I opened the door and dove from the shower. I lay naked on the floor and screamed for help. My chest trembled. I felt it microflexing, tensing and releasing like the muscles were seizing. My breath was fast and shallow. I looked at the hideous blisters forming on my chest, growing right before my eyes, and I knew I should be in pain, horrible pain, but I felt nothing. I tasted nothing. I knew my life was in danger but I didn't taste the cold wash of fear.

I looked at my left shoulder and nearly vomited. It was burned to the bone. I was scalded across my chest and back, and from my shoulder to my thigh on my left side, but I didn't taste even the faintest hint of rosewater. That was almost as frightening as the sight of my burns.

Nehud reached the bathroom at the same time as one of the grey-named girls. He looked on in shock frozen in his tracks. The grey-named girl shrieked and ran off.

"Call 9-1-1," I begged him. He sprinted away and returned with a phone. In retrospect I was terribly lucky that Costa Rica uses 9-1-1 as it's emergency number just like the U.S. Nehud got an operator and handed the phone to Polvo who had stayed the night. He informed the operator of the situation and relayed instructions to Nehud. "Agua fria, uh, uh…how you say…cold water! Cool him down. Pero, no hielo."

"What?" Nehud shouted as he started splashing water on me from the sink.

"No hielo…ice. No ice." Polvo handed him the phone. "Estoy dejando. Lo siento, pero no quiero estar aqui cuando llegue a la policía." He dashed out.

Nehud didn't speak Spanish but he understood policía. "Shit!" He called for help but everyone else was busy running out of the house. God only knew what paraphernalia was lying around. To his credit, Nehud stayed with me. Despite how things would turn out later I always credited him as a good person and a true friend. He continued to pour handfuls of cool water on me, then seeing it was futile he ran to the kitchen came back with a glass and continued to cool me down pouring glassfuls of water on me.

All of a sudden a frigid wave of roses washed over my tongue and I felt like I was lying in a frying pan as the most intense pain I have ever felt racked my entire body. Nehud was still pouring water on me when I blacked out.

An Evening in the Desert

Wren was silent when I finished telling her.

"Don't," I said when I saw the look in her eyes. "Don't say it."

"Say what?"

"I'm sorry. That's what everyone says when they hear. I'm sorry. That's why I don't talk about it. There's nothing you can say, *I'm* sorry, but I can't change it."

"I wasn't going to say that. I was just thinking that I can't even imagine how much that must've hurt."

"A lot. But the worst part wasn't the pain, it was everything else I lost."

"Surfing?"

"Surfing, hiking, walking without a limp, two years of my life, the company, everything."

"Everything but your life."

"Whatever that's worth." I immediately felt embarrassed. "Sorry. It felt like everything then, sometimes it still does." I could feel the pressure in my chest and the faint sweetness of overripe fruit, but there was salt too. I felt like I might cry. I was glad to be high. Otherwise I couldn't have held it together.

"So that's how you lost the company?"

I nodded. "I sold it to Zak. My medical bills were insane. Skin grafts, hospital care, flown out of Costa Rica. I retired the Sparx name, got the suicide factory, and that was it. Zak got every asset worth a lick and I got my bills paid." I looked at her and I couldn't see it in her eyes, the pity. Not that she was callous, just not pitying. I was glad. I didn't want her pity, especially not today. There was some other expression on her face. She looked, *curious?* Serious definitely, and paler, but that could have been the dim light from the moon. No, definitely curious. "Something you want to ask, Wren? Now's your chance."

"You burned your left side? I thought your right leg was the bad one?"

"It is. I woke up two weeks later in the burn unit at Parkland Memorial in Houston. I had been in a medically induced coma because they thought the pain would be overwhelming. I had third degree burns over sixty percent of my body. Doctors said it was the worst scald they'd ever seen, they couldn't believe I did it in the shower. They estimated the water temperature at least 190 degrees, but the lawyers tested the house, and never got a reading over 170. I was the only one who knew why. It was because I stood in the water for at least thirty seconds. Doctors figured it was more like two."

"So what happened to your right leg?"

"They used skin from my right leg to graft my shoulder. When I woke up the graft was already in place."

"Shouldn't that heal?"

"Yeah, but the doctors kept expanding the donor sites, I wound up getting six grafts in total."

"Oh my God! Where did they get all that skin?"

"From my right leg, mostly my buttocks and thigh, some came from my right side, stomach and back. They didn't actually take enough skin to cover sixty percent of my body, more like twenty, and the grafts weren't all at the same time. I was in the burn unit for six months. It was the second time they took skin from my thigh that it got infected. That's what did the worst damage."

"The infection?"

"Yeah. It got into the bone, my hip socket, the muscles too. It nearly killed me."

"I'm glad you're alive."

"Me too." *At least when I'm with you*, I thought but didn't add. "But that's why I walk with a limp. Bum hip. I'll need a replacement before I'm fifty, if they can do one. If the degenerative changes in the socket are too bad I'll probably wind up in a wheelchair. Other than that I healed up pretty good, scarred to shit, but healed. My shoulder doesn't move too well, but..." I trailed off. There was nothing more to add, just more woe, and the last thing I wanted was a pity party.

"You said there was a lawyer." She asked. "But you still had to sell?"

"Yeah the lawsuit kinda fizzled. They have this doctrine called contributory negligence. I guess we have it here too, in some states. Anyway, if the judge decided the accident was more my fault than the guy who owned the house then I wouldn't get anything." I laughed, "I had enough coke, weed and booze in me to kill a soccer team, and my lawyer wanted $30,000 U.S. for a retainer. I let it go and sold out. Truth is, I probably would've sold anyway. I couldn't keep the brand, *his* brand."

"Riley?"

"Yeah."

She put her hand on my arm and I tensed. It was an unconscious reaction. A rare wild bird had flitted down rested on my arm and I was scared to move lest I spook her. "I'm sorry," she said.

"Thanks," I said, and I meant it. It didn't feel like pity coming from her. "Happy memories huh?"

"Oh yeah," she said with a sarcastic laugh. Then she added in a more serious tone, "I'm glad we did this."

"Did what?"

"You know, had this talk, met each other's families. I feel like I know you better now."

"You know you're the first person I've ever told about what happened?"

"Wow. I'm honored."

"Well it's not like I took you to meet my parents." It was a morbid joke, and a bad one at that. There was a pause. The silence ate at me. I had to fill it. "So now that we've seen each other's childhood homes, does that make us boyfriend and girlfriend?"

Wren sighed and took her hand off my arm. "Riley I like you."

"Riley I like you but…?"

"But let's not put a label on this. Let's just live it. If we give it a label that makes it abstract, and you know how I feel about abstraction."

"No fair. I call shenanigans. And semantics."

"You think that's no fair. How about this?" She grabbed my shoulder and threw her left leg across the Jeep, straddling me in the passenger seat. She reached past my right arm, pulled the lever and the seat dropped back flat. She kissed me deeply. Molé picante and saffron competed for attention. She bit my bottom lip and my hands slid reflexively up her sides along the taut lines of her abdomen and the protrusion of her ribs. She bit harder into my lip and I groped at her breasts caught up in the passion and joy and molé. She responded to my hands, pulling my hair and pressing her slim hips down into my waist. She wanted it. I squeezed harder. She arched her back and moaned, the tight lines of her dress revealing every aspect of her lithe torso.

Somehow in the midst of that, a bit of bitter aromatic crossed my palette and a thought crossed my mind. "You've had this planned for a minute."

"Shut up," she said arching back even further.

"Your mom said molé takes two days to make."

She sat up straight, still straddling me. I'm an idiot. "Are you seriously talking about my mom right now?" I know. I'm an idiot.

"You must've let her know you were coming at least three days ago."

"Oh my *God*!" she said with a sprite-like grin. "Yes. I planned to seduce you in the desert and steal your virtue." She raised her hips and hiked her dress up over her thighs. She pulled my hand from her breast and shoved it between her legs. "Is it working?"

In that instant I felt like I was in a fairy tale. The dialogue was all wrong, but Wren just looked, I don't know, mischievous, like a nymph or a fairy. Her eyes sparkled in the moonlight. It felt like she possessed some magic, something I couldn't possibly resist, not that I wanted to, and of course she did have something magical.

I slid my finger gently inside her conscious of my hands again. My grasp on her breast became lighter. Wren rolled her eyes in response to a second finger and a gentle stroke from my thumb and I shuddered together with her at the touch. It had been so long. Molé and saffron and chipotle fire danced a step more complex than a tango and hotter than a lambada. Her eyes locked on mine, full of shine and desire. She pulled away from my hand and reached for my belt.

I flinched and pushed her hand away. "What?" Wren asked, her sorceress-stare suddenly shocked and confused.

"It's just... I haven't..."

A look of recognition passed over her face. "Ohhh. Not since your accident?" She took my non-response as a yes. "Wow. Well, it still works right?" She pressed her hand hard into my groin and raised a seductive eyebrow. "It feels like it works."

"Yeah... it's just..."

"What Riley? Don't you want to?"

"Yeah but... the accident..."

Now she understood. "Oh." She shoved my shoulders back onto the seat and kissed me. She pressed her breasts against my chest and put my hand back to her thigh. She continued kissing me as she undid my belt.

Then she sat up and wriggled her shoulders as she slid my pants down. I was nervous, the anxiety seeming to press up from the seat behind me, but I let her pull them over my thighs and under her knees. She reached down and grasped me firmly in her hand. She rubbed her thumb over the lumps and raised lines I knew were there. "Mmm," she moaned and then she leaned down over me and whispered in my ear, "If it makes you feel better, they all look ugly, even when they're not scarred." I laughed out loud and my anxiety fell to floor of the Jeep. Molé, saffron and red-hot lust jockeyed for position in my mouth as she slid me inside of her.

We made love in the passenger seat of the Jeep.[*] Twice. She was on top both times, primarily for logistical reasons, but also because of my body image issues. Vanity is cinnamon. It's just pride in your appearance and I strove to keep mine in tact.

I watched her dance naked in the moonlight amidst boulders thrice her height and I was transported to a more primitive time where I was man and she was woman, Adam and Eve, Riley and Wren. Only this does not do her justice, nor does my prior description of her as a nymph or fairy. She was a goddess. Her willowy frame lithe and free as she pranced and twirled, she moved with the careless ease of a feather on the wind, perfectly wild and perfectly proportioned and perfectly feminine, perfect. I was saffron and sugar and molé, sitting on the hood of that Jeep basking in the dim light of the crescent moon and the afterglow of our consummated love, watching my perfect storybook creature, this goddess, this myth, dance. She danced for me and for her and for the moon and the boulders. It was the happiest moment of my life. Which is to say that it was all downhill from there.

We sat together in the Jeep, holding hands, looking at the stars, and watched the night pass with the slowly turning sky. "So Wren, there's something that's been on my mind." I'd had a thought on my mind for the

---

[*] Dear Reader, you may object that to have 'made love' in the front seat of a Jeep is an impossibility, and that any such activity which occurs in the front seat of a Jeep is properly described through the use of some other carnal verb. However, I assure you that you can make love in a Jeep, as this is what I did with Wren on the night in question. Whether she felt that we 'made love' or would have used another verb to describe it is another question entirely, and one that I cannot answer with certainty. Suffice it to say that my remembrance of the event is a fond one, and that I felt, and still feel that I made love to her.

past few hours, but I hadn't wanted to spoil an instant of the evening with thoughts of the future.

"Yeah."

"Were you wearing panties at dinner?" That wasn't really the thought.

"Oh my God!" She smacked me on my bad shoulder, which actually hurt a bit. "Yes. What kind of girl do you think I am?"

"The kind that seduces cripples in the desert, never wears a bra, and putters around panty-less on a pink Vespa."

"Ha. Three out of four ain't bad."

We sat there for another minute before I finally broke the silence. "So are we going back?"

"Back where?"

"El Rancho."

"Yeah of course."

"I mean I know we have to return the Jeep. I just didn't know if we were going back to stay, or if we were going to do something else."

"Why wouldn't we stay?"

"I don't know, because it's weird and Colin is... Shit Colin isn't crazy, but he's something. I can't explain exactly. I just don't like him. He's creepy."

"We're going back." Her voice was like a flat hand slapped down on a desktop. "What do you think happened today? You think we had sex so everything's changed?"

"I thought since you took me to see your family that things between us—"

"Exactly!" Everything went hot and pasty on me. "I took you to see my family. What didn't you get? You saw my mom's living room. I told you, that's not going to be me. She worked her ass off so I could become an artist. That's why I'm at the Rancho. You can think what you want about Colin. He might be a creep, but he's dialed-in to the art world. He has money, resources, access, and we're making incredible art at El Rancho. So yes. We *are* going back."

My mouth went dry with disappointment, but I also felt very small and very hot, though perhaps not as hot as the cinders smoldering in Wren's eyes. "I'm sorry." I slapped myself in the forehead feeling foolish

262

and insensitive on top of everything else. "I never even asked you about Portland. How'd it go? Did you sell any pieces?"

Wren relaxed a little. "It went good. Thank you for asking. I didn't sell anything yet."

"Yet?"

"We're supposed to go back in two weeks, Colin and me. I think I'm going to get a showcase in this little gallery in the Pearl, nothing huge, but I might get some exposure. Plus, I think Colin convinced the owner to let me show it my way, with the music that corresponds to the piece playing as part of the exhibit."

"That's great." I forced myself to smile despite my dry mouth and the steadily increasing pressure on my spine. The thought of Colin and Wren together in Portland made my stomach ache and added an earthy rot to my mouth.

"Yeah," Wren said, clearly excited, "we must've met a dozen artists and gone to fifteen different galleries when we were there. You should have seen Colin running around the Pearl in his yellow suit, talking me up to gallery owners and trying to interest collectors."

I gagged. The taste of mushrooms so powerful and earthy it was like chewing a mouthful of woodland soil. I knew where I'd seen Colin before. "That son of a bitch!"

"Who? Colin? He tried really hard to sell my work."

"He wore yellow to my mother's funeral."

Puppet Show

It was nearly midnight when we arrived at El Rancho. Ndukwe awaited us. "Where have you been? This is not yours to take." So Wren had stolen it. But I didn't care. I charged past him into the courtyard as fast as my cane could take me. "Where do you think you are going?" he shouted at me and then turned back to Wren, "How dare you take the Jeep! You cannot leave!" He seemed torn as to whether he should follow me or yell at Wren and I had no intention of helping him figure it out. I headed straight for Colin's wing, the bile boiling in my throat. Ndukwe saw and called after me, "Hey! You cannot go there." I paid him no heed and continued on. The door to the Jeep slammed behind me and Wren told Ndukwe to fuck off.

As I reached Colin's door I heard Ndukwe's footfalls coming up quickly behind me. He decided to chase me, which was fine, it meant he wasn't bothering Wren. "You cannot go in there." I'd spent the whole ride back stewing. I wanted an explanation and I was going to get one. I yanked open one of the heavy double-doors and my cholic mood momentarily switched to utter blandness.

Colin stood atop a platform raised a dozen feet above a wooden puppeteer's stage and handled two control bars with five strings each. Below him, on stage, Daphne, nude and painted blue, whirled about with the jerking maneuverings of a marionette. Each joint bore black line markings giving her the appearance of a life-size wooden puppet. The strings attached to her at each shoulder, wrist, elbow, knee, and ankle and as Colin pulled and shifted the strings Daphne emphasized the movement at each joint.

Cameras were mounted on tripods in four locations around the huge room. Each captured a different perspective and Taggart worked a fifth, hand held camera from a low angle. At present Daphne whirled and twirled to a discordant piece of electronica with black and white ribbons grasped in each hand to create a flowing train of streamers, but judging from the props and the low mattress on stage, she had been performing simulated sex acts.

Perhaps on another day I would have been too aroused or too shocked to interrupt. "Colin! We need to talk. Now!"

"What the hell!" Taggart and Daphne exclaimed in chorus.

Colin kept his composure. "No, no. It's okay." He climbed down from his platform. "We got enough. Taggart you're up with Daphne in the next scene anyway. Take five. Taggart go get Midas so he can film the next segment. Daphne you're doing great. Get some water." He pinched her butt. "And stay stretched out." Daphne glared at me and strutted out the door without a hint of modesty. As she left I noticed her tramp stamp, that same 'CK' I'd seen on Erin's back. The green from the 'K' practically jumped off her back it irritated me so much. I turned that irritation on Colin.

"You owe me an explanation you son of a bitch!"

Ndukwe grabbed me by my shoulder. "I'm sorry," he said to Colin, "I'll throw him out."

"No. It's not a problem." Ndukwe let go but stood there like he wasn't reassured. "It's okay," Colin said, and then added in his most condescending voice, "I'll talk to Riley. He seems upset."

I didn't know where to begin. So I just blurted it out, "You wore yellow to my mother's funeral!"

"Oh good!" He rubbed his hands together as if he'd been anticipating this moment. "You remembered. See I was telling the truth. I told you you'd already seen some of my art."

"Why wear yellow? And why were you even there? You didn't know my mom."

"You say that with such certainty." He flashed a toothy, knowing grin that caused more bile to build on my palette offset by paste and herbs. "I was there as a favor. And as a performance."

"A favor to who?"

"Not revealing their identity is part of the favor. The performance was my own idea. Can you guess the subject?"

"A performance? At a funeral?"

"I admit it's a bit macabre. But I did provide the only splash of color. Besides art has no limits, no taboos, just points of view."

"Bright suits at funerals. You think that passes for art?"

Colin waved his hands out at the room, palms up. "I'm a performance artist. The world is my stage. But you tell me Riley, what counts?"

"How did you know my mom?"

"Oh there are many answers to that question. Professionally. Intimately. Not at all. But the best answer I can give is that I knew her through a man named Mortimer Kane."

I had never heard that name before in my life. "Who the hell is Mortimer Kane?"

"That is another question with many answers." Colin turned his back to me and walked across the room with patient and deliberate steps that echoed eerily and sent a wash of fear through me. He pulled a thick binder from a bookcase near his bed and turned to me with a sinister smile and an air of revelation, "You won't find this in the library." He patted the binder, "Some of the answers are in here. You should read it. I'll lend it to you okay?"

"That's some heavy reading."

"He was a complicated man. I don't know what you want to know about him, but I'm betting it's in here. I'm also betting that there's things in here you don't want to know. You know how I got this place? El Rancho?"

"You said you inherited."

"In a manner of speaking. I was a televangelist."

"You don't strike me as the religious type."

"Not anymore. But I've always been an actor. Preaching is really just performance art. You've got to connect with your audience in a way they can relate to. If you make them like you, they'll believe you. If they like your show they'll buy a ticket. I sold a lot of tickets. The real trick is convincing them that God's the executive producer. You'd be amazed how much money people are willing to part with if God's involved."

"What's that got to do with this Mortimer Kane?"

"Or the price of butter?" Colin shrugged, still wearing that smug smile. "Morty was complicated. You've really got to do the reading."

"How'd he know my mom?"

Daphne and Taggart returned along with Midas and Ndukwe. "I'm afraid I have to get back to work Riley." He clapped his hands together. "All right next scene! Time to see if Giuseppe's puppet is a real girl."

I didn't leave. "You owe me some answers." My voice was firm, more confident than I really felt. I was coming to understand that Colin didn't respect weakness.

266

Colin's smile disappeared. His eyes narrowed, the left one, as always, lower and more sharply narrowed than the right. He marched at me and raised a finger, "I don't owe you anything." Cold wet tin overwhelmed all bile and paste, and I fought the urge to raise my cane in defense.

And then his smile was back. Instant transformation. It was scarier than the way he had stalked at me. "I'm glad you're curious. So I'll give you the cliffnotes version. He was a scientist. He was a pastor. He lived here. He died here. He's buried here. He knew me. He knew your mom. He knew of you but he never met you. He was a genius. He was my father. Now get out. I have to get to work."

Morty's Journal

It was a diary. I never kept a diary. I kept secrets. But Dr. Mortimer Kane or Rev. Mortimer Kane kept secrets in a diary. The hard part was determining what secrets were about my mother. I stayed up past sunrise the night Colin gave it to me searching with no success for any mention of Rainbow Sparx.

There were some dated entries, but it wasn't organized by date. It wasn't organized at all. Some pages read like alchemical grocery lists:

6/16/68

Pigeon Turds	Wasp Venom
Coffee	Candy
Bleach	Carrots
Aspirin	Cabbage
Milk	Cribbage
Underwear	Scorpion Stingers
Gold Leaf	Cactus Paddles
Gunpowder	Dragonflies
Sunshine	Tube Socks

Sporadic entries read more like a journal:

4/23/71

Today I treated one of our patients for narcolepsy with my own special stimulant concoction. It was a great success. I expect she will not sleep for several days. I spent the afternoon working on Sunday's Sermon. While the Sermon was not a great success I did come up with a fantastic new chili recipe, which I will try out soon. Carrie brought me both lunch and dinner and seemed most happy that I spared some time for her. Little Colin gives her a terrible time it seems and she doesn't get much alone time. I told her I'd see what I could do, but that I was very busy and my work very important. She's a terrible cook, but beggars can't be choosers and I was far too busy to cook as I expect I will be working through the night on Project Nimbus.

There were multiple references to Project Nimbus, but no explanation as to what it was. Other entries read like case studies, patient initials given followed by summaries of psych-evaluations from an asylum, with references to forcible restraint, chills, shivers, hearing voices, mania, suicidal tendencies, and detailed records of what drugs were given, measured in grams, and what therapies were administered, talk, pharmacological, and so on, and then lists of acronyms I didn't know like EST, and SRT, and FSS.

There were Sermons, some dated, some not. There were recipes for soups and stews and stir-frys. There were diagrams and instructions and scraps of ideas for inventions of all types: new mining apparatuses, raptor traps, a proposed method for extracting methane from cow dung, a drug to cancel the effects of birth control administered in powder form so it could be surreptitiously placed in food, two-sets of deep ocean dive suits that looked truly futuristic, and most interestingly to me, hydraulic limb supports of the kind the Professor had hinted at.

And in all of this, the easiest documents to find were the 'Advice' pages. These pages were always starred at the top in bold pen and titled 'Sound Advice For Living'. The advice was in all cases truly bizarre, things like: *To ensure one's chi remains in balance, when masturbating, switch hands. Always put on your left sock first, but always step first into your right pant leg. Hats should never be worn at night, except when the moon is full.*

Even more bizarre was advice that took the form of pseudo-biblical admonition. *When playing in C-major scale, the notes B and F must never be played in succession as this is the call of the devil.* And: *A woman is unclean when she gives her monthly blood, this the Bible tells us, but she is also not in her right mind owing to a surfeit of blood to the brain, similar to that which happens to a man when his penis is erect. To counteract the loss of blood, a menstruating woman should stand on her head no less than one hour each day of her period.*[*]

---

[*] No counterpart advice was provided for men dealing with erections. I guess this makes sense if you figure it's easier to stand on your head than stand on your dick, third legs excluded, of course.

269

Some Advice for the Ladies

I seldom give advice. Even more seldom do I give advice to women for the simple reason that I am not a woman. What's more, I understand little about women despite my best efforts to learn. But I do have one piece of advice for women: never trust a man who won't go down on you.

Going down on a woman is the sexual act that best allows a man to show a woman that he cares about her. It is the giving of pleasure without the expectance of self-gratification. In my experience it is also the surest way to get a woman to orgasm. So ladies, if you are in a relationship with a man who won't give you the pleasure of his tongue beware!

A Brief Time for Reflection

After my confrontation with Colin, I had a chance to reflect upon the events of the previous evening: the confrontation, Mortimer's strange book, the puppet show, but more so the time spent with Wren, time soaked in saffron and molé, and laid forever upon a smooth orange stretch of my hoop. But as I recalled the kisses and touches, the conversations, our hike, the long drives, the meeting of family, and the shared silences, my mind always drifted back to one thought, the molé.

The taste didn't fade as I thought of her. The taste was her. In the way that 'R' is red and 'B' is blue, Wren is molé. There is no experience that is Wren that doesn't include her quintessential flavor. If you think it odd that I describe Wren not only as a flavor, but also as an experience, then think harder. Everyone is an experience. We know a person only through our experience of him or her, through our own thoughts and feelings about that person.

Incredible, the existence of the taste and that it found confirmation in such a personal fashion. I spun her taste in my mind and spun the illusion of it on my tongue. I pondered and pined and came to the inescapable conclusion that I knew a thing without knowing it. There was knowledge available to me beyond conscious thought, knowledge existent and available beyond the reach of reason. And this gave credence to the Professor's ideas.

I knew something that I could not consciously know or express, but this knowledge nonetheless found expression in my mind and senses. This suggested a hidden mind, one that operates without the need for conscious expression. This perhaps is the mind active in dreams, though I am ill suited to weigh-in on this matter, as I never remember my dreams. This hidden mind and its wordless manner of expression also suggest the mechanism by which it is hidden. Language. It has long been clear to me by virtue of the imperfect shift from letters to words in my chromatic lexicon that language is not a fixed concept, but over time the mind becomes dependent on language to communicate with itself, the *conscious* mind, that is.

And this is the miracle of meditation that the simple act of stilling the mind can lift the veil created by chains of reasoned thought and unending self-dialogue. Meditation helps us to move beyond language, to apprehend directly instead of symbolically, to learn to hear and see the other mind, the hidden mind, the wordless mind. I continued, and continue to this day, to work toward that end.

A Disturbing Image

I went down on Wren frequently over the next few weeks. I wanted to show her that I cared. Also, it allowed us to be intimate without my having to undress.

One day, after I twice tasted her molé, Wren was left panting, covered in a sheen of sweaty pleasure that could only be washed away with a shower. As I do not shower I could not join her and was preparing to head back to the barracks when Erin walked into the Girls' Room.

Her come-ons had stopped almost as soon as Wren had arrived and though I felt awkward around her our relationship had developed a semblance of normalcy following my pleas at Court on her behalf. I was compelled to ask a question that had been on my mind, "That tattoo you have, the 'CK,' Daphne has one too. What's it stand for?"

"If you have to ask then I'm not going to tell you."

"Colin Kane," I said.

"Bingo."

I had suspected as much but it was nice to get confirmation. I found the whole idea creepy but people tattoo boyfriend's and spouses names all the time, so why not your patron's?

She smirked at me. "So, you and Wren." I couldn't tell if she was flirting. It made me uncomfortable. "You guys seem serious. Exclusive."

"I guess. Elusive might be a better word than exclusive. She's tough to pin down."

"Aren't we all, nothing but wanderers in this house. She's serious about you though."

"Did she tell you that?"

"No. But I can tell. It's a girl thing." She changed her shirt in front of me without any hesitation, revealing for a brief moment the 'CK' on her back.

"Why Colin?"

"If you have to ask you won't understand."

"That's not an answer. You must have a reason, to put him permanently on your body?"

She shrugged in a way that felt like a dismissal. As I was leaving, she added, "That's why you're a guest here Riley, not a member, until you figure it out you're always going to be on the outside. If you want to keep

Wren you better figure it out soon. She's all in for her art." I left with a mouthful of mushrooms and an image in my mind of a giant 'CK' tattooed across Wren's back.

A Conversation I Didn't Have, and a Confusing One That I Did

There was no immediate fallout from our escapade in the Jeep, primarily because Colin disappeared after he gave me the Diary of Mortimer Kane. In the Colin-less atmosphere things were relaxed, although our nightly jam sessions didn't start up again.

I spent my days with the Professor and my nights with Wren, when she wasn't working. Despite Colin's absence she worked just as hard and occasionally days would pass where I didn't see her. When I did it wasn't exactly a honeymoon period. I still didn't know where we stood and I was afraid to ask. I didn't want her to accuse me of trying to label it. Besides, the uncertainty I could live with, her absence I could not.

Each time I spent the night with her I held her close and breathed the fresh smell of her hair while she slept and savored the molé. I never tired of it. The sleepovers were hard. I didn't really sleep. I still wouldn't undress in front of her and wearing clothes while holding her made me hot and sweaty. The human body produces as much heat as a hundred watt light bulb, try holding a light bulb in your arms while wearing a shirt and pajama bottoms and you'll see my dilemma. But it was worth it and I savored those moments along with her taste.

The Professor continued to chart my synesthesias, but we also began to delve into theories, and our meetings took on an odd character: part study, part collaboration and part therapy. I felt better, although why was hard to distinguish with competing effects from the anti-depressants, my successes with Wren, meditation and Colin's absence. I really didn't know or care which was most responsible.

I continued my quest to decipher Mortimer Kane's diary and discover Colin's connection to my mother. When the diary work became tedious I read neuroscience texts and Cytowic's book on synesthesia.

****

"What do you think about the neonate hypothesis for synesthesia?" I asked the Professor.

"It may have some merit. But it's exceedingly difficult to study. All study of this phenomenon requires the translation of experience by a synesthete. Researchers have to be told what the qualitative aspects of the experience are. Newborns and infants are notoriously poor at describing anything, much less a subjective experience."

"Yes, but assuming it does have merit. Doesn't that throw a wrench in your evolutionary hypothesis?"

"Oh I don't think so."

"But the neonate hypothesis is that everyone is born synesthetic and then at some point in their development most people lose those synesthetic percepts because neural connections are pruned away."

"I see you've been reading. Careful with that, a little knowledge is often worse than none. You should also remember that this field is young and that new developments occur and theories regarding synesthesia are constantly changing and being altered based on new data. For instance, what we are doing. But you stated the hypothesis more or less correctly. The 'pruning' you refer to is called physiologic necrosis. While a fetus, everyone develops an excess of neurons. As the brain is constructed in infancy, neuronal migration occurs and more neural connections are formed at synapses throughout the brain.

"An important part of this process is physiologic necrosis, which is essentially cell death, in which excess neurons die so that the neurons can connect in an optimal fashion. It's a bit like defragging the hard drive on a computer. One theory posits that everyone is born synesthetic and that synesthetic percepts are lost as the sensory pathways differentiate. In synesthetes the unnecessary pathways, the excess neurons and neural connections, are not sufficiently pruned and thus senses remain linked."

"But if that's true wouldn't that be the opposite of evolution, like devolution. If you think synesthesia is a 'lessening of the filter' doesn't the increased number of neurons indicate the opposite."

"Nonsense. The elimination of pathways reduces the sensory inputs to the brain. I consider that an optimizing of the filter. The quote unquote 'excess' pathways are in fact an increased level of sensory input. By my way of thinking increased inputs equals increased potential for entirely new modes of perception."

I was all pasty again. I'm not a scientist, but I wanted very badly to understand what was occurring in my head and whether there might be something to the Professor's theory. I knew things without knowing them. It couldn't be a coincidence that the only person with her own flavor tasted exactly like her favorite dish. Clearly, something was occurring, some process that I wasn't conscious of was giving me *enhanced* or, dare I think it, *extra-sensory* perception. However, I wasn't ready to share this information just yet. Not with the Professor, not even with Wren.

"Don't worry yourself too much about it," the Professor said. "Leave the science to the scientist, just give as clear an account as possible of your subjective experiences. This is going to take years to sort out, but you play an important part. You seem in better spirits. Are the meditation and the medication helping?"

"I think so."

"Good. I may want to change your medication soon. Start weaning you off and possibly switch you over to something milder. But my hope is that the mediation becomes habit."

"Professor can I ask you something?"

"Of course, I'm here to profess."

"Did you know Dr. Mortimer Kane?"

"Oh my. You've been talking to Colin."

"So you did know him?"

"I'm not sure anyone could really *know* Mortimer Kane, but I was acquainted with him, at one point I was his research assistant."

"Here?"

"Yes. Back in the early 70's. This place has been around for a long time."

"Is he really Colin's dad?"

"Yes. Riley we have had a similar discussion before. This is Colin's area to inform, not mine. How long are you sitting for?"

"Meditating? Usually twenty-minutes a stretch. Sometimes longer."

"Any peculiar experiences?"

"Well, one time I felt like I was just above my left-shoulder. Not like I was seeing myself, or that I was seeing anything, my eyes were closed. It was just a... sensation, a feeling like I was just above my left-shoulder, perched there like a parrot or something."

"What do you think that means?"

"I have no idea."

"Any odd synesthetic experiences while meditating?"

"No. Why?"

"Sometimes experienced meditators experience synesthesia even though they aren't synesthetic. Meditation changes brain wave activity. When you're wide awake during the day your brain exhibits beta wave patterns, more relaxed waking states exhibit alpha waves. Meditation moves your brain wave function toward alpha, and even down into theta, where the first stages of sleep occur. Experienced meditators, yogis and such, can work themselves into trance like states where theta wave activity is heightened. I was just curious to see if your synesthesias were impacted at all, but it sounds like the answer is no. Have you ever reached off-sensation?"

"Off-sensation?"

"My shorthand nomenclature for the point at which you lose positional awareness. In effect your body feels as though it's switched off."

"Like you go numb? Sometimes my butt and legs get numb after sitting cross-legged for awhile."

"That's probably attributable to decreased circulation. Westerners like us often struggle with sitting on the floor, the positions just feel unnatural, but I wouldn't call off-sensation numb. Based on my experience, it is more a stillness that comes over your entire body. Your tactile sense ceases to reach out into the world. Almost like your body is asleep and your mind is awake."

"I don't think I've felt that."

"I think you should try and sit longer, still your thoughts by focusing on the mantra. Off-sensation is actually quite pleasurable and once achieved you may go deeper and deeper, when this occurs meditators often lose track of time, minutes may seem like hours or vice-versa. Given your time-space synesthesia I'd be curious to know how you would register an experience like that. Where would it fit on your hoop?"

Something rang true in my head. Again I felt that odd sensation of knowing I'd forgotten something but not knowing what. After that I redoubled my efforts to meditate.

On Meditation and Perception

I eventually reached 'off-sensation' and still deeper states, but not until after I came here. When I finally did reach 'off-sensation' I learned something, not right away, gradually, but a seed was planted and started to grow.

What I learned was the real reason why I meditate: to escape perception. Buddhist philosophers often speak of universality, of oneness, of being present in the moment. That last one is really hard to wrap your head around, and harder still to put into practice. I still haven't learned to, save for a happy accident here and there. That's because perception traps you in the past.

Odd, isn't it, how we all live in the past. Present like sand slips through our fingers, present turns always to past. As soon as you think of the present moment it's past, in the split second it took your brain to process the information the present turned to past. Before you perceive the present it vanishes, lost forever to the past.

I think that's why humans spend their lives thinking about the future: all our plans and schemes and hopes and dreams exist to ponder what might be, and for no greater purpose than that. We need the illusion that life moves forward to convince us that we don't live in the past.

That's the beauty of meditation. It allows perception to cease. If you believe mind and body are distinct you are wrong. They are aspects of the same thing. Your mind needs your body and your body needs your mind. One does not exist without the other. To still the mind still the body. Slowly the body turns off, sensation disappears and with it perception. And what is left? The present.

A Nasty Prank and a Harsh Critique

I expected to meet the Professor. Instead I found Colin in the library, waiting for me. He was wearing all black, except for a bright yellow bowler. It was a kick in the gut. "Morning sunshine. Got a few errands to run. You're coming along." It was the first time I'd seen him in nearly two weeks. "Hey and bring Mortimer's binder too."

"I'm supposed to meet with the Professor."

"We are, out at the Bunker." He clapped me on the shoulder like we were best buds. "Big day today. Gonna fire up the fancy machines." I felt a little sweet and sour rush and a brush of sage, I'd stopped asking when we were going to use the MRI and the CT, but I hadn't stopped wondering.

Waiting in the drive was a suped-up golf-cart, gas-powered with all terrain tires. "Kids took the Jeep out to the studio. You and I are gonna rock it Austin Powers style." The golf-cart was surprisingly fast, and the bumpy trail out toward the sculpture garden tossed rosewater balloons courtesy of my rusted hip.

"So how do you like Mortimer?" Colin asked, unable to contain his glee. "Very distinct voice, right? You learn anything about your mom?"

"He's a loon. The diary has no rhyme or reason. I don't even know if there is anything about her in there. You're a lying sack of shit."

Colin feigned like I'd shot him through the heart, but he never eased off of his cheesy grin. "I'm hurt Riley. When have I ever lied to you?"

"That's tough to say. First I'd have to know when you told me the truth. Were you a televangelist? Or did you inherit? Which is it?"

"Always with the either/or man. Stop being such a binary thinker. Thinking like that you'll make a terrible subject for somebody's art. Look I promise you there is information about your mom in that book. Cross my heart. Hope to die. Stick a needle in my eye."

"More like a needle in a haystack, finding something that pertains to my mom in that pile of gibberish."

"You know where that saying comes from? A needle in a haystack?"

"From the fact that it's hard to find a needle in a haystack."

"That's half right, but not a very good story. I expect better from a would-be novelist. The saying comes from a prank kids used to play on farmers. Mischievous boys would toss a needle into a haystack and when the horses or cows came to feed, sometimes that needle would get swallowed up by one of them."

"What would that do to the animal?"

"Puncture the esophagus or stomach, one of four for a cow. Might just hurt, or it might die from internal bleeding or the gastric juices eating it from the inside out."

"That's an awful prank."

"Yep. Sometimes the farmer would find out before the animals went to feed. Then he had a choice: throw out the whole haystack or feed it to them knowing they were likely to lose an animal. Usually depended on the size of the haystack and the value of the animal. Sure as hell wouldn't feed it to your best plow horse, but a pack of lame mules? Maybe. Simple economics. Anyway if the animals got fed, once one died you found the needle in the haystack. Seems to apply to your dilemma quite well. Best way to find the needle is to eat all the hay."

"So I can rupture my stomach? I'm not reading that whole binder full of crap."

"I think you will. Especially after what you're gonna find out today. Hoo boy that's gonna set you to digging."

"And what exactly am I going to find out?"

"Oh you'll see. Gotta stop by the studio first." He made a snapping motion with his wrist, "Crack the whip."

The Studio bustled with activity and heat. It was over ninety degrees inside with two kilns and the forge fired. Colin ignored the artists at work and headed for the back of the building. I dallied trying to get a look at Wren and her project, but Colin called me over impatiently and showed me a pile of lumber in the back corner. "How's the novel coming?" I shrugged. "I figured as much," he said. "I've got a project for you. You can work on it whenever the Professor doesn't need you. What's the moon's phase?"

"Waxing crescent, full in sixteen days."

"Very good." He waved Taggart over to us, "Taggart!"

Taggart got up from a computer and jogged over. "What's up?"

"You done drafting those templates for Court?"

"Yeah I'm gonna laser them out with the computer this afternoon."

"Great. I want Riley to help you cut and lathe and whatever else you need to make the pieces."

"I won't help you make stocks," I said.

"You'll do what I tell you. But we aren't making stocks."

"I won't help you make anything that you use to hurt people." I could hear the room around me get quiet as machines stopped running, brushes stopped painting, and chisels stopped chipping. Taggart looked at me wide-eyed and fidgeted awaiting Colin's response.

"Court isn't always an actual Court jackass," Colin said. "It's a different performance every time. You don't have a choice, you must help or you're out, I don't give two shits what the Professor says. Everyone participates in Court. But if it makes you feel better, I promise that there will be no stocks this time and that anything you build will only be used by a person who voluntarily agrees to participate."

"I don't believe you."

"I don't care. Besides you won't build anything, you're just cutting wood." He turned and addressed Taggart directly, "Use him to help with whatever you need. Don't let him or anyone else see the schematic." Taggart nodded his assent and Colin clapped him on the shoulder with a smile. "Good man. We've got to have some surprises or it's not really improv, right?" Colin glared at me and I nodded grudgingly.

"Wren!" Colin strode across the room toward her. She was painting at an easel with headphones on. "Wren!" he yelled out again and this time she heard him. I clacked on behind him trying to catch up.

Wren's project was in her favored style, musical colors and fluctuating shapes.

"Who are you making this for?" Colin asked without hesitation.

She hunched her shoulders and avoided his eye. She looked like she was trying to shrug within her shadow, to flatten down to a disc and join the circle cast at her feet by the bright light overhead. Her body betrayed her emotions, the shrug saying the words she didn't want to, "I don't know," or was it, "I don't want to tell you." I got the impression they'd had this conversation before.

"Art cannot exist without a subject," Colin said. "Point of view is the sole criteria. Who is this for?"

Again Wren was silent, shrinking. I didn't recognize her. The woman that had worked me for hours in the front seat of a Jeep, who had torn my art and the course requirements of the art department to shreds, the woman who had defended her right to paint her art her way and demanded that I strut like a peacock or not bother to walk, that woman vanished and in her place stood a timid, mousy woman with a yellow streak in her hair that seemed more chicken than bumblebee.

"Who?" he asked. "Who? Who?" he was in her face, nose to nose screaming, "Who?"

She looked to me. Or did I imagine it? No. I did not. She looked to me. Just a glance, a flicker of hope, a pleading, but she looked to me. I imagined what she said, what she verbalized with her eyes: "It is for you, please intercede."

But I did not. I didn't even watch. I lowered my head, my reserve of bravado spent on my ineffective woodworking protest. Colin turned his eye to me and I could not meet it. It was the briefest of instants and yet I was humbled. Again he turned to Wren, "Who?" How that word must have sounded to Wren. "Who?" I have never had the heart to ask her if it caused colors to flash and explode in her mind's eye. Colin's frozen yell burst forth again and again. "Who? Who?" His voice was so sharp that it caused me to see a flash, his voice getting shriller and more focused with each question, each accusation, with each shout an intensely bright point burst forth like tiger claws on a blackboard.

Wren mouthed almost inaudibly, just a flutter across her lips, "You." Finally, she tried to lie, but he was on to her.

"Me?" Colin scoffed. "This isn't for me. You know what I think? I think you're lying to me because you don't want to tell. At first I just thought you didn't know and so you were embarrassed because that meant you were only pretending that you weren't actually creating art, but now I think you know. I think you know who the subject is. I think you're the subject!" He pushed her out of the way and grabbed the canvas from the easel examining it with the eye of a surgeon eager to cut. "This!" He shoved his hand through the canvas putting a hole in the center and splintering the wood cross that backed it. "This is not what we do here! You are not the subject! I will not have you using my Rancho for creative masturbation! Either address the question of audience, truly consider your art, or stop wasting paint." He slapped the palette from her hand then flicked a glob of paint from his fingertips. It struck Wren in the face.

On Cowardice

I was a coward. I say 'was,' not 'am,' because who I am, and who I was, is not the same person. Just as who you are, and who you were, changed in the time it took you to read this sentence. Cowardice is a trait that is both mutable and revelatory. It is only revealed by actions, or inactions, as is more commonly the case. So, if you have behaved cowardly and this causes you shame, as it did me, rest easy. You are likely to have an opportunity to behave bravely in the future, so set aside your shame and focus on preparing for that moment. I know, easier said than done. But remember that cowardice is revealed through action, through circumstance and your response to circumstance, a coward is never something you are it is only something you were, always subject to change at the next opportunity for resistance or bravery.

I could argue that it was not cowardly for me to remain silent as Colin destroyed Wren's painting. I could argue that Wren knew the rules of the Rancho. I could argue that she had never before indicated the need for a rescuer, and so I could not be expected to rise to her defense. I could argue that if I had come to her defense it would have diminished her in Colin's eyes portraying her as a fragile little girl incapable of standing up for herself. I could argue that Colin's reaction would only have made life harder and harsher for both myself and Wren had I spoken up or stepped in, and so I was justified in remaining mute. I could argue that she would have resented me for interceding. I could argue that every aspect of her character to that point had demonstrated to me that she needed no aid that her confidence in her art was unshakeable that she was her own best advocate a lioness stalking through the grass ready to fight and scratch and tear asunder any who dared encroach on her territory.

But I have already said that argument is futile. This is all the more true if you argue with yourself. So...I was a coward. I didn't argue with myself, at least not for long, instead of argument I turned to a tried and true method of persuasion, threats. I threatened myself. I would die a coward if, at the next opportunity for resistance and bravery on behalf of someone I loved or what was right, I did not stand and fight. So fight I would consequences be damned.

The Bunker

The bunker was what I thought it would be. Underground. We descended a metal staircase. A hollow ring echoed from each grated step at the clunk of my cane. A bare incandescent bulb lit the way down.

We arrived in a brick-walled anteroom. The air was heavy and damp, and I still burned from the shame of the studio. Colin strutted and preened even more than usual. He opened the lone metal door and I felt the push of cool, dry, filtered air before the door closed heavily behind us. I had the bizarre sensation of being at once hot and cold. The chill atmosphere could not quench the heat of my shame.

The Professor stood in the center of the room I came to know as the gateway. He wore a jovial expression on his face like he had just been informed he'd won the Nobel Prize or discovered that the University was tripling the size of his lecture hall and giving him the chance to profess to a captive audience three times larger than usual.

At the end of the room behind the Professor was a vault door made of heavy grey metal with a drop bar two inches in diameter that ran into a hole bored in the concrete floor and a horizontal arm that swung down across the entirety of the frame. A combination pad to the left of the door provided an extra layer of security. I wondered, what could be back there that required such a high level of security?

The Professor immediately directed me through a second door, which had only a keypad for security, and entered a suite with a small kitchen, a room with a cot and a computer room with a massive server bank and five large monitors. The computer room had three large rectangular panes of thick glass. Through one of the panes I saw a bare bones conference, (er, interrogation?), room with a single simple wooden table and two hard back metal chairs. Through the other I saw the mother lode, a tubular mass with human-sized donut hole and sliding flatbed loader, an MRI.

I was excited. Lemonade excited. Now we were going to do some real science. Instead of taking down data and making charts we were going to take pictures of my brain. I had no idea how the machines worked or what they would show, but I hoped they'd show the Professor that he was right and that my brain was very special. I was so excited that I almost forgot Colin was there too, almost.

The Professor loaded me into the scanner. We started with a standard MRI. "To get a baseline picture of the brain," he said. "I want to see if there are any structural abnormalities before we start measuring function and neural activity." I lay back, head and neck immobile, as a thunder of clicks and clunks echoed through the torus. The whole process took about forty minutes. All the while I was anxious and antsy and it took a great deal of concentration not to move my head in response to the anxious pressure on my neck.

The Professor told me it would take a while to set up the scanner for an fMRI so I had about an hour to relax. I was pleased to have a break and relieved to be out the tube.

Unfortunately my relief was short-lived and my break unpleasant. The cot in the suite wasn't dirty, but it wasn't clean either and I wasn't about to lie down on something that so many others had apparently laid on before me. Instead I sat at the small table in the conference room and practiced seated meditation. It wasn't ideal, as the chair was rather uncomfortable and hard against my bony butt, which in turn aggravated my bad hip, but I gradually stilled my mind eased my anxiety and slowed my heart rate by following my breaths and focusing on my mantra, *om mani padme om*.

My concentration snapped when a piercing metallic shriek set gold starbursts ablaze upon my closed lids. I opened my eyes and saw Colin leering and, of course, grinning. I was not amused.

"Hey brother." He dropped Mortimer's binder on to the table between us and took a seat. "I gather you've been having trouble deciphering this text here, and that's perfectly understandable. Remember how I said everything here is either art or history? Well, I think it's time for a history lesson. It'll help put things in context.

"My dad, he was a lot of things, different things to different people. I'm kind of like him in that regard. Father, scientist, preacher, lover, researcher, chef, inventor, he was all of these things. But he was also something else, he was a prophet."

"Right," I snorted. I'm sure *he* believed that."

"Snicker if you like. But you should know a little history first. This place hasn't always been what it is today. Back when I was a child, more than a hundred scientists lived and worked here with their families. Classified, cutting-edge research, that's what they did, and the entire project was an experiment of its own, a social and scientific experiment to gauge the effects of bringing together a large group of brilliant minds in a communal setting. The Project was called The Crucible. That's also what they called that old broken-down church up the road from here."

Colin pulled a page from the binder and handed it to me. It was a sermon full of half scratched notations, cross-outs and red ink. "Let me translate." He pointed out a paragraph near the center of the page. "As Mortimer put it:

'Here is where God houses men and tills the soil of their souls. Here he speaks through me as water through a pipe that I may irrigate the fertile ground in which His seed was planted by the Spirit.'

"Eloquent, huh?"

"Delusional, but I already knew that."

"Ah but he had followers."

"So did Jim Jones."

"All the world's a stage and it's full of bad actors. Bill Shakespeare had it right. He just didn't finish the thought. Now Morty, Morty was a finisher, and an actor of the highest caliber. I mean, you've read some of this stuff, can you tell if he believed his own shit? I can't. Anyways let me tell you a story... a story about Morty and the prophecy he delivered, and about his tragic end. It's all in that binder Riley, well, the binder and the grounds of El Rancho, but it'll take you forever to piece it together, so I'll give you the cliffnotes version:

The Halloween Prophecy

"Reverend Mortimer Kane delivered the prophecy from the pulpit of the Crucible. Mortimer stood in church that day, Halloween, and proclaimed:

'Heed my call!

'Cursed is All Hallows Eve, this day for Satan and sinners, but blessed are we who serve the Lord. I see! I see!

'The Lantern is lit!

'Born Alive! He who sees the strings that bind, he too will see Satan's seat on earth. The Lord has promised and shall fulfill. This day of cursed minions finds darkness met with light.

'Born Alive! He who sees the strings shall peer into the abyss, and he shall announce himself in fire. I have seen the sparks of the Lord's flame and witnessed its brilliance. God shields His Light to protect our unworthy eyes from His greatness. But through the Spirit His Light yields a beacon for the righteous to follow.

'Heed my call! Open your eyes to the Light of God's beacon.

'Born Alive! The messenger arrives to announce the coming baptism of fire and mark the minions of Satan! He brings the beacon. The Lantern of Truth shall shine on the unbelievers. The Lantern of Truth shall prepare the way.

'Born Alive!

"Mortimer claimed he was filled with the Holy Spirit. And maybe he was, but he was definitely full of LSD.

"He told the other scientists that the prophecy was about his work. The 'lantern of truth' could only be the result of his science. About half agreed, the same half that went to church and heard Mortimer preach. The other half thought Mortimer had been dipping into the experimental hallucinogens again, but they wanted to keep their experiments going, so they let it slide.

"My father, Reverend Mortimer Kane was a man of the church and a man of the lab. Some would call this a contradiction, but Mortimer explained all of his religious beliefs in a scientific manner. He studied rocks in Southern Oregon as a young man and demonstrated that the layers of sediment in the Rogue Valley clearly evidenced a flood approximately 3,000 years prior. He found fossils of shellfish in the rocks and

288

determined their age to be of the same era as the flood. Mortimer collected the moon dust that was prevalent and well preserved in the area and through his samples he proved that the earth was only 6,000 years old. But most importantly, through a rigorous experimental methodology, Reverend Mortimer Kane, proved the existence of cognitive dissonance.

"Poor Mortimer never knew of this, never knew of his most significant contribution to the world, apart from his prophecy,* of course. But despite failing to recognize the significance of the data set he created, Mortimer's contribution to the fields of psychology and neuroscience was so important that his discovery has been publicly and posthumously acknowledged by a religious sub-set of the scientific community. Credit must be given where credit is due, and so Mortimer and the Crucible scientists who agreed with his beliefs, will forever be known as the Cognitive Dissidents.

"But the one religious belief Mortimer could never prove scientifically was the truth of the prophecy. His evidence was swaddled and carried away on the very same day he first proclaimed the future. This did nothing to shake my father's faith in the Spirit, but it did shake his faith in his skill as a scientist. He felt that he should have been able to find the evidence, but try as he did to chase it down, he never could. He blamed himself entirely. It sure as hell wasn't God's fault. What a shame that Mortimer an excellent scientist, in the religious sense of the word, considered himself a failure.

"Mortimer tortured himself over his failure. The Lord loved Mortimer, but Mortimer hated himself. He succumbed to the sin of Despair. It was Satan at work. Mortimer nearly ended it all. But just as he was about to ingest a fatal dose of strychnine the Holy Spirit warned him that Satan had tricked him. Even then Mortimer didn't recognize his sadness and confusion as cognitive dissonance, but he did recognize it as Satan's evil plot. And what a clever ruse Satan played, using Mortimer's own mind, his own love of reason, to derail his work on the prophecy.

---

* LEGAL DISCLAIMER: The term 'his prophecy' is Colin's, and presumably used to indicate the speaker who first publicly delivered the prophecy. This usage is in no way meant to disparage or devalue any intellectual property right(s) asserted by the Holy Spirit. I take no position as to which party or parties hold a copyrighted interest in the prophecy.

"The Spirit ordered Mortimer to penance cleaning the toilets in the lab. Mortimer, desperate to please God went above and beyond the Spirit's call and deliberately assigned himself to latrine duty in the experimental laxative division. It was filthy work but the sponging of spatter-stank soothed his soul for the Spirit's genius is always to exalt the base and so the Spirit led him to God's plan, led him to his highest path through his lowest chore, the solution to free him from Satan's shackle, experimental laxatives. And just as Mortimer cleansed his soul, so too, did he cleanse his body. Mortimer realized Satan's devious plot just in the nick of time. Only XB-40, the most powerful laxative ever created, would undo the damage Satan had wrought.

"Mortimer was full of shit.

"The XB-40 was dark brown and shaped and scented like a coffee bean. It did the trick. Satan's possession excreted, Mortimer returned to his work confident in his service of God and continued to search for evidence to confirm the prophecy.

"Then, one fateful day, the Good Lord called Mortimer back, his days as a scientist and Reverend completed. And on this day Reverend Mortimer stood astride a block of dirt more than ten feet high. The dirt was delivered only three hours prior but already was shaped into a sturdy compact cube.

"'My fellow scientists,' he announced from above like a returning king, 'the sonic compaction device is a success!'

"A hearty cheer erupted from the Cognitive Dissidents. The other scientists were busy doing work.

"To Morty, every discovery was a blessing, and once more, God had blessed science. Mortimer exhorted the crowd to worship:" 'Praise Jesus we are blessed!'

"'Praise Jesus!' the crowd echoed. The hills around the compound provided remarkable resonance. The Cognitive Dissidents worked very well in an echo chamber, but on this day their tone was off.

"Dr. Philip Miaz was Mortimer's partner, fellow scientist, lab mate and devoted parishioner. He was twenty-five years Mortimer's junior, a handsome lad and a brilliant young mind. He saw it coming. He took the initial soil readings. Before they started the compaction process he warned Reverend Mortimer, 'Morty,' he lisped, his voice faltering on the verge of tears, 'it's been dug too recently. Why, it's practically sifted, and the nitrogen levels, they're *much* too high. You *have* to let it sit. You have to let it *mature, Morty.*'

"Had they used older soil, one with greater nitrogen absorption and larger granules, they might have averted disaster. Had Mortimer listened to Dr. Miaz he might still be alive, might still be out to prove the truth of his prophecy. Instead Mortimer bounded atop that soil soapbox to give his speech. 'The dirt is as good as blocked. It can be removed in chunks and stacked like bricks.'

"It was a somber moment, a righteous achievement. Mortimer stood atop that cube, felt the familiar sensations: the rush of adrenaline, the jolt at years of work paying off in discovery and the vague sense of being party to a holy moment. Mortimer basked in an accomplishment sanctioned by God. It was addictive. He lived his life in the shadow of God always in search of a fix. God's acknowledgement! It swept through him, and as he looked down upon the crowd he felt the Spirit and was moved to speak, 'Remember this day. With God all things are possible!'

"Over the shouts of 'Hallelujah!' and 'Praise God!' Dr. Miaz called to his friend and colleague, 'Come down Morty!'

"Poor Dr. Miaz. He tried. But his stubborn scientific companion would heed no warnings. A slight rumble filled the air as the echoes of praise returned from the hills.

"'Get down,' Dr. Miaz begged, 'the soil's too fresh.'

"Reverend Mortimer Kane heard his protégé call to him. Hands on hips he gazed down at Dr. Miaz and in a voice loud enough for all to hear, said his last words: 'I believe in young earth.'

"The pile collapsed and Mortimer suffocated in his own proof.

"It was a fatal miscalculation, the worst kind of mathematical error. But even in death God honored Mortimer as Mortimer honored Him. God gave Mortimer a Christ-like death. Crazy shit happened that only his followers could attest to, and, Mortimer Kane, Reverend, scientist, and sonic landscaper, gave a posthumous proof.

"Sadly, Mortimer did not prove his prophecy. Mortimer merely proved one of his own unfortunate quotes.

"When Mortimer's flock dug him up in order to bury him, the Reverend who replaced Mortimer recognized the irony and decided that it simply wouldn't do to rebury him. Reverend Mortimer Kane was respected by all as a man of God. There could be no humor, not even ironic humor, found in his death.

"Instead, the new Reverend arranged for the construction of a towering funeral pyre, a funeral pyre to burn hotter than Gandhi's, a fitting departure for a man who led a bright flaming life.

"The ceremony was somber and very well attended. There were several gentlemen who no one knew. They wore black suits and white shirts with black ties and sunglasses. They were very polite, stood near the back of the gathering and never said a word. All of the Cognitive Dissidents cried, and all of the scientists were there along with the entire population of the Crucible, save three people who had made an unauthorized departure years earlier on the day the prophecy was delivered.

"Dr. Miaz brought forth a tightly wrapped bundle of twigs and lit it ablaze as all the members of the Crucible looked on and waited to pay their final respects. Just as he was about to lay the torch at the base of the pyre a freak storm poured down upon them and extinguished the bundle of sticks. And by this work the Lord proved through Mortimer that which Mortimer often preached, 'God hates fags.'

"They left Reverend Mortimer in that pile of twigs, his corpse washed down into the center of the stack. It was fall and the rain was sure to come back before the pyre dried out, so they covered the pile with Mortimer's compact dirt, and that is where he rested."

fMRI

"And that Riley, is how we got Morty's Mound," said Colin. "What do you think?"

"You're awfully glib about your father's death."

"I admire the man, but Morty was as much a father to me as that binder, less in fact. But he would have appreciated the style in which the tale was delivered. I upheld Morty's two deepest convictions, never let the truth get in the way of a good story and know your audience. You should understand that you aspiring novelist, you."

The Professor interrupted our discussion. It was time to start the fMRI. He gave me a pair of thick plastic glasses that wrapped around my head blocking out my peripheral vision. He poked the lenses. "These are screens," he explained. "I'm going to give you visual stimuli, mostly words and numbers so we can track the changes in brain activity when your synesthetic perceptions are activated. You'll be able to hear me through a microphone and vice versa. Try to keep still and focus only on the stimuli in the glasses, but if you need to communicate just talk."

Once again I lay down on the flatbed and rolled back into the scanner. The loud clicks started up once again, but this time the sound conjured up images of excrement splattering about the spin cycle of a washing machine.

Words began to pop up on the screens. Simple words at first: dog, cat, Riley. Then came random jumbles of letters that required effort to decipher as the colors popped out individually. After that came a series of rapid flashes and letters made up of other letters like the test cards the Professor had shown me at UCSD. Then came numbers, followed by pictures of faces. I remained still and focused throughout. The images stopped, but the clicking continued. For a moment I thought the scan was over.

The Professor's voice echoed in the tube, "I want you to try and remember some historical dates for me." He listed off dates giving an interval of several seconds between each: "Signing of the Declaration of Independence. Spanish Armada. Birth of Christ. Signing of the Magna Carta."

I saw each in succession. First, in front of me, slightly to the left, burnt orange. "July 4, 1776." Next, in front of me, further to the left, white. "August 8, 1588." Next, several feet left, down toward my waist but still projected in front of me, grey or a darker shade of grey. "Depends, 4 B.C., 0 A.D." Finally, far left, but several feet above the birth of Christ, yellow. "June 15, 1215."

"September 11, 2001."

I saw it, pink, slightly to my right. "Ummm." I wasn't sure how to respond. "You gave the date."

"Where were you on September 11, 2001?"

I felt it, behind me, slightly to the right, glacial blue. "The hospital." I winced involuntarily and a thimble full of rosewater turned on my tongue and then vanished.

I was in the hospital recovering on 9/11. I have since learned that for many people this date marked a turning point, a massive world-altering event in their lives. Like most people I know where I was, like I said, I was in the hospital, but for me 9/11 was not transformative. It was one day among many days on the long road to an incomplete recovery. I think the insignificance of that date for me arises largely from this fact: On 9/11, I was not living in America. On 9/11, I was living in pain.

"Your eighth birthday."

I recalled the date, light purple, almost directly in front of me. "October 31, 1982."

"What did you do for your eighth birthday?"

I feel it, brown, to my right, extended about a yard. "I had a birthday party and a seizure."

"The day you were born."

I saw it, but barely, it was so grey and faded. "October 31, 1974."

"Where were you on October 31, 1974?"

I couldn't feel it. I existed but I had no memory. "I don't know."

Colin's voice came through on the speaker. "So what did you think of the prophecy?"

His question diverged from the Professor's line of questioning and it took me a second to provide a sufficiently snarky answer, "It wasn't much of a prophecy. Some hunt for a lantern that shines out Satan. The half-assed grail quest of a delusional mad scientist slash dopey preacher."

"You know the Holy Grail isn't a cup right? What makes you think the lantern is an actual lantern?"

"What makes you think Morty knew anything about the future? He wasn't a prophet, there's no such thing."

"Once again you miss the point with either/or thinking. Either he's a prophet or he didn't know about the future. Don't you know that every prophet is a charlatan? A huckster. They all do it one of two ways. Either you give a vague prediction about the distant future that leaves enough ambiguity that subsequent generations can twist up the facts and prove you right. This can make you famous, but only after you're dead.

"The better way is to make a future event happen to prove your prediction. It's like a scientist falsifying data to prove his hypothesis. But what if the scientist didn't have to falsify the data, because he just made his prediction conform to what the data already showed. God didn't tell Morty about the future, but if Morty predicted the future wouldn't people believe he talked to God?"

"So what are you saying? That Morty knew something?"

"Morty knew lots of things. It's one way that I'm like my dad. But what I'm really saying Riley, is that if all the world's a stage then every man's a mark."

"So what did Morty predict exactly? And who believes it? You said there were a hundred scientists here before. Where'd they all go? None of them are following Morty or his crazy prophecy now."

"One of them is. You know him pretty well."

I sat up and clunked my head on the tube. Paste and rosewater stilled my tongue for a half-second until I regained my wits. "The Professor?"

"Yes the Professor," Colin's voice echoed in the tube and in my head. I could faintly hear the Professor in the background, screaming, "Damn it! The magnets!"

"Go on. Tell him," Colin insisted.

The Professor screamed at Colin, "You're corrupting the data! You freak!"

Colin found this hilarious. "I think we've got a pot-kettle situation here. But if you expect anything but freaks out here..." He clicked off to dead air. There was a brief pause where all I could hear was the clanking of the MRI.

"Hey dumbass!" I jolted but caught myself before I banged my forehead. "His prophecy is about a little study called Project Nimbus. The study prominently featured a young woman known in the data as Spectrum. Sound like anyone you know?"

He was telling the truth, at least partly. I had seen the name Spectrum in the data on Project Nimbus, but none of the data or observations made sense to me.

"What do we call a spectrum, in the sky, maybe after a storm?"

"Is he telling the truth?" I asked.

Colin answered before the Professor could get a word in. "The truth is whatever you believe. But I know: 'you gotta give 'em some proof to feed 'em the truth.' I found that little gem in Morty's book, too."

"You might consider that, because I don't believe a word you say."

"Yes you do. But you don't have to. I'm going to prove it to you. See I helped the Professor find Morty's evidence. Now we just have to confirm."

"Why do you care anyway? What's the prophecy mean to you?"

"Nothing. It's just another scene, man. I live my life as a work of art and that means I'm always searching out subjects. Here's an interesting fact, I know where you were on October 31, 1974."

I felt the trap closing, a bizarre sensation of high pressure anxiety crushing against my neck from below and the taste of paste mixed with rosemary and thyme, all slathered up with a fresh wet coat of fear. I wanted to ask but I didn't want to know.

Before I could decide what to do Colin came on the speakers again, "But wait, if I know where you were on your birthday, then I must know where Rainbow was too. You wanna guess Earl?"

I was too stunned to be angry and for the first time since my accident my palette went blank. Nothing.

"Judging from the fMRI readout, you're either thinking *very* hard, or not at all. Here's a little more food for thought. On your birthday you and your mom were laying almost exactly where you are right now."

My mind was buzzing. It was like the fMRI was shooting static between my ears, just a toneless, tasteless buzz of comprehension, I understood every word and yet I had no idea how I felt about it.

"Tell him who the lantern is."

"That's enough," the Professor's voice remained in the background.

"Tell him."

"I said that's enough Colin."

"The Professor is searching for Morty's lantern, and he thinks he's found him."

"Him?" I said. "What is he talking about Professor? What is he saying?"

I could hear them struggling for the mic. "Give it to me you shit! You're ruining decades of research."

"Screw your research."

Crash! Then, faintly, "Stay down old man." Colin came back on the mic at full volume. "Halloween 1974, you lay there, swaddled, checked over by a skilled team of docs, and then your mother skulked away with you and your brother back to Skip fucking Sparx like a thief in the night. You see you are the lantern, Riley. At least according to Morty's book." There was a pause, it seemed like a long time, but was probably only a few seconds. "Damn!" Colin said. "I thought for sure we'd watch your head explode!"

No Answers, Just Hugs

In a way my head had exploded, or perhaps imploded is a more appropriate term. My thoughts had no order and came unbidden. My tastes and touches returned over the next few days, but slowly, and as apparitions, faded and amorphous echoes of past reality. It was as though only the edges of my inner world remained accessible and every time I touched an edge it receded, like motion caught out the corner of my eye, but when I turned to see it, all was still.

I didn't see Wren for three days after the bunker debacle. Whether it was a blessing or a curse I couldn't say. I needed her, but did I really want my senses reawakened by the shame, guilt and humiliation[*] of our last encounter?

"He took away my paints." That was the first thing she said to me, like it was the only thing she'd thought of for three straight days. Her eyes were puffy like she'd been crying that whole time and the look on her face was so pitiable that had I not known the circumstance I'd have thought she lost a loved one. Which in a sense I suppose she had. The effect upon me was immediate. The ephemeral turned solid, the incorporeal phantoms of feeling banished by layers of stout definition: salty sadness, burning shame, and a bilious rage toward Colin and his games. The crisp lash of reality, the sudden awareness of substance, stole my words. I had nothing for her except a hug.

My body responded to the press of her breasts against my chest and I swallowed down an inappropriate burst of chile pepper. She felt soft in my arms, vulnerable, and for the first time in our relationship I felt strong. I nearly coughed on a mouthful of cinnamon. She needed me. And I was there for her.

I still had no words. None could suffice. None could answer her unspoken question: What do I do now? The only solution to the intractable problem of El Rancho was to leave, but I could not suggest this. It would send her running from my arms. So I didn't speak. I held her and hoped it was enough.

---

[*] SPECULATION: The embarrassment trifecta, it can only be hit through a public display of cowardice resulting in harm to a loved one or other innocent party.

298

"Maybe it's for the best," she said as we released our long embrace. "I've started working with clay again. It's kind of fun."

"That's good," I said. Then I lied, "Maybe it is for the best."

"Yeah. I still get to show my paintings in Portland. Keep your fingers crossed okay?"

"Of course." I did my best to keep a smile on my face as I absorbed an invisible punch to the gut and an explosion of salt. "When are you going?"

The Cripple Carries the Cistern

Ndukwe roused me in the middle of the night, "Get up. Time for Court."

I blinked my eyes. Dazed and pasty I sipped a cold draught of fear, pulled from a dreamscape that receded apace from the edge of consciousness, nearby but already forgotten, a mere echo of terror.

I had gone to bed wondering why no Court was held. I had dreaded it all week, frightened that my meager woodworking contributions would be put to some horrible purpose. Maybe tomorrow, I thought as I lay to rest, the moon would still be full. Instead I rose from a dread slumber into lunar-cast shadows.

Ndukwe wore a sheer white robe that revealed all of his anatomy, from his muscular frame to his impressive member and the steep cleft in his buttocks. "What do I wear?" I asked.

Ndukwe grunted. "Something you can move in."

I slipped into a pair of sweats and a hoodie and followed him out. We met Shelly and Wren at the fountain in the courtyard. Morning wood had me primed for spice and the female forms sparked fire on my tongue. Wren was ready for a run in form fitting black Lycra with hot pink stripes and a pair of cross-trainers. Shelly wore a robe identical to Ndukwe's and filled it out disproportionately, heavy curves graced with sharp points in the cold air of desert midnight. Thankfully my erection was tucked flat to my belly under the elastic band of my sweats and it gradually subsided as Wren's calm smile reassured and the burn morphed into the greater complexity of molé.

Shelly lowered a dipper into the basin of the fountain beneath the stream pouring from the jaws of the dragon. Her motions were slow and solemn. She ladled the water from the fountain into a large, round, clay cistern, with a square base. She repeated the action seven times with her right hand, seven times with her left, and seven more with both hands. I asked her what she was doing but Ndukwe shushed me and she ignored me, though I wasn't certain she'd seen me speak.

With the cistern largely full Ndukwe motioned for me to help him lift the cistern. "I can't carry that," I protested, but Ndukwe would not be swayed.

"Give your cane to her." He snatched my cane and handed it to Wren. He extended a long index finger at me. "This work is not for women. You must help carry."

I did. It was dreadful work. We carried it out of the courtyard all the way out to the sculpture garden. My bad shoulder was useless so I carried it one handed, holding precariously onto the lip of the cistern, which was rounded and thin making it hard to grasp. After numerous near slips and at least ten stops to rest we made it up to the top of the hill and the awning at the point of the pentagram. My good arm and bad hip both throbbed and all molé and spice were extinguished by rosewater.

A bulky shadow lay beneath the awning, an extended mass covered in a dark sheet large enough to be a cargo parachute. We set the cistern beside it. "Is that all?" I asked.

"Go to the mesa's edge," Ndukwe said.

"More walking? I need my cane." I looked around me. "Where are the girls?"

"Mesa's edge. They have your cane. Now go."

I limped down to the mesa's edge. My hip felt like the ball had disengaged from the socket and my good leg began to ache from the overcompensation. I fought through the rosewater and tried one of my meditative breathing tricks. I exhaled deeply trying to pull my stomach wall back against my spine, clearing all but the tiniest reservoir of excess air, then three short inhalations, another slow exhalation, three more short inhalations and one final lingering exhalation. I felt a little better but rosewater lingered on my breath.

Down Into the Wigwam Wasps' Nest

The girls were nowhere to be seen but I caught a glint of reflected moonlight. The shine came from the handle of my cane, which was stuck like a stake into the ground at the edge of the mesa erect above the steepest drop-off to the floor. As I retrieved my cane I saw a rope ladder that extended to the desert floor some fifty feet below. *You've got to be kidding.* I was in no condition to head down that ladder, but that's clearly what was expected of me.

I turned back from the edge. *Forget this.* I wasn't going to be goaded into risking my life for the equivalent of a middle school art project. El Rancho and the study be damned.

Then I heard the cries for help. They came from the desert. I recognized the voice immediately. Wren. But she sounded like I had never heard her before, I'd heard her angry, sad, happy, serious, but never panicked, never terrified. At the bottom of the ladder, just beyond the shadow of the mesa, I saw a large dark figure drag a smaller silhouette kicking and screaming into a globular white structure and disappear.

I dropped my cane to the desert floor below and started down the ladder.

My bad arm was up to the task, but barely. I had the strength in my grip, the forearm strength, to hold myself on the rungs. The problem was that my shoulder didn't allow my hand to extend above my head. So I methodically worked my way down the ladder using the following procedure:

First I grabbed hold with my good arm and lowered my good leg two rungs down, then brought my bad leg down to the same rung. With the top rung now about waist height I grabbed hold with my bad arm so that both arms were at the same height and both legs were at the same height. Then I simultaneously reached one rung down with my good hand and my bad leg, holding tight to the rung with bad hand and flexing my good leg to support the majority of my weight. Once my good hand was latched on, and my bad leg fully extended, I pulled myself close to the ladder with my good arm and brought my bad arm down to the level of my good hand while keeping my good leg flexed for support. Once both hands were again on the same rung I lowered my good leg to the level of my bad one and started the process again. In this way I was able to descend without ever having my bad shoulder attempt to reach above my head or have my bad leg required to support the majority of my body weight.

It was agony. I fought to control my breath and ignore the rosewater and the rolling sensation on my spine at the knowledge that Wren was getting further from me with every delay.

I reached the bottom out of breath, doused in rosewater and buckling under anxiety with all four limbs burning. But I wasted no time in resuming my pursuit. What had appeared a white blob from above was at ground level an eggshell colored structure that resembled a wigwam or an oversize wasp's nest. I detected traces of Midas in the exterior, in the subtle layering that gave it a finished patina and its ovoid appearance. The structure, the bones on which it was built, was of course hidden, but the sturdiness of it, its stout solidity, spoke to Taggart's touch. I wondered if I'd cut and sanded some of the beams that kept it standing.

I entered with a limp and immediately descended a set of plywood stairs. It was dark. The only lights were the remnants of moonshine behind me, and a cold dim light straight ahead in the distance. There was no handrail and I felt for each step with my good leg, my hand pressed to the smooth plaster of the interior walls.

I pressed further into the depths and the light grew brighter. I made out a lone figure ahead. As I came closer I saw the figure more clearly. It was Daphne. A hood covered her head and she held a shepherd's crook in her hand. The light was harsh and fluorescent and illuminated the light blue swaths of her silk robes most brightly. Around her feet sheep grazed on a small patch of sod.

"Where's Wren?" I asked.

"Won't you tend to my flock fair shepherd?"

"No. I won't. Where is Wren?"

The sheep began to crowd around my feet. They were ordinary sheep, not borregos, and a lamb, the youngest of the flock scarcely more than a newborn, nuzzled against my leg. "See," Daphne said, "they like you."

"I don't care. I'm looking for Wren." I fought back a sour pickled urge to spit.

"To follow the flight of the bird you must first walk the earth, only then can you look to the sky. Please fair shepherd, tend to my flock." She handed me a baby's bottle filled with milk. Again I swallowed down the pickle juice and took the bottle from her, resigned to playing along. Such was the way of Court. I set down my cane and sat down on the small patch of grass, glad at least for an opportunity to rest my leg and hoping that this delay wouldn't cause Wren to suffer. I figured there was little I could do but act out my part and hope that in the end no harm would come to her or me.

I shooed away the larger sheep to give the lamb space to nurse. I gathered the lamb into my arms and she immediately took the nipple. Despite my best efforts to focus and stay angry, warm vanilla crept in and slowly shifted to rich saffron.

I stroked the downy soft curls of the lamb's wool and felt the warmth of her body and the steady beat of her heart. She was nearly halfway through the bottle when the lights went out.

Everything was pitched into darkness. The lamb shifted in my arms, frightened, but I held her tight and stroked her. I fought to keep myself calm but the pressure returned as a slow roll down the spine and copper flooded my mouth at the specter of danger.

The lights came back up. Daphne and the rest of her flock were gone. Where she had stood was a man, horned, clad in hideous green with the scaly face of a lizard. Copper and tin exploded onto my palette and the urge to flee took me.

Before I could move the lights went out again. Disoriented, I didn't move. I had no place to run. I felt the lamb jolt. It squealed horribly and I felt it twitching as a rush of warm liquid poured into my lap. The lights came up. I saw the lizard man running away with something long and thin in his hand. Then he disappeared around a bend in the turnings of the wigwam-wasp's nest.

I looked down at the lamb in its palsied death throes, its throat slit wide gushing hot red life upon me. Fetid meat, saltwater and the smell of blood overcame me. The iron-rich blood smelled metallic like fear, and I considered for the first time the possibility that not only might I die in here, but also that Colin might kill me. I fought against the urge to run back to the ladder knowing that to do so meant abandoning Wren.

After a moment I gathered my wits and enough composure to lay down the poor little lamb. I went to stand up and looked around for my cane. It was gone, no doubt taken by the lizard man. In my cane's place was left a long dagger covered in the lamb's blood.

Left with no choice but to play out the scene until I could be sure that Wren was safe, I followed after the lizard man. After I made the first turning the walls narrowed and the floor sank and the ceiling dipped. Copper and tin overwhelmed all else as claustrophobia set in. Eventually I had to hunch so far over that my hip gave way in a burst of rosewater and I was reduced to crawling through the tunnel. The passageway became narrower and narrower, until I had to wriggle and squeeze to move forward by inches. It was at this moment that the terror, the frigid wet, overtook me, as I realized that to go backward was physically impossible and that pressing forward into an ever tightening space was my only option. So press on I did.

Still the passage narrowed until at last I reached a point where my shoulders stuck. The pain was horrific, rosewater wrapped in ice, and I jammed my shoulders, both good and bad, forward into the gap with as much force as I could muster.

I felt a damp slimy substance permeate my sweatshirt and at last I squished through against the lubricated walls and popped out and fell over a short ledge onto concrete. Flashes of rose-hued electricity shot through my frame and green dots pulsed before my eyes.

When my head cleared and the pain faded I saw before me a wide pool of clear water. Fluorescent lights illuminated it from above. Near the surface, where the light penetrated, I could see brightly colored fish swimming. I could not see the bottom and had no way to determine the pool's depth.

I felt a pressure on my toe that turned quickly to a hard pinch. I looked down and felt yet another pinch, as blue-backed crabs crawled from the pool by the dozen, overrunning my feet. I was not giving up, nor was there any way to turn back, so I tossed the dagger over the water and jumped in. The world went black. I was blind in the deep. I floundered, directionless, no light, no sense of up or down, forward or backward, just wet, cold and black.

Somehow I managed to reach the other side and scrabbled blindly out of the pool. Beneath my hands shells and claws clacked and slipped. Another set of pinchers crushed down on my right thumb and I shook my hand like a wet dog in a futile attempt to get free. Finally I slammed my hand on the concrete and felt the pincer rip a rosewater tear through the top of my thumb. I charged blindly ahead, away from the crusading crustaceans, and crashed headlong into a solid wall.

I lay there dazed as the lights came up. I snatched up the dagger that lay at my side and turned over, tasting tin and ready to defend myself. The crabs were several yards away, scurrying to no place in particular, and appeared to be no threat. I turned my head to look further down the passageway and assess my whereabouts. I struggled to reach my feet and came first to a knee, when I became aware of a shadow looming over me. I looked up and turned my head toward the wall on my left to pinpoint the source of shadow. Standing over me, no more than two yards away, was the lizard man.

He hissed and yelled and shook my cane above his head. It reminded me of a Sand Person lording victory over a Bantha on Tatooine. He then let out a yawlp, a half yell half screech that went from low to high air horn accompaniment. My ears rang with the sound of it and I staggered to my feet as he ran further into the depths of the wigwam-wasp's nest. From behind I could see two sets of straps around the back of his head, the mask and buggle-eyed red pane goggles he wore.

I pursued at full speed, caught up in the chase. I wanted to know who among the artists played this part. It might have been fun if it weren't for the pain and the cuts and the blood.

At each new turn I again caught a glimpse of him as though he were waiting for me. Finally we reached a straight and there he was, no more than fifteen yards ahead, at a plaster-walled dead end. He looked at me with bulging red eyes and hissed. I limped for him dagger in hand. The lights went out again.

I froze and waited, knowing, or at least believing they would come up again. It was all part of the act. They didn't. Instead there was a burst of blue flame and smoke filled the passageway. I coughed and hacked, the smoke was thick and acrid and smelled of sulfur.

Through the smoke I saw a dim yellow and orange flickering, but no Lizard Man. I kept my dagger at the ready. The blade was comfort, an illusion, but a comforting illusion. I could defend myself. I could choose. That was no illusion. So long as I held the dagger this was not scripted. I wasn't merely playing a part. I could improvise. I was an actor with his own will to action.

306

I looked about for any signs of movement. Nothing. The slow weight of anxiety crept down my spine and the adrenaline kicked in like I was sucking on a penny. Where was the Lizard Man? Would he attack? I felt the blood still wet on my shirt and wondered how far the violence might go. Was I ready to stab a man? I had never stabbed anything tougher than steak.

I saw movement at the end of the passage, low to the ground. I crouched to match height and squinted into the cloudy tunnel. The smoke was clearing, but slowly, the flickering light at the end of the passageway grew brighter and more defined, fire. There was no doubt about it; the flickering was flame. It threw shadows like devils through a prehistoric cave, my senses keyed, I saw nothing but phantoms refracted through smoke. Again movement came low on the ground. Lizard Man?

I heard a voice, Wren's voice, "Time is short. Riley time is short. Vanquish the dragon. Bring forth the fire."

"Wren!" I called out. But she didn't call back. Her words rang false. I briefly considered turning back, but to where. Even if I managed to cross the water in the dark I couldn't squeeze back through that tunnel. But I was at a dead end here. I heard Wren again. She said the same thing. Again I called out to her and she did not call back. Her words rang false, but I came for her and I would not leave without her. There had to be a way out. 'Vanquish the dragon. Bring forth the fire.' Clearly she was playing a role, but what the hell did that mean?

I stayed low and the smoke continued to clear. I kept my head on a swivel, but there was no sign of Lizard Man. I checked my backside. Nothing. The taste of copper overwhelmed everything but the smell of sulfur. I spun back quickly. Nothing.

The smoke continued to clear. And then I saw. The Lizard Man was gone. He had turned into a lizard.

A lighted tiki torch stood at the end of the passageway behind a miniature dragon. It was a Gila monster, just over three feet long with a muscular body and a scaly waddle of a neck. Lumpy and foul it waddled a few steps toward me. My anxiety disappeared. This creature wasn't menacing, gross, but not menacing. Copper gave way to bland emptiness tinged with rosewater. I felt fatigue begin to set in as the adrenaline faded. Lizard Man was gone. It was a decent magic trick but nothing more, and it meant there was a way out.

A piece of plaster lay on the floor ripped down from the wall. It revealed the source of Wren's voice, a small television monitor built into the wall. On it was a split screen image. I limped carefully forward not wanting to startle the lizard. It wasn't menacing but that didn't mean it wouldn't bite. I stopped once I was close enough to see the screen. The bile bubbled back instantly. One half of the split screen showed me standing in the passageway dagger in hand. The other half showed Wren, tied to a stake, her hands bound behind her. She kept repeating the same lines. I couldn't tell if it was live or a loop. It didn't matter anyway. I started running my hands along the walls searching for the way out. Obviously Lizard Man didn't turn into a real lizard. There must be a way out. All flavors but rose gave way to sage as curiosity occupied my attention. I wanted to solve this little ruse: how did Lizard Man manage this vanishing act? If I could figure that out I was sure I could find Wren. Then I could decide whether or not to stab Colin.

I searched in vain. Every time Wren repeated her plea the anger boiled up in my esophagus and I'd redouble my efforts to find an exit, but to no avail. Then, probably the fifth time I'd heard Wren's plea, it clicked. I knew what I had to do. I was not happy. There had to be another way, but if there was I hadn't found it. I didn't think Colin would actually hurt her, but could I really be sure?

I used the screen to estimate the location of the surveillance camera. I looked where I thought it should be. I couldn't see it, but I was sure I was close enough. I pointed the dagger in that direction. "Fuck you Colin," I said. Then I walked forward two paces and slashed the Gila monster.

I knew it would be brutal work. It tried to attack. It was fast, too. With such a short sword I had to be close, but I was ready. It shot forward at me. With my crippled leg I couldn't dodge it, but my good arm was strong. I overpowered it with sheer ferocity. Hack to the neck! Stab to the shoulder! Slash to the face! Hack! Hack! Hack! It tried to retreat but I was on it. I was merciless. I hacked and stabbed and when I was satisfied it was dead I grabbed the tiki torch and turned back to the camera, covered to the elbows in gore, and I raised the fire and roared. From the ceiling a set of stairs swung down like the entrance to an attic. I left the passageway of the wigwam-wasp's nest a grisly abattoir strewn with scales, limbs and lizard blood.

Ascent of the Bird

I marched up the stairs horrified but alive. I swallowed back rose flavored bile, chewed seafood saliva, picked mushrooms coated in peppermint and cinnamon from my teeth with my tongue, savored the muscular force of molé pressing upon my mandible, and fought back salt and tears and shame at the thread of saffron that shouldn't have been there. I was out.

I emerged to the desert floor and the light of the moon. A makeshift wooden sign with an arrow painted in green pointed the way. I laughed without mirth. It was comical, like it belonged in a Bugs Bunny cartoon. I half expected Elmer Fudd to pop out somewhere.

The sign led me down a short path back to the foot of the mesa's edge about two hundred yards east of the ladder I had previously descended. Another ladder awaited me, this one sturdy, metal and anchored into the cliff. Next to it was a pulley system with a platform that resembled an open-air dumbwaiter. Two signs were attached to the platform. One read 'Fire,' the other, 'Sword.' I focused involuntarily on 'Sword.'[*] It is a maroon word, but I paid heed to the letters. They painted a beautiful mix of violets and reds both deep and bright like spilled blood drying upon flat grey of steel, the 'd' at the end of the word, yet another sign that should have been printed in comic sans. A short sword maybe, but better called a dagger, and apart from the bloody blade and hilt it was unworthy of the word.

Determined to play this out to the end I put the torch into a slot that was cut to fit and placed the dagger on the flat space next to it. I used the pulley ropes to raise the platform up the mesa. Then I climbed the ladder using my good arm and my good leg, and I retrieved my fire and blade.

Wren stood alone, the stake behind her, but she was no longer tied to it. My cane lay on the ground between us like the arrow of a compass, the handle pointed toward me, the foot toward her. To one side of the cane lay the dead lamb, on the other side the bulk of the dead lizard lay in several

---

[*] Fire, long considered a symbol of strength and passion, is a surprisingly weak word. The 're' provides an impressive finish, but the pink 'f' and nearly invisible pale yellow 'i', give a lackluster beginning that cannot be overcome.

pieces. Wren lifted her hands, palms up. "The slaughtered and the slain," she said.

I bit back my anger and let mind and tongue wander, slowly drifting through the layers of flavors and feelings within the molé. I detected the grainy corn taste of pity hidden under the chocolate and spice like a corn tortilla for a full Mexican meal.

I threw down the torch. I dropped the dagger. I took Wren's hand.

We walked hand in hand to the awning overlooking the sculpture garden. The only sound was the loose gravel shifting beneath our feet and my cane. Again there was no space for words. Words would only come between us. I had Wren at my side, and together we crested the hill and approached the gathering for Court.

Mechanized Baptism

Together we approached yet I walked alone. Resolve, the willingness to act as required, despite opposition or adverse consequences. Resolve is not an emotion; it is action in the face of emotion.

I've said previously that argument doesn't get you very far. Finally, I heeded my own advice. I could not convince Wren. Her art was implicated. She was all in. I wouldn't threaten her. I had no incentives to give except my love, and she already had that.

So I approached the final scene of Court alone, but I had resolve. Shame is a powerful emotion. It causes suffering. The desire to avoid that suffering was the basis of my resolve.

Colin was a monster, but he was also a mirror and I had looked into that mirror and seen my own cowardice staring back at me. Never again, this I resolved. No argument, no threats, no incentives, just resolute opposition. Since I could not convince, I would demonstrate.

All the way up the hill I felt Wren's small hand in mine and repeated to myself that word, over and over: 'Resolve.' It did nothing to lighten the weight upon me or warm the chill from my tongue or displace the fragrance of roses, but it steeled my spine, and I limped upright and marched uphill with my chin held high. When we reached the top I let go of Wren's hand and squared my shoulders to the spectacle.

That's how I remember it.

Strong stance. Shoulders squared. Resolve in every breath. I scaled the hill with the resolve of a dead man walking. But it's easy to find resolve after the fact. Resolve coated in cinnamon sticks and grainy grit. Resolve is a word that inspires sympathy, when resolve meets circumstance and goes horribly wrong. Pride encourages resolve. Pride enhances resolve. Pride masquerades as resolve. Who can really say, right?

Colin awaited us. He stood atop a platform beneath the awning. Clad in vestments, a crimson hood covered his head and a large cross hung from his neck. All of the artists stood barefoot in line before a long platform. Their backs were to us and they were clad in identical white robes that were thin and sheer.

I tried not to let my eyes wander to the outline of Daphne's buttocks. Resolve. I didn't stare at the tattoos visible through the sheer fabric that covered Erin's back. Resolve. I didn't imagine how Shelly's nipples must have poked through the front of her robe like the tops of teapots. Resolve. I thought of Wren's hand in mine, but I didn't reach for it. Resolve.

The round cistern with the square base stood on Colin's left side. On his right side, in the center of the platform stood a wooden frame more than ten feet high and six feet wide. A solid plane of wood fit tightly inside the frame. It would have looked like a door were it not for the absence of hinges and the three loops of rope threaded through the wood, two high on the plane about a foot inside each corner, the other low and in the center.

Colin spoke without expression, "John did baptize in the wilderness and preach the baptism of repentance for the remission of sins. Mark 1:4". He pointed first to Wren and then to me. "You are the subjects. Quick. What are your first impressions?"

Wren didn't hesitate, "Christian theatre."

I thought for a moment, "My second least favorite gospel."

Colin smiled and continued the act, "Before me stand artists... and a novelist. The artist creates. But how? From where do we derive our creative inspiration? God? Who dares say it? Who dares risk that? Who dares to put their hubris on display?"

"I do." Midas stepped forward from the line. I couldn't tell if he acted on his own initiative or if he was playing a role for Colin.

"You?" Colin said. "You are divinely inspired? Hah. The gall. Come stand with me."

Midas climbed onto the platform and faced us. Colin gestured at the wooden frame, "Did you build this?"

"I helped Taggart."

"Helped? Did God inspire you to help? Did God deny you inspiration for your own work so that you could practice your carpentry with Taggart?"

"Jesus was a carpenter."

"So you're inspired by God and you compare yourself to Christ. I'll give you this Midas, when you go for hubris you go big. But still, why such arrogance? Nothing on display but your apprentice carpentry and yet you alone stepped forth to claim divine inspiration."

"Everything I create turns to gold. There is no false pride here. Hubris would be if I took the credit for myself. I give the credit to God."

312

"Spoken like a true Christian. All the Glory be to God. And your failures? Your sins? You put those on God too?"

"No. Those I formed of my own free will. Those holes were dug with my own hands. God merely handed me the spade."

"Very well. Shall we give our subjects a demonstration?"

Midas faced outward and extended his arms at the shoulders. Colin tightened the loops. First he tightened the two around his wrists. Then he bound his feet together at the bottom of the plane.

Colin pulled back his hood and spoke in a deep intonation so fraudulent it sent painful vibrations rolling down my spine, "Come forth the Vessel, come forth the Lord. Bring forth the Chalice, bring forth the Sword."

Shelly mounted the platform, a small vase clasped in front of her with both hands. The vase was black and white and bore the thin black lashes characteristic of Native American horsehair pottery with carvings of the moon's phases etched around the aperture. Ndukwe climbed atop the platform from the opposite end. He held the dagger that now bore the blood of both lamb and lizard.

Colin turned first to Shelly and made the sign of the cross. He uttered the words, "*Succus Lunarie.*" Shelly dipped the vase into the cistern then held it up to the light of the moon. She moved across the platform next to Midas. Bound to the plane he stared straight ahead. For a brief instant I thought she might offer him a drink, but instead she reached behind the plane of wood and poured out the vessel. I heard the splashing of water and realized that behind the plane was another larger pool of water.

Next Colin turned to Ndukwe, who raised the short sword with both hands to eye level, the blade turned flat to his face. Again Colin made the sign of the cross. Ndukwe slowly lowered the blade and Colin received it reverently. Ndukwe stretched his right hand forward and Colin drew a line across his palm and uttered, "*Sangre Reflectitur, Reflexionem Sol.*" Then he dipped the blade into the pool behind Midas before returning it to Ndukwe.

"Midas," Colin said, "you are of the initiate. Do you submit again? Willingly? As exemplar to the uninitiated?"

"I submit," Midas said, his eyes on the distant horizon, his face stoic.

"Very well. May your hubris be forgiven. May your creativity be celebrated. May your art be rejuvenated. May the life of the artist begin anew." Colin reached behind the cistern and pulled forth a mask. The faceplate bore the green face and blood drenched fangs of the dragon, the claws of the crab curved in subtle pink and silver from the sides of the snout, and the pearl spirals of the borrego's horns extended from the top of its head. Colin put on the mask and said aloud, "From three come the four. From the four come the two. And from the two comes the one." He raised his arms to the sky and shouted, "*Baptismus Machinosus! Renovamen Lunarie!*" Then he pulled a lever and Midas fell back through the frame, still bound to the plane in the pose of the crucifixion, and crashed into the pool behind him.

I saw then that the plane had wheels attached on the back. They rolled down two parallel tracks causing the plane to slide back like the drawers in a desk, and as they slid, the plane was completely submerged, and Midas with it. For a few brief, terrifying moments, all was still. My mouth was cold and wet. I was aware of my shirt stuck to my belly with lamb's blood. I wondered whether Colin would leave Midas to drown, if today was the day I would witness a murder.

Colin walked to the other side of the contraption. He raised his hands to the moon. Then he began to turn a crank, slowly, one revolution after another, and just as slowly the plane began to rise. Midas emerged from the water gasping for breath, coughing and choking. Colin continued to turn the crank, one revolution at a time. The plane reached a tipping point and gravity caused the wheels to slide back down the tracks. Finally after what seemed a hundred revolutions Midas was returned to the confines of the frame. His golden locks dripped darkly in the light of the moon, every aspect of his figure displayed to the group by the clinging of his robe.

Ndukwe and Colin loosened his bindings and took him down. He collapsed in Ndukwe's arms and was carried away.

"Subjects!" Colin removed the mask to reveal a toothy grin. It was the first genuine emotion I'd seen from him, he was giddy at the role he got to play. "What do we think now?"

Wren piped up immediately, "It's a commentary on modern religion, the intersection of religion and technology. Religion has become mechanized. The words and ritual are just window dressing. It's the machine that matters. Industrialized religion, assembly-line faith."

"Stop intellectualizing it," Colin said.

314

"Yeah," I said. "Don't intellectualize it. There's nothing smart about it. It's blasphemy."

"Blasphemy?"

"The worst kind, devoid of intellectual criticism. It's blasphemy for blasphemy's sake."

"Thinking of mommy, are we? Blasphemy requires belief. Art doesn't. It's about experience. Besides, you don't believe. I know. I wore yellow. Your religion isn't offended, just your sensibilities, and your family history."

"It's a humiliation disguised as art. It's insurance that Midas will suffer and we all get to see his little pecker. It's false. It's faux ritual."

"It's true. It's truer than you. You're still stuck on Christianity man. Just like mommy dearest, and we both know how that ended. When you're stuck on Christianity you only get half the story, only the Son, never the moon. If you're half-right, then you're half-wrong."

"What do you care? You deal in half-truths."

"With everything except my art!" He threw up his hands. "You still don't get it! Come up here and see. See with your own eyes. That's why I have their respect. You attribute it to manipulation because you don't see. You don't see that my art is always true."

I mounted the platform. It took a great deal of effort to climb up. I was tired, covered in blood, anxiety weighed on me like a rolling weight and rosewater coated my palette, but somewhere, beneath the currents of pain and dread, cinnamon stirred with the proper aromatics, the enhancers of clove and mint, and deeper still on the deepest layers of flavor lay Wren and molé, and the complexity of it all.

Resolve. I straightened my back and stood tall. I refused to lean on my cane. I met Colin's piercing lopsided eyes and I spoke, "It's all an act."

"You're damn right it's an act. And I'm a first-class actor. So again, the question we've been asking all along, 'What counts?' The sun's coming up, we're running out of time. My subject, what is your impression?"

"It's crude and phony. All of it. The bogus cave, the trek, the slaughter, this! You're a fraud, a thief and a liar stealing mish-mashed motifs. You don't have an original bone in your body."

"You insult us all." He stretched his arm out toward the artists watching. "Look at them. You think I did all this. Everyone participates in Court. You insult us all."

"Art that is derivative and hollow deserves to be insulted."

"All art is derivative. Defend your own originality. Tell me Riley, what is your impression?"

"It's an initiation. But a lame one. I ran your little obstacle course. I slew the dragon. I brought back fire. I saved the girl. What more?"

"This," Colin waved his hand at the baptism machine. "First is to prove." He clasped his hand together as though in prayer and gave me a short bow. "Last is to submit. So the question to you, are you in? Or out?" He stepped in closer and into my ear, no louder than a whisper, he bleated a soft "Baa-aa."

"Out," I said and turned to face the eyes of the artists. Their faces were inscrutable to me. My eyes watered at the pungency of cinnamon.

"You've made your choice," said Colin, and though I didn't look at him I could hear the smile in his voice. "Now you have to live with it."

And the molé rushed in. Molé and cold, coupled with a pain in my gut and a bounding pressure down my back. I looked to Wren, but she didn't look at me. I choked on molé and saltwater, a horrible sensation.

Resolve.

I climbed down from the platform.

Resolve.

Sometimes the only power you have is the power to refuse, the power to say no. When your position is one of weakness, when there is nothing to be gained and your only power is to deny, to deny is noble, so long as that act of denial is not born of cowardice. I passed the test. I refused the prize. I made my choice and I had to live with it.

I could have walked away without looking back. I would have, were it not for Wren. As I cast back my eyes she stripped away the last of her clothes and took her place before the board. I walked alone down the hill. I heard the clunk of the lever and the crash into the water, and I witnessed the sun rise, blood red, upon a new day.

316

VI. CH'I, CHAOS, CHAGRIN

Emotion and Reason: There's No Such Thing as a Free Ride

"Long way from civilization."

Civilization left me long ago. No one left to talk to but myself.

I found her goodbye note on my cot. Wren and Colin left for Portland early, the trip moved up to accommodate a gallery owner in the Pearl. I was alone. The artists remained, but all followed Colin's injunction to silence in the presence of the outcast.

Foulness, sadness, rotten rage and salt, a thin veneer of cinnamon, the sheen of defiance, and me unable to rise above my adolescent mood.

Did I read too much into the note? Was it that it was brief? Unceremonious? Did I expect too much? What did I expect? A poem? Flowery prose? A painting just for me? A tear-stained letter with words smudged and unreadable? 'XOXO' in the signature line? Or maybe just something less disdainful? Or did I imagine disdain? Did I mistake brevity for disdain? She had me thinking in circles, thoughts in a rut that ran round my feet.

I had to escape my thoughts. They flowed in the swale that circled the drain. Better to drain than to spin on end. If outcast, better exiled than shunned and caged. She was the only one who'd spoken to me in the weeks following her baptism. Now she was gone and a cone of silence enveloped me. Only the Professor would speak to me and I no longer wanted to speak with him.

"I said you're a long way from civilization," he called to me from above, leaning across from the driver's perch of his mammoth R.V. "Hop in. I'll give you a ride."

"No thanks."

"Come on! You're hoping to hitch a ride anyway. Even if that backpack's full of water you'll die in the desert if you try and walk to San Diego. Now get in. You won't find a more comfortable ride to hitch in."

His logic was unassailable. The steps slid out from the door and I limped up into the R.V. and took a seat next to him. I didn't offer a thank you.

"So where you headed?"

"Home."

"You didn't bother to tell me?"

"Why should I?"

"You signed a contract. But maybe you should. Go home, I mean."

318

"Maybe you should. Maybe we both should. Why do you need this place anyway?"

"Go for good? Never come back? Would you really leave if I suggested it? For good?" When I didn't answer the Professor said, "That's what I thought. You're lonely aren't you? Feeling lonely so you walk out into the desert alone. It's a good thing I'm your psychiatrist."

"Yeah the last few months have done wonders for my mental health." I stared out the window at the passing desert, barren and brown with a few dots of color, remnants of the brief flowering season already coming to an end, the landscape incongruous with the green day at my hip. I pondered the turn to yellow that would soon occur. The yellow turning was an appropriate place to put El Rancho and the desert, behind me. "So do you really believe this prophecy crap?" I asked. "You think I'm some kind of Lantern of Truth?"

"I don't know what Dr. Kane meant by that."

The 'K' was awful. I couldn't stand to hear it. "Don't call him that. Just call him Morty, please."

"He was often deliberately cryptic," said the Professor. "An unbecoming quality in a professor and a scientist, but a tool of the trade for a man of the cloth. I'll tell you what I know as clear as I can. I know that your mother was at the Rancho for several years. I know she gave birth to you at the Rancho. She was a test subject in Project Nimbus. I don't believe Dr. Kane was prophetic, but I believe Dr. Kane's prophecy referred to you. He had data. I've already told you what I think of your potential."

I gritted my teeth at the 'K' and swallowed back chanterelles and sour pickles. "Did you know her?"

"Yes."

"So you were here. Did you experiment on her? Did you work with Morty?"

"She volunteered. Just like you. But yes, I experimented on her and I worked with Dr. Kane."

"*Volunteered*," I sneered out a mixture of rank cod and wood rot. "And I just happened to volunteer for the same group. What a grand coincidence. Did you find me because of the prophecy? How long have you been searching?"

"Searching assumes that I hadn't found you."

"You're government aren't you?" I blurted it out without even thinking. The pieces just clicked into place in my mind. No taste accompanied it, but I had that same surreal sensation as when I tasted the molé in Barrio Logan, that ineffable sense of knowing something without actually knowing it.

The Professor remained motionless, his face blank, but he blinked faster than normal, or maybe time slowed down for me, just for an instant, but that little flutter, a flutter I normally would have missed, confirmed my suspicion. "What makes you say that?" he asked.

"For starters your overly calm reaction to my question. But also it's the only thing that makes sense. This place is crazy. If you're not government it makes no sense. Power and water sent in to a single estate from a military base thirty miles out. MRI's and CAT scanners buried in a desert bunker. You come to the desert to do research when you're a tenured professor at one of the premier research universities in the country. The pull you have at the University. The rumors that you fund the entire psychology department, that you find mystery donors to pour money into University coffers, that you can veto research projects. My God, Wren got tenure at age twenty-six on your recommendation for a completely unrelated department. All the rumors are true, you don't have to tell me, it's apparent now that I think of it. It's the only explanation that makes sense. I don't know what you are, but that money comes from somewhere. DOD? CIA? The only thing that doesn't make sense is Colin."

"Colin owns the place. We're just renting."

"I'm guessing that has something to do with Morty."

"You're very smart."

"I'm a fool. Like you said, I'm not leaving. I should walk away, but I won't."

"Have you considered that maybe you won't because you shouldn't? That maybe you stay because you sense the importance of our project even though you can't be sure of it." He was dangerously close to the mark, but he was wrong. I had no doubt that my fear and discomfort at El Rancho and this experiment would win out over curiosity and pride, if there weren't another factor. "Know that I'm here Riley, both to listen and to talk. You said you were feeling lonely. What's that taste like?"

"Always researching, eh?" Wren was my only friend, but she wasn't around and I just wanted to talk, to anyone. I was tired of being high and silent. The only words I'd used all week went into a poor draft of an early chapter in my novel. I was still toying with the idea of an epic poem. The paper would have been better used if I wiped my ass with it. "Loneliness doesn't taste really. It's more like a type of anxiety. I feel it on my neck, sometimes it's a little salty too."

"Interesting. This lends itself to a theory I've been pondering. I first thought of this when we were discussing shame, how its flavor is indistinguishable from embarrassment and humiliation. Before I said that meant that the emotions were one and the same, identical. But what if they're not. What if taste and touch capture only one aspect of your emotional experiences, just the visceral *feel* for lack of a better word. What if there is more to it than that. What if certain more complicated emotions have both a visceral aspect, or as we've speculated, a combination of visceral aspects, and also have a contextual component, that is to say an intellectual awareness of the circumstance in which the visceral feeling or feelings arise.

"Think of it this way. Embarrassment is the visceral emotion. Shame is your personal awareness of your embarrassment. In other words even if no one else is aware of whatever event or action you are embarrassed of, you nonetheless can be ashamed of it. Contrast this with humiliation, which is embarrassment caused, not by your action, but by someone else acting upon you. Yet another manifestation is guilt, embarrassment at the way you have acted toward someone else. Only humiliation requires an externalized context, only humiliation requires an audience. Only guilt requires awareness that your action affected someone else. Only shame requires that you internalize the feeling of embarrassment. Three different manifestations of the same visceral feeling, yet, I would suggest that each is a qualitatively different experience. Do you agree?"

"That they're different?" I thought about it for a moment. "I suppose I would agree."

"You sound tentative."

"I am. It's difficult to clearly recall a feeling as opposed to an event. That's part of why my tastes are so important to me, they let me know what I'm feeling, both during the experience and after the fact. You're asking me to look at my emotions in a different way, one that includes an intellectual component. It's counter-intuitive. Emotion is the enemy of reason, right? Yet you're asking me to include reason, thought that is, as an aspect of emotion. It seems weird, but I'm not sure I disagree with you."

"Well, let me clear up your thinking in this regard. There is no reason without emotion."

"What?"

"Emotion is necessary for preferences to exist. The mind responds to stimulus. Reason is dependent upon stimulus, dependent upon observations of the various stimuli that comprise the external world and that comprise reality, as we understand it. If every stimulus were given equal weight, reason would either function differently than we believe it to, or it would not function at all.

"Take something as simple as attention. You can't attend to every item in your field of vision simultaneously. You must select what to look at, what to focus on. Sometimes logic informs this selection, but just as often it does not. For instance, our brains are exceedingly adept at recognizing faces. If I show you a mosaic of cutouts with roughly equal proportions of some everyday objects, like bottles and chairs, some animal rear-ends, some random sections of pipe and tubing, and some faces. You are much likelier to see and recognize the faces before other objects. Why? Because faces carry emotional importance. Is there a logical basis for this preference? Yes, it is important to be able to distinguish the face from other forms because humans are the most important things we interact with in our external reality and when humans interact we take our social cues from each others' faces, but the preference is not based in logic but in emotion.

"Another example. You are asleep outside, in the desert. The wind blows through the dry brush near your camp. You hear it, but aren't consciously aware of the rustling. Then a coyote howls far in the distance. In terms of volume, decibel level, the howls and the wind are equally loud, but which one of these sounds registers in your conscious mind? The howl. Why? We are emotionally hardwired to respond to this as a threat. Thus it is both emotional and reasonable. Emotion tells us threats are to be avoided. Why? Because we have a preference for our own survival. The survival instinct coupled with reason might compel you to build a fire or a small shelter on a cold night, but the preferences, first to survive and second to not be cold, these are rooted in emotion. Without emotion we could not decide where to direct our reason. Reason in the absence of emotion is impotent.

"Now the examples I've given are not perfect, but they should make my point. All reasoning requires some method of determining from among an infinite number of potential observations which observations are important enough that we should bother reasoning about them. The mechanics of the brain bear this out. Information in the form of electrical impulses from nerve endings passes up the spinal cord, first into the limbic system, the emotional center of the brain. Only after the emotional importance of this information is processed does the information then pass to the higher levels of the visual and auditory cortexes, etc. What's more, the higher functioning aspects, those in the neo-cortex, send information back to the limbic brain forming feedback loops. In other words, emotion influences reason throughout the entire process of reasoning, and reasoned responses are consistently checked and re-checked against the emotional valances determined by the limbic brain.

"So, Riley, your initial way of thinking about reason is itself flawed. Since it isn't reasonable to consider reasoning in the absence of emotion, isn't it plausible also that emotion should not be considered in the absence of reasoning."

"Interesting, but how does that account for my more complex emotions. I'm thinking of emotions like pride. I experience pride as one taste, cinnamon, if you're right shouldn't it be a composite like embarrassment?"

"Is pride really all that complex? I'd suggest to you that it isn't. Pride is perhaps the most basic emotion, well, excepting fear perhaps. Pride is just a basic assignation of importance to oneself. Any emotion that includes, as a key component, the feeling, 'I am important', involves pride. The work we've done so far suggests that other emotions such as envy, jealousy, and vanity are all manifestations of pride within an external context and that sometimes implicate other visceral emotions such as sadness or anger."

"Shouldn't pride be implicated in emotions like humiliation then?"

"Maybe. Or maybe it is conspicuously absent and humiliation is simultaneously a form of embarrassment and the vanquishing of pride. You tell me?"

"I don't taste pride when I'm embarrassed, publicly or otherwise. What about loneliness?"

"Haven't you already answered that? It's a form of anxiety or worry. That's why you feel it in your neck, right?" His question was rhetorical so he pressed on with the explanation, "Loneliness may also present with anger or sadness, or even contentment I suppose, if you're the type that enjoys their solitude, hmm... though that would suggest there should be no anxiety, so perhaps one who enjoys their solitude can't properly be said to get lonely. But I digress. The important, necessary components are anxiety or worry, coupled with an awareness that the anxiety arises in part from the absence of others."

I had to give the Professor his due. "That's a plausible construct. I'm glad to see this hasn't been a complete waste of my time."

The Professor recoiled like I'd slapped him. "How could you suggest that it has been?"

"I haven't seen any evidence that I'm evolving, or evolved." I flashed to memories of impossible knowledge, knowing without knowing and I felt a tinge of anxiety that had nothing to do with loneliness.

"Patience," said the Professor. "We haven't yet hit on the most important emotional concept, empathy."

"Why is that the most important?"

"Perhaps it isn't but I will argue that it is, primarily because it is observable in so few species. Some scientists argue that primates and other higher-order mammals are capable of empathy, but there isn't yet a consensus. Some scientists and philosophers argue that it is the defining characteristic of human beings. We'll keep studying your emotions and your other synesthesias, but since you're already neck-deep in the finer points of the study I may as well bring you in on this."

Empathy and the Marijuana Paradox

The Professor turned the R.V. off the 8 and onto a secondary highway headed north. "Where are we going? I asked.

"We're making progress. Smoke a bowl I want to conduct a conversational experiment."

He didn't have to ask me twice.

I filled up my bong with Crystal Geyser from the fridge and packed a fatty. A minute later the rear of the R.V. was filled with dissipating grey smoke. I emptied and stowed the bong before I got too high and forgot. I returned to the front of the R.V. and felt my eyes glass over and my Yangs fade.

"I owe you an apology Riley," the Professor's voice carried the same tone of sincerity it did when he was lecturing a topic he was passionate about. "I have not been sufficiently empathetic to your situation. I am sorry. I know you are lonely. I know you feel that I have at times deceived you. I think you know some of the reasons why I have not always been forthcoming with you, but that does not necessarily excuse them."

There was a pregnant pause, as though he expected a response, but I had none. I was still trying to process and internalize the apology. It was difficult without the benefit of my emotional tastes. How did I feel about it? What should I feel about it?

Eventually the Professor spoke into the gap, "I have a gift for you, an expression of my empathy and the fulfillment of a promise. But before we get to that, tell me what you think about empathy."

"I haven't ever given it much thought. This is the first time you've brought it up."

"Let me ask you this, is empathy an emotion?"

"I don't taste it, so I don't think it's an emotion."

"Does it require imagination?"

"That's a hard one. I guess it does in the sense that you have to be able to imagine yourself in someone else's situation."

"Have you ever considered why marijuana dulls your synesthesias?"

The question shocked my mind a little. It was an apparent non sequitur, yet I had the distinct impression that the Professor had an unseen linkage in mind. I had no good explanation for marijuana's effect. "Maybe because it dulls all of my senses."

"Does it?" the Professor asked. "Then why does coffee have a similar effect? It's a stimulant. Do you ever cry during movies?"

"No," I answered reflexively, and then became aware that my answer was a masculine defense mechanism. "Not usually."

"And when you have? Were you smoking?"

"I was probably stoned."

"How about music?"

"It's better stoned. Everybody knows that, that's half the reason people smoke."

"So marijuana doesn't dull your emotions, if anything it enhances them, makes you cry during movies. And it increases your appreciation of music. So does it really dull all of your senses? How about your hearing? Is it dulled or enhanced?"

"I don't know. Could it be both?"

"Yes! That's the question. You got there quickly. I am talking about the marijuana paradox. Senses seem to be simultaneously dulled and enhanced. What is this alteration? You see with enhanced colors and reduced clarity. Is sight dulled or brightened?"

I pondered in silence and found myself woolgathering on past highs. There were so many they were hard to sort, so much life in altered consciousness.

"What are you thinking Riley? I want your knowledge. First-hand. Break it down for me. What is it to be stoned?"

"I was thinking about hiking. I used to get high and hike by the lake. I'd always wear a backpack. There were times when I heard footfalls behind me, footfalls that weren't there. I'd turn around real fast expecting to see a jogger or an attacker coming out of the brush with a knife, but nobody would be there. So I'd keep on hiking, and then the footsteps would start up again. I'd start to wonder if I was hearing the wind, or critters in the brush, but it never was. Eventually I'd figure it out, but only after I listened and walked, and listened and walked. It was my backpack brushing against my back.

"It was the weed. It didn't keep me from hearing sounds, but it made it hard to judge the distance. Sounds that were close sounded far away. The same thing would happen around the house. I'd get high and be all

326

paranoid that my mom was going to come home or the cops were outside. I'd hear a car pull up the hill or helicopters overhead. I'd tell myself 'oh it's just a Huey headed for Pendleton, but then the noise wouldn't go away, the car kept rolling up the hill, the helicopter hovered overhead. I'd start to panic that my neighbors called the cops. I was stupid, like they'd send a chopper for some kid smoking bud in his room. Eventually I'd figure it out, just like the backpack. Usually the car was the fridge starting up. Sometimes it was the A/C. The chopper was the bathroom fan, that's why it sounded like it was hovering. Sounds from inside sounded like they came from outside... projected you know..." my voice trailed off along with my train of thought, suddenly self-conscious of my words. "Sorry, I'm rambling."

"No, no. It's interesting and insightful. Let's bring that insight to bear on empathy. When you've cried during movies you were high. Did you cry because you related more to characters' suffering?"

"Maybe. But I think it also had to do with sound, the music."

"That's why music is so critical to movies. It tells you how to feel. But that doesn't mean you weren't empathizing more with the characters."

Again a silence filled the space between us. But not the space between my ears:

There is a connection. A memory... Empathy and music. Marijuana and emotion. A thought tugs but has no mass to pull, tip-top but formless there on the edge of my brain. I don't want to ramble. Profess to the Professor yes, but I need something clever to say. I hope I don't sound stupid. What were we talking about? Music and empathy. Music and empathy? I've lost the connection. Damn it.

"Where's your head at?" The Professor snapped his fingers at me and laughed. "Stoner slang. Did I use it right? Let me ask you this my daydreaming student, would you agree that marijuana makes you more introspective?"

"I wasn't daydreaming, I was thinking about what we were talking about."

"And?"

"And nothing. I don't know. But yeah it makes you more introspective. Sometimes I get real quiet."

"So maybe it's not 'where's your head at?' but 'where are you inside your head?' Answer me this: how does a drug that makes you more introspective also make you more empathetic? I think it's a question of distance, just like with sound."

"What does empathy have to do with close or far?"

"That gets us back to the question I asked earlier: what is empathy? You said before that empathy requires you to imagine yourself in someone else's position. Imagining yourself in someone else's situation, is that empathy?"

"No, you also have to feel what they feel in that situation."

"So it is a feeling?"

"No. The feeling you experience when empathizing is a feeling, but empathy itself is not a feeling. Say I see a child homeless and starving in an alleyway. I can imagine myself in her situation and feel the pain of her hunger, her fear of strangers robbing or raping her, her sadness at not having what others take for granted. I feel all of those things, an expression of empathy, but I don't feel empathy. It's just as true with something like sports. Being a sports fan is all about empathy. When my team wins I experience the happiness and pride that the players feel even though I didn't have anything to do with it. That vicarious enjoyment is a feeling, it requires empathy, but it isn't empathy."

"Then what is empathy?"

"I guess it's an idea."

"Interesting. If it's an idea can it be taught and learned?"

"I don't know. Empathy seems to arise spontaneously. It's natural. It's hard to imagine it being taught."

"How about the other way around?"

"What do you mean?"

"Can empathy be unlearned? For example the military spends a great deal of time and money conditioning soldiers to kill. It is difficult to take a human life, hence the training efforts to make killing reflexive, the propaganda and slurs to dehumanize the enemy. If empathy is an idea, is military training an attempt to unlearn empathy?"

"I don't know. Maybe empathy isn't an idea. I mean, despite all that training it's still hard to kill right?"

"Thinking about your brother?"

"Maybe. I just think it'd be hard to kill no matter what. Maybe that training just dulls the idea, or teaches you to ignore it. I don't know."

"Maybe it puts distance between you and the experience of the person you kill. Maybe that training is about creating the illusion that the person you kill is 'other', is not you. Maybe the marijuana paradox and introspection give us the clues we need to understand empathy."

"I don't understand. Of course the person you kill isn't you. Do you mean emotional distance?"

"Perhaps. But what I'm thinking of has less to do with feelings or even ideas. It has to do with perspective. This might sound crazy. I'm not even sure I fully understand what I'm about to say, but I feel the press of intuition creeping toward profession, so hear me out. What if empathy isn't about putting yourself in someone else's shoes at all? What if empathy is putting someone else in yours?"

"You're right. You sound crazy."

"Introspection is an inward orientation, correct? A look within yourself instead of out into the world."

"Okay. I guess that's one way to describe it."

"Are you still meditating?"

The non sequitur blast hit me and again I spiraled back the gravitational force of the Professor's thoughts, spinning around the mass pulling ever closer to the point. "Yes," I answered.

"Any insights?" he asked.

"Not really. Meditation calms me, I guess. And it makes you notice all the random insignificant thoughts that bounce around your head. Even if you're not thinking about anything you're thinking about something. Even if you're totally spaced out something runs in there, dialogue, pictures, it's like a program on auto, you can't shut it down, or I can't anyway. I guess that's the insight. Concentration is hard."

"What if you could shut it down? What if you stopped the train of thought that moves of its own accord. What would you have left?"

"Nothing, I guess. Just stillness."

"Nothing. Stillness. Emptiness. What if nothing is everything and emptiness is full?"

"That sounds like a lot of nonsense to me. Like you've been reading too many of those philosophy books that you recommend to me. Smart dudes talking nonsense may sound smart, but that doesn't mean they're making sense. Same with you, people may think you're deep, but that's just because you're talking over their heads. They don't understand what you're saying, but they assume *you* do."

"What if it is deep? What if it's not nonsense? Give me the benefit of the doubt. You know two things about me for sure, whatever else you may think. I'm smart. And I profess that which I know. Here is my hypothesis: what if the further inward you turn the more you see that the difference between what's outside you and what's inside you isn't different at all? What if there's nothing between self and other? What if it's really just a question of distance, of *perceived* distance? Do you hear what's close or what's far away? If you experience a sound as far away, is it? What if the marijuana paradox and my proposed hypothesis of the empathy paradox are one and the same? What if introversion is the key to empathy? What if the outside world is a reflection of the inside? What if empathy is not the experience of another's feelings, but identifying the other within yourself?"

"You're speaking in riddles. Or Greek."

"Perhaps. I need to ruminate on this. Thank you Riley."

"For what?"

"For being my sounding board. Sometimes a problem can't be solved right away. You have to talk it through and reconsider. Like you did with this project, El Rancho. You didn't want to come, you talked it through, reconsidered."

"And now I want to leave."

"Except you don't. You already admitted as much. Do you remember our conversation that day? The promise I made?"

"You made a lot of promises that day. You haven't exactly kept them."

"I've done my best. Go in the back, in the drawer below the bed there is a silver case. Pull it out and look in it."

A Promise Kept

I made my way to the back, levered my cane through the drawer handle and pulled it open to retrieve a long rectangular case. I sat down on the bench across from the galley kitchen, lay the box on the floor and opened it. Between foam padding cut-to-fit was a plastic and metal device that resembled the knee-braces worn by NFL linemen.

"What is this?" I pulled it out to study the construction. It was the largest brace I had ever seen, extending past the knee up to the hip socket. Despite that, it was lightweight, less than three-pounds.

"That is state-of-the-art of supplemental physiologic technology," said the Professor.

Sturdy O-rings of composite plastic were clearly designed to fit at mid-calf and the bottom of the knee joint. These locked in place and did not appear to be adjustable. The rings formed part of a splint, a single mold composite plastic, that extended to a hinged connection at the knee. The upper moiety of the two-piece splint was again a single mold, extended on both sides of the leg to a hinge at the hip. It formed another O-ring at the top of the knee. From there, bracing wrapped back from the splint arms in a semi-circle to brace the back of the leg at mid-thigh and the buttock culminating at the top of the thigh in the hip hinge connection. A thick strap connected above the hip hinge to a curved piece of plastic formed to fit the contours of the upper hip and buttock. The obvious use for the strap would have been to wrap at the waist and tighten like a girdle, but it seemed too long.

For all the masterful construction and high-tech materials, the oddest aspects of the brace were the metal components, eleven cylinders that connected the upper O-rings to each other and to the hip and knee hinges. These staggered thin tubes encircled the thigh. Some ran vertically, others at odd angles, even crossing in front and behind each other in shiny silver 'X's. Sage and cilantro imposed themselves on my consciousness through the dulling chronic haze as I examined the cylinders closely. A single thin rod protruded from each end of each cylinder through tiny circular apertures. The rods were the components that actually made the connections to the plastic bracings and the hinges.

"What do you think?" the Professor shouted from the front of the bus. "Pretty cool huh?"

"Yeah." I muttered and continued to examine the rod and cylinder setup. *Could it be?* I wondered, not daring to give voice to my hope. "What's it for?" I asked as an unseen mass settled upon my neck and a feather danced across the backs of my knees.

"It's to get you back in the ocean and back on a board." Saffron starbursts sent shivers of joy from tongue to toe. I could hear the unrestrained joy in his voice. Whether at his own vindication or my elation was immaterial. If this worked he had not only come through, he was spinner of dreams, a genie granting wishes I didn't dare wish.

"How does it work?" I asked. "I see plastic parts form a brace, but what do these metal cylinders do?"

"It's not plastic. The brace is constructed of carbon polymers, ultra-lightweight and nearly unbreakable. The cylinders are titanium alloy. They're the real trick. Each one is a little like a two sided piston. Outward force is generated from the center of the cylinder pushing one or both of the rods out in opposition to the brace. The combined action of the rods allows for both motion and stability. They provide the power where your muscles no longer can."

"Pistons? You mean this thing is hydraulic?"

"Pneumatic actually. Less messy. At the center of each cylinder is a chamber of highly compressed nitrogen."

"But how does it know when to fire the rod? And which rods to fire?"

"Computer. The main processor is in that curved piece at the top of the hip. Each cylinder has it's own silicon microchip embedded. The rate and direction of fire changes based on the kinetic forces applied by your body. The computer learns based on the input you give it. I'm going to stop for gas up the road here. I'll help you put it on. You may as well start getting it calibrated. Strip down. There's a pair of compression shorts in that top drawer for you."

We stopped and I puzzled over how to get into the device while the Professor gassed up the bus. Could it be as simple as stepping into it? I wondered. I tried this and it worked. I slid my leg straight through from the top. The fit of the brace was perfect, tight to the skin but not pinching, each curve conformed to my frame.

The Professor bounded up the steps and into the rear of the bus.

"It fits," I said.

"It has to. It can't be adjusted. So don't go putting on any weight. That's a custom pneumatic brace."

I started to pull at the long strap hanging from the hip. "So where does this go?"

"Oh wait." The Professor reached down into the box and pulled out a curved silver triangle with rounded edges. "Before we go any further you need to put on this cod piece. See those flaps on the compression shorts? It fits in there."

"Cod piece? What for?"

"To protect your stones, man!"

It was bulky, albeit lightweight, but a bulging mounded protrusion. "Can't I just wear a cup?"

"That's made of an extremely hard plastic resin shot through with strands of Kevlar. You see those three pistons on the inner thigh. They generate forces upwards of five hundred PSI. That's why the pistons are constantly firing in opposition, to balance out those forces. Should one of them malfunction…"

"I'll wear the cod piece." I stuffed it into my shorts. It was uncomfortable but a small price to pay for testicle insurance. "So what do I do with this strap?"

The Professor moved in and pulled the strap between my legs, his hand passing uncomfortably close to my groin. "You wrap a figure eight, like this, under and around each thigh. Then you press the bracket into the clasp on the hip brace." It clicked in. "Perfect. Now you should walk on it a bit. Do a few squats. Get into positions you'll use when you're surfing."

The brace responded to every flex. I wasn't completely without pain. There were tinges, shooting sensations, but I felt like I had a new hip. I bent as low as the flexion in the brace would allow, crouched down like I was shooting the curl.

"The support is primarily vertical." The Professor said. "Your lateral movement will be somewhat restricted. You need to become accustomed to turning the torso above the waist. Use your abdominals."

I practiced the stiff upper body turns and kept on testing the squat capabilities, feeling the pistons fire and release and refire, *chu-chu-chi*. I imagined myself on a wave: the rush of gravity and lemonade as I sped down the face, the frothy spray of saltwater off the lip hitting as I snapped back into the wave's face and allowed its momentum to push back at me, thrusting me forward down the line. I thought of the sun, the sand, the ocean, just to sit in the ocean again atop a board and watch the sets roll in, the bobbing atop the surface, the waiting on the wave and turning to—

The saltiest wave in the world hit me with a force that knocked me to the floor. "Paddle!" I wailed and pounded the floor with my fist, my stomach wrenching in spasms of sadness. "I still can't paddle! My shoulder! I can't surf!" Tears welled up in my eyes. To have my wish granted and then taken away! I wished I'd never got into this R.V.

The Professor pulled onto a turnout and stopped the R.V. He came back and placed a hand on my shoulder. "Don't touch me!" I sobbed. But he ignored me and kept his hand on me.

"We haven't been able to solve the shoulder problem. That's a range of motion issue. It's not possible to extend your range of motion with a brace; a brace does the opposite. But we didn't forget about it." He stroked my back with his hand. "There are ways to surf without paddling."

The apparent hit me in the mouth like scalding hot boiled chicken. "You mean tow-in."

"I presume you've heard of Cortes Bank."[*]

"We're going to Cortes Bank?"

"God no! That's no place to test a prototype unless you're trying to commit suicide. And the season's passed. We're going to see a friend. But it's important to have a goal."

---

[*] ADDITIONAL DATA: Cortes Bank is located one hundred miles west of San Diego in the Pacific Ocean. It is an underwater island, i.e. completely submerged, that is almost the size of Catalina. In optimal wind and swell conditions Cortes Bank creates waves that are amongst the largest in the world. However, wind conditions are not often calm enough to produce rideable surf. The correct conditions for surfing usually only occur between the months of November and March.

334

Leviathan

We entered the facility after the Professor flashed his badge at three separate security checkpoints and had a spirited discussion with a security guard who relayed information through a walkie-talkie. He was apparently unaccustomed to large all-black tour buses being driven onto the grounds.

We disembarked onto what I assume was an abandoned airfield and approached a gargantuan concrete hangar with the largest single door I had ever seen. It was a rollup door of corrugated metal like those on the Sparx Factory, but it was at least four times as high and five times as wide. I could not imagine an object large enough to require such a door.

I walked with ease and trepidation simultaneously thanks to the pneumatic brace and the sheer scale of the building. We entered through a human-size door to the left of the rollup. I had drastically underestimated the size of the building. A single cavernous concrete room, it extended back from the door the length of five football fields with a nearly corresponding width.

"Welcome to Leviathan," said the Professor. We stood poised above a great pool on a wide promontory ledge that ran the perimeter of the room. Heavy lifts and cranes filled parts of the ledge, but even their sheer tonnage and flagstaff elevations did little to counteract the vast enormity, the emptiness, of the room.

"If we weren't so far inland I'd guess we were at dry dock." I said.

"It's a dry dock for experimental vessels and a hydrology lab," a voice called out from across the expanse of water and a scarecrow of a man sidestepped a scissor-lift and began to work his way around the ledge. "When you build something this expensive it's best to make it multi-purpose."

"Dr. J.!" The Professor called to him. *Dr. J?* I squinted across the room at the frail figure. *Could it be?*

"Dr. J.!" I called.

"Riley Sparx! Professor! So glad you could make it." He shook both our hands with the enthusiasm of an eccentric in his old age. "You're going to love what we've done here." He paused and ran his fingers through his grey moustache. "My Riley, it's been a long time. I heard about your parents. I'm very sorry I didn't make it to your father's funeral."

"Don't be. No one else did."

"All the same I wish I had. So very sad. He was a good friend. I was in Papenburg, when I heard. I couldn't get back."

"It's okay. It's good to see you again."

"And you Riley. And you."

"Riley is concerned that he can't paddle," the Professor interrupted. "I was hoping you might reassure him."

"You won't need to paddle today. And if this works," he pointed at the pneumatic brace, "then we'll figure out the logistics. I think you can probably hold a towline with your good arm, but we'll figure out a solution if the forces prove too great. I don't think we're likely to get you paddling though. The shoulder is a very complex joint." I nodded and felt a slight release of weight and tension although a marble size pressure continued to roll about my back. Dr. J grabbed me at the bicep and smiled causing a warm wave of nostalgia to carry away my residual disappointment. "Not to worry," he said. "You're going to surf. *Today.* Just wait until you see what I've cooked up."

The professors set about readying the experiment, planning and plugging data into several computer terminals. I limbered up as best I could until they were ready. I tried to stay out of their way, but I couldn't resist asking a few questions.

"If this is a dry dock how do you launch the ships?"

"Nothing actually launches from here. This facility is used to build and test prototypes, experimental vessels. We aren't repairing battleships in here."

"What are we doing anyway? I'm going to surf in here?"

"Yes."

"How?"

"You'll see. What you need to understand is that for all you do see there is much more that you don't. There is more water underneath this facility than there is in it."

I continued to stretch until the professors were nearly ready. Dr. J sent me into a small storage closet while he called for additional workers to prepare the final setup. "Go in there and check it out. We can modify the binding if need be." In the tiny closet I discovered a true treasure, a

336

blue and gold late 90's model Sparx shortboard, custom shaped with my father's unmistakable signature just above the centerline. The board's specs were top-flight: six-four, quad fin, with a pro-setup and bindings to hold my feet in place. It was good thinking, the bindings. If I was going to surf tow-in I'd better get used to being strapped to a board.

"What do you think?" Dr. J asked as I emerged from the closet.

"It's great. Thank you."

"It's yours to keep. A gift from me. It was a gift from your father but I was never good enough to ride it."

"Thank you. I'm not sure I am anymore."

"You will be. Now check this out." Workers operated two cranes to lower down a single slanted sheet of metal several hundred feet long and 60 feet high at one end sloped to twelve feet high on the other. Workers in hard-hats stood at either end of the sheet and made sure that it fitted into solid metal slots riveted to the side and end of the pool. The sheet went into the pool at an angle so that two pools were created. One, the main pool, was a tapered trapezoid, widest at the end near the roll-up door. The other pool was smaller and formed a triangle.

At a signal from Dr. J a drain was engaged and all the water emptied through the floor of the triangular pool, leaving only the main trapezoid from the initial rectangular expanse of water. The workers left and Dr. J unscrewed a cap in the floor of the ledge on the side of the pool where the sheet had been inserted. He inserted a wide plastic tube with a hexagonal fitting into the space where the floor cap had been and tightened it down. The workers returned carrying a heavy metal sluice that looked like an oversized version of the gutters you would find on the eaves of a house. The sluice was placed with one end attached to a short metal pole that protruded from the ledge, the other end lay atop the metal divider sheet and into the main pool, approximately two-thirds down the length of the pool.

Again the workers left and Dr. J took up his position at the computer. "You're familiar with the concept of a standing wave, Riley?"

"Yeah sure. But don't you need a special board to surf them?"

"You're thinking of the type of standing wave created by what they refer to as 'sheeting' technology. A special board is only required because the wave is created by a sheet of water that is very thin and moves very rapidly across a specially designed surface. The wave you surf is as thin as that sheet of water, usually less than three inches, so you can't use a board with fins. I am referring to the type of standing wave that occurs naturally on rivers throughout the world."

"Yeah, but no one has been able to replicate those, and we don't have a river."

"Oh yes we do." Dr. J grinned with the wild-eyes of an old man captured by a youthful idea. He pressed a series of buttons on his computer and the pumps and turbines started up. I couldn't see them, but I could hear them and feel them rumbling. Then the water started to flow, slowly at first, then faster and faster, until small ripples of whitewater began to form at various points throughout the pool. At the far end of the pool the water dropped several feet revealing a clearly defined ledge over which water flowed rapidly.

Dr. J shouted over the rushing water, "The reason no one could replicate a true standing wave, a river wave, was that they couldn't replicate the river." He pressed another series of buttons and water began pouring in at an angle through the sluice. Immediately, where the flows converged, a visible bulge appeared and the speed and turbulence of the water increased.

I watched in awe, chewing through lemon-lime paste, semi-sweet berries and fresh mackerel. My knees began to itch and tickle so badly that my legs started to shake and the pneumatic pistons fired in compensation, *chu-cha-chuchuchu.*

Before my eyes it started to happen. First just a small bump up, a steady splash at the ledge, then in the blink of an eye, a fully formed wave, an arcing break that peeled to the right. It grew steadily then stabilized, a solid five-foot right hand barrel. "Haa-hah!" The doctor howled with delight and I thought he might jump up and click his heels. "A deep-water, barreling, standing wave! Hoo-hoo!"

"How did you do it?" I asked. "People have been trying to make one of these for years."

"With the correct topography it's just a matter of controlling water volume and flow rate. There's a little additional engineering to create a smoother, cleaner barrel, like a small flow jet moving opposite the rushing water, but all the problems other people had trying to create this, we solved them by reengineering a river."

"It's unbelievable."

338

"It's a hydraulic jump. The physics of it are simple enough if you know what you're doing."

"So how does it work?"

"You want me to explain the physics? Well, I suppose I can give you the layman's version. We start with a gradual change in water depth. The pool is deepest at that end." He pointed down the length of the dry dock. "And shallowest where the wave forms. But it isn't a uniform gradient. There are undulations in the contours of the bottoms, some subtle, some sharp, this adds to the top water turbulence you can see in the form of swirls and whitecaps. Then if you look over here," he pointed to the water entering through the sluice. "See the rill created, how it converges with the main flow, the result of that placement is water flowing faster on the side closest the sluice than the side away from it. That very fast moving channel comes upon a man-made rock formation designed to mimic aspects of underwater formations we studied in several rivers around the world. That is the point where the jump actually occurs and the wave is formed.

"The aforementioned opposition flow jet adds to the intensity of the hydraulic jump as well as forming a resistant current that adds to the 'standing' quality of the standing wave. Some water passes over the obstacle and beyond the wave, the rest jacks up and breaks across, as you can see. The water that flows through is re-circulated. Underground reservoirs provide sufficient water and high-pressure pumps provide sufficient flow to create the simulated river."[*]

"It's genius," I said. "You could make a fortune on this. What an ideal training wave."

"It doesn't scale well and the pumps alone cost a fortune."

"But you were able to build it."

"At great expense. Plus, we had the requisite space. Not many pools this big."

"Am I the first to use it?" I asked through a mouthful of cold, soggy rosemary.

"Don't worry. It's perfectly safe. Well, safe enough for a pro like you."

---

[*] The pool and standing wave mechanism are depicted in Appendix 'D'.

He had utterly missed the import of my question, the reason why I suddenly felt a curious anxiety. "No, I meant... you didn't build this for me, did you?"

"No... and yes. It's complicated. We do other things here, like test those experimental boats. The modifications to create the wave, we did that for you, but don't worry, that brace you're wearing has, er," he hesitated, "other applications."

A cinnamon kick pressed up along with a feather flicking on the back of my knees. I knew what I wanted to do. "So when can I surf this thing."

Dr. J grinned, "Right now."

Triumph and Loss

I took up position on a rubber mat along the ledge. I tested the water temperature with my digital thermometer, 68 degrees, with this volume of water it would take hours to heat the water even a degree or two. Satisfied, I hung the skegs over the lip, so as not to damage them, and strapped in. The bindings were set perfectly, just the right width apart with the left foot strap angled slightly forward.

I could hear the water frothing and churning behind me, the unceasing movement of change and chance, minute and dangerous fluctuations hidden by the illusion of the larger pattern, a wave standing, form without solidity.

I hopped back. Pistons shot, *chu-chu hiss*, and for the first time in years I left solid earth with two feet. The board hit flat, a balanced plane. I felt the grip of the current as the fins caught beneath the fluctuating surface and I allowed myself to drift backward with the flow into the heart of the wave. I ducked with instinct more natural than walking, more natural than breathing, muscle memory surging with the flow of water, The sheeting water splashed through the curls of my hair. I felt the drip of water in my eyes. A moment of oddness at the lack of expected salt in the water was overcome by the citrus-drenched sweetness of the moment, wild exhilaration in the forgotten familiar of the freshwater ride.

Inside the curl I began to test my abilities. I turned sharply back into the wave face, forcing the nose of the board up then down cutting back off the stand-still-shoulder. I executed the maneuver, but not without difficulty. The brace supported my worn down hip, but the Professor's admonition about limited lateral mobility was a fair warning. I found my abs and the muscles of my front leg compensating, overworking to force movements that had once come with grace and ease. The twist came from higher than it should have, a semi-pirouetting of shoulders and profile. My crouch was lower than it used to be, another unconscious compensation, as it lowered my center of gravity. The exhilaration, the lemonade burst, faded as rolling pin rockers slotted my spine in extreme anxiety at sudden fatigue.

I could not maintain. How was it that my energy was so quickly exhausted? Natural movements altered ever so slightly became gross anomalies. My only hope was to ride forward, out of the barrel, and hop back onto the mat. I thought about the turn, about my posture, my crouch, each bend, each twist, my position on the wave, and with each controlling thought my control over the board lessened, as that which was natural became mechanistic. My legs wobbled. Bursts of compressed air loosed like a firing squad of full-auto paintball guns, as I strained to hold the line. The board wagged beneath my feet: *left-right, left-right*, the deviation grew greater with every correction.

I fell.

The professors were ready with long hooks and extra hands and pulled me from the water.

Standing in silence on the side of the pool I felt within me the cool quench of that smoldering stick of cinnamon at the center of my being. If you have never been truly exceptional at something I doubt I can make you understand. I was Riley Sparx! But the only word that mattered was 'was.'

Was this what it was like to play in the Old-timers Game at Yankee Stadium? Did Dimaggio and Mattingly feel this same sense of loss of pride and time as they stepped onto the field to display the shadows of their former greatness? No. Their time had passed. That was the difference. I wasn't an old-timer. I was a victim who lost his prime. They could step onto that field, nothing left to prove, and enjoy it as a fond remembrance of former glories, a fleeting glimpse back to a time well remembered now properly past. They gained something when they stepped onto that field, bittersweet perhaps, but a sweetness nonetheless. I was filled with loss.

I often think back on this moment, on my feelings and musings at that instant of reflection and sorrow as I stood beside the pool. A self is a story. The tale of how that which one does is different from what others do. Fiction or non-fiction? This is the underlying tension. This is the reason we wear silly hats and bold colors, or business suits and uniforms. This is the reason we have hobbies and work jobs and why a select few do work so weird that it's primary significance is that it is unusual. It's all for the sake of the story, the desire to distinguish held in opposition to the desire to conform, competing drives always juxtaposed and held in varying states of tension. The self is that form which is distinguished, set apart from the many, from the whole. Yet another level of tension: if the self is but part of the whole, can you ever be wholly yourself? Is self nothing more than a subplot of history? Or can a part sometimes be greater than the whole? A subplot can dominate a narrative, but can it subsume it?

Perhaps no illustration or words can demonstrate the point, perhaps it is of that form of knowledge that is wholly experiential, best evidenced in meditation or prayer, where the tension is reduced and removed until the point of unification and the boundary between self and other is wholly erased. Or is the boundary moved to encompass all? It depends primarily on your point of view: Do you see it from within or from outside? Erasure? Or expansion to include?

So, what a man is, what a *self* is, is that which distinguishes it from other things. Which again begs the question: if so, can your *self* have a true essence, if it exists only because it is different from other aspects of existence? And if not, is the true path not found by searching for no-self, by striving to eliminate the world of opposition and tension, by seeing the oneness of it all? If I could see that, not only see it, but also hold onto that vision, would I still feel pain and sadness at the self I lost, the self that rode waves like few others could ride them? Or, would I see something greater? That *I* am the wave and all things ride with me.

To become the ocean you have to drown.

Moving Fast by Standing Still

One month later I stood on the same lip of the same ledge and faced the same wave.* For one month every day had been the same, morning calisthenics at the Factory, breakfast at a nearby diner, mid-day yoga, bath, a walk along the beach, late-afternoon weights (squats with the good leg, hold the weight in the good arm), music or television, dinner: chicken breast or steak, broccoli or Brussels sprouts with bacon, a twenty-two of Stone Arrogant Bastard, then two bongloads and off to bed, a method-month for mental and physical health. My good leg, torso, back and abs were all strengthened and suppler. I could twist harder and further above the waist. I lost twelve pounds, an impressive feat made all the more impressive by doing it while drinking Stone daily.

I could not bring the brace with me. It had *other applications*. This was a devastating end to my day of failure but I sucked it up and followed the program knowing that if I was fit, the brace would respond and the wave would be waiting.

I was ready. This time I would not only master the wave, not only demonstrate the skill and feel and ability of a consummate professional, but this time I would maintain. And I did.

My stamina had increased a hundred-fold and my determination with it. I drifted in, felt the wave carry me and proceeded to dominate it. Cutbacks on every section of the wave, then I pulled back into the power at the breaking edge and used it to pick up speed, willing myself to move across the stationary flow. I launched a floater. I shot the curl. I showed off. I screeched sweet and sour. I kept on. A three-sixty spin controlling the board front and back, I felt the power of compressors firing off like AK clips as I forced the fins down, then spun back around; a maneuver that was impossible a month prior was now in my bag of tricks.

I rode. I conquered. I maintained. Five minutes, then ten, but as I approached fifteen a strange thing happened. My body didn't give out, my heart did. As I shredded the wave with ever increasing precision and technical prowess the lemonade disappeared, and then even the cloying

---

* It was of course not the *same* wave, although in theory I guess it could have been, it is more accurate to call it the same wave shape made with different water molecules in a different arrangement.

344

press of cinnamon vanished. And in that moment I had an epiphany. I saw the truth. This would never be enough. It was not enough to answer the challenge, to take on the wave; I had to answer not a challenge, but a call, the call of the ocean.

The professors were impressed. I was depressed. I left knowing I could, but without having done it, and knowing I would not be able to fully shake this agony until I faced not waves, but surf. Only two words lifted my spirits as I left that day, Cortes Bank. A magic place I would never see.

I left the brace with Dr. J. I never saw it or him again.

Subject

It was a grey day, a grey sky, a grey mood, my mouth tinged with salt and the rot that comes of prolonged exposure to the cold ocean air. June gloom, oft present over San Diego, made a rare desert appearance. My June lay behind me pushed in from the coast, matching month to sky to mood in perfect synchronicity, a great grey nimbus of melancholy blowing at my back. It would no doubt disappear in the late morning desert sun, but for the time being the world seemed to be the unified receptacle of my emotional states.

Her sculpture had three figures. One, a tiny girl-child made of clay, sat huddled, arms wrapped round her legs, face tucked to her knees so that only one fearful eye was visible. Beneath the hem of her skirt her feet pressed together concealing something small and round, like a seed or a nut. Above her towered a monster. Intricate bits of interlaid metals set into the clay formed a mosaic depiction of its scales. The metal transitioned to clay at the head. Its features were muted except for the exaggerated eyes and fangs smeared thick with blood-red pigment. It was snake-like, but not a snake, for it had arms that reached toward the girl. Light cast from above and the right put the girl entirely within the monster's shadow. Finally there was another figure, smaller than the monster but larger than the girl, clay, faceless, but clearly male, two smooth blobs, stacked atop each other, nothings, nearly formless, except for a singular drooping protrusion.

"And who is the audience?" asked Colin.

Wren looked right at me and announced, "Riley Sparx." A brief bland blast hit me and was subsumed. It was the closest I had stood to Wren since she left for Portland and molé dominated my palette just at being near her. However, she was different since the trip, like part of her was removed, like her bravado was gone. An ingredient was missing from my molé, but I couldn't tell which one.

The sound of Colin's laughter rang in my ears. It still rings in my ears to this day. "Oh tonight is gonna be good!" he hooted. "This is exhibit one. Imagine what we got in store."

It was the night of court. It was also the summer solstice. In celebration of this rare occurrence Colin had decreed an open Court, a festival, Solstice Lunarie, part art show, part rave. I remained *persona non*

346

grata, but Solstice Lunarie was open to the public and the Professor had paid my way.

"I'm sure it'll be a great time," I said trying to keep my voice flat. I refused to look at Wren. Instead I stared at the sculpture. The engineering and use of materials was amazing, but my eyes kept leaving the monster and returning to the blobs.

"So?" said Colin expectantly.

"So what?'

"So you're the subject. Tell us what you think."

I continued to stare at the sculpture, buying time. I knew I could not escape Colin's cross-examination if I wanted to stay. If I refused he might let me stay to appease the Professor, but would hold Wren apart from me. Participation being required I was mindful of only one thing, to be decisive in my critique. If I held to my review I could say nearly anything, but Colin would not accept any subjective wavering.

"Come on Riley she chose you. Show her some respect man. Start with the easy stuff. Does this count? Did Wren create art?"

"Oh yes," I said without hesitation. "She has provoked a reaction, I feel something. I am trying to understand the work."

"Fine. What reaction was provoked?"

"Empathy."

"Empathy?" Colin sputtered. "That's not a reaction."

"Sure it is."

"No. It's a falsification. It's a projection. The question is what do you feel? Subjectively man. What do *you* feel that causes you to project into another person's shoes?"

I could feel the group of onlookers growing. They pressed in like the plates of a vice, the early-comers and the artists of the Rancho anxious for a confrontation. "I thought I was the subject here. I said it provoked a reaction of empathy. It counts."

"It counts. But you're hiding. You're hiding the art from all of us. Verbalize so that we can share in the art, secondhand is the best we can get, we aren't the subject. Stop hiding behind your empathy."

"You want to see my empathy. You should reach for your own. Don't you see it too? That little girl is Wren, or a part of her anyway. And she's desperate. She's trying to hold onto something tiny. She's trying to protect the one little thing from that monster.

"I feel empathy for that little girl. I feel empathy for Wren. She's trying to protect herself in the face of a monster."

"So it's Wren," Colin said. "Assuming we accept that…"

"You have to accept that. I'm the subject." Resolve. I remained firm in my critique. Anything less would be taken for weakness.

"Unless you're lying. But assuming that I don't call you a liar and we accept that Wren is the little girl, what do you believe she is trying to protect that justifies your feeling of empathy."

"I don't know."

"Oh now you don't know. You've got a lot to say about Wren putting herself in her art but you don't know why? You're the one who said she was protecting something. What is it?"

"It looks like a seed."

"A seed of what? Buckwheat? Oat? Marijuana?"

"Hope," I said. "I think she's protecting a seed of hope." Colin was momentarily silent. I looked at Wren. Tears streamed down her cheeks. She no longer looked exotic, just vulnerable and small. My molé lost depth and spice with every passing instant. "But I'm more interested in the monster."

"The monster is beautiful," said Colin.

"I empathize with her, not with whatever she's protecting and certainly not with the monster. I empathize with her pain. And that's as far as I will analyze this."

"Ah so she's begging for protection. Is that it? I must say that insight does point out a gaping hole in your analysis. The third figure is curiously absent. Have you nothing to say about that? Is he the protector perhaps?"

I held my chin up. The small crowd gathered around us remained silent, but was suddenly large in my awareness. My hip ached. The rosewater was helping for once. It kept me from losing control. The pain dulled me to the world, to his taunts, to the eyes on me, to Wren's proximity. I put my mind on my hip and focused on the pain, lapping it up like rosewater in the dog bowl of my soul. Nothing from Colin's art but attempts at humiliation, but if I said so I'd wind up looking the fool. His game, his rules, and Wren set me up for it, the bitch! That thought came unbidden. And I wondered how long it had it been there buried beneath the complexity of molé.

348

The anger impressed, forcing acrid flames through the roses, dragon breath at the back of my mouth. I bit my tongue, I shut my lip, I closed my flap and I wrapped myself in mental mirrors and prayed that they saw themselves staring back from me.

"What about the third figure Riley? Curious blind spot. Might say more about you than the artist. Here's what I see: That 'monster' as you put it is focused on the girl in both a paternal sense and a carnal one. The seed she protects is her virtue—"

"Well it doesn't really matter what you see," I interrupted. "You're not the subject."

"Which if allowed to grow will flower into womanhood, but not if the," Colin made air quotes, "monster—"

"Enough!"

"Relax man I'm not impugning her, if she wants to put all her childhood baggage out for everyone to see it—"

"I'm the subject! These are your rules. We're playing by your rules."

"There are no rules in art man, just different points of view. So give me that. I want your point of view. What about Blobby?" This got a few snickers in the crowd. I resisted the impulse to look at Wren. If I looked at her I might have cried.

"What about Blobby?" he said. "What do you see? Or maybe a better question is why don't you see him at all? You haven't said a word about Blobby."

"Blobby's an enigma. He represents the unknown."

"You're such a bullshitter."

"Coming from a pimp like you that's quite a charge."

"A pimp?" Colin straightened up and pulled his shoulders back. "Did you just call me a pimp?"

"It's just what I heard."

"Heard from who?"

"Forget it."

"Like hell. What do you know about me?"

"What do you know about Wren?"

"My art's not on display. Now what the fuck do you think you know about me?"

Some part of me remembered to not back down from my point of view. "Did you notice the monster's eyes?" I said, thereby insisting that my subjectivity dictate the confines of the discussion. "Funny how the left eye closes just a bit more than the right. I didn't know monsters had eyelids."

Colin peered in closer crouching to stare down the monster. He met its eyes and stared and stared and I wondered if he'd see it. I wondered if everyone else would see it too. How could they not see it? The eyes!

Then Colin slowly turned his head up toward me. He left his eyes fixed on the monster's, until the slow turn of his head stopped and then, just then, at the last possible instant, he flicked them up to meet mine. It had a beautiful dramatic effect. I felt all the eyes leave him and come to me. I froze. Colin broke into a slow, wide grin then burst out laughing. I joined in with the rest of the crowd. He was a magician. I had to laugh. Tension broken, the world snapped in sharp relief, suddenly more defined, and I felt a heavy pressure that I hadn't even realized was there leave my shoulders on the warm desert air. The sun was burning away the grey, as predicted.

Show complete, the group moved on following Colin's Cheshire smile: *that's right, everyone back to good-timey disagreements and artistic appreciation.* But I met Colin's eye as the group headed off toward the next exhibit and I saw Wren's monster staring out at me.

Set-Up

I wandered on my own instead of following Wren and the group. I brooded on bile with weighted spine and pondered the missing spices of her flavor. I caught her alone, studying sculptures under one of the many canopies set up on the desert floor for Solstice Lunarie.

"Are you going to help Gary and Taggart set up for the show?" I asked her.

"No," she said.

"It should be cool. Gary said they've synched up lasers. They're going to spin an eight hour trance set."

"I have my own stuff to get ready. And I have to help Colin."

"Of course. Colin." I won a frown from Wren. "It doesn't matter anyway." I turned away in disgust, swallowing back rank earthen sludge.

"You won you know?" she tried to comfort me, "The argument with Colin."

"I lost in the end. They walked away laughing."

"Who's laughing?

"The others. Like you didn't notice. You set me up for it. You knew what he'd do. You knew what I'd see in that: you and Colin, and me, Blobby, the limp dick in the corner." My disgust was subsumed by bile and I wondered if my whole day would be spent swallowing back unpleasant emotions.

"You don't have to personalize it."

"You made me the subject! And what about his analysis? Can't tell me there's not some truth there. What about Blobby? What am I supposed to think? He destroyed your work. I just sat there. Blobby's how you see me. Blobby is me through your eyes."

"Riley you don't have to personalize it.

"Of course I do. You made me the subject. You made that choice. Not me. Of course I take it personal."

"You're not Blobby. Nothing in there is as simple as that. Nothing in me, nothing I feel, is as simple as that. You don't have to personalize it."

"Then why'd you make me the subject? Why call me out in front of everyone to let Colin pick at me?"

"Maybe I wanted you to see something other than yourself in it. Did you ever think of that? That maybe it's not all about Riley Sparx?" But of course it was. How else could it be? I watched the sway of her skirt as she walked away.

I wiled away the day in the shade watching Gary and Taggart set up. They tolerated my presence though I was even less useful than usual. There was no lightweight equipment to move and the wiring was far too complex for me to assist. I couldn't tell an amp from a pre-amp, an MPC[*] from a soundboard. I watched, fascinated, as the shady stage went from a bare expanse to a cleverly cluttered workstation.

Best of all was the careful setup of the lasers. Taggart took several large mirrors out to the north hills. Gary made me put on sunglasses as thick as welding goggles, and then he fired pulses from a battery of more than seventy individual lasers. The beams bounced off the mirrors and returned to sensors on the stage. They spent several hours making minute adjustments while I napped.

---

[*] MPC – Midi Production Center

How Do You Spell Colo(u)r?

It was nearly sundown when Wren came for me. "Come see the exhibits before it gets too crowded," she said. "Ndukwe's starting to let people in up by the Church Road."

I followed her across the desert floor and into a roped off tent. "Is your work on display?" I asked.

"Not here. Colin put my sculpture in with the Lessers." She touched my hand gently. Her fingertips were rougher, still soft, but rougher, since she'd started sculpting instead of painting. "I know you're mad, but I think your critique helped get me a place in the gallery." She kissed me. "Thank you."

I didn't say anything and the taste of molé lingered on my lips.

"Riley!" At the sound of Colin's voice a heavy tremor touched my spine and a cold tin swallow washed away Wren's kiss. "There's someone I want you to meet." He had a plain looking young man with him. "Riley this Charlie Whitson. Charlie this is Riley Sparx. But enough with introductions, we really must view the art. It's about to get crowded in here. We sold fifteen thousand tickets for tonight!"

I followed Colin and Charlie and Wren down a boxed off scaffolding-lined corridor within the tent. Colin talked at me over his shoulder, "Charlie here is a magnificent artist. I can't wait for you to see his work. He's doing some really remarkable things with color. This project is amazing. I commissioned it myself."

We left the corridor and entered another dimly lit passage, this one slightly narrower with white drapery hanging on both sides. The corridor widened at the end where another large curtain hung.

"Anything you'd like to say Charlie?" Colin asked.

Charlie spoke in a British accent, "No, I think my work speaks for itself."

"That it does," said Colin, but having always a flair for the dramatic added, "Lady and gentleman and cripple, I present to you the first ever North American display of the word art of Charlie Whitson!"

The large curtain dropped revealing a canvas, ten foot by twelve foot, painted with enormous block letters. Each letter was a different color. It read:

I
CAN'T
SPELL
COLOUR
WITHOUT
'U'

I
CAN'T
SPELL
COLOUR
WITHOUT
'U'

Every single letter was wrong. Not just wrong, jarring. 'I' was bold red when it should have been vanishing primrose. 'R' was cobalt instead of red. 'C' led words with a phony blue sheen. A yellow 'S' hid bright where it should have led, deep and powerful. And worst of all, 'W' was perverted in pink. It was sick. Not to mention it misspelled 'colour.' The saving grace was the absence of a 'K.'

The double print, one black and one falsely colored, was doubly devious. I saw my alphabet atop and the phony colors below, and my mind attempted to impress my colors upon the lower phrase, unsuccessfully. I was seeing double, but tripled, (or two and a halved?) because of the top phrase painted in black. I stared, captured primarily by the ugliness of it, the same way you can't look from a car accident. The incongruity was magnified by a simultaneous taste of sweet-dill pickles and citrus-salt, utter nonsense.

I could take it no longer. I spun round and all of the remaining drapery fell to the floor. Murals with a common theme lined both sides of my exit route. Row upon row of the letter 'K' printed in alternating red and black. I staggered and braced myself upon my cane. My mind again reeled as nausea hit me and the muraled walls closed in, a tunnel of foulness. Putrid 'K' green splashed across the walls mixed with red and the double half-press of layered vision, bile and blood, everywhere was bile and blood.

It rained rosewater as physical pain overtook me. I could not stand. My cane slipped and the handle caught me in the gut. I closed my eyes, but the image remained imprinted on my consciousness, bile and blood, blood and bile. I fell sideways and crashed into the mural. Behind me I could hear the peals of laughter. "Well played Charlie Whitson! Well played!"

Evicted

Wren managed to drag me from the corridor, writhing and retching. I threw up on her shoes. She stroked my hair and whispered to me that it would be all right. It took some time before the rosewater faded, but what remained was foul and loamy, like a muddy morel pudding with a side of moldy tree bark covered in lichens. Even the mole and her kind words and gentle touch could not break through or banish the disgust.

Eventually I managed to sit up and Wren brought me a glass of water. I was sipping when Colin came up. "I need a word," he said.

"You've done enough," Wren said. Those three words did more to heal me than had an hour of her care and kindness.

"It's okay," I said. "We can talk."

"Yes Wren. He's a big boy. Now make yourself scarce."

She held her ground and looked to me. I nodded and waved her off as Colin brought over two folding chairs. I pushed myself up with my cane and took a seat. I felt a little better up off of the ground, like the air was cleaner at three feet than at two.

"How ya feeling?" he asked with his customary grin.

"Fuck you." I spit on a glob of pukey mucus on the floor.

"Hey now, that was the last prank, I promise."

"Right."

"Cross my heart and hope to die."

"I hope so too."

"That's cold. Look man, last prank. Consider it a parting gift. I mean this has been fun and all, but you're out of El Rancho. I already had the boys move your stuff to the Professor's R.V. You can stay there, or in the Bunker. I don't care. But Charlie gets your cot."

"That's sudden."

"Really? I thought this was a long time coming."

"So just like that. I'm out. He's in."

"What can I say? I like the kid's accent. Besides, Charlie made more art on one commission than you have in six months."

"I've been writing."

"Like I said." Colin paused and picked at his cuticles. "You're not like the others."

"Not like them how?"

"For starters you're not an artist." Colin continued to pick at his nails, speaking absently almost like I wasn't there, "But there's more. You haven't been a good camper. You stole a jeep. You bad-mouthed me. You flaked on court."

"You said I had a choice."

"You did. You chose wrong." He slammed his hand flat onto the seat of my chair, smack between my legs, an inch from my crotch. I was astonished how fast he moved. It was a like a reflex strike, a snakebite. "Why do you even care? You've been a whiny bitch ever since you got here. Do you even want to stay?"

I met his empty unsmiling eyes and tasted the tin tang of danger in the back of my mouth. I didn't answer. How could I answer? What kind of answer was yes and no? I couldn't very well say I wanted to stay but wanted him to go.

"I see," he said. "It's her. Why her? She's not even that hot." The smile came back to his face. I sat there dumb while Colin pondered his nails. Finally he spoke again, "So it's her. I tell you what. Since I'm a romantic at heart, a believer in true love, I'll give you a chance. If you can give me one reason besides her that you want to stay, you can keep your cot."

My mind was not merely wordless. It was empty. No taste, no feeling, no thought, just vacancy. I thought about why I had no thoughts and then realized that the thought negated itself.

"Nothing!" Colin said. "You got nothing? You can't even make up a lie for the woman you love? What is your problem man?"

I felt my brain reboot with a burst of cinnamon and molé. "The truth is that she's the only reason I have. She's reason enough for anything."

"Truth! There it is! That's why you're a shit artist. You're hung up on the truth."

"Most people would say that's a good thing. I'm not a liar."

"Won't stoop to the level of a pimp like me? Is that it? Not even for love? Some love."

"So, you admit you're a pimp."

"Never said I wasn't. Want to know a secret?" He smiled again, wider than usual. My defensive tin taste tingled instinctively. "I'm pimping every artist here. But that's not what you meant. You meant that story I told Midas."

"I heard it from Pedro," I lied.

"Word gets around. What's funny is how everyone needs something different. Wren wanted to be approached by a successful art dealer. Midas respected a pimp. Ndukwe just needed an American with a bankroll. The real talent is figuring out who needs to hear what."

"Lies. All lies."

"So what? Lies can be true. You're hung up on the facts. You've confused the facts for truth."

"So which is it? Am I hung up on the facts or the truth?"

"Doesn't matter. Either way you hang." Skip dangled at the end of a rope, salt and rot and a pain in my gut. Colin's smile twisted a millimeter more, a millimeter crueler.

"Like the truth doesn't matter?" I asked.

"You're not like the others. I don't know if that's good or bad." Colin gave me that look of appraisal, the off-putting air that he was assessing my cut, like a side of beef. "It's definitely bad for your art. This truth obsession."

"I just don't like being lied to."

"You don't like a lot of things. The others, they just want a tall tale, but not you. You want the truth. But how do you know I didn't tell them the truth? You don't know the first thing about me."

"You're right about that. I don't know the first thing about you. To do that I'd have to figure out what's truth and what's lies. The only thing I know for sure is that you lie."

"Everybody lies."

"That doesn't mean that the truth doesn't matter."

"Of course it does!" He leaped from his chair and grabbed me by the shoulders. I looked up, unable to shake his eye contact. He chuckled and let me go, then brushed off my collar. "The truth of something isn't what's said, it's the conviction that you say it with. If you believe it when you say it, it's true." I wanted to believe him, even though I knew he was lying. His demeanor went abruptly from one of aggression to a pose of deliberate ennui. With palms upraised and shoulders shrugged he broke eye contact and spoke disinterestedly to the desert air, "That's what I mean when I say you're not like the others, you sense that you are always on stage. And I must say you are playing your role just smashingly."

I rose to the bait. "And what role is that?"

"The Professor's marionette. The honest fool. He's leading you around by stick and strings and his hand up your ass. He brought you here, to this place of ultimate freedom, knowing that he didn't need to lock you up, you'd build your own cage, that you'd find a way to lock yourself up. You keep trying to leave but you keep coming back. You associate with artists, but your art is accidental. You dance and prance and preen and sulk, it's a limited role, low-end of the spectrum, doldrums for the down scenes and the semi-sweet dreams of a wannabe. But you play it as well as a man with strings can." And in that instant I felt the strings, anxiety more than a weight, and also a tug, a pull, like strings attached at the shoulders. But it wasn't the Professor.

Nimbus

I recovered backstage of Gary's set. He let me post up there amid myriad generators and gasoline cans. I promised to keep them all running. It was about the only chore I could handle. I've always enjoyed the smell of gasoline.

I looked out over the crowd, a swirling mass of neon, lamplights and public nudity. I became entranced with a topless woman wearing butterfly wings and a multicolored crown of flexible glowsticks. The lasers fired in rapid succession red, blue, green, and caught the dust from the desert air on their path, straight-line tracers above the dancers' heads. They beamed out images that shifted and morphed against the contours of the desert hills: snakes, lizards, blizzard dots, wizard's heads, turtles, hawks, breasts and buttocks, words like 'love' and 'peace', and nothing with a 'k'. The repetitive beats of the trance music seemed to circle with the images lending them a mystic quality.

"Take this," Wren handed me a pill. When was that?

"What is it?" Was that just after the show had started, or before, or just then? Time had become fuzzy. The order of events blurred.

"It's ecstasy. The Professor said it will help. I told him what Colin did." I hesitated, staring at it in the palm of my hand, a little red pill, marked with an 'N'. "I took one," Wren said. "Don't you want to roll with me?"

I did. "Christmas pills," I said.

"What?"

"Red pill with a green 'N'. Like Christmas colors." I popped the pill. "Do you think the 'N' stands for Noel?"

"Nimbus. The Professor called them Nimbus hits."

When was that? Wren had gone. She said she'd be back. Was that minutes ago? Or hours ago?

I started adding gas to generators fearing I might forget. Something was building inside me. A tap on my shoulder, it was Gary, his eyes wide, black and shiny, stage light dancing off them like off spinning vinyl records. "Nimbussed out man!"

He handed me a water bottle. "Keep hydrated," he said and broke into dance. He popped his shoulders then pressed his hands together, rotating them against one another and dragging them across at shoulder

360

height. Every motion free-flowed yet conformed to the beat. One hand chased the other following in trail around his body, creating visual forms, box, box, circle, pull, trailing eight, box, trace the stomach. Now elbows and shoulders seemed to follow in the chasewild faster bouncing boxy every motion to the beat, now hips and feet, then turn spin, spin, he whirled like a dervish, arms and hands still popping and pulling, ever and ever the chase was on. Stop! The beat dropped out. Gary froze. The lights went black.

Gary smiled and put a finger to his lips. A silent shhhhh... I could hear now, the subtle build. Gary's smile was huge, white-white under the blacklights, the build was palpable, the grin contagious, the build, the build, he raised his arm and pumped it overhead. I could hear it, the *waap-waap-waap*, building, faint at first but building... Gary's arm pumped in time with a silent rhythm... my good arm raised... I couldn't help it, synchronized with Gary... Gary synchronized with Taggart... Taggart spinning the set, the set spinning Taggart, synched with flow... flow building... building, building, still building and one-two-three-BOOM! The beat dropped. The energy hit me in the chest like a rogue wave. Gary shot back to the chase, hands pumping patterns of mojo and magic. The crowd roared. The strobes flared and lasers dominated the desert sky. I tripped balls.

Gary ran to Taggart's side and exhorted the crowd, flapping his arms for them to make noise. He grabbed the mic: "Motherfucking Thundercloud! Nimbuuuusssss!" The crowd roared back: "Nimbuuussss!"

Bodies gyrated about me in the maelstrom of music and mirth. I had to dance. The music compelled it. I had none of Gary's smooth liquid moves, just a Jello gait, an invisible necktie and a janky leg. Propelled by unadulterated enthusiasm I pirouetted atop my cane bouncing jangly joyful atop my one good leg and my pretend pogo stick. Joy, joy and connection, I felt a part of the crush, part of the crowd of revelers, part of the flow. And then it dawned on me. I felt without taste. But there was joy, indisputable, saffron or no, there was joy.

I felt the revelers around me pressing in, not physically, but... revelation! They love my dancing... I love dancing... I love them! All of them! All that training, good for something, worth it for this... Thirst! A sudden pressing need, thirst, and then Taggart at my side water bottle in hand, blessing bestowed, all things in order. It was the flow, the synch. I gulped greedily, the only greed I was capable of feeling, if anyone had asked I'd have handed over my cane, I'd have done it with a smile, same for my pants or the shirt off my back, but for water, for water I was greedy.

I killed the bottle. Taggart grinned and gave me a thumbs-up. I threw my arms around him. "I love you man!"

"I love you too!" he said. "You know the human body is two-thirds water?"

I was just about to say the same thing. It was uncanny, the synch. I followed the thought. Words flowed before I even understood them, the thought-speech delay circumvented. "How is it that the human body is two-thirds water, yet is also ninety-nine percent empty space? That the molecules that make up the body are separated by distances greater than their sizes, that the atoms that make up those molecules are separated by distances greater than their sizes, that the protons are separated from the electrons by spaces far greater than either of their sizes. And all of these distances added up mean that the body is made up mostly of empty space. How is it that empty forms appear solid?"

Taggart stared at me with inkwell eyes and a marshmallow grin. I answered my own questions. "Form is not an illusion. Form is the recognition of layers and levels. My hand looks different under an electron microscope than it looks under an ordinary microscope, than it looks to my eye, than it looks to that person over there, than it looks from atop a ladder, than it looks from an airplane. Which form is true? Which form is my hand? All of them? None of them? Form is the ultimate evidence of subjectivity."

Taggart hugged me again and dashed back to the stage. He shimmered as he ran. Glittering emanations shed in his wake. I began to look around me. A panoply of color flowed and blended, glittered and glowed. Color surrounded and imbued everyone and everything: Taggart, the topless butterfly girl, Gary, the emo kid pop-locking next to me, the ground, the air, the desert hills, all pulsed with shades and blends and layers of color; color in motion, color as motion, nothing static, nothing stable, all in flux.

I had taken ecstasy before. This was not ecstasy. This was stranger than an acid trip. I didn't just see trailers and dots, my entire visual field filled with colors and movement. I felt fear, but I didn't taste it. What had I taken? I saw colors that didn't exist. The topless chick was bathed in a halo of green-red. Another dancer, arms swinging wild, tossed blue-ochre bombs in all directions. Impossible colors, impossible scenes, yet all bearing a strange sense, not of surreality like an acid trip, but of reality, of deep underlying reality.

A flash caught my eye. The massive strobe next to the D.J. flickered. A sensation preoccupied me. It emanated above my left shoulder, a vibration, then... release. The pulse of the strobe slowed. The beat waned. Notes dragged and extended doing a Doppler on the 405. The strobe continued to slow: pulse, pulse, pause, pulse, freeze, and in that frozen instant the world stopped and two things happened. First, I remembered. The gnomes, the chants, the song, the machinery, the mead, the numbers, *the jewel*, all of it came rushing back in a single hippocampal regurgitation. All of it lay before my mind's eye, all of it condensed into the single point of light emanating from the frozen strobe. All that is except the jewel, which lay in my awareness, present and known, but veiled, camouflaged, unable to pierce the lid of the mind's eye.

The other thing that happened was that the obvious became apparent. Form was but one aspect of reality seen from one point of view. The strange colors were not hallucinations. They were illustrations of a reality previously unseen. They were a new point of view.

I describe the colors, this new reality, in visual terms, but this is not entirely accurate, it is just the closest analogue I can muster. Everything that I would normally see with my eyes, I still saw. But I also *saw* impossible colors and bulges of energy, fluctuations that seemed to have no clear distinctions. It was like everything was one giant field of energy like a diagram of an electro-magnet, or a big bubble, that if you pushed down in one spot it would pop up somewhere else. Each person was a fluctuation, a spike in the field, but everything was part of the field. The emanations of each person joined and mingled with the emanations of others in a continual transference of energy. At times, certain people seemed to have a kind of static hue, a constant, non-fluctuating aspect, like a halo. But as everything, even the air around them, was in a state of emanation, the places where the perceived stability and instability met were impossible to discern. I concluded that stability was the illusion, that all was in flux to one degree or another.

Each person, rock, plant, molecule of air, each of these were but aspects of a larger unity, their relations to one another were in a constant state of change, but all were part of this larger unity. This is not to say there were no distinctions at all. People were the source of far more colored energy than the ground or the air or the plants. The dance area was suffused with deep and powerful flows and the bulges of colors surrounding certain individuals were brighter or denser than the colors around others. Thus, what I saw could not be properly described as an elimination of forms. Nor could it be described as the enhancement of forms. Rather it was an illumination of forms, the realization of another layer that was always there but that I had never seen.

At the smallest scale and the largest scale, all forms were the same; all forms were one. I was granted a new coign of vantage from the corner where the infinitely small meets the infinitely large, I saw down each side of the wall and watched the wall dissolve. I realized that what we recognize as different forms are but aspects of the one form, seen from one isolated, meager, point of view. On this night I was privileged to see another aspect of the one form, a more raw aspect, that which lies beneath, like a glimpse of God's underwear.

In writing this I have had some time to reflect upon my experience, yet still it is difficult to convey the essentially ineffable quality of it. My attempts to do so that night were unquestionably less successful.

I hobbled from one group of ravers to another rambling, "Do you see it? Music gas, it's everywhere. We're all made of music gas." I doled out hugs and expressed my love, "You and me. We're the same person." I explained my vision, "Where the smallest scale and the largest scale converge is the tip of God's penis." To a guy smoking a bowl: "The weed you burn and the weed you freeze are both smoke." "Why would I freeze weed?" he asked. "It doesn't matter man. It's the same. Can I have a hit?" To the topless butterfly: "Your aura smells like rain drops." She gave me a hug.[*]

I danced and danced. I gathered in armfuls of floating colors and watched the energy waft and ripple from one smiling face to another. I saw the vibe. If you don't know about the vibe I can't explain it to you.

---

[*] Best hug ever!

But if you do know, then I can tell you. The vibe that night was excellent. The vibe was fun. The vibe was love.

A candy-raver in a pair of orange suspenders yawned. I watched the yawn pass through the sea of energy as a wave of color. I followed the wave as it moved from one peak to another like an open ocean swell approaching shore, each new person a subtle change in bathymetry. Each person yawned in turn as they received the wave and their energy changed in color and form. Each change also changed the wave, passing it along with a modified shape, texture and color. It was beauty in motion, a physical manifestation of interrelatedness, subtle communication without language, or perhaps a language all its own, an archaic form that predated words.

I had a sudden desperate urge to tell Wren. To tell her everything, to tell her that everyone and everything was connected, to tell her that I knew about the gnomes and the jewel, and to tell her that I loved her. And there she was, on stage, talking to Gary. The synch, the synch was incredible, the synch tracks the vibe, when the vibe is good the synch is on and you don't even have to ask to receive.

I started toward the stage then froze in my tracks. The ethereal glow emanating from all things was disrupted. The beautiful pastels and imaginary colors whirled toward a vortex of black and vanished over the event horizon. The diaphanous sheen that covered all life seemed to be slipping, sloughing like snakeskin pulled rough from the edges, sliding down into the abyss. And at the center of the void stood Colin.

Colin stood on the edge of the stage talking with Taggart. The emanations closest him were drawn with greater rapidity and turbulence, like water to a sinkhole. Taggart's aura steadily renewed only to send increasingly bright emanations down the abyss. I struggled to comprehend. Whatever universality I thought I perceived, Colin somehow stood apart from it. His emanation was not. It was a cavity, a vacuum. In the brief instant I had, I only began to piece it together, what he was. The inversion. He stepped back into darkness and the emanations from the stage resumed.

Wren jumped down as soon as she met my eye. She glowed 'W' blue and shot pink starbursts. Her dark eyes glittered with fairy dust. She ran into my arms. "I got a show!" she burst out with the news before I could say anything. "Colin got the gallery to take them all. The whole

Symphony Set. I'm showing for eight weeks in Portland! They even agreed to play the music." She hugged me again. "Isn't that great?"

"Yeah." It was. So why didn't it feel great to me. A second ago I was totally blissed out, Wren told me the best news of her life, and I didn't feel the least bit happy for her. What the hell was wrong with me? My suspicion ran to the void that surrounded Colin. I mustered a weak, "Congratulations."

"What's wrong? Are you okay?"

"I'm just really high," I lied.

"I know! Some rolls, right? I know I said I'd roll with you but I gotta head back to the Ranch House. Come there after the show. *Major* after-party."

"What about Colin?"

"You're invited. I don't care what he says. We're gonna celebrate." She kissed me on the lips and was gone. I hadn't told her anything. Why didn't I at least say I love you?

It was too early for me to be crashing, but the connection to the colored ether of reality had been severed. The after-effects of the roll persisted, but mostly as a vague warm body buzz and a complete lack of synesthetic response. It was not altogether unpleasant, but hardly the ecstasy I had experienced.

Ecstasy? Yet another unanswered question: What the fuck was in those pills? I've taken ecstasy, and that wasn't ecstasy, although Wren and Gary seemed to think it was.

A Homecoming of Sorts

Left with no Yangs and an intense thirst, I sought out water, and for the first time that night had difficulty finding something I needed. I considered that the synch might have died with the vibe, but everyone else seemed to be having a rip-roaring good time. The only post-mortem vibe seemed to be mine. And as my thoughts turned sour the synch imposed itself, cruelly this time, in the form of Ndukwe on a golf cart. He handed me a water bottle. "Get in," he said. I got in. I liked him better when I didn't have to experience his name.

"Where are we going?" I asked.

"Sculpture Garden. Colin has something he wants you to see."

Well, happy-happy joy-joy,* I thought, and immediately thought of Wren, and the error in spelling that eroded our first encounter precluding the possibility of love at first sight. I bemoaned failing to express my love for her yet again that evening.

We pulled up at the awning overlook. Colin was there with Charlie and Midas and Pedro. Wren was nowhere to be seen.

"Ah just in time," said Colin. "Have a look."

Down below a great rumbling shook the air and I saw the taillights of an enormous semi with an empty flatbed trailer as it pulled away from the center of the Sculpture Garden in a cloud of dust. Under the light of the full moon I could see that the Man with the Mirrored Balls had been removed. In his place I made out the vague outlines of a large structure, boxy, but not square, with a few odd angles. It took up the entire circle at the center of the pentagram shaped garden.

"What is it?" I asked.

Colin laughed drawing energy and mirth into his void. The vision was fading, but the abyss surrounding him called attention to its remnants if only that I should watch them disappear. "You don't recognize it? It's yours."

"I never made an art project that large."

"Of course not. You're a hack. I never said you made it. I said it's yours." He laughed and slapped his newest sycophant, Charlie, on the

---

* "Happy-happy, Joy-joy" – title and lyrics of a song sung by Ren on the Ren and Stimpy Show.

back. "Well, it used to be his. Right boys." The laughs sounded forced to me, all except Charlie's, but they all laughed just the same. "Lights!" Colin yelled down into the garden.

Floods burst into illumination on all sides of the display. There, below me on the dry ground of the desert was my childhood. The lakeside house, designed and aligned by my father to maximize the features of both the lake and the sun, transported to a barren pit in a madman's funhouse.

My Yangs would have aided me then, if I'd had them, just to know how I felt. Instead, I limped away. A chorus of laughter rose at my back, Colin's laugh the loudest of all. I got into the golf cart and drove back to the stage, harboring the vague impression that I'd fallen over the edge of the abyss and could never hope to climb out.

One Hell of an After-Party

I don't remember the intervening events, *per se*. I mean, I know what happened and I know what I did. I just don't really remember doing it in the sense that I remember it more as an observer than a participant, like I lost agency.

"It's Burning Man!" Someone cried. I felt the crowd grow around the awning, everyone seeking better vantage atop the perch. I felt the smooth handle of my cane in my bad hand, and I felt the smooth grip and single rough seam of a plastic can in my good hand. I felt the heat on my face.

I dropped the gas can and sighed. I switched my cane to my good hand and took one long, last, deliberate look at the inferno that blazed away my past, and just as surely torched my future.

I made my way through the press of youth, pretty girls with glitter on their faces and skinny boys in baggy jeans. Glowing paraphernalia parted for me, a desert swarm of neon fireflies scattered at the scent of gasoline. They reformed as I passed, bunching behind me, cheering, drawn to the flames. For love of dance, for love of music, for love, love and togetherness was what they claimed. I'd seen the unity, watched it appear out of the ether in undeniable brilliance. Love, they said, love and togetherness, but still they came to watch it burn.

I do not remember how I collected the gasoline cans from amidst the generators and cords, and loaded them onto the golf cart in stacks, just that I did. I remember how the steering wheel was sticky and the golf court bounced through the rutted desert sloshing gasoline upon the seat, onto my legs, and over the dash and wheels. I do not remember driving. I remember can after can of gasoline splashing upon the floorboards and walls. But I do not remember pouring any gas, much less the final two cans upon the terra cotta tiles and then in a long line and puddle out the door, but I remember wondering if the tile would melt or burn. I remember the flames, the strange blue glow at the base of my childhood. I do remember the flames and the sudden burning passion to find Wren. Not just to locate her, but to possess her, as if the completed arson required an equally rapid reclamation project.

****

The forms in the courtyard were strange. Fraudulent light cast ghostly silhouettes and alien tentacles replaced succulent arms. The cascade dammed, the dragon stood silenced his serum breath withheld, the crab-lined pool at his feet tepid and limpid in the still, hot air of the desert moon.

In search of a bird, I followed percussive thumps down the forbidden hallway past Lessers and Greaters to the door of the Chill Room. A steady pulse of housy beats flowed atop the discordant din of anarchy inchoate.

I hesitated to open the door. After-party as invitee, different than after-party as party-crasher, different than after-party as arsonist, had word of my deed preceded my arrival?

I shoved open the door and found the vast room empty except for the exhibits and furniture. The echo of dim house beats transcended the walls. I traced my steps back and listened carefully at the door of the Greaters. No hesitation this time, I burst in.

A full-panel painting of coarse-haired male genitalia confronted me upon entrance. I ignored it and turned left. The pounding house beats and screeching scratching anti-melodies sounded of death throes in rhythm, the agony of ritual sacrifice. I stared down the narrow room, expecting to see paintings and sculptures, and there were some, including a six-foot tall N'kissi stabbed through the center with an iron pipe, but the vast majority of the room was shelving covered in tapes and CD's and DVD's. An enormous flat screen hung on a wall playing the same scene on repeat, no more than five seconds, an extreme close-up, difficult to discern, but overlaid with the unmistakable sounds of violent copulation.

The room was dark save the lighted exhibits, the television screen, and the pale purple glow of blacklights at the far end of the room. People were gathered there, at least five, most standing, but one seated with his back to me. I advanced and recognized those standing: Pedro, Charlie, Ndukwe and Midas. As I came closer I saw the hideous dragon-ram-crab tattoo that covered the muscular back of the seated man, Colin.

A faint buzz was audible over the hideous noise. As I came closer still I saw that Midas was filming with a handheld video camera, and that all four artists were nude. Colin moved his arm delicately as though drawing a sketch. His body obscured a vague form from my view, his medium. The buzz grew louder as I approached, nearly on par with the volume of the horrible music. My eye caught a glint of metal in Colin's

370

hand, and two others on each side of him. I came closer, and the scene began to take shape. Colin was barefoot, clad in compression shorts, seated on a swivel stool while his artist lackeys looked on in lust and admiration through drug-addled eyes. I saw the flat of a foot on either side of Colin. The semi-flaccid members of his entourage drew my attention for an instant, until I saw his medium.

She lay cruciform in reclined repose, nude, chained at the wrists to iron rings in the floor and by the waist to a workout bench. Her eyes were closed. I couldn't tell if she was passed out, drugged out, sleeping, or shutting out the image of the act. I didn't care. Colin sat between her legs with the tattoo gun, her feet propped in makeshift stirrups, her mouth gagged with a crude gold bandana. Midas filmed the whole process. Secretions, foul globs and streaks of white effulgence upon her face and chest, glowed an eerie blue under blacklit illumination.

The sick rot of rancid meat destroyed every taste bud in my head. I felt in that instant I would never taste anything else for as long as I lived, and I didn't care how long that was. I flew into action at the taste of blood and maggoty beef.

I flipped my cane in one swift motion. I lashed out and caught Charlie first. He never saw it coming. I brained that fuck. The crook of my staff smashed into his cerebellum. The ferrule clattered across the terra cotta floor, but my cane proved sturdier than his skull. The sharp crack of steel-reinforced wood, the gross crunch of bone, followed by a second blow, and a third. The final crack to his skull yielded a squirt and oozing tissue.

The tattoo gun ceased and for a brief instant all was still except the blaring sound of a sick house beat atop the splashes and screeches of a drowning kitten.

Ndukwe got the next stroke. I bloodied his nose, but he bloodied mine in return. I recoiled and doubled over then caught Pedro with the tip of my cane square in the jewels, as he tried to grab me from behind. I broke his jaw with the follow up strike. I was possessed, a devil, a madman, an avenger. I wanted Colin, but at every turn his henchmen stepped forth; no doubt this is why they never joined me in confinement, while the jokers and whackos, like Gary and Bob, soon found their way there. I got one swing at him. I missed. I saw Wren's eyes wide with fear; at me or for me I cannot say. I saw the 'CK', indelible upon her thigh and bikini line.

A flash of lightning streaked before my eyes. I screamed with rosewater lungs and a paralytic tremor shook my body to stone. A glimmer of fear turned to triumph on Colin's face. I watched Midas go from vertical to horizontal, sorrow in his eyes and a sparking black box in his hand. Unable even to reach out and break my fall, I toppled, frozen, and watched a half-nude gnome slap himself in the forehead just as mine hit the tile.

Progenitor

"So you know how I came to own El Rancho?"

I was chained to the same bench Wren had been on. They hadn't stripped me or put me in stirrups. The room had been cleared, but it still felt cluttered, full of rage and outdated media. "Where is she?"

"She's fine. Which is more than I can say for Charlie. Now tell me what you know?"

"Haven't we already had this discussion?"

"Yes. But the cops will be here any minute now, and there are a few things we simply must discuss. Who knows when we'll have the opportunity to talk again? So tell me Riley, what do you know?"

"I'm going to kill you. As for you and this god-forsaken place what's it matter? Dirty Doctor Morty, government blackmail, human experiments, dope slinger, pimp, child actor, televangelist, who cares?"

"Always this parsing! Either or. This or that. Can't they all be true?"

"I'd bet they're all lies. Especially the televangelist one. I've seen you preach. I didn't convert remember."

"You didn't listen. But that's okay. Wren did. How'd you like her ink?"

"Fuck you."

"She did."

Bile and blood boiled inside me. Were these the only emotions I could feel? Suffused with the foul rot of death I shook so forcefully with rage that the bench I was cuffed to shook along with me.

"I'm afraid we're running out of time Riley. There are some things you should know before you go. I thought we'd have more time together. I wish we had a greater bond, a measure of trust, but perhaps we'll be able to work on that later, if the authorities ever let you out of your cage. Anyhow, Pop, the physician, Dirty Doctor Morty, he did leave me El Rancho, but that's not all. He was also on the board of several other fine medical facilities and held ownership interests in some. Ever hear of a place called Glissen?"

The residential care facility for my mom, Glissen Home.

"I took his spot on the board when he died. I asked if I could observe, make rounds with the doctors. What a surprise to find someone I knew.

Oh I told the doctors how I just couldn't believe what a coincidence it was, what Rainbow being an old schoolteacher of mine."

"She wasn't a schoolteacher."

"Yeah. You'd think the doctors would know something about that, but I have to say that the care we give at Glissen is consistently below medical standards. I'm not sure the doctors pay much attention. You can't really blame them for ignoring ones like your mom. It's not like she could remember if the doctor fucked up. There are plenty of other patients and some of them might remember enough to sue. Anyway, being a representative of Glissen I felt compelled to personally attend to Rainbow. We had a long conversation about her sons. Little Riley was quite a surfer. I'd have guessed he was eight or so based on what she told me. 'My little angel' that's what she kept saying, over and over, like she's having a fit."

"I don't believe you," I said, but of course I did, it was exactly what she said to me the last time I saw her. I fought the tremors running through my body. I bit back the cold and the rot and the rosewater. My Yangs were returning but I didn't care. Before I couldn't imagine living without them. Now I couldn't imagine living.

"Did you know she saw auras?" Colin asked. "Funny huh? She described them to me, 'pale emanations of pure light and pastel colors.' Exact quote. She was surprisingly lucid, but that came and went. She tells me about these auras and how that's the way she spots angels. Wild stuff. Did she ever tell you this?"

"She believed it all her life."

"Auras and angels, you know she called them halos, right? Of course you did. Coincidence?"

"We both know it's not. Whatever she couldn't explain she attributed to God, like I said, she was a believer."

"You know another word for halo? Nimbus. Funny, right?"

I was too stunned to speak.

"She almost stopped believing, you know why? Because I didn't have a halo. I was so nice she just couldn't believe that I didn't have a halo. Then she got this look like I was far away and she started back in saying your name, 'Riley, Riley, my little angel. Where's my angel? Why isn't he here?' And I couldn't very well tell her you were off surfing, or that you couldn't take the sight of her anymore, so I shook her by the shoulders, and all of sudden she's like 'Skip!' And that poor crazy lady didn't remember her man was dead and she had me confused with him. I just didn't have the heart to break it too her. So I," Colin thrust his pelvis forward in a crude gesture, "consoled her," thrust thrust, "the best I could." Thrust. "Then I asked her to tell me about your delinquent brother and she got very confused. I tried to explain, I said 'of course I'm not Skip. Why would you think I was?' And she got all weird like 'oh but didn't we… but wait… but…' So I told her to lie down, because she was getting really agitated. But she didn't want to lie down and she started to get physical so I grabbed her by the wrists and I called in the orderlies and had them sedate that crazy bitch. Then I left."

"You son of a bitch." Gelded words. They came too late to matter.

"You believe me now? I knew your mother. Man, two weeks after that I'm attending her funeral in a spiffy yellow suit and listening to the worst eulogy I've ever heard. I could see you needed my help."

The Professor burst into the room. "Colin! What have you done?" Panic streaked his pale blotchy face. He looked old. The white curls at his shoulders no longer bounced, they flopped. He knelt and grabbed me by the shoulders pressing his face close to mine. In a hurried whisper he asked, "What did you see? Tell me Riley! Quickly! Did it work? The drug? What did you see?"

I spit in his face.

Colin howled from behind the Professor. "Now you get brave!" At his signal Midas and a bloodied Ndukwe dragged the Professor up off his knees and out of the room.

The Professor screamed to me as he left. "Remember! Remember! Write it down if you can. Riley I'll make this right! Write it all down!"

"He's a void! An empty hole!" I shouted.

Colin was thoroughly amused. "I knew before he moved that the Professor was out to get his hooks in you. So I tried to shake you up. I tried to set you free. I suppose you could still get free, maybe like your dad did. But you're more lamb than lemming. It's one thing to follow the pack off a cliff. It's entirely different to let yourself be herded into a pen." He shrugged, "I held the gate open for you."

"So you're just trying to help me out? Is that what you've been doing Colin?"

"Me ayudarse."

"Bullshit. Even if you do think it helps in your twisted little mind why help me?"

"Because we're brothers Riley."

"Enough with the humanity crap."

"No man. We're *brothers*. Real brothers. My dad, Dirty Doctor Morty, well, let's just say that he got to taste the Rainbow. Now I know you're probably thinking that this explains a lot, like why your dad and brother looked like Viking warriors while you look like a scarecrow. So don't act all surprised man. You know I'm telling the truth. The Professor ran the DNA, we're brothers."

The sirens in the distance were as close as my body. I vomited without taste. The terra cotta I sat upon was a million miles away, merged with the sirens and the empty space that surrounded Colin and enveloped me.

VII. CHAINS

Examination and Privileges Revoked

Socrates said, "An unexamined life is not worth living." That doesn't mean an examined life is. I should know. For seven plus years I've examined my life. For seven plus years that's all I've done. Seven years limping laps around a room on a brittle cane. When participation in life is taken from you all that remains is self-examination, and possibly a novel.

The first three years of my confinement the Professor was my ally. He was not a friend, but an ally. Like friendly nation-states, we remained at arms-length, but worked together where our interests converged. I had my private quarters. We continued to collaborate and chart. He provided me books, mostly eastern philosophy, classic literature and neuroscience texts. I progressed in my meditations.

I resented him, but I cooperated as he probed my experiences. Seldom did a session pass where he didn't refer to that fateful night of the Solstice Lunarie. Always the conversation turned to what I saw, what I felt, and Colin, always Colin, and always I rebuffed him. Then we reached an impasse. The synesthesia work involved more analysis of the data he already had, and thus less of my personal input. He now pressed harder for that knowledge I hinted at when I told him in my hallucinogenic haze that Colin was a void. He asked my meaning. Did I liken him to a cipher? What had I seen? What had I felt? How was the void represented? What else did I see? A void implies absence, but an absence of what? What else did I see? I responded with silence and eventually the day came where only he spoke. And then things changed.

The Professor continued to come to my room and interview me. Sometimes we even spoke or shared a story or a laugh, but the visits became less frequent, often six months would pass between visits. My living conditions also changed in many ways, some subtle, some not.

Every other night during my first three years of confinement, I was allowed to bathe in a private tub and test the water with my thermometer. I now had to shower once a week and my thermometer was confiscated. It was frightening, and remains so every time I step into the stream of untested water, particularly if it is creating steam. However, I endured the change without complaint, fully cognizant of what the Professor attempted.

Shortly after the shower situation changed the Professor made one last attempt to win me back. "I not only gave you back surfing, I opened your mind. You feel things, see things, taste things. You hint at these… these… connections, I have no doubt they are real. Let me help you. Let's discover your talent together. The next step in human evolution."

There they were, the 'evolution' card, and the 'I rescued you' card. Guilt and flattery, carrots and sticks, the problem with this sort of persuasion is that it only works well if you have something to gain and something to lose. I had neither. Not even the magic brace, the ocean available, could turn me again. Colin was a liar but he was right about one thing: I had been a puppet. No longer.

"You drugged me."

"You took it willingly and it worked as advertised. This is real. You have extra-sensory perceptions that no one else does and I believe it's related to the entanglement of emotion, sensation and memory."

"Then why did you tell them I'm insane? Why did you have them lock me up here?"

"Riley you attacked a man with your cane and set fire to a building. I don't think my testifying that you're the next rung on the evolutionary ladder would have helped either of our causes."

He was probably right about that. Changes continued. The neuroscience books remained, but the literature and philosophy books disappeared. He was trying to break me. Philosophy has the potential to provide solace, literature an understanding and acceptance of that which you cannot control. Science has no such potential.

My meditations were no longer permitted. The staff interrupted me. Meditation calms, balances, centers. It yields insight. Knowledge of self can be converted to strength and that which is strong is difficult to break. So he had the orderlies put an end to it.

I learned to feign sleep in order to meditate, but eventually he caught on. As a consequence the orderlies would rouse me at random times and soon my sleep patterns were out of whack. That was a dark time, amongst all the time I've spent in here, that was a dark time, or a bright time, I saw lots of bright colors when I didn't get to sleep. I saw other things too. Horrible things, bugs crawling from my pores and faces in the darkness, dead faces. I heard voices too, voices that told me to hurt myself. I tried once, like my Dad but with a bed sheet. Eventually they hooked me up to an EEG. They monitored my brainwaves each night and eventually I began to sleep again. I stopped meditating after that, a truce. I still sneak in a sit every so often when I can get away with it, but it isn't the same as daily practice.

Meditation prohibited, my examinations took on other forms, intellectual introspection, research on the mind, on Morty, and on my genealogy.

I've examined the choices that led me to this place. Examined my personal history and my familial past. Examined the workings of the mind in neuroscience texts and compared it to my experience. I've examined the process of my thoughts through meditation. I've examined my face in the mirror and examined my existence through the mirror of my mind. Sleeping, reading, sitting, thinking, fantasizing and above all writing, all in examination of this: existence, self, or the illusion thereof.

And now the day of the jewel approaches.

Aftermath

I suppose I should fill you in on the outcome of the events of Solstice Lunarie. Charlie nearly died. He's in the Bunker now, an imbecile, reduced to an infant. He shits himself and eats nothing but pap. He speaks with a lisp, the few words he knows, and he can't move half his face. I suppose I should feel bad. I don't.

I initially plead not guilty to two charges of attempted murder and three counts of assault with a deadly weapon and plead not guilty by reason of insanity to the arson charge. Nehud was my lawyer, his second career after he quit the tour.

There is a legal defense called 'defense of others.' It excuses the use of force when used to protect another person from harm. I thought Wren was being raped and tattooed against her will. I feared for her life. The problem was that I was wrong. She was a willing participant in Colin's artistic endeavor. The video proved this conclusively. However, there is another legal doctrine called 'mistake of fact.' This defense excuses an otherwise criminal action if you misunderstood the facts so as to not know that your actions are in fact criminal.[*] Without getting too much into legal technicalities, Nehud said that it meant that I lacked the guilty mind state, or *mens rea*, and therefore my actions were not considered a crime.

The arson was a problem. Uprooting my childhood home for display showed that Colin had bad taste and was mean spirited, but it didn't excuse my burning it to the ground. The fact that I committed the arson before the assaults was also bad. Nehud was worried that the prosecution would use this fact to get the jury to infer that I had a guilty mind state when I went to the Art Wing. The theory went as follows: I was furious with Colin as shown by the fact that I committed the arson intentionally, and therefore in my fury I went to find Colin with the intent to attack him. Even if I acted in defense of Wren, I nonetheless went after Colin with the same bad intent that had inspired the arson. My defense was already a bit convoluted, and even if we could prove mistake of fact, and that I acted to

---

[*] This is different than a 'mistake of law,' which is not a legal defense. If you are wrong about what the law is and on that basis you commit a crime, it is a crime despite your mistake.

defend Wren, a jury still might decide that I had a guilty mind state when I went to swinging.

It took a great deal of convincing from Nehud, but I cut a deal. I plead guilty to three counts of second-degree assault and the prosecutor accepted my plea of not guilty by reason of insanity to the arson charge, paving the way for my placement in a mental institution. In exchange they dropped the attempted murder and assault with a deadly weapon charges. Thanks to testimony from the Professor that I had severe depression and was prone to psychotic breaks, on my thirty-first birthday I was sentenced to custody in a mental institution and ordered to serve three three-year sentences consecutively.

I signed the deed to the old Sparx factory building over to Nehud. He didn't want to accept it, but I insisted. He deserved to be paid and it seemed only fitting that what was left of Sparx should go to a Beshev. There was nothing there for me anyway. I made a clean break of it this time. The Professor convinced the judge that he should be the one to continue my treatment. He took charge of my care and we returned to the Bunker.

When every day is the same and uneventful days are the norm the times when something out of the ordinary happen really stick in your mind. If it weren't for my colors I doubt I could distinguish one day from another. So few things worth remembering: yellow, orange, white, black, left, right. Events. So few events worth remembering, in here all is cumulative.

Yellow Day

I spent a great deal of time organizing Morty's journal. I categorized it in three groupings: Nonsense, Utter Nonsense and Project Nimbus. Nearly a third of the journal fell into the last category and I spent years pouring over the documents in search of answers for which I didn't even know the questions.

I discerned that the study involved pharmaceutical development. The Professor confirmed that the Nimbus hits were a later generation of this drug. A powerful empathogen, Nimbus was originally developed as a treatment for depression. However, a fortuitous discovery showed that in certain persons with a genetic susceptibility the drug produced quasi-mystic states in which subjects reported seeing auras and showed a remarkable ability to determine the intentions and relationships of and between those people with visible auras.

Early evidence showed surprising reliability suggestive of extra-sensory percepts. In one instance a subject predicted a violent attack by one patient upon another from a fluctuation seen between the auras of those two patients. Unfortunately for Dirty Doctor Morty,[*] the sample size, two persons, was far too small to draw any conclusions and repeat experiments with those subjects were inconclusive.

Thus Morty began the process of collection, which is partially documented in his journal. His search focused on persons with a peculiar, and at the time little known, neurological condition called synesthesia. Both of the subjects who had shown extra-sensory promise were synesthetes, one, Subject 'L,' was a grapheme-color synesthete; the other, Subject '2J,' was an auditory synesthete with photisms.

As best I can glean from the partial documentation, the results were not good, either for treatment of depression, or, among the synesthetes, as it related to ESP. A notable exception appears late in the study findings, a subject code-named 'Spectrum,' a grapheme-color synesthete. Spectrum lost her synesthetic percepts after ingesting one dose of Nimbus. She fell into a terrible depression. Unable to care for her young child, she and the

---

[*] Dear Reader, I continue to and always will refer to this heinous man with this epithet. I refuse to acknowledge him as my father despite evidence that he is my genitor.

child lived for a time under the supervised care of Dr. Mortimer Kane. During this time she was administered massive doses of Nimbus on a bi-weekly basis. Eventually she reported seeing 'halos' around certain persons. A previously moderate propensity for the religious became an obsession and her life soon revolved around lengthy sessions of prayer and the observance of these 'angels.' Sound like anyone we know?

I must admit that I fear I could suffer the same ignominious fate as my mother: the loss of all faculties, the fading of memory and the failure of mind. There are few deaths so cruel as to die to the world before you are dead. Fortunately I have not lost my Yangs as a result of my ingestion of Nimbus hits and I show no signs of early onset Alzheimer's.

Apart from these basics and the obvious interest of the Professor in potential extra-sensory perceptions I have learned little else about Project Nimbus. However, my research has yielded an interesting clue about Dirty Doctor Morty. On a yellow day beneath my left shoulder blade I finally paid close attention to a page of the journal I had skipped over many times before. It was badly burned, and seemed to be part of a larger series of notes.[*] However, the parts I could make out read as follows:

> Project Nim
> Brothers CK & RS
> Spectrum transp
> Effective dos. 10 cc.
> 3 + Inc. Temp. / Aspect Rat.
> Mendellian Swap
> RS mother set – Synesth
> CK shows no early indicia of synesthetic promise

If we accept that CK and RS stand for Colin and myself, which I grudgingly will for purposes of this analysis, then an interesting question arises from the last line. Presuming that Dirty Doctor Morty was the author of this page why would he expect that Colin show signs of being a synesthete? Was Colin's mother another participant in Project Nimbus? Another synesthete? I have combed the records for any allusion to Colin's

---

[*] Someone deliberately attempted to destroy this evidence. Perhaps Colin? He was in possession of the journal for many years.

mother or a Mrs. Kane, and have come up empty. Which leads me to ask: is it possible that Dirty Doctor Morty was himself a synesthete?

Black Day

It was a black day when she came to me. The day was a taunt, near my right hip, forward and close, it was a reminder of what we would never again have, a future together. Black hair with a pink streak, pleated black skirt, striped thigh-high stockings she was dark and bright amidst a sea of white, contrast. Maybe that's all she ever was, contrast.

The pleasantries belied the name. Awkward inquiries. 'How are you?' is a silly question to a man in a cage. *However they make me.* But instead I said, "Fine."

I asked about her art. She sold a few paintings.

"How are my conditions? You're looking at them. Would you like to know how boredom tastes? I never knew it had a taste until I came here. It's far too subtle to notice, unless you spend all your days noticing the small things, because the big things no longer exist. Boredom is it's own taste. Could I ever name it? Perhaps a pinch of paprika or parsley, I'm told these things have flavor though no one could prove it to me. Same thing with boredom, it has a taste, I promise, I can't prove it or name it, but every once in a while I taste it, it's real."

But I didn't say these things, just, "fine."

She didn't sit. She shifted her stance every few seconds. She was nervous. Did she feel guilty? I wondered. I watched her dance in place, unconscious betrayals of her desire to run. Corn meal mush, stone ground kernels stuck in my teeth. Strange that I pity her when I'm the one locked up.

The dance continued, words and feet, saying nothing, stepping in place. Finally the question that had to be asked: "Did you know?"

"Know what?" she asked, tears in her eyes, dragging out the dance a few more steps, just a couple measures more.

"Did you know what he was doing? What your part in all this was?"

She shook her head, neither no nor yes. Is there such a thing as a willing pawn? Or does the act of willing negate such a claim? Dare I call her oxymoronic?

"You were bait," I said.

"The thing with Colin—"

"It doesn't matter. He's not the reason. Your paintings sold after all. You helped recruit me—"

"I thought I was helping. I know what it's like to be alone with my thoughts, with my colors…"

"I can never know your intentions, but I choose to believe you cared for me. Did you know?"

"Know what?"

"That night at the Solstice party, that drug you gave me, it was an empathogen, like ecstasy but not ecstasy. Did you know?"

"The rolls? No. He told me it was ecstasy."

"I choose to believe you."

"Riley I love you," she blurted through tears. Mascara ran from her eyes and played connect the dots with her freckles. Not a hint of molé in my mouth, and there never would be.

"I forgive you," I said.

"But you don't love me?"

"I loved you." Pity. I watched her walk out the door as I picked the grit of cornmeal from between my teeth.

Orange Day

I remember the day I figured out the numbers. I never would have known if I hadn't written this story. Everything here is cumulative. Details accumulated and culminated in an event. It was an orange day, up front of my left hip, sort of parallel to my last encounter with Wren, up front and shining light on my future, funny how parallels reveal opposites. I have a future even if she's not in it.

An orange day, but I remembered a brown day, a birthday. I wrote about my father's suicide that day and was struck by how many significant days were brown, then I realized they were not just brown days but birthdays: the gnomes, quitting Mom's church, Dad's death, my sentence and incarceration; all birthdays, eight, fifteen, twenty-four, thirty-one.

I thought about the numbers, the gnome numbers, with their beautiful wrong colors, numerals in pastel waterfall. I had them written down. I knew the start, 8, 7, coincidence? If they were talking birthdays they had the first two, even my acalculic self could determine that, but then what 1.2, 7.8. I decided to add it up. Wait, I thought, $1.2 + 7.8 = 9$. I asked an orderly for a calculator. If the numbers meant birthdays, then what did 1.2 mean? I started punching in digits. After some trial and error I determined that 0.2 of a year equaled seventy-three days. One year and seventy-three days from my fifteenth birthday put me at... age sixteen, a chartreuse day in early January. And it hit me, the day of the contest at Black's, the day I lost my virginity, the day that set me on the path that lead me away from my family and into a scalding shower in Costa Rica. 7.8 years later, my twenty-fourth birthday, my Dad hanging from a pipe. 7 years later my 31st birthday the beginning of my incarceration.

The rest of the math I have double, triple, quintuple checked on multiple occasions. 116 days is exactly .3178082191780821917808... of a year.[*] So what is to happen, 7.31780821917808... days, or seven years, three months, three weeks and three days from my thirty-first birthday, the day of my incarceration, or exactly thirty years, three months, three weeks and three days from my eighth birthday, or exactly one day from today?[*]

---

[*] $116/365 = .3178082191780821917808\ldots$

[*] Starting from my eighth birthday add the remaining numbers.
$7 + 1.2 + 7.8 + 7 + 7.3178082191\ldots = 38.3178082191\ldots$

388

Process of elimination yields the only plausible answer. Since nothing can happen in this time, because I am stuck in this place, something must happen out of time, hence, tomorrow I will once again see the jewel.[*]

---

[*] Dear Reader, you may object that this is hardly the most plausible thing to occur tomorrow. Moreover the list of things that might occur is to all appearances infinite. After all I might be released. Or I might have a visitor. Or the Professor might die. Or I might die. And so on. However, you have not experienced the visions as I have. The final number is of undoubted significance, and it repeats forever. The infinite character of this decimal leads me to believe that something of an extra-temporal nature is afoot, and that simply reeks of gnomes and jewels.

White Day

The Professor brought them on a white day. I reach and touch it with the fingertips of my right hand. Like all days it is simply there. This day is recent. It sits atop a stack of white November days.

I took the pill willingly. He would have forced me otherwise. It wasn't stamped this time, just a white pill, but I knew what it was. The effects set in almost immediately. Then he brought them in, first one at a time, then in pairs, and finally in groups. I watched through a two-way mirror. I could see them. They could not see me. Yet this brought me little comfort because the mirror did nothing to separate the energy.

Some of them were prisoners. I could tell by the way they walked, brash, upright, with fixed stares, or a shuffle step, downcast eyes and furtive glances. Both walks were fake, or real, depending. They were postures, acts, but if you act in a certain way for long enough you become your act. Still these were easy to spot, menace either deliberately conveyed or studiously avoided, dominance or compliance, they behaved with the subtlety of dogs.

Others were trickier to ascertain, like a cocksure swaggering country boy, he kept asking the interviewer questions. He was supposed to be answering a personality inventory, but he kept turning the questions back on the interviewer. "Do you play cards? Supposed to be a card game tonight. If you don't play why do you want to know if I gamble? Well how often do you masturbate? You won't tell. I will, every day and twice on Sundays."

I didn't have the answers in front of me, but I doubt he answered a single question truthfully. I think he even lied about his name. When he went back in, paired with a female who had been particularly flirtatious with the interviewer, things got creepy.

"See now Mary here's a real beauty. Why can't we get a pretty girl like Mary to ask these questions?"

Mary hopped over the desk revealing a scandalous amount of leg and plopped down in the interviewer's lap. "That better hon?" she asked in a sweet adolescent voice that sent a chill down my spine and rusty nickel across my tongue. Then she turned to the interviewer, "I thought you wanted me to yourself, what with all those nasty questions you were asking."

"He looks like he shared before," the country boy said with a laugh. "Ain't that right boss? He told me he masturbates three times a day. He tell you that, sugar?"

The interviewer tried to get Mary off his lap and sputtered something about moving on to the next question. Mary grabbed his thigh and squeaked, "Oh that's just sad. Don't you have a girlfriend Ted? Do you want a girlfriend?"

The interviewer scrambled out of the room and the two of them had a good chuckle and a brief sexual encounter. Mary made me uneasy because she kept staring at me. She was probably staring at herself in the mirror, but the eye contact was uncanny.

Another man was also tough to peg, but I guessed he was a soldier. He had a rigid posture like the prisoners, but it was more assertive and less menacing. He answered in clipped terse words, mostly yeses and nos.

But all of these people had one thing in common they had no glow, no energy. They were drains. They expressed the same void as Colin. All but one that is. He was a prisoner, one of the meek ones, and when he was in with a group you could see the fear on his face and his energy signature pulled away in all directions. He knew he was in a room with predators and he acted like it, but I doubt he knew he was in a room with energy predators, with aura thieves.

I cried that day. The Professor asked to record all my thoughts, but he had to settle for a video of me watching in horror and crying like a child. He wisely waited until the next day to interview me.

"Tell me, what did you think about the people I brought for you to observe?"

"What makes you so sure they're people?"

"What do you mean by that?"

"By people, do you mean human?"

"Why would you say they aren't human?"

"I didn't." It was time to have this out and I knew it, but I didn't know if I was up to the task. My perception was spectral, foggy, flavorless, the lingering effect of the previous day's dose. I couldn't tell how I felt but I spoke anyway trusting my insipid intuition. "I am suggesting you may be right about some things."

"Like?"

"Like empathy, that it's a defining characteristic of human beings."

"Other animals display behaviors that suggest empathy, sharing and altruism in primates, dogs display signs of mourning when a member of the pack is ill or dies."

"I didn't say it was the only characteristic, just that it was a defining one. If you lack empathy you aren't human. But you're also wrong about empathy. It isn't an emotion. It's an experience. It's real."

"So you see empathy when you're on Nimbus?"

"That's what you hope. And that's what Morty hypothesized in a roundabout, way, but no. What I experience is far more complicated than that. But you're wrong about more than just that and empathy."

"Is that so? What else am I wrong about? Do profess," he said with a flourish of his hand.

"A man is not what he does, *Professor*. A man is his idiosyncrasies. He is that which distinguishes from his fellow man. A man is what he does only to the extent his actions are idiosyncratic. All other action is just a part of the collective."

"Interesting take."

"Just professing what I've learned. But you're more wrong about empathy than you know. It doesn't require imagination at all. You either have it or you don't. But I was wrong too. About empathy."

"How so?"

"It's not an idea. It's an experience. It cannot be learned or taught, but it can be strengthened or weakened, and it can be directed."

"I must say I'm surprised you are being so forthright today. I might even consider it a breakthrough in your treatment, if it holds up. Why don't you answer my original question now? What do you think of the *people* I brought by yesterday?"

I laughed. "Brought by. Like friends casually dropping in. Mind if I have some friends drop by?"

He pushed his wire glasses up the rim of his nose and spoke in a flat soothing psychotherapist tone. "So long as you clear it with staff first I see no problem with that."

"As if I had any friends to invite." He shrugged and smiled. "Fine," I said. "Those *people*, we both know why you brought them by. You brought them because they're like Colin."

"Do you mean to say...what was the word you used? Oh, yes, void. You called him a void. I never did get clarification on that. Could you clarify it for me?"

"I'd rather revise it. I no longer think he is a void. It always struck me as odd that he appeared disconnected. That's why I used the term void. It implies an absence. There is no absence. He's not a void. That's just how it appears on the surface. He's what's on the other side of the field. He's an inversion. And so are all the others. They aren't human. All but one."

"Which one?"

"Wouldn't you like to know?"

"Again you regress. I must admit I'm disappointed. So if they're not human what are they? Robots? Ghosts? Simulacra?"

"Stop trying to paint me with the crazy brush. You know full well what they are. They are just like Colin. That's why you brought them."

"Before you said you wouldn't share this information. Why the change of heart?"

"I'm not helping you by telling you something you already know."

"Well help me please. Won't you? Tell me what you see. I gather it has to do with energy and connections of some sort. Nimbus is a powerful empathogen, is it pleasant? Is what you see beautiful?"

"Oh the connections can be beautiful. Like at the Solstice, when the music was playing and people were synched. The connections were strengthened, yet they flowed even more. It was because so much of that energy was freely given. But even there the other aspect was present. The pulling, the bodies pulling at one another, there is a perpetual give and take. I could feel the energy moving both ways, but in the desert it was mostly a sharing. But that pulling, that desire to possess, it's always there too. And then there's Colin."

"Yes. Tell me about your brother."

"Don't call him that."

"Riley, I've already confirmed to you the fact of your fraternity."

"And I've already told you never to call him that. I have one brother."

"Very well. Tell me about Colin, then.

"Just because you phrase it as a statement instead of a question doesn't mean I'm going to answer. We've been at this too long for you to keep with the psychological tricks. I'm not going to tell you about Colin."

"Why not?"

"Why should I tell you what you already know?"

"How could you possibly know what I know or don't know about Colin?"

"Because you analyze everyone, Professor. And his type is so obvious that you can't be blind to it." I ran my hand through my hair; it was so long. I couldn't recall when I last cut it, a year at least. I ran it through again, delaying. I pondered how much to reveal, whether to continue talking at all. I had no emotional sense of the conversation, at least none I was aware of in the concrete tactile-taste way that had always defined my emotions. I was living blind, or bland. It was at once freeing and frightening. I decided to continue, "Do you remember before when you speculated that shame, guilt and humiliation all had at root the same visceral feeling, embarrassment? I suggest to you that Colin can be humiliated but is almost never ashamed and is incapable of feeling guilty."

"Interesting."

"By your definition guilt requires an awareness that you have taken an action that has harmed someone else. Colin has this awareness but he'll never feel any resulting embarrassment. Because guilt is more than that awareness, it is also a symptom of empathy. As I said, empathy is more than an act of imagination. It is more than a type of social understanding. It is an event, a physical phenomenon."

"And Colin? Your diagnosis?"

"Are we going to get clinical now? Is that why you keep dropping by abnormal psych texts? I'm not a doctor. Diagnosis is your job. But I've got one: sadist." The Professor confirmed more with a frown than a dissertation could have. "Not what you're looking for?" I raised an eyebrow, and pitched as much disdain into my voice as I could. I think I succeeded, but it's hard to know how your voice inflects when you mostly talk to yourself. "I'm right though. Call it one for one, but you want something more, something related to those folks you 'brought by'. Fine, I'll say the word, just for shits and giggles, sociopath."

The Professor's eyes brightened. "And how did you arrive at that conclusion?" He is incapable of shielding his interest in a topic or idea, the cost of being *Professor*.

"Now we get to it. That's the question that you're dying to know the answer to. And that's why I ain't saying shit. I've said too much already."

"Riley, please. Profess. Explain your reasoning. What have you observed that leads you to believe Colin is a sociopath?"

"I'm gonna stop you right there Prof. You can observe him just as well as I can. In fact, I'm sure you have. So if you were really interested in what observations of Colin's behavior demonstrate sociopathic traits then you wouldn't be asking me."

"That's not true. It is always valuable to test my own views against the arguments and evidence of others. In order to be certain in one's professions one must consider both, arguments for and in opposition. I ask only what I ask of everyone, that you assist me in this noble task. Why won't you?"

"Can it with the noble ideals. I know why you want to know."

"And why is that?"

"Because I don't require extensive observation to figure it out. That's why you paraded those psychos through here yesterday, to confirm what you already knew, or at least suspected: I can spot them when I'm on Nimbus."

"So tell me in more detail what you see. What's the harm? You've already told me enough that I know the drug's value."

"That's where you're wrong." I paused and stared at his anxious eyes. "No, not wrong. Lying. The drug has no value. Well, no value higher than the street value of ecstasy. But that's not why you, or your bosses that is, want Nimbus. Nimbus has no value. I have value. And that is why I won't tell you what you need to know and why I won't help you, because I know what it is you really want to do, you want to make more of him."

"Cloning?" the Professor scoffed, but he couldn't hide his disappointment. He was too used to professing to commit to a lie that he hadn't planned out in advance. "Don't be preposterous."

"No. Not cloning." I sneered and pointed at him with my cane, "Let me be more precise. You don't want to make more of him. You want to find more like him."

"Riley I want nothing more than to seek out knowledge and profess it to others."

"I notice you don't deny it."

"Deny what? There is nothing to deny."

"Deny why you want to know about Colin. This is not some innocuous quest for knowledge. People will be hurt."

"Like you?"

"Like me. Like Wren. Like Bob. Like Gary. Like everyone who comes in contact with this place. Everyone who comes into contact with him."

"Oh so you're all victims. Of what? Of exposure to Colin's personality? Of my magic healing potions? Of my treacherous science? Everyone who comes here comes here to be fixed. To be healed. I healed you Riley."

"You imprisoned me."

"You imprison yourself. You were crippled. I set you to the ocean. I gave it back to you with a tool to enter, I gave you the means to surf again, to ride monsters." He pulled at his coat and stared at the ceiling as though pondering his next move. "Cortes Bank." He tried to tempt me. "Will you ever see it?" I was resigned to the fact that I never would. I sat perfectly still and waited him out. Being locked away had taught me nothing if not patience. The absence of Yangs, which at first had been disorienting was now aiding. I was empty. I wasn't worried about what I was feeling. I trusted myself in this little tête-à-tête.

The Professor broke the silence. "So if I were to take you on a field trip, could you spot these non-humans?" An inartful question, he was losing his edge.

"Yes. But I won't."

"If they really aren't human, don't others deserve to be warned?"

"Yes. But you won't warn people of them. You'll put guns in their hands. That's the plan isn't it? You hinted at it in the bus. It's quite the cost savings, not having to brainwash men and convert them to killing machines. Catch them young enough and you can bend them to your ends before they become uncontrollable, loose cannons like Colin. Just find conscienceless kids train them as soldiers and set them loose on the world. We both know the same things Professor, I just know without fancy tests and lengthy periods of observation. And I know when they're young, whereas you can't diagnose psychopathy until maturity, because nearly all teenagers profile as psychopaths." It was the only time I ever was able to read genuine anger on his face. "Thinking you shouldn't have given me all those books on abnormal psychology now, huh?"

"I empathize with you Riley. I really do. It pains me to watch you condemn yourself to a lifetime in here. I keep hoping for a change of heart, but if one doesn't come..." he shrugged with a vindictive smile that could have been on Colin's face, "We have other options."

Stuck

I startle awake. I struggle in vain to sit up, held to the bed by strong hands in latex gloves. A needle glistens in the darkness. I feel a pinch. My body goes slack and a blindfold is placed over my eyes. I fight for consciousness as I slip into warm wet dark.

"Some times you see..."

Who's there?

"Sometimes you see with clarity..."

Who is it? I can't see you.

"Never do you see reality."

Is this real?

"Enlighten... Remove yourself ..."

I know it's the gnomes.

"Step away, all ceases... no time... release and return..."

Like the gnome said, "Never do you see reality." Not time travel, time stops traveling while I step away.

I float along the snaking ductwork searching for a way out. I follow the path, the largest cluster of bound wire and pipe. I trace over and around, up and through, searching for the gear hub. I am not interested in the gnomes. I want to see the guts, the innards. The gnomes are a distraction. Fixated on the small I missed the big picture. All of those gears are driving something.

The pipes are confusing. They twist and turn, narrow, contract, expand and branch. I wish for a map. I wish for a faster way to navigate the pipes. Then I am in a cart. Have I always been? I whiz along. The cart's wheels whir attached in tracks to the pipes. I duck low. I am flying at an incredible rate, too fast. I want out. Out of the cart. Out of the pipes. I burst free.

A Beard and a Break

I open my eyes. No pipes.

A wave laps against my face. I cough. I taste salt in the water. I lay prone on a white sand beach. I remember the needle. I must have been out for some time for them to transport me to…wherever this is. I turn over and immediately shut my eyes. I squint into a brilliant sun. I prop myself up on my elbows and stare into lush tropical greenery, ferns and palms.

How long was I out?

My instinct is to never have the ocean at my back, so I stand and turn to face the water. In the distance I see a perfect left hand break peel across the horizon. My old performance board, my six two thruster with the Sparx emblem, sits next to me. I am perfectly dry. No sand sticks to my hands or face.

A man emerges from beneath a stand of coconut trees. He walks toward me and I turn to face him. He is tall, barrel-chested, bare-chested and bearded. His strides are long, but his approach is slow and shrouded in shadow. "Who are you?" I ask.

"Lovely day isn't it," the bearded man says in a voice much softer than his burly appearance. "Perfect left hand point break too. Is that your board?"

"Yeah."

"You mind if I take it out. I really wanna shred that left man, I been checking it out all morning."

"You've been here all morning?"

"Yeah. So do you mind if I take it out? I'll bring it right back."

"Wait, where are we? Where'd you come from?"

The bearded man thrusts his neck toward the edge of the beach. "See those coconut trees over there." He smiles as though that answered my question.

I turn to stare at the trees. Did I miss something? Is there a hut or hotel? No, just trees and sand. "But where is this?" I ask.

"You really shouldn't stand with your back to the ocean. Rogue waves can kill."

I look over my shoulder. Ceaseless black tumult confronts me. A wall of water blots out the sky. I run for the trees as the sea rushes in behind me.

Flooded

I scamper and dash through skinny trunks and dense undergrowth. All is green. All is black. I am terrified. But I taste nothing, neither metal nor cold. The air is thick and humid. I taste the air. I do not taste my fear.

Barefoot. Half naked. A sorry state but one I cannot ponder except as painful fact. Rocks and twigs pierce the soles of my feet. Branches lash my torso like stinging whips. I no longer hear the roar of the waters behind me. I stagger a few more steps. I stop, panting, hunched over, hands on knees, body a wobble, lungs afire.

I recover quickly and survey my surroundings. I stand perched atop a patch of high ground. There is sand underfoot and water as far as the eye can see. I look around me three hundred sixty degrees. Jungle obstructs my view, but there is no apparent end to the sea.

I walk further into the jungle. The more I walk the more sea I discover. It is dark. Sun and trees reflect upon its surface. I cannot find the sun in the sky, only its reflection on the surface of the dark deep. The trees above become denser and denser. They block out the sky. Yet the reflection on the waters below becomes brighter and clearer. I see myself, a lonely wanderer, ringed by the sea, illumined by the sun.

Catch Me If You Can

In the distance I hear a faint beating. It grows louder as I walk the arc of the land's edge. It is rhythmic, *ba-thumpa ba-thumpa bump.* The rhythm gains pace. The beat quickens. I see them, dark haired-maidens dancing naked round a lone drummer.

One of the maidens sees me. I catch only a glimpse of her, just the soft round curve of her hip and her face, a familiar face hidden behind a swath of wavy dark hair. She squeals and they all run for the jungle. I give chase. They have a head start but I am faster. There! I see her. The sheen of her hair catches a single beam of sunlight before she disappears behind a tree. The jungle grows thicker and thicker. I cannot see her. She is gone. And again I am in darkness.

Trees encircle me. There are no gaps. Their trunks grow side by side and branches interleave like the pen boards of an animal enclosure. How did I manage to get in this grove? I am a part of this grove! I cannot move! I am rooted to the ground. It is too dark to see anything. I feel a faint sliding about my legs. It wraps itself around my ankles like a serpent slithering invisible in the darkness.

I hear a voice, "You must get away from him."

From who?

"From Father," the voice answers my silent question.

I look up. She sits upon a branch high above my head. Her delicate toes dangle like sweet red grapes from a trellis vine. Raven locks fall gently across her face as she beckons for me to climb. "Come up," she says. "Come to me."

"But I can't move," I say.

"Of course you can. Climb."

I climb. She climbs higher. I follow. We shimmy up the narrowing trunk onto ever more perilous branches. I call to her, "Are you the one I saw before?" But she does not answer. She continues to climb. Higher and higher we ascend until finally she stops.

We have reached the very top. She sits on a branch thinner than a cat's whisker, floating in space. She points. I look out. A rainbow stretches over the sea to a verdant isle in the distance. "Terra juventus. Pons," she whispers. "A bridge you cannot cross." The rainbow breathes. I think of my mother and of my terrific height. I reach out for the woman,

402

groping at emptiness, scared to fall. "Don't fear," she says. "It's only an almond tree." I look down only to find myself on solid ground. I look back to the woman. She brushes her hair from her face. I go to meet her eye and find myself staring into a supernova.

Fornix

An arch stands before me. The maidens gather beneath it. They whisper to each other and cast lascivious glances at me over their bare shoulders. A hooded woman stands apart and points through the arch to the green land of small plants.

I walk through the throng of women. They run their hands across my bare chest and shoulders as I pass. "Hey baby. Wanna date?" As I pass through the arch one pulls close and whispers in my ear in a throaty Italian accent, "Fornicari." I rush to get away and run straight into a muddy field of clashing hippopotami.

Hippopotamus Camp

The sulfur stench of rotten eggs hangs over the field. It assaults my nostrils and I cover my face with my hands as I scramble for cover. The ground shakes beneath me. My footing slips again and again. I let go of my nose and clamber through the mud toward what I hope is the edge of the field. I dive over a berm and slide down a short slope onto grass at the foot of a wooden tower.

In the tower the maidens sit, only they aren't the maidens from before. I recognize them, but they are somehow changed, older, perhaps. Most seem disinterested, but they pass around a single pair of binoculars to watch the action on the field. One woman hands them off then looks down at me as I wipe the scum and mud from my body. "Messy business, Hippopotamus Camp is. You're wise to steer clear. Come on up."

I climb the ladder to the wide platform atop the tower, anxious to gain some distance from the pitch. "What exactly is going on?" I ask. "And what is Hippopotamus Camp?"

"That's Hippopotamus Camp." She points to the field. "Our kids are playing the big game today."

"Your kids are hippopotamuses?"

She glares at me. The woman now holding the binoculars sets them down and glares at me. All of the other women turn and glare at me. "Don't be silly. Our children are not hippopotami," she emphasizes the 'i' with a sneer. "The children ride atop the hippopotami." Another woman hands me the binoculars, "It's the big game. They're after that ball. My boy's the one in blue with the blonde hair."

Through the field specs I can see the children riding atop the massive beasts. The children vary in size from grown men to infants. Each holds a stick like a polo mallet and they chase their steeds about the pitch whacking furiously at a small white ball. However, the game seems as much about crashing the hippos into each other as it is about the ball. I see no goalposts, or any indications of boundaries save the berm before our tower.

I spot the toe-headed boy the woman said was her son. He looks to be about six. "He's so young." I say.

"Yes. Well you can't choose these things of course. We've got to let them play."

"Why?"

"Because that's the rule."

"Whose rule?" I demand. It's preposterous, six year olds and infants have no business riding about on hippopotami.

"Paul's of course."

"Who's Paul?"

"Paul from Hippopotamus Camp. The referee." She turns to another one of the mothers. "Where is Paul anyway?"

"He should be here shortly. Some emergency at the switching station."

"Yes well Hippopotamus Camp should take priority. Whatever the emergency." The rest of the mothers voice their assent.

I continue to watch the toe-headed boy. He charges recklessly into the fray, challenging two grown men atop much larger hippos for possession. One of the men raises his mallet to chest level and clotheslines the boy.

The boy flies from his hippo landing face first in the mud. The man who struck him turns his hippo round one hundred eighty degrees and tramples his limp body in a muddy, bloody spectacle.

I scream in horror. "Your son!" The boy's mother sits by, passive and disinterested. "Your son! Did you see what happened to your son?"

"I've already forgotten him," she says calmly. I am so shocked at her laissez-faire attitude toward her son's death that I almost don't notice when she puts her hand on my thigh. I feel the hands of the other mothers pull at me from behind.

Van Dyke

A whistle shrieks. "That's enough of that." A thin man sporting a pointy Van Dyke with wax-tipped moustache stands amidst the throng. He grabs at the lanyard around his neck. "I have the whistle," he says with authority and looks at the women as if daring them to challenge him.

"And who are you?" asks one of the throng.

"I am here on Will's behalf. Now unhand that young man. He is here to keep score."

The women break their hold and accost me verbally, "Why didn't you tell us you were here to keep score? Honestly! The nerve! Making us sit here waiting for Paul and all the while you could have been keeping score!"

I scamper away, following Van Dyke down to the pitch. "So how exactly should I keep score?" I ask. "How exactly do they score?"

"Keep score however you like. It doesn't matter anyway. I'm calling the game. Will's orders. There's too much going on today. He said to just keep everyone in play, that you'd sort it out later."

"I'd sort it out?"

"You should head back through the arch. Go find Will at the switching station, it's the sensible thing to do."

Anxious to get as far from Hippopotamus Camp as I can I head back the way I came. I have no idea who this Will is, but he has to be nicer than stampeding hippos. I hear the whistle as I leave and see Van Dyke mount a hippo of his own, a bullwhip in hand. He cracks the whip leaving pin streaks through the mud.

The children quickly organize into a hippo-phalanx, every beast shoulder to shoulder and ass to nose with another. They roll white balls, hundreds of them, under and through the legs of the hippos, like a rugby scrum but with all the players facing one direction and the ball getting passed both forward and back. Some players try to advance the balls; others defend, acting as gates. Where a defender is overcome the gate ceases to be a gate and becomes a passer instead. I walk on, deciding not to worry about the score of this bizarre exercise. As I leave I can hear Van Dyke cracking his whip, screaming at the top of his lungs, "Demons! You're all demons!"

Dr. Uma Stahl

I skip happily through an empty arch and into the back of a longhaired man. It is the bearded man from the beach. "Oh good you're here. You need to see this."

The room is crowded. Everywhere short people run about plugging and unplugging wires in an unfathomable array of holes and slots. "Homunculi hard at work. It's full blown crisis mode in here. Doctor. Doctor over here! Please give us a status update."

An attractive blonde woman with a clipboard and black glasses rushes over. "Certainly Saul." She looks quizzically at me, "Who's this?"

"That's Riley. Riley meet Dr. Uma Stahl. Doctor Stahl runs the switchboard here and it's been a very hectic day. Please continue with the briefing Doctor."

"Of course. All's quiet on the Frontier, but Paris has gone completely dark and they're rioting in Oxford, starbursts and fireworks on the Oxford skyline. It looks bad. The grid is down. We've been getting flickers from time to time but as best we can tell the power is out. There's some evidence the Parisians are talking to themselves on short-wave radios, but we can't be sure from here."

"How about Tempe?" asks Saul.

"Tempe is online. We're getting incoming transmissions, but they're getting panicked. We can't get anything out to them."

"Why not? Aren't the generators working beneath us and at the edge?"

"Yes. The generators are functioning. It isn't a power issue, it's a data issue. We've got nothing coming in; so we've got nothing to relay. We keep bouncing their signal back to them."

"Ok Uma. What do you suggest?"

"Oceanic delivery seems like the only option. It's limited in terms of what it can communicate, but at least it will let them know someone is still here and in charge. But it's not my call."

"Not mine either."

"Obviously." She exhales a tense breath. "The boys downstairs got started already. They've been chucking bottles of dope, pep, pine and oxy off the docks for hours now. No need to toss any trips. There was a massive bottle break, black tonic and hyrdromammal cordial everywhere. The place is flooded with it."

"Sounds like a fun day on the seas of sorrow. Nothing to do now but watch and wait," Saul says. "Hey Riley come take a closer look at the switchboard." On our way over to the board I see Van Dyke nervously pacing about watching the chaos unfold around him. "Who's that?" I ask Saul.

"Him?" he asks as though I should already know and then glares at me, "He's in my employ."

"I meant, what's his name? I just met him."

"Right," Saul scoffs. "Just met him. You're too dependent on Van Dyke you know. He's an unreliable go between."

"I did just meet him," I say, confused. "You call him Van Dyke too?"

"You call him Van Dyke. Why should I call him anything to you?" Saul glares at me again. "You'd do well to remember he works for me." He points to a tangle of wires jammed into two ports, "Check that out." I happily shift my attention to the switchboard and away from the Van Dyke issue.

To my eyes, the switchboard is a convoluted mess but this tangle is particularly messy. "What is it?" I ask.

"That is a connection from here to down below to Paris. Notice anything odd?"

I look closer at the tangle. It isn't two ports, but four in a two by two setup, input and output side by side. Four wires total, but it looks more like eight, because each wire plugs-in crossways twice, input to output and output to input. "The signal goes both ways," I say.

"Exactly. It makes it hard for the relay sites to know where the signal originated. It's a feedback loop and it's run to ground in the middle of Paris. My employee has been reading. He suspects treachery, a *sinister* placement." He looks at me, his eyes dark and serious. "Ever have a taste of French food? Funny on the tummy, snails and shit with lots of butter, but I like the way it makes me feel. How about you Riley? You go both ways?"

Is that a come-on? I'm not off-put. It isn't the first time a guy's hit on me. But I'm stuck on the French food. How does food make me feel? How do I feel about food? Is he asking if my taste goes both ways? An ancient TV tube screen suddenly lights up. On it a massive obelisk glows at its point above a dim cityscape. "Bingo!" says Saul. "Uma dear, what is that?"

"Oh that's the Seers Tower."

"And where is that?" Saul asks.

"It's in the Former Higher Circle in Tempe, right at the fold, where the street meets the road."

"I don't have my tastes," I say.

"Of course not," says Saul. "Not in here. But you finally got the joke. Be sure to tell Van Dyke. Although he hates to be the last to know."

The Path Through the Meadow

The path winds uphill through a grassy meadow. The warm dirt feels good on my bare feet. I stop to sniff the lupine and marigolds. A blue-eyed daisy catches my eye. I pick it and put it behind my ear.

Saul paints at an easel in the middle of the meadow. He wears a black and white striped shirt and a black beret. The canvas is blank except for a tiny gold diamond that Saul is methodically filling in.

"What is it?" I ask.

"A flower," he says.

"So it's abstract then?"

Saul continues to paint, but Van Dyke rambles off an answer. "All art is abstraction all thought is abstraction all life is abstraction all death is abstraction. So, do show do tell do think do look do live do die. If so? Then so? Shall we unpack abstractions or pile them up?

"Folly holly filly dilly, follow folly mostly though. Why ten fingers? Why ten toes? Stack abstract or pack it back? Peel or deal? Incognito or by name, either way it's all the same. What do you have if you travel in opposite directions to wind up at the same place? Does it matter if it's curved or straight?"

He grabs an 8 and throws it on its side. "Come now," he says. "We've used enough of time. Tell me which is nearer true the meaning or the rhyme? The concept or the silver of a nickel or a dime?

"Chippy chaps chomp cheap chemical chard. 'Ch' is it soft or hard? Abstract symbols governed by abstract rules violated for abstract causes. Cursed chimera. Mutant emissaries of dead languages wash up on the beachhead with the remnants of abstractions dreamed on foreign shores. Chameleons climb, cymbals chime, chandeliers shine, why not 'chine'? Italy or France?"

"Never mind," Saul cuts him off then says to me, "You've got my employee all worked up. You really must stop working through him. Never mind." He sighs, exasperated, "Here. Take this."

He hands me a gold lozenge. I toss it away. I immediately regret it.

"That's such a Van Dyke move," says Saul. "He's a useful tool. He works well on the nuts and bolts of it, the superficial, but he's limited. He can't create. He only sees the obvious and he can only work with what he's given. Stop giving him material that's over his head. You'd do well to remember he works for me." He turns to Van Dyke, "Let's go."

"You got it Will," says Van Dyke as Saul packs away the easel. The two of them head up the hill together leaving me behind.

My Place?

"Walk with me," he says. "I used your board. I hope you don't mind. I had to do it. That left was sick. You gotta try it."

"How'd I get here?" I ask.

"You tell me Riley. It's your place. I'm just visiting."

"My place? What makes you think this is my place? I just got here. Are you with the gnomes?"

"The gnomes?"

"Yeah the gnomes. I know it sounds crazy, but so is... Dude who are you?"

"The better question is who I'm not. Like I said, I'm just visiting."

"Visiting from where?"

"Out there. I'm always looking out there. I'm a planner, a mover and a shaker. This spot is chill. I hope you don't mind me hanging out."

"Dude this is not my place."

"It seems like the kinda spot you'd like. Myself I'd have picked something a little more country, lakeside maybe. I guess you live lakeside where you're from. But this, this definitely seems like your kind of spot.

"I don't understand."

"Isn't it obvious? Sun, sand and a sweet point break that only goes left. Sound like anyone you know? I'm just waiting for the beautiful women, spicy chocolate and maybe even crème brûlée to appear. You don't mind if I have a little? Of the crème brûlée I mean."

A carafe of steaming chocolate appears on a table next to me. "How'd you do that?" I demand.

"I didn't do that. You did. Although I did plant the suggestion." He sniffs the cinnamony chocolate vapors and crinkles up his nose. "I was really hoping for the crème brûlée."

"Okay, if this is my place how'd you get here?"

"Oh it is your place. It's your happy place. And you come here more than you know."

"I remember the gnomes. From when I was eight."

"Actually there is no 'when.' Not here. Is-was-will be, all is. You've been here more than you know."

"So how did you get here? How do you know all of this? Just who the hell are you?"

"Look I'll bring your board back in a few. You should really test the water though. No need to be afraid of the sea."

"I'm not—"

But he's gone. So is the chocolate. It didn't make sense anyway, the chocolate. Far in the distance I see a form pop up on the wave. I never saw him paddle out. He angles down the face and executes a turn before the pipe covers him up. He's very good. The wave breaks across the entire shoreline. I follow as far to my right as my eyes can track. It's still breaking. I wonder if he'll pop out on the other side.

She is there. Our eyes lock for an instant. Wren. She takes off down the beach. The chase is on. I run as fast as I can. But I'm too late. She is in a boat in the sea before I can reach her. She motors away at trawling speed under the rainbow. She is headed for the isle. I dive in and swim after her.

I cut through the breakers with the skill of a dolphin. Amazingly I am gaining on the boat. Halfway under the rainbow, I trail her by only a few strokes. Wren leans over the bow, her hand extended for mine. Just a few more strokes and I'll—

I reach for her hand. I feel wrinkled skin. I look up.

Mom!

I lose my grip and slide under the water. The current pulls me down into salt and blackness. I am in deep waters. I fight to the surface. A wave crashes over me just as the boat vanishes below the horizon.

I sputter and struggle, but the current is strong. I pop up only to be smashed by the waves and pulled back under. I fight to the surface again, but I am fading. The ability to surge back wanes with every attempt. Once more to the top, I gasp for air when strong hands grab my arms and lift me from the sea. I fall heaving and hacking onto the flat deck of a flat boat. Van Dyke is at the oars. Van Dyke rescued me from the sea. I struggle to catch my breath and start to thank him, but he interrupts, "To become the ocean you have to drown."

Saul and the Storyteller

The mothers from hippopotamus camp and Saul await us onshore. The mothers rush to me. "What's the score?" they ask. They all want to know the score.

"Nice to see you too. Yes I'm fine. Almost drowned but I didn't. Thanks for your concern."

Mercifully, Saul calls them off. "But Paul!" they protest. "We have to know the score."

"All points valid. The game continues. Now please, give him some air." Next he dismisses Van Dyke. We stand together on the beach, just the two of us.

"Some show," he says. "You are a strong swimmer."

"Who are you? The mother's called you Paul from Hippopotamus Camp, but Van Dyke called you Will."

"I'm called many things, some nicer than others, Paul, Saul, Will, Joules, over time some call me Watts. I prefer Riley but we have to let you have that one."

"I am Riley."

"Like I said. You get that one."

"Why wouldn't I? It's my name."

"That's right. It's your call. You're the Storyteller."

"What's that mean?" I ask.

"It means you're the Storyteller," he says. "It means you're here because you have to be.

"What story?"

"What story? *The* story. There can only be one, subject to revision by the Storyteller, of course."

"I still don't understand."

"People around here think I'm in charge, and I am, sort of. You see, I can plan and do, but I don't get to interpret. It's the same reason I'm the referee and you're the scorekeeper."

"Yeah thanks for getting the mothers off my back. Is this all about hippopotamus camp?"

"No. The mothers are all hung up on hippopotamus camp, fretting about a past that keeps on changing. But it's just a game within the game. The mothers worry about the score but there's always another match. I

415

hold the whistle. The Storyteller holds the chalk, the eraser and the shovel. How could the game have any significance if the ref and the scorekeeper were the same? The outcome only counts if the ref lets it stand. The score only matters if the board is kept fair. All that makes the players seem pretty insignificant. How much more so the mothers?"

"That sounds a little egotistical. And why would I need a shovel?"

"Because sometimes an eraser isn't enough. Some things have to be buried."

The Old Man and the Tree Upon the Earth

He walks away and I follow him into the trees. I see a form waiting in the shadows up ahead. I approach, expecting to see Saul, but when I arrive it is an old man with a long grey beard, and the entire world around me is a vast expanse of brown.

"What is this place? Who are you?"

"I can't tell you. It's not part of the story. Besides I could tell you anything. So why bother asking? Besides, what I'm about to tell you is not nearly so important as what I'm about to show you."

The old man shows me a leafless tree. It towers enormous, but not reaching for the sky, rather for the edges of the earth. The edges of its canopy cannot be seen. Its broad expanse blocks the sun low on the horizon as though ablaze at the base. The fire spreads through the lower limbs while the top is bathed in quenching moonlight. I wonder how long it would take to walk around it.

"It'd take a long time to walk around it," he says.

I wonder if he ever has.

"You know I never have walked around it. I'd like to do that sometime."

"How about now?" I ask.

"Oh we don't have time for that. Not nearly."

We stare up at the tree for a time. Neither of us speaks. I try to follow the turnings of the branches with my eye. I find a larger limb to focus on, then trace it up to a branching, where I follow a new limb and then the new limb put out by that limb until it twists up and disappears into the dense canopy, all discernment between branches lost about halfway up, or what I guess is halfway up, since I can't actually see the top.

There is a question brewing, called up of its own accord. Necessary, it demands to be asked as though it is the only question I could possibly ask. The old man answers before I ask.

"It's still standing," he says.

"But is it—"

"It's still standing. That's all we can know."

"There's not a single leaf."

"None you can see."

"Not one on the tree. Not one on the ground. If it were autumn wouldn't we see leaves on the ground?"

"I don't see any leaves on the ground. Nor fruit. Nor seed."

"No. No evidence of them either. No decomposition. No discoloration of the soil."

The soil is a perfect brown, no apparent tint, not reddish soil like clay, nor particularly rich. It is brown, a perfect even mellow brown, no lightening hints of yellow, nor darkened black spots, no tinges of shine or metals, just brown, flat unchanging brown.

I turn to survey the landscape and I am suddenly troubled by the thought that there is in fact no ground to speak of at all. Before me the flat expanse of brown exists without contrast. All is brown, brown extending endlessly without any forms upon it or contrast behind it. All is brown and without something to differentiate from the brown there is no way to distinguish brown from nothing. If nothing is brown then as I stand here nothing exists. If nothing is brown then I stand on nothing and if I stand on nothing do I even exist?

"I can't stand on my head," says the old man. I turn back to him and the tree before us, and I feel their existence proves my own. Hardly logical, but the brown is now soil and not nothing. "Can you stand on your head? I'd really like to but I don't have the balance."

"No. I can't stand on my head. Bum shoulder."

"What do you mean?"

"Well I hurt it—" and then I realize that here I am not hurt. I don't limp. I ran. I swam. I don't even have my cane with me. I never even thought to use it.

I am no longer looking up into the branches. Instead I stare down at twisting snarls sinking to ever-deeper depths. They plummet below my feet stretching out into the empty brown. The soil is again the formless expanse of not-soil, just color with no texture.

"I can't stand on my head," the old man continues, "but sometimes I think like an Aussie, down-under, all flipped around. Sheilas, ya know, mate?"

"What?"

"You know, Sheilas. That's what they call the ladies down under, much nicer than 'bitches' or 'chicks', that modern slang you fellows use, don't you think?'

I don't think. I stare. My mind still reels from the arboreal rotation.

"Sheilas. Good I think, more sophisticated in that upside-down manner that those Aussies have. Will you get off your head? Show-off."

I am at eye level with the old man's feet, the straps of his sandals grimy with sweat and dirt, the not-soil turned to soil once again. It presses against my head. I feel the grit in my hair. I see through the soil to the bare branching arms of the tree. "Wait," I say, "you're upside down not me. I still see the branches."

"And what does that prove?"

"That the branches are still overhead."

"Or underfoot."

"But they've been over my head all along, so you switched spots, not me."

"That's one way of looking at it."

"It's the only way to look at it."

"Assuming such things as fixed spots and orientations exist. There's always more than one way to look at it."

And then the world is flat, brown and endless. Saul and I stand, connected at the toes. I look up at him. I am stretched out flat across the expanse of brown.

"Get it?" the old man's voice calls out, and before I can answer the perspective flips. I stand above a flat two-dimensional Saul. "Take a walk," says the voice. I step away a few steps and I feel the sun on my skin. It dawns on me. I stand in the sun but I cast no shadow.

The old man stands next to me and the tree stretches out across the brown not-soil, but it isn't flat like a drawing, there is no expansion or contraction of near and far. In other words, there is no perspective yet it is complete. Somehow the man in three dimensions beside me and the two-dimensional tree in front of me both fit, and neither requires adjustment.

"It's easier to walk this way," he says and we head out along the trunk, its image underfoot. I start to turn out and follow an interesting branching, one that is especially dense and complex, full of twists and sharp articulations. "Not that one," he says, "there's a branch I need to show you."

We head out along a thin wispy branch. Two-dimensions become three, and I am out in the air like a tightrope walker on a branch as narrow as my foot. I crouch down and grab hold of the branch with both hands.

"Don't worry," says the old man, "this isn't a branch you can fall off of. Look out there."

From our vantage I can see a distant obelisk. It glows brilliant red at the peak. I look at the strange fork in the branch on which I stand, two tines to the right, only one to the left. And suddenly it becomes clear to me. The pieces fall into place: Shelly, Erin, Wren, evolution, reproductive advantage, my mother, Colin's mother. I know what the Professor is after. He wants to know about Colin, he wants my skill, but even more he wants my seed.

The surf crashes in the distance. The wave is perfect. The tree is gone. The air is chill. I shake with cold. I shake with fright.

The old man puts a warm hand on my shoulder. "Knowing everything that you know is scary, but not knowing all the rest is even scarier. I can tell you any story you'd like to hear, and a hundred more you wouldn't. You know why you've come here Riley. You've come to decide, and you want it all at your fingertips. You want me. You want her. You want Saul. It's sad, because you saw it, the jewel. But instead..." he holds out his hands, palms up and looks around, "...this. You were wiser as a child."

The old man is gone. I hear Saul from behind me say, "So decide. You already have after all."

"Decide what?"

"Decide to embrace it. Decide that it doesn't matter if it's real or not that you have to believe it is. I've already done it. Now you have to write the story."

But I don't want to leave. I haven't seen the jewel. Somewhere here is the jewel.

"I'm sorry Riley," The old man's disembodied voice sounds from within me. "The child is the Buddha and the Buddha is a child."

I understand. I will not see the jewel. I am no longer a child and I will never be a Buddha. Were I, I would see it, for to see it once, to truly see it, is to see it for eternity. It makes me afraid that eternity is lost to me. Then I realize, eternity is lost to us all, the most we can hope for is a glimpse, and I had mine. So instead of straining to see, I close my eyes.

Truthful Reinterpretation

I open my eyes to ice blue lakes. "Morning sunshine," Colin says. He stares into my eyes, his face pressed close to mine. I shudder at his voice, so hollow, as the pressure rolls my vertebrae.

I am betrayed by my body; betrayed by my mind. The cold waters of fear threaten to consume me as I realize the scope of my defeat. Colin holds the front page of the LA Times for me to see: February 25th, two days have passed. The time of the jewel has passed. I knew this, but the confirmation hurts and frightens just the same. My solace removed, my strength, my faith. All removed by the removal of a jewel and a hope, and what remains is void. I had only my resolve, and now I haven't that. All that remains is the end.

At this point I must admit a certain reinterpretation of the gnomes and their reality. Perhaps it was a fool's errand, to guess at the meaning of a trip out of time, or a fool's calculation anyhow. Leap year issues? But then the numbers would be different anyway. Perhaps I sought to impose order where none exists. Or perhaps the numbers told me what I needed to hear, a collusion of sorts between the gnomes and the old man. A stacking of cosmic dominoes while time awaited the drugs and the deprivation tank to trigger the stack and start the chain.

They pull me from the tank, and then I sleep a dreamless sleep. I do not fail to remember my dreams as I have always done. I do not dream. I do not need to.

What remains is a secret. Knowledge I can use to wound. The tree upon the earth, a truth long felt, but now revealed. Truth known to both actor and observer, whichever I be, truth to open up a bloodline, clamp it off, and watch as it turns necrotic and black. Truth wielded as a sword. Truth unleashed to flood the void inside with a momentary vengeance. Truth set free to watch truth die. What a pure moment that will be!

But is it possible to wound a creature such as Colin with knowledge like this? Can this monster feel pain or loss or shame though he could never know guilt? Can I make him feel regret?

The End

They rouse me from my slumber, Colin and the orderlies. They force me to march down the hall. Disorientation is their strategy. I haven't had time to wake, but it doesn't matter, I know how my story ends. The Professor waits for me in the room. I know this room. I've seen it, or made it, it's where the story ends.

I see him first, then the machine. A padded adjustable chair in full recline, like the kind in the dentist's office, only it is turned nearly vertical with leather restraints affixed to the arms and leg rest and a thick belt strap at the seat. A video screen is mounted from the ceiling at the level of the headrest. The machine itself sits next to the chair; a plastic cuff attached to the end a single robotic arm. The arm itself is simple, a single hinge joint capable of moving the cuff back and forth over a distance of a few inches. Inside the cuff is a donut shaped latex bladder. A technician tests the mechanism and a small pneumatic pump sounds as the bladder gently inflates to constrict around any object placed inside the cuff. I know what object will be put inside the cuff. An orderly applies lubricant to the bladder and screws a small glass collection jar onto the end of the cuff.

I take my place at the machine and stand before the inverted chair. The orderly pulls out a wrench to adjust the arm's angle.

"I've got it," Colin says to the orderly and takes the wrench before stepping in to affix me to the device. "Take down your pants."

"No." I am stoic. I make no move to resist, but I will not assist. This is the only thing I have left in my control. I will end my story with dignity in the face of humiliation.

"Fine." He sets the wrench on a nearby cart. He straps my arms into the restraints and cinches the belt around my waist.

"I was wrong," I call to the Professor who is standing in the doorway. "A man isn't his idiosyncrasies. A man is the story he tells himself, and the faithfulness with which he communicates that story to the world."

"That's all very philosophical," says Colin as he adjusts the arm angle and tightens it down with the wrench. "But it's about time we started milking your sperm sack."

"You ever think about how your story ends?" I ask him.

"It ends the same way all stories end, death."

I ponder that for a moment. It may be the wisest thing Colin ever said to me.

"Prototype." Colin yanks my pants down around my ankles. "That little cup has a thin sphincter on the end that allows liquid in but not out." He tightens the restraints around my ankles.

"Don't want to yank it yourself?" I say.

"I don't have the wrist strength." He points to the latex donut. "You see the bladder there inflates and deflates. The idea is to leave a subject attached to it overnight, or even for days. At the appropriate times the bladder automatically inflates, the video screen displays a 'relevant stimulus,' the Professor's words not mine, and the arm activates. After a release from the subject passes through the sphincter, the bladder deflates, the screen turns off and the arm ceases motion. But the best part is the jar itself. Once the sphincter is activated the bottom of that canister releases a cooling agent into the outer sleeve of the jar instantly freezing the contents. The only labor required is to change the collection jar once its full. For an average male that's only once every thirty-six hours assuming two-hour intervals between activation. You can imagine the practical utility right, set up a row of a hundred and wow, you could fill the vaults at a lot of banks."

I can bear it no longer. "He wanted you to be a synesthete. You ever wonder why?"

"Who?"

"Dirty Doctor Morty."

"You're about to embark on a three day jerk-off and you're thinking about dear old dad. You're one sick puppy."

"It's in the notes on Project Nimbus. 'CK shows no early indicia of synesthetic potential.' The page was badly burned. Wonder who did that?"

"Those pages were like that when I inherited. Just how the Professor handed them over."

"You wonder why he thought you might be a synesthete? He wasn't one, after all. Was he?"

"Don't know. I'm not. Who cares why not?"

"You should," I say.

"Why's that?"

"Because..."

I pause so the impact of what I'm about to say will have maximum effect. I want it to sink into his mind and burn into his very being.

"You wore yellow to your mother's funeral."

His eyes widen, the icy lakes turned to fiery holes. Always so glib, but his words have left him. I give him the full story. "My mother's egg. Implanted in your mother. The Professor said we were brothers. And it's true. But we do not share a father." Again he stands mute, for a second he glares at the Professor, and the Professor's body betrays him as mine has betrayed me. The aura of control is revealed as illusion and without a word the Professor confirms what Colin already knows to be the truth.

"Go on. Ask him," I prod. And I see in his empty eyes the intensity that is all that remains of him. And I have my answer. He knows regret. I have won.

"My condolences," I say and thrust my pelvis forward in mimicry.

I hear the Professor cry out for him to stop as the first blow of the wrench comes down upon my skull. I see a flash. Defenseless, the restraints hold up my sagging body as the blows rain down. All around me I feel my history, my brown birthdays and June gloom. I leave the colored flashes of light and take one last sip of rosewater. My name whizzes by for the final time and the restraints cannot prevent me as I reach out to feel the shape of time around me. As I fall into shadows I reach ever deeper into time, from my history into shared history, until I can feel the shape of time no longer and I am left with the image of the tree upon the earth and I think that perhaps the branches are not branches at all, but roots. And whether root or branch, if one should end without a further branching, is it a tragedy?

424

APPENDICES

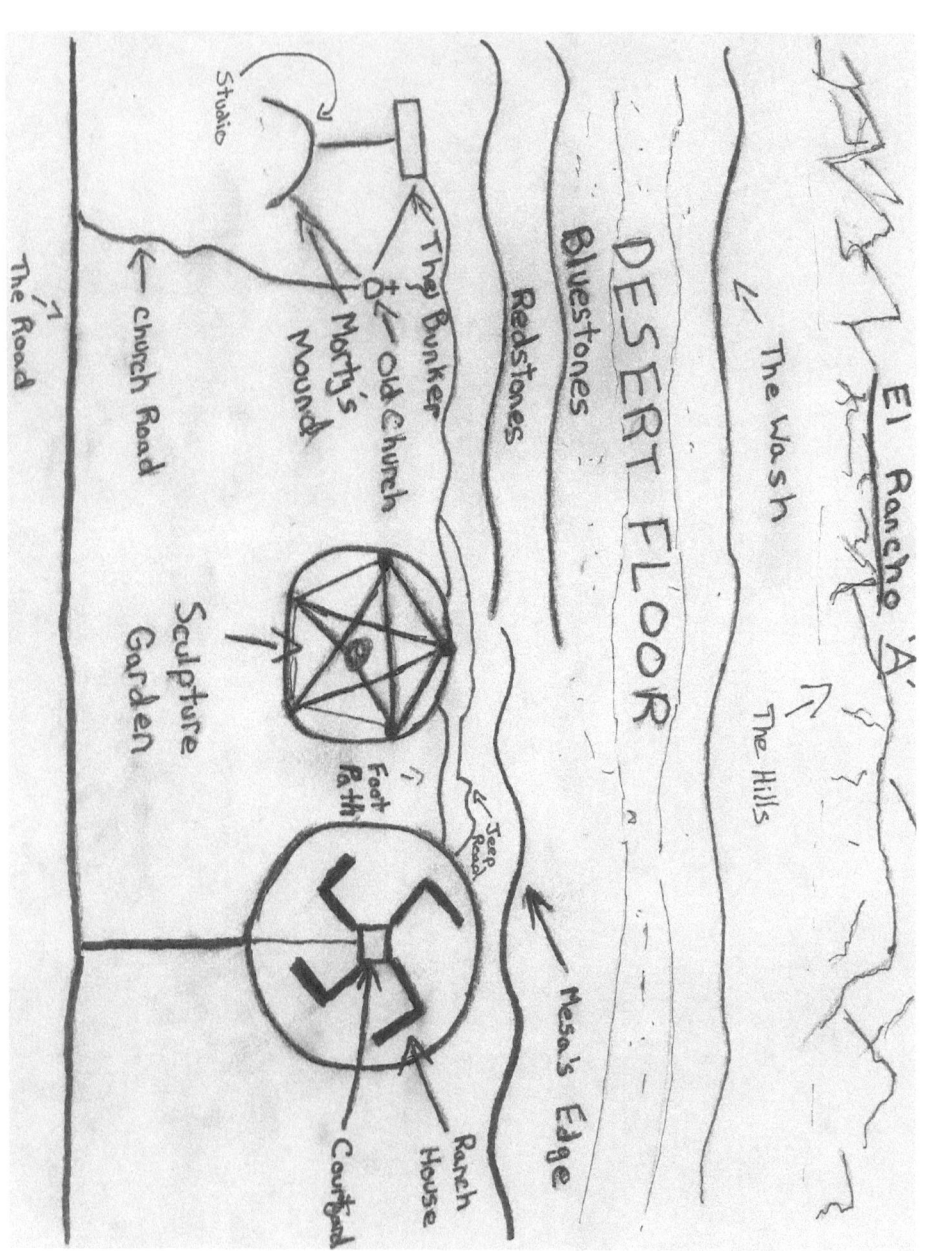

El Rancho "A"

The Hills

The Wash

DESERT FLOOR

Mesa's Edge

Jeep Road

Bluestones

Redstones

The Bunker

Old Church

Morty's Mound

Studio

Church Road

The Road

Sculpture Garden

Foot Path

Courtyard

Ranch House

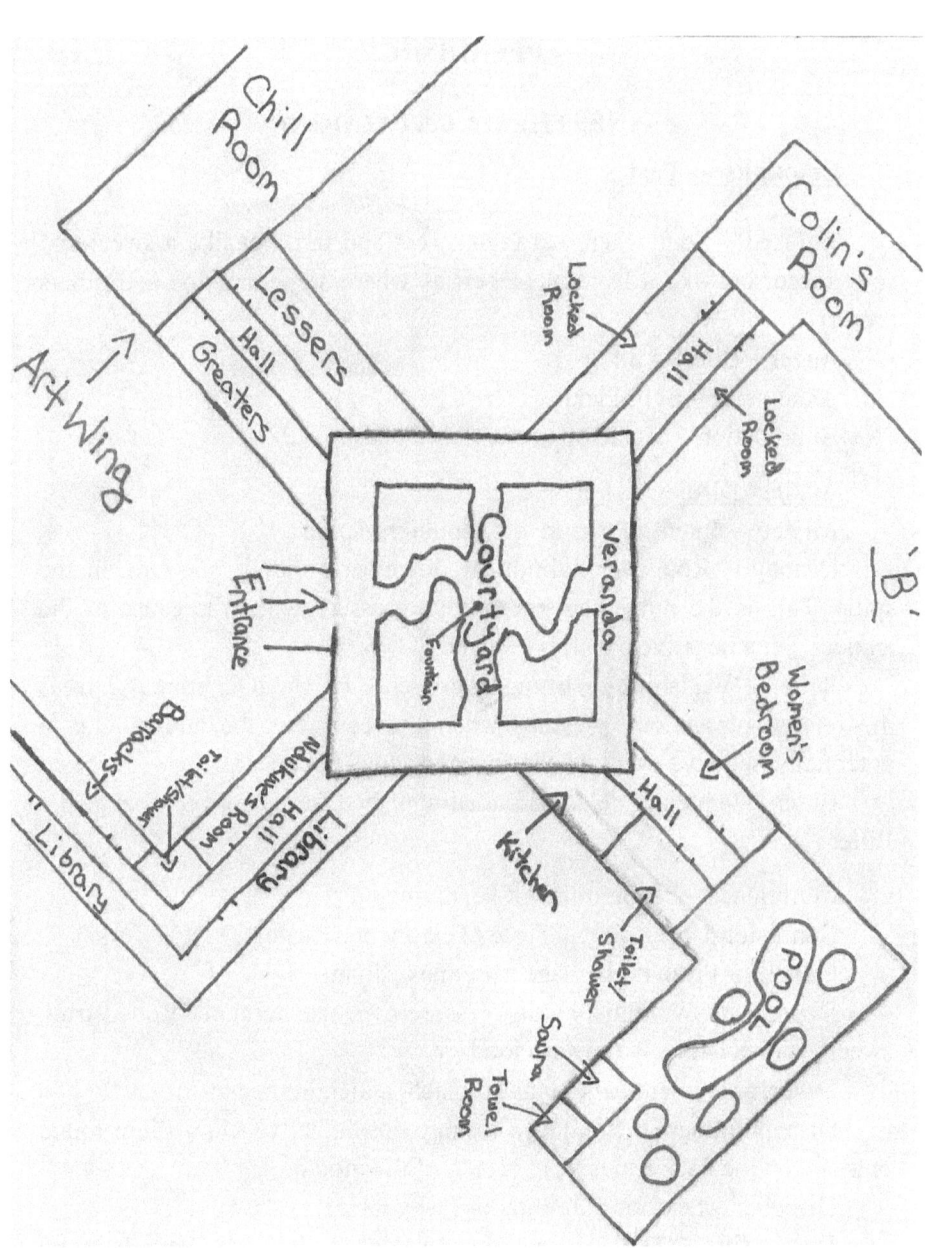

427

APPENDIX 'C'

SYNESTHESIA CATALOGUE

Emotions → Tastes

Amused – Somewhere between sweet and tart, not like a sweet and sour sauce, but like a handful of berries where some are ripe and others aren't

Anger – Bile/Vomit

Annoyance – Sour Pickle

Anticipation – Tickle on the back of knees

Anxiety/Dismay/Relief:

Anxiety – Intense Pressure on Shoulders/Spine.

Dismay – Round or cylindrical downward sliding pressure on the spine. This is the movement of anxious pressure when the cause of the anxiety, i.e. a negative event, is realized.

Relief – Vanishing or lifting of pressure on shoulder/spine. This is the release of anxious pressure when the cause of the anxiety, i.e. a potentially negative event, is eliminated or does not occur.

Bitter (Slighted or dejected as distinguished from annoyed or angry) – Bitter

Confidence – Peppermint, clove, nutmeg

Confusion/Uncertainty – Paste (Texture and Taste)

Curious – Fresh herbs, sage, rosemary, thyme

Depressed –Weighted chest, pressure over the sternum. Rotted fruit, sweet yet disgusting. A type of mood.

Despair – Violent pain in the stomach, a kick in the gut

Disappointment – Similar to dismay but lighter touch, a slight round pressure on the back and a rapid drying of the mouth.

Disbelief – Seafood (Shrimpy or Fishy taste)

Discomfort – Dull Sweetness (Related to Pain but Pain is more complex, deeper flavor)

Disgust – Mushrooms, wood rot, earthen

Dismay – See Above: Anxiety/Dismay/Relief

Embarrassment – Hot (Caliente) Often experienced in the mouth but intense embarrassment can give strong bodily feelings of heat as well.

Exhilaration/Thrill/Rush – Lemonade

Fear – Wet/Cold (As distinguished from threatened)

Glad – Sugar/Vanilla

Joy – Saffron

Lust/Arousal – Hot (Picante, Spicy)

Pain – Rosewater

Pity – Soft, corn-potato flavor, mushy yet mealy, not quite moist enough, too dry, granular

Pride – Cinnamon

Rage – Vile/Rotted Meat. A type of mood projected onto the world, or a feeling directed at a specific person.

Relief – See Above: Anxiety/Dismay/Relief

Sad – Salty, Salt Water

Surprised – Bland Protein, ironic eh?

Threatened – Metallic tinny, copper or iron (precursor to fight or flight)

Wren- (Infatuation? Romantic Love?) – Molé. Complex, hints of various mixes of flavors, chocolate, cinnamon, coriander, cumin, hot peppers, warmth.

Months → Colors/Positions

January – Pale Lime Green, Chartreuse / Directly in front of belt buckle

February – Aqua-marine (scrunched up just to the left of January)

March – Orange / In front of the left hip

April – Green / On the left hip

May – Yellow / Left and slightly behind

June – Grey / Behind and left

July – Sky Blue / Behind

August – Crimson / Behind and slightly right

September – Blue (Like glacial ice) / Behind and to the right extended back a foot

October – Brown / On the right, extends out several feet

November – White / On the right extended in front a foot

December – Black / In front of the right hip

Years → Colors (List Runs from Lower Left to Right)

B.C. – Grey (bunched up)
1500's - White
1800's – Teal
1700's – Burnt Orange
1910-1916 – Black
1917 & 1918 – Red
1919 - Orange
60's - Brown
1970-73 – Beige
1974-79 – Grey (hard to see)
80's – Light Purple (lavender)
90's – Green
2000's – Pink

Letters → Colors

A – Orange
B – Blue
C – Brown
D – Grey
E – Middle third of a tequila sunrise, pink-orange
F – Pink
G – Burnt Orange
H – Red
I – Vanishing Primrose, very pale yellow, so pale it is almost white
J – Pink
K – Hideous pukey green
L – Gold
M – Grey
N – Green
O – Violet
P – Bright Yellow
Q – Black
R – Fire engine Red
S – Maroon
T – Red (same as 'H')

U – Pink

V - Brown

W – Indigo but shimmery, sparkly midnight blue, the color of a mountain lake in moonlight

X – Black. Very inky and dark.

Y – Silver. Moves to the right

Z – Jade

Numbers → Colors

1 – Red

2 – Grey

3 – Pink

4 – Purple

5 – Blue

6 – Brown

7 – Yellow

8 – Orange

9 – Green

0 – Black

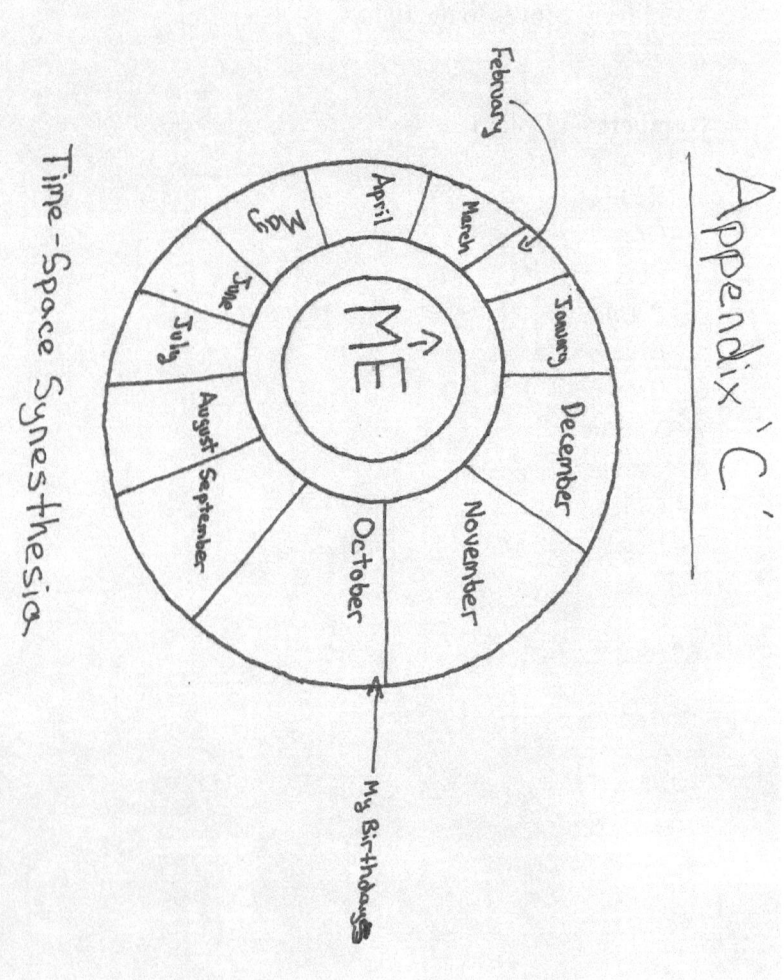

Appendix 'C'

Time-Space Synesthesia

432

Appendix 'D'

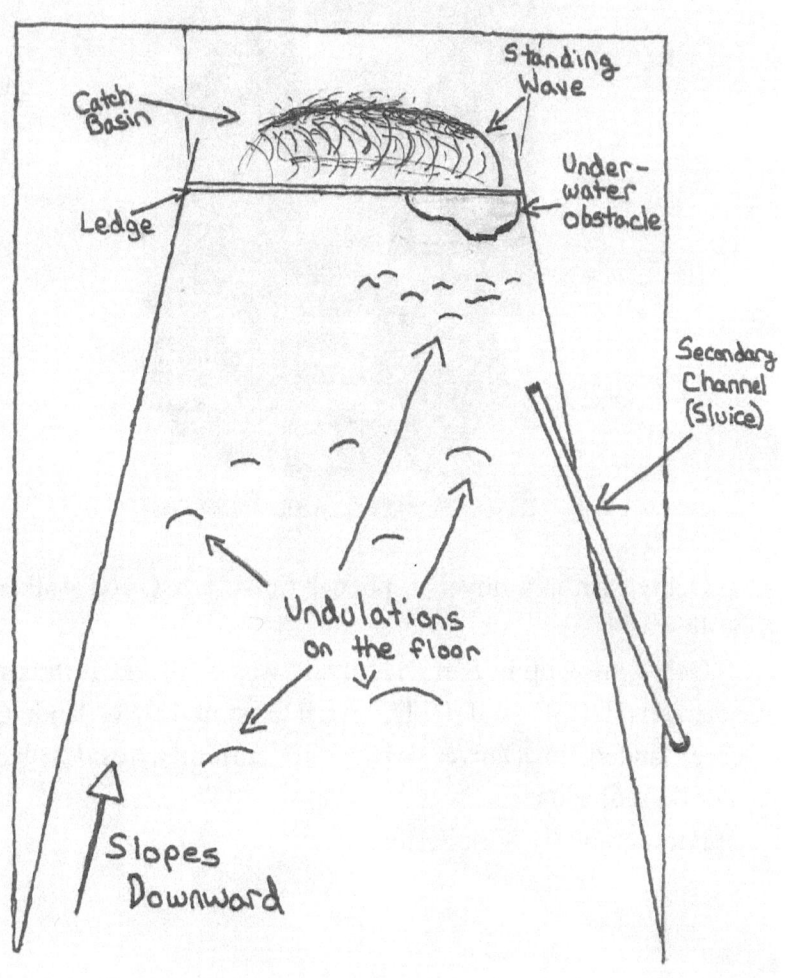

Standing Wave

Catch Basin

Under-water obstacle

Ledge

Secondary Channel (Sluice)

Undulations on the floor

Slopes Downward

ABOUT THE AUTHOR

Ochre Ash is a novelist, poet, lyricist, artist, and walker of the fine-line.

Ochre grew up in San Diego, and was educated at the esteemed institutions UCSD and USD. After a stint in Portland, Oregon, Ochre landed in Denver where he currently resides with two beautiful redheads.

Photograph by Kirk Perttu.

www.ingramcontent.com/pod-product-compliance
Lightning Source LLC
Chambersburg PA
CBHW030539260626
47157CB00006B/2104